EX
LIBRIS

Romance Treasury

THE ROMANCE TREASURY ASSOCIATION

TORONTO · NEW YORK · LONDON
AMSTERDAM · PARIS · SYDNEY · HAMBURG
STOCKHOLM · ATHENS · TOKYO · MILAN

These stories were originally published as follows:

THE CHALLENGE
Copyright © 1980 by Kerry Allyne
First published by Mills & Boon Limited in 1980

A GIRL BEWITCHED
Copyright © 1981 by Marjorie Lewty
First published by Mills & Boon Limited in 1981

KING KIELDER
Copyright © 1982 by Margaret Rome
First published by Mills & Boon Limited in 1982

ROMANCE TREASURY is published by
The Romance Treasury Association

Story Illustrations by Muriel Hughes
Book Design by Charles Kadin
Printed and bound by Arcata Graphics
Kingsport Tennessee U.S.A.

ISBN 0-373-04182-9

Printed in U.S.A.   A182

CONTENTS

Page 9

THE CHALLENGE
Kerry Allyne

Page 191

A GIRL BEWITCHED
Marjorie Lewty

Page 403

KING KIELDER
Margaret Rome

The Challenge

Kerry Allyne

Debra desperately needed a job and gratefully accepted one from elderly Eleanor McAllister. She'd never worked on a cattle station before, but she would try anything!

Handsome Saxon McAllister, however, thought she was a conniving adventurer and made her life miserable. Yet tough as the work—and Saxon—were, that wasn't what made Debra quit.

It was because she couldn't risk a repeat of the past: Saxon meant too much to her....

CHAPTER ONE

THE BRISBANE Royal Show! Debra Armitage had loved it ever since that day ten years ago when, for the first time, she had been fortunate enough to be included in the party taken from the orphanage. The crowds, the excitement, the thousands of exhibits, and the numerous pavilions filled with pedigreed animals of all breeds, shapes and sizes—she loved it all. But mostly it was the feeling of the country which reached out to her every succeeding year she had been lucky enough to be taken or, more recently, had paid the admission price herself, as she came through the turnstiles and once again stood on the concourse leading to the show ring.

The feeling was there in the exhibitions of farming machinery, the giant displays of primary produce, the livestock, and by no means least the farmers and graziers themselves—almost always uniformly dressed in fawn cord pants, white shirts and ties, and if that wasn't enough, there was the bush hat set well forward on sun-bronzed faces to finally distinguish the country born and bred from his city cousin. It was that once a year time when the primary producers of Queensland came to show and be judged on the fruits of their labours, and Debra wouldn't have missed it for anything.

At twenty-two years of age, her long dark hair swinging well below her shoulders, wide violet eyes outlined by thick black lashes and set in a piquantly heart-shaped face, she had long since left the orphanage behind her, but still she set aside this one day of the year for the Show. Even though this particular year was different from the rest in that three weeks ago the small firm for whom she had worked since leaving school had reluctantly been forced to close their doors owing to the prohibitive scale of rising costs and she, along with the rest of the staff, had found herself out of work, she still hadn't been able to resist the attraction.

It had been a worrying time since then, scanning the newspapers for a suitable position and finding none—where were all those jobs that had seemed so prolific only a couple of months ago?—and seeing her meagre savings dwindle rapidly as she went about her daily business of living without a wage to sustain her.

She supposed it had been an unwarranted extravagance to spend the day at the Show as she had done in previous years, but had consoled herself with a philosophical shrug of her shoulders and the thought that a few dollars either way wasn't going to make much difference if she couldn't find work within the next few weeks.

As the sun sank quickly below the city skyline and the myriad lights of the exhibition grounds sprang to sparkling life for the evening ahead, a chill wind began to whistle around the buildings, lifting discarded bags and paper refuse of all descriptions into lightweight missiles as it sent them whirling and scurrying down the roadways until they finally drifted to rest among others of their kind in ever mounting piles nestling in the corners and crevices of stairways and gutters.

Debra hugged her denim jacket closer to her slender form and wished she had thought to also bring a sweater with her to slip on over her thin cotton shirt, but the weather had been gloriously warm that morning when she had set out from the small bedsitter she rented in Mortimer Terrace, with no hint of the keen invader which had just begun to blow.

Now she hurried along the roadway, intent on mingling with the crowds in the main ring to watch the rodeo events and so gain a little warmth from the nearness of the other spectators, past the swimming pools which had looked so inviting earlier in the day with their winking and blinking blue waters, but which now sent involuntary shivers down her spine at the thought of submerging in their cold depths.

It was then that she saw the little girl—eight years old, or nine at the most, dressed in pale blue jeans and a sunshine yellow polo-necked jumper, her dark pigtails flapping behind her as she chased a break-away red balloon which skipped and flew with the breeze in front of her. With hardly a hesitation she scaled the fence erected around the pools and, arms outstretched, made one final lunge to grasp the teasing novelty, slipped on the wet surrounds, and tumbled headlong into the shining water.

Debra rushed forward spontaneously, looking about her to see if there was anyone else who had witnessed the child's predicament, or if there was someone accompanying her, but these particular stands were closed for the night and there were only a few people still making their way to the ring on the far side of the walkway and no one who was obviously trying to locate a missing child.

Pushing through the gateway, Debra dived into the pool immediately she saw the girl come gasping and flailing to the surface—a sure indication she couldn't swim—and with a couple of strokes had reached her side and clasped her under the arms.

'Whatever you do, don't panic, darling,' she urged with a reassuring smile as she tossed her own streaming hair back over her shoulders. 'Just hold on to me and we'll have you out of here in no time.'

Either the child was too shocked to do anything other than what she was told, or else she was an extremely cool-headed youngster—but for whichever reason Debra was very grateful, for slim arms obediently twined around her neck and together they managed to inch their way over to the steps and out of the water.

A few seconds later Debra had taken hold of a small hand and led her charge back through the gateway just as a rather plump little woman wearing an expensively tailored jersey suit came hurrying around the corner, her fading blonde hair slightly ruffled by the breeze and her blue eyes casting about her worriedly. On seeing the two of them dripping with water she came to a shocked standstill and spread a hand agitatedly across her chest.

'Prue dear, whatever's happened to you? You really shouldn't have gone rushing off like that,' she scolded in distraught tones.

Contrite pixie brown eyes peeped upwards from beneath spiky lashes. 'I'm sorry, Grandma, but the wind blew my balloon away,' came the solemn explanation between bouts of shivering. 'Then I fell in the pool while I was trying to catch it and this lady,' she indicated Debra who was gritting her teeth in a supreme effort to stop them from chattering as the wind cruelly pierced her wet clothing, 'dived in and pulled me out.'

Two warm hands caught at one of Debra's cold wet ones. 'Thank heavens you were around, my dear!' Prue's grandmother gave a heartfelt sigh of gratitude. 'I can't tell you how appreciative I am. I couldn't have faced my daughter again if anything had happened to Prue.' She gave a shiver herself at the thought, but the sight of the two shaking forms before her soon had her returning to more immediate priorities with a bustling concern. 'But the pair of you must be frozen standing in this cold wind! This way,' she urged them lightly forward in front of her, 'I'm sure they'll have something to warm you at one of the first aid stations.'

By the time they had both been handed a hot drink and were wrapped in thick blankets, Debra began to feel a little less chilled as she sat on a bench next to Prue in the tent while they both cradled hot mugs between their fingers. After ensuring herself that they were as comfortable as possible under the circumstances Prue's grandmother turned to Debra with an apologetic smile on her lips.

'Goodness, I'm all a-dither! You must think me very discourteous, I haven't even introduced myself yet,' she said with a nervous fluttering of her hands, and proceeded to rectify the omission with a hurried, 'I'm Eleanor McAllister, and this is my granddaughter, Prudence Wayland.' A regretful look at Debra's saturated clothing and she continued, 'I'm terribly sorry we've spoilt your evening at the Show. You must let me make it up to you.'

Having given her own name in return, Debra discounted the suggestion quickly. 'Don't think about it, Mrs McAllister, it's not that important. I'm only pleased I was around to notice Prue when she fell in.'

Eleanor McAllister's eyes blinked rapidly. 'Oh, yes, otherwise there could have been very tragic consequences. How could I have told my daughter and son-in-law?' She shuddered dramatically before turning to her grandchild and wagging a finger at her remonstratingly. 'And I hope it taught you a lesson too, Prue. You really must keep away from swimming pools until you've learnt to swim, dear.'

A downcast head nodded dismally. 'Yes, Grandma,' Prue agreed dutifully before asking in an even more woeful tone, 'Does this mean we won't be able to see the rodeo and stunt motor-cyclists after all?'

Her grandmother stroked the damp hair back from her face consolingly. 'I'm sorry, darling, but you'll have to miss it tonight, I'm afraid. Perhaps we can come tomorrow night,' she offered in lieu.

'It's not held on Sunday night,' Prue reminded her disconsolately.

'Well, Monday, then.' Mrs McAllister was becoming a little flustered.

'Can Debra come too?'

The innocent question brought a hasty disclaimer from her rescuer. 'Oh, no, I can easily come another time on my own if I want to. There's no need for you to invite me to join you.'

Completely impervious to her protestations, however, Eleanor McAllister immediately agreed with her granddaughter. 'That's a very good idea. Of course she can come with us,' she concurred happily. 'After all, we do owe her a night out since we ruined this one, don't we?'

'Really, you don't have to do that, Mrs Mc-Allister,' demurred Debra again in embarrassment. 'I can...'

'But I'd like to, my dear,' Eleanor interrupted equably. 'I feel it's the least I can do to repay you in some measure for your prompt action. In the meantime, though, I think I'd better see about doing something to get you both back to the hotel before you catch your death of cold,' she concluded, walking to the tent opening.

'You don't have to bother about me, Mrs Mc-Allister,' Debra began a protest once more. 'I don't live all that far away and I can catch a taxi.' A small lie since she didn't have the fare, but she didn't want Prue's grandparent thinking she was beholden to her for having retrieved her young relative from the pool.

'I couldn't let you do that!' Mrs McAllister sounded genuinely horrified at the idea. 'What would your parents think of me if I showed my gratitude by sending you home soaking wet? No, you must come back to the hotel with us and have your clothes dried first,' she insisted.

About to dissent for yet another time, Debra saw Prue's shoulders lift, an impish smile tug at her mouth and her head shake fatalistically, and she started to smile resignedly herself. Eleanor McAllister obviously wasn't about to be gainsaid!

Meanwhile, her self-appointed benefactor had slipped out of the tent and called a white-coated official over.

'Bill, could you call a cab for me, please? Prue's had a slight accident and I'm taking her back to the hotel,' she explained. 'You might also let Saxon know where we've gone too when he comes out of the restaurant. He's attending the Breeders' Dinner there tonight and I told him we'd meet him afterwards.'

'Be glad to, Mrs McAllister,' the man agreed helpfully. 'And I'll go up to the office and ring for a taxi right away.'

The fact that Eleanor McAllister had mentioned a hotel had led Debra to surmise that the McAllisters might be visitors down from the country, but the easy familiarity with which the older woman had addressed the official—and his readiness in recalling her name—now had her wondering just *who* the McAllisters actually were!

In the taxi it was a constant battle to keep the water from spreading over the seats, although the blankets which Mrs McAllister had promised to return as soon as possible did absorb quite a large portion, but it was with relief that Debra felt the vehicle pull up on the marble gravelled forecourt of the imposing Panorama Hotel. Nothing but the best, she thought with a wry smile, and of course none other than that which had long been known as *the* city resting place for members of the grazing fraternity.

She was even more relieved when they had finally crossed the dimly lit foyer in their squelching shoes under the speculative eyes of the staff and a few lingering guests, and had reached the anonymity of the elevator which swiftly rose to the tenth floor and the extensive suite of rooms reserved by her companions.

An involuntary sneeze from Prue decided who would be using the bathroom first, and Eleanor

McAllister hurried around making sure her grand-child had everything she needed and that she didn't take too long before being vigorously towelled dry and dressed in pyjamas and a prettily patterned dressing gown.

'Just hand me out your wet clothes when you're undressed and I'll ring for room service to have them dried,' Debra was instructed as she entered the bath-room in turn. 'Meanwhile, I'll find something warm for you to wear until they're returned.'

Debra smiled her thanks and closed the door be-hind her, only too pleased to be able to remove her wet and uncomfortable clothing, and especially her denim sandals which were beginning to rub her feet pain-fully. When she passed her clothes out to Mrs Mc-Allister she was given in return a long pale blue silk nightdress, and a matching empress-line quilted housecoat with a high mandarin collar, which she ac-cepted gratefully.

The streams of delightfully hot water from the shower dispelled her last feelings of coldness and af-ter rubbing her hair as dry as possible she donned the provided night attire and padded back into the sitting room in bare feet.

Prue was laying full length on her stomach on the carpet, engrossed in an action-packed Western on the television, a plate of sandwiches and a glass of hot milk beside her. Eleanor, in the act of pouring a cup of coffee, returned the pot to its tray and hurried for-ward, picking up a blow dryer from the low table as she did so.

'Here, you dry your hair with this and I'll pour you some coffee,' she said, handing the brush to Debra while she bent and plugged the power cord into an outlet next to the tan and cream upholstered sofa. 'There's chicken and ham sandwiches here too if you'd like some. I had them brought up when the clothes were collected.'

Declining the offer of anything to eat, Debra sat down and switched on the brush, pulling it through the long fall of her hair while her hostess poured another cup of coffee and placed it in front of her together with the sugar and cream.

'I don't suppose your parents would have expected you home by now, anyway, would they?' Eleanor queried conversationally as she pulled her own cup closer and sank down on to the sofa. 'Although you can give them a ring if you would like to,' indicating the cream telephone on a table beside the television.

Debra switched the brush to the other side of her head before answering slowly. 'That's very kind of you, Mrs McAllister, thank you, but I live on my own. My—my parents are dead.'

Both sets, in fact, she pondered sadly. Her natural parents in a boating accident when she had been six and a sudden vicious storm had swept in from the horizon to catch them unawares, swamping their small craft in a matter of minutes, and leaving Debra as the sole survivor for the rescue boat to pick up because she was the only one they had ensured was protected by a lifejacket.

Then had come eighteen months in the orphanage until Matron and the doctor thought it advisable for adoption to take place, whereupon she had been taken into the loving hearts and home of Rose and Jack Armitage for a period of two wonderfully reassuring years, until they too had been callously wrested from her. There had been a storm that night as well—a circumstance which had produced many nightmares for Debra over the years whenever wild weather occurred—and the car in which they had all been travelling had been struck by a falling telegraph pole, crushing the front of the vehicle with ridiculous ease and sending Debra into a state of shock as the chilling scream of tortured metal grated on her ears as she had lain on the back seat.

After that there had been no more talk of adoption, neither the doctor nor Matron considering it prudent after two such traumatic disasters in her short life, and although her early experiences had left no physical scars the wounds went deep all the same, with the result that Debra had never again allowed anyone to become *that* necessary to her existence, and now made certain she kept her inner feelings and emotions very much on the defensive.

'Oh, my dear, I'm so sorry,' Eleanor brought her out of her reverie sympathetically, a compassionate hand patting her arm. 'You must find it very lonely. Have you no other close family?' And upon receipt of a negating gesture, 'Even though there are so many people in the city they do tend to be such impersonal places. Everyone's so busy rushing about and looking after their own business, they never seem to have time for anyone else. Although I look forward to coming down to Brisbane every year for the Show, I have to admit that after a fortnight I'm only too ready to return home again.' She gave a small pleased smile at the thought, but immediately followed it with a doubtful, 'But, this time, only if I can get some satisfaction from the employment agency on Monday. I've been doing the rounds of them for the past week and they still haven't been able to find anyone suitable, so I'm beginning to doubt whether I'll have any better success on my last few days here.'

'It must be very frustrating when you only have such a short time to hire someone,' commiserated Debra, thankful that the conversation had veered away from more personal topics.

'How true! You have no idea how hard good staff is to come by in the bush these days,' Eleanor informed her in a resigned tone. 'I've been advertising in Acacia Crossing, and just about all points north, south, east and west, for over a month now without results, and it isn't even as if it's what you would call an exacting position. Secretarial mainly—shorthand, typing, a little book-keeping, that sort of thing—with perhaps a couple of odd jobs thrown in . . . like driving Prue to and from school each day, taking notes for me at some of my committee meetings, helping to prepare stud catalogues . . .'

Acacia Crossing! That was in the Channel country in the far west of the State. Debra stirred her coffee pensively, an as yet only half formed idea coming to light at the back of her mind.

'I suppose you're after someone who was born in the country and has had first-hand knowledge of that type of work,' she suggested diffidently.

Eleanor took a sip of her drink and shook her head emphatically. 'My dear, at the moment I feel I would be willing to settle for anyone who knew the difference between a typewriter and a calculator, no matter where they were born. It's just that with my committees and such I don't have time to help Saxon myself.' She paused, then smiled with twinkling honesty, 'Besides which, I just don't like office work.'

A responding smile caught at Debra's soft mouth, bringing a sparkle to her long-lashed eyes before they clouded again and she proposed hesitantly, 'I don't suppose you'd care to—er—give *me* a try...would you?'

'As Saxon's and my secretary, you mean?' Eleanor queried with a frown, looking somewhat taken aback.

Now that she had actually made the suggestion and seen Eleanor's reaction Debra found herself wishing that she had left well alone. Just because her companion confessed to experiencing some difficulty in finding someone suitable there was no reason to believe that she was ready to accept just anybody for the post. Now, with a deprecatory lift of her shoulders, she chewed at her bottom lip doubtfully.

'Well—yes—that was what I meant,' she finally conceded in low, apprehensive tones. 'I know I've never worked anywhere but in the city before, and—and my shorthand is only of my own devising—I was never actually taught one of the accepted forms,' she admitted truthfully, glancing at Eleanor to gauge her response to such generous candour. 'However, I do have references to say I'm a competent typist and clerk. Not that I'm attempting to have you believe I'm the best available, of course, but at least I've always tried to be conscientious and I've never received any complaints about my work,' she concluded with a shy, self-effacing smile.

The face of the woman next to her cleared almost magically. 'But of course you can have the job, Debra, if you think you'd like it,' she exclaimed happily. 'If that's the type of work you've been doing I'd be only too pleased to have you come and work for us. But aren't you already employed?'

For the first time since being out of work Debra was pleased to be able to answer in the negative. 'As a matter of fact, I'm not at the moment,' she revealed. 'Up until three weeks ago I was employed at a small manufacturing works not far from where I live, but with prices and the cost of labour going so high these days the owner couldn't compete with the larger concerns and he had to either shut down or face the likelihood of going bankrupt. Naturally, he chose the former,' she shrugged understandingly.

'That's marvellous!' cried Eleanor, and placed her cup and saucer on the table with an enthusiastic clatter. 'Not about the poor man having to shut down, of course,' she was quick to disclaim, 'but that you're free to start immediately. You'll be able to come back with us when we leave during the week.' Here a rueful smile pulled at her lips. 'Although I expect Saxon will have some extremely pertinent remarks to make about my precipitance in engaging someone without the benefit of an agency's recommendation. But then I'm used to lectures on my impulsiveness,' she smiled again, unconcernedly this time.

'You're sure you wouldn't rather wait until you've had a word with him about hiring me, Mrs McAllister? Until I can show him my references?' Debra asked anxiously, not wanting to cause trouble between Eleanor and her husband, and preferring to start off on the right foot herself.

'No, dear, of course not! I only meant it in fun,' Eleanor hastened to dismiss the worried look from her face. 'Saxon usually allows me a free hand in these affairs and I'm sure he'll be as pleased as I am to have finally got the matter settled so satisfactorily. Nevertheless, there is one thing you'll have to change.' A warm friendly smile dispelled any wariness her words may have created. 'You'll have to stop calling me Mrs McAllister and make it Eleanor instead,' she instructed. 'We're just not that formal in our part of the world.'

Unaware that there had been an interested spectator for the latter part of their conversation, and preventing Debra from immediately replying to Eleanor's behest, the two on the sofa now found Prue swivelled around on the floor to face them as she enquired interestedly,

'Is Debra going to live with you now because she pulled me out of the pool, Grandma?'

'Not exactly for that reason, dear,' the older woman laughed. 'But because Saxon and I need someone to help with the office work and so forth now that Noreen's left, and Debra has come to my aid—once again—by suggesting that she take over in her stead. You'll like that, won't you, because it will be Debra driving you to school each day now.' And she explained for Debra's benefit, 'Prue's staying with us for the next three months while my daughter and her husband, who are both doctors, are attending some important seminars and conferences overseas in connection with their medical research.'

'Mmm, I'll like that,' acceded a pleased Prue before turning back to her absorbing film, but managing to forgo its pleasures for a few moments longer in order to add over her shoulder, 'The last time I was out there all Noreen could do was to tell me to be quiet and stop talking all the way to town. You won't do that, will you, Debra?'

'No, I won't do that,' came the smiling concurrence. 'In fact, I'll probably have to ask you for directions because I won't know the way.'

'Oh, that's easy,' Prue discarded such a problem airily. 'You just turn left at the main gate and keep on that road for the next seventy miles. You can't get lost,' she finished absently, the television screen inexorably claiming her full attention once more.

A gulp and a weak smile were all Debra could summon in return for this casually imparted piece of information. She *could* drive, of course—Matron had helped her to get a licence during her last year at the orphanage and had allowed her to use the Home's vehicle on rare occasions after that—but seventy miles was probably the sum total of the distance she had driven to date, and she could only hope that her driving ability was such that she could safely transport Prue into town and back again each day.

Moments later she ran experimental fingers through her hair and switched off the brush. 'I think it's just about dry now, thank you very much...Eleanor,' she murmured gratefully, and watched as the other woman prepared to return it to her bedroom.

She had only just disappeared from view when the door to the hallway opened and a man walked into the room, his air of rugged masculinity making Debra's indigo eyes widen in amazement. Surely this wasn't Eleanor's husband! Why, he couldn't be more than thirty-three or four at the most, she guessed. She had been expecting someone much older.

As her glance travelled the powerful line of him back to his suntanned face and her vision encountered an interested and appraising pair of eyes beneath a wide forehead and gold streaked dark blonde

hair, she suddenly remembered the mode of her dress
and her cheeks flushed warmly as she unconsciously
hugged the housecoat about herself more closely. It
was a strong, good looking face returning her inspection, the eyes a clear blue and ringed by surprisingly
dark lashes, the nose well formed, the mouth wide and
curving, the chin square and assertive.

Successful, determined, self-assured, and disastrously attractive to the opposite sex, were all descriptions she abruptly found herself applying to the tall
stranger, but for some unknown reason the minute
those thoughts flashed through her mind an entirely
different feeling surged through her body—one of in-
stinctive challenge—and to her absolute amazement
she discovered her own chin to be inclining upwards
and her eyes defying his even before he had time to
utter a single word.

On hearing the door close Prue swung round once
again, but this time scrambled to her feet and rushed
across the room excitedly.

'Saxon! Did they tell you that I fell in the swimming pool and could've drowned if Debra hadn't
come in after me?' she relayed her adventure happily
now that she was safe and dry again. 'We had to come
home in our wet clothes all wrapped up in blankets.'

He smiled down tolerantly at the animated face, his
large hand resting affectionately on her shoulder. 'You
were lucky there was someone around to help you,' she
was told in a deeply smooth voice. 'I hope you
thanked—Debra—for her timely assistance.'

Prue glanced towards the girl on the sofa and back
again, a slight frown puckered her forehead as she
tried hard to remember. 'I think I did...but I know
Grandma did if I didn't.' She tugged hard at his wrist

to ensure she had his full attention before divulging her most impressive piece of knowledge. 'And now Debra's going to live with you at Wyeera.'

'Is she?' he counter-questioned in a slow drawl, along with a sardonic look at Debra which had her colour deepening furiously as his mouth took a decidedly cynical turn. 'How convenient! And in return for only one good deed too.'

By her puzzled expression it was clear the conversation was passing over Prue's head, but it definitely wasn't going over Debra's and she jumped to her feet in embarrassed confusion.

'It wasn't—it isn't—quite as it sounds, Mr McAllister,' she stammered and clenched her hands into stormy fists at the mocking look of disbelief she received in response to her statement. But before she could explain further Eleanor made her reappearance in the sitting room doorway.

'Ah, Saxon, you're back. Have you met Debra yet?' she smiled, and when it became evident that no such initiation had been made, went on, 'Debra, I'd like you to meet my stepson, Saxon. Debra Armitage.'

Which solved the relationship riddle that had been puzzling Debra for the last five minutes, but which introduction she acknowledged with only the barest movement of her head in return for his even briefer nod.

'I've hired Debra as our new secretary so she'll be coming home with us when we go,' Eleanor continued rapidly, and causing Debra to wonder if she was trying to pre-empt any objections he might raise. 'Or has Prue already told you all the news?' With a knowing smile for her young grandchild.

'Prue had already informed me in an—er—round-about way,' he admitted in a lazy tone, cool eyes flickering speculatively over Debra's stiff house-coated figure. 'And is Debra also staying here with us until that time?'

'No, I'm not, Mr McAllister!' The words burst forth from her with a burning resentment for the con-struction he was choosing to place on her presence. 'It was only at Eleanor's insistence that I came to the ho-tel at all. Immediately my dry clothes are returned to me I shall be on my way,' she took pleasure in telling him tartly.

'I couldn't possibly have allowed her to go home dripping wet,' his stepmother added her own point of view. 'Especially not after having spoilt her night out for her.'

'So we're taking her again on Monday night,' Prue revealed yet another of her items of importance, and promptly gave a sneeze.

'It doesn't sound as if you'll be going anywhere on Monday night,' Saxon grinned at his niece's woebe-gone expression. 'In fact, young lady, I think it's high time you were in bed.' He swung her up in the air and she clung to him piggy back fashion. 'Otherwise you won't have recovered enough to come to the Lion Sa-fari tomorrow.'

Prue's eyes rounded with delight. 'Are we really going to see the lions?' and without waiting for an answer, 'Are Grandma and Debra coming too?'

Immediately Debra was shaking her head in a vehe-ment denial, while Eleanor laughed after the retreat-ing figures as Saxon carried his burden into the bedroom, 'No, your uncle can take you this time. After the walking I did with you at the Show this after-noon I shall enjoy having a rest tomorrow.'

'Oh, okay,' the happy acquiescence came floating back to them. 'I'll be able to tell you all about it when we get home instead.'

With a thoughtful expression on her face Debra picked up Prue's glass and plate from the floor and placed them on the table as Eleanor reseated herself on the sofa.

'Eleanor? I hope you didn't think it was an impo-sition for me to ask if I could be your secretary's re-placement,' she spoke her anxieties aloud.

'Good gracious, no! I was only too pleased to ac-cept your suggestion.' Suddenly she smiled in under-standing. 'You're concerned about Saxon's reaction, is that it?'

'Well, he didn't seem exactly overjoyed with the idea,' Debra recalled ruefully.

'But only because I'd sprung another of my sur-prises on him, that's all. Not for any other reason,' Eleanor was quick to assure her.

Debra only wished she could feel as confident as her companion sounded. To her mind there had been other emotions, besides surprise, evident in the facial expressions and voice tones of Saxon McAllister, but before she could put her suspicions into words a knock sounded at the door which proved to be room service returning the dried and pressed clothes, together with the freshly laundered blankets.

Gratefully gathering her own apparel, Debra for-sook any further conversation in order to hurriedly slip into the bathroom where she stripped off her bor-rowed raiment and dressed swiftly in her own, and feeling far more assured and secure once she had done so, and grimacing as she slid her reluctant feet into her still damp and cold sandals. With Eleanor's carefully folded clothes draped over one arm she returned to the sitting room and, to her misgiving, found that Saxon had apparently been prevailed upon to drive her home himself when she noticed him withdrawing a car key-ring from his pocket.

Deliberately ignoring him, she turned to his stepmother. 'Thank you very much for the loan of the dry clothing, Eleanor,' she said appreciatively. 'Now, if I might use the phone, I'll ring for a taxi and take myself out from under your feet.' This last for the benefit of the man behind her.

'There's no need for that, the car's only just down-stairs,' a deep voice cut in firmly.

Debra sent him a smile of gibing sweetness. 'I wouldn't dream of putting you to such trouble at this late hour, Mr McAllister. So, if I could...'

'But of course Saxon will drive you home, dear,' inserted Eleanor this time. 'It's no trouble at all, is it, Saxon?' She looked to her stepson for confirmation.

'Not if we don't stand around here discussing it for the rest of the evening,' he conceded with a drawling kind of impatience.

'See? Saxon doesn't mind,' she laughed, and walked to the door beside Debra. 'And we'll pick you up on Monday night for the Show at about—hmm, seven, I think—if that's all right with you.'

Debra stopped moving and swung to face her. 'Really, Eleanor, there's no need for you to take me with you on Monday,' she protested anxiously, and attempting to prove to the man behind them that it hadn't been her idea that she accompany them. 'Missing tonight's events just wasn't that important.'

The other woman had different ideas, however. 'But I have to see you some time to make final arrangements about you coming home with us, so it might just as well be at the Show,' she proposed lightly.

Faced with this seemingly incontrovertible logic there was nothing for Debra to do but give in, which she did with as much enthusiasm as she could manage. Not that she didn't want to meet Eleanor, but rather because if it could possibly have been avoided she would have preferred not to endure an evening laced, as she was sure it would be, with Saxon McAllister's somewhat disparaging innuendoes. The less contact she had with the man the better, and for more reasons than one, as far as she was concerned.

Her goodbyes said, she accompanied him to the elevator in silence, thanking her lucky stars that it was stationary on the floor above and didn't take long to reach them. After they entered the softly lit cubicle Debra watched covertly as Saxon pressed the appropriate button for the underground parking station with a strong brown finger, her thoughts involuntarily recalling the dissatisfaction he had displayed on learning of Eleanor's decision to hire her, and perturbingly creating last-minute doubts as to whether she had done the right thing by accepting.

She could, of course, just telephone in the morning and say that she had changed her mind, even though she believed at least Eleanor and herself could work well together, but—catching frosty eyes surveying her thoroughly and not a little derisively—wasn't that exactly what *he* wanted? Inexplicably just the thought of the smug pleasure it would probably afford her companion should she let him coerce her into yielding was enough to have her squaring her shoulders and returning his gaze defiantly. Come what may, she was going to keep the position Eleanor had given her, whether Saxon liked it or not!

CHAPTER TWO

SECONDS LATER the elevator doors opened automatically to the view of a low roof, concrete stanchions, and rows of neatly parked vehicles of every colour and description. Debra preceded Saxon from the compartment and stood waiting for him to indicate in which direction they should proceed, then, when he started off down the right-hand lane with a long supple stride, found it necessary to break into a trot every so often in order to keep pace with him. That was, until her damp sandals began chafing again, and she lagged behind so she could lessen the friction by moving more slowly. It was a moment before she realised he had stopped and was waiting for her, hands resting lightly on lean hips, his expression unfathomable.

'I'm sorry if I was walking too fast,' he apologised, but to Debra's mind sounding as if he wasn't experiencing the slightest touch of remorse at all.

She shrugged indifferently. 'It wasn't that. It's just that my sandals are still wet and they're rubbing my feet.'

Now his expression was all too clear. It was definitely mocking. 'Sorry, sweetheart, but you'll find I'm nowhere near as obliging as my dear, unquestioning stepmother. I have no intention of offering to carry you,' he gibed hatefully.

Debra drew in a sharp infuriated breath. As if she would *want* to be carried by the likes of him! Her violet eyes flashed indignantly as she bent to wrench the discomfiting footwear from her feet.

'Oh, don't worry, Mr McAllister, I can assure you no such thought crossed my mind. It would never occur to me to suppose you capable of such a gallant act,' she smiled caustically as she stormed past him on bare feet until she was some yards ahead, whereupon she swung back to face him, a sandal-dangling hand perched on each of her own hips this time. 'Not that I'd wish to be accused of rushing you, of course, but...' a nod of her head indicated the rest of the cars in the line and she demanded pertly, 'which one's yours?'

Even after they had driven up the ramp and had joined the rest of the vehicles traversing the city streets Debra's heartbeat was still suffocatingly fast and hard against her ribs as she remembered the savage look on Saxon's face when he had paced towards her in the parking area. For a time she had wondered if he intended removing the provoking look from her face physically—making her quail at the thought—but he hadn't, fortunately, he had merely pushed past her in tight-lipped silence to unlock and drag open the passenger door of a white sedan, then had proceeded to slam it ruthlessly shut only seconds after she had nervously slipped in front of him and on to the dark green leather seat.

Seeing only her own worried reflection when she stared out of the side window she turned her head to the front, her fingers intertwining agitatedly in her lap. This was no way to start with a new employer. If she was really honest perhaps she could admit that

maybe—but only maybe—Saxon did have some jus-
tification for his behaviour. It must have seemed very
suspicious for him to return to the hotel and find that
Prue's rescuer was already ensconced as a member of
his staff. Perhaps she should have tried a little harder
to explain the circumstances instead of taking um-
brage as she had. Impulsively she twisted in her seat to
face him, speaking quickly, before her courage failed
her.

'Look, Mr McAllister, I'd like to explain about...'

'*Don't bother,* Miss Armitage! I'm not interested!'

His interruption was uttered with such harsh finality that she slumped back dejectedly, her thoughts
turning despairingly inwards again. It was no use, she
sighed quietly, he was determined to...

The sudden blaring of an impatient car horn behind them had her glancing up curiously when she realised they weren't moving, even though the traffic
lights at the crossroads directly in front of them were
green, and she swung a puzzled look towards the man
next to her. His eyes never wavered from the windshield, but she surmised he must have sensed her baf-
fled interest because she could see the corner of his
mouth beginning to edge upwards satirically.

'How about you keep your mind on one thing at a
time, Miss Armitage, or have you forgotten you're
supposed to be doing the navigating? You did say we
turned at this set of lights, didn't you?' he enquired
goadingly.

For revenge Debra was tempted to refrain from
telling him until the drivers behind them were really
irate, but the glittering gaze she intercepted dissuaded
her from this course of action.

'Turn right, and then first on the left,' she told him hastily, deducing that it wouldn't be at all smart to ride Saxon McAllister too hard unless one was extremely confident of what his reaction was likely to be. In his anxiety to be rid of her she wouldn't put it past him to drop her off at the next convenient corner and leave her stranded. Her statement at the hotel about ringing for a taxi had been pure bluff.

One thing she was certain of, though, she had no intention of apologising for not having previously advised him of the direction they should take at the lights. The last time she had attempted to apologise for a misunderstanding she had been very curtly squashed. She wasn't going to put herself in such a position again!

Presently she was pointing out the old terrace house where she lived and which had been converted into small bed-sitters capable of accommodating half a dozen single tenants. After the gracious refinement of the Panorama Hotel it was difficult to see the time worn building with anything but critical eyes. The stonework was pitted and dirty, the railing fence had obviously seen better days, and the drab curtains at the windows offered no promise of any improvement inside.

As soon as the sedan pulled up beside the curb Debra hurried to free herself from the seatbelt and thus preclude the necessity for her escort to emerge from the car, but the belt proved stubborn to her unpractised manipulations and by the time she had finally extricated herself from within its confines Saxon was already holding the door open for her to alight. She did so in a rush, scooping up her sandals from the floor in one hand, and immediately making for the house even as she thanked him perfunctorily for the lift. She was equally anxious as he was for them to part company.

There was no chance for him to reply, however, for another figure suddenly appeared from within the shadows of the darkened porch and she sighed despondently to hear an all too familiar voice complain in a softly hurt tone, 'I've been waiting here for you since eight-thirty, Deb. Why didn't you let me know you wanted to go out tonight? You know I would have taken you.'

Errol Pemberton! Why did it have to be *this* night that he turned up for another of his rejection scenes? Debra had dated him a number of times some months ago, but there had never been anything serious on her part, so when he started to become extremely possessive she had thought it best to call the whole thing to a halt. Unfortunately, this was easier said than done with someone of Errol's unfaltering persistence. Not terribly tall, lean and brown-haired, he sometimes reminded her of a terrier, for once having got his mind set on something there was no way he was going to abandon it again without a long and furious tussle. So far she had tried to get her message across without hurting his feelings too much, but now she was beginning to wonder whether he had any sensitivity to *be* gentle with!

A pointed glance for Saxon McAllister failed in its intention to let him know his presence wasn't required in such a personal matter, for he appeared disposed to ignore the mute hint, because he only leant back more comfortably against the car with his arms folded across his broad chest and an annoyingly amused look on his face. With an inward groan Debra turned her back on him, a slightly nervous hand flicking her long hair back over her shoulder, a major effort required to keep her voice cool and controlled.

'I'm sorry you've had a wasted evening, Errol, but I did tell you the last time you rang that I wouldn't be seeing you again,' she reminded him steadily.

'But what went wrong, Deb? You know I love you, and we were so right together.' His voice grew stronger as he began to repeat his habitual claims.

Debra paired her sandals in one hand and thrust the other into the front pocket of her jeans, hoping it would give her an air of unassailable conviction. 'But I don't love *you*, Errol,' she tried to impress on him decisively, all too conscious of the indolent figure at the curb. 'Sure, we had some good times together, but you can't expect them to go on for ever. I'm sorry, but you just weren't right for *me*!'

The dark brown eyes which had been shaded in the hazy glow from a street lamp two doors away suddenly lost their soulful quality and, to Debra's surprise, became almost rancorous.

'He is, though, I take it?' he questioned bitterly, his head nodding past her to indicate the third presence. 'What's he got that I haven't . . . more money?'

'No, of course not!' she denied promptly, but when an unconscious sideways glance from beneath curling lashes showed one of Saxon's brows to be ironically challenging her statement, she flushed and amended wryly, 'Well . . . probably. Although that has nothing whatever to do with . . .'

'Hasn't it?' Errol's disbelieving query cut across her denial swiftly. 'Then it must be something just as rewarding, otherwise he wouldn't be bringing you home in such disarray!'

'Oh, don't be so damned ridiculous!' she snapped back at him in embarrassment, knowing full well that Saxon could hear everything that was being said. 'I'm not wearing my shoes because they're wet!'

'Huh! That's a good one,' he snorted sarcastically. 'Especially since it hasn't rained for the last three weeks. I suppose your make-up was washed off in the same fanciful but convenient shower, was it?'

'No, in mine, actually. At my hotel,' came the bland intervention which had both of them staring speechlessly at the newly approaching figure, one in wide-eyed dismay, the other in a return to sorrowful wretchedness.

Debra was the first to break the tension-filled silence, but not until she had given Saxon McAllister a wrathful glare which should have felled him to the ground.

'There was no need to say that!' she hissed at him furiously. And to Errol, in an attempt to dismiss the implied inference, 'It wasn't anything like you're imagining. He's just my—my new employer...'

'In a manner of speaking only,' Saxon again put in a sardonic-sounding correction, and it was only his clasping his arms firmly around Debra's shoulders and pulling her back to rest immovably against his muscular shape that stopped him from being dealt a stinging slap from his absolutely incensed captive when he went on to add implicitly, 'Although she will be moving in with me next week.'

One look at the size and height of the man confronting him and Errol knew he was beaten. Not that it had ever been his way, but he wasn't such a fool as to resort to physical arguments with someone who made him feel a puny dwarf.

'So it's all settled, then,' he murmured defeatedly, and had a strangled noise issuing from Debra—the only sound the pressure of Saxon's forearms would allow as they lay against her throat.

Her struggles to be free of the enveloping embrace when she saw the look of hopelessness descend over Errol's face as he turned away were unexpectedly, but efficiently, stilled by Saxon suddenly spinning her around and his hard hands cradling her cheeks.

'There's no point in keeping it a secret, sweetheart,' he proposed softly, holding her somewhat bemused gaze steadily, but not too bemused to note that he said it clearly enough for Errol to hear. 'It is all arranged that you're coming home to Wyeera next week, isn't it?'

The aggravating lift to the corners of his mouth had her glaring at him and renewing her attempts to pull free in order to explain, but he apparently had no intention of allowing this to happen, and to prevent her spluttered, 'You—you...!' from eventuating into the onslaught it was evidently going to be, his firm lips closed over hers with a ruthless domination which effectively cut off her words and had her frantically endeavouring to break the surprisingly disturbing contact.

Except perhaps in order to annoy, Debra had no idea why Saxon should be going to such lengths to convince Errol there was some deeper relationship between them than actually existed, but the effect he was having on her emotions was quite illogical. When he finally released her she was quick to pretend a nonchalance she was far from feeling by looking anxiously around for Errol—only he was nowhere to be seen—and thereby giving her breathing a chance to resume its normal tempo. This proved to be only momentary because Saxon's next words had her pulse rate climbing alarmingly again.

'Earlier this evening I had thought you were only extremely calculating in keeping an eye open for the main chance,' he denounced bitingly, his eyes cold and contemptuous. 'But in truth you're nothing more than a cold-hearted, conscienceless little bitch! You weren't going to leave that poor devil any pride or self-respect, were you?'

Debra was so unprepared for his scathing words that for a moment she was too shocked to answer. But when she eventually did she hurled her own censures back fierily, her breasts rising and falling rapidly against the thin material of her shirt.

'*I* didn't leave him any pride or self-respect!' she repeated in stunned disbelief. 'Don't you think the shoe's on the other foot? I was under the impression it was *you* who saw to that with all your suggestive insinuations and presumptuous kissing!'

'By which means I at least left him with enough dignity to believe he'd been thrown over for someone else!' Saxon retorted icily. 'If you'd had your way you would have wiped the floor with him in your desire to prove you'd rather have no company than his!'

Debra's fingers curled about her sandal straps indignantly. How dare he have the audacity to tell her how to conduct her personal affairs!

'Of course I wouldn't have wiped the floor with him! If I had, maybe it wouldn't have taken me almost two months to break off with him,' she retaliated pungently, her eyes wide and sarcastic. 'But just because he thinks he's in love with me, it doesn't mean that I have to accept his company whether I want it or not. I don't happen to like possessive men, and if you consider that's being cold-hearted and conscienceless then it's just too bad, because that's the way I am!'

'Precisely!' he endorsed with an anything but pleasant smile. 'But if you're planning on bringing any of your hard-headed little philosophies to Wyeera, then I feel it only fair to warn you,' his voice sharpened and grew colder, if that was at all possible, 'that although Eleanor may have hired you, it will be me you'll be answerable to while you're on the property, and I don't appreciate my staff causing unnecessary upheavals. You catch my drift, Miss Armitage?' One well-shaped brow peaked expressively.

Up until that moment Debra had thought she would be in Eleanor's charge, and his revelation to the contrary caught her off guard. Although, she mused ruefully, if she had taken the trouble to think about the matter at all, it shouldn't really have come as such a surprise. Saxon McAllister wasn't the type to relinquish any of his authority on his own property, and especially not to a woman, not even if she did happen to be his stepmother. Determinedly she made her features relax into a tantalising smile and set about doing some warning of her own.

'I believe so, Mr McAllister,' she finally answered his question, and refusing to let any of her inner turmoil show. 'However, if you thought that your little attempt at sabre-rattling was going to have me throwing up my hands in horror and charging for the nearest telephone to let Eleanor know I'd had second thoughts about accepting the position, then I'm afraid you're going to be very disappointed. You receiving *my* message, Mr McAllister?' she concluded with dry provocation.

Two broad hands were pushed into the back pockets of his pants and his dark blond head lowered in sardonic acknowledgment. 'How could I fail to? You make it so disgustingly obvious! Having caught Eleanor in a weak moment and feeling beholden to you for saving her granddaughter, you're far too coldblooded to surrender your advantage and miss out on an opportunity you apparently feel will be to your benefit just because of a few discouraging remarks from me. I do hope, though—for your sake,' and Debra really didn't care for the emphasis he stressed on those words, 'that you have the right qualifications for this post you've so eagerly acquired for yourself. Otherwise...' Now it was his turn to smile, and the fact that it boded no good for herself still couldn't quite prevent her from appreciating the magnetism of his personality when the tautness left his expression and he looked as vitally attractive as he did at the moment. 'Otherwise, it's more than likely you could find yourself regretting the overly hasty decision you made tonight. I presume you've had previous experience on a cattle station, and that you're familiar with the work?' he quizzed mockingly.

Debra suspected he was as aware as she was that the work wouldn't be familiar in the slightest, but as she had no intention of telling him so to his face she merely hunched her slim shoulders offhandedly beneath her denim jacket.

'Office work is much the same anywhere, Mr McAllister, and Eleanor knows my qualifications. Why don't you ask her if you have any doubts?'

A forceful hand ensnared her chin before she had a chance to evade it. 'Never doubt that I won't, sweetheart.' He lowered his head to within inches of hers and had her catching a soft bottom lip apprehensively between her teeth at his unnerving proximity. 'But her replies had better be more commendable than yours, because I have a natural antipathy for sharp little females who think they only have to spin some pathetic hard luck story for everyone else to chivalrously overlook their inadequacies. So, believe me, those qualifications had better be good, or I'll make sure I'm personally responsible for turning your life into such a hell that you'll think I'm doing you a favour in accepting your willing resignation!' he revealed his ultimate objective inflexibly.

'Oh, is that so?' Debra gasped stormily as she twisted out of his hold. 'Well, unfortunately for you, I don't happen to give up that easily, so do your damnedest, Mr McAllister, and we'll see whether I hand in a willing resignation or not, won't we?' she gibed as she whirled for the steps leading on to the porch. And turning back to add in a tone which conveyed an overwhelming confidence which was actually non-existent, 'What's more, *I* don't like arrogant males who trade on their physical size and strength in order to intimidate those smaller than themselves! So perhaps you'd better watch out too, in case I decide to make your life such a hell that you'll think I'm doing *you* a favour when I finally decide to leave!'

His eyes narrowed consideringly and he raised one hand to sketch a taunting salute. 'Okay, sweetheart, I accept your challenge...but I also give you fair warning.' He paused and his eyes wandered over her waiting form slowly, mockingly. 'For someone like you I won't necessarily be fighting fair or reputably, and you can take my word for it that there'll be no concessions made because you're a female,' he informed her meaningfully.

About to insert her key in the lock, Debra spun round, her lips pouting impudently. 'You don't say!' she jeered. 'But then, if allowances were to be made because of my sex, you would first need to be a gentleman, and as I've already intimated once before this evening, we both know you would never fit into that category, don't we?' she smiled sweetly.

If Saxon intended to reciprocate he wasn't afforded a chance to do so because the front door was suddenly thrown wide, spilling pale yellow light on to Debra's surprised face, and a large woman positioned herself in the middle of the opening.

'I'll have that key, thank you, young lady,' she smirked triumphantly, and had snatched it out of Debra's unsuspecting fingers before she could protest. 'I told you what would happen if you didn't come up with your back rent in a hurry. Well, I re-let your room today...to someone who pays in advance!'

'B-but you can't do that!' Debra stuttered in her mortification. It had been humiliating enough to have Saxon McAllister witness the scene with Errol, but this was even worse. 'I told you I'd pay you as soon as possible, Mrs Jenkins. As soon as I could get another job, and—and now I've got one.'

'You're too late!' The ring of satisfaction in the woman's tone was quite noticeable.

'Don't you have a lease?' queried Saxon sardonically, moving to Debra's side.

She shook her head despondently.

'I wouldn't give a lease to the likes of her,' Mrs Jenkins sneered spitefully. 'Madams like that give the place a bad name, what with all the men they bring round. There was one of them hanging about all this evening but I see she's apparently found herself other fish to fry. No, I wouldn't give her a lease, the only reason I let her have the room at all was because she found me in a weak moment and I felt sorry for her.'

'That's not true!' Debra burst out resentfully. Mrs Jenkins had never experienced a weak moment or felt sorry for anyone in her life. 'You practically begged me to take the room because, at the time, you couldn't find anyone else who would pay the rent you were asking for such dingy accommodation. I only agreed because you said you were going to improve it . . . except that you never did.'

'You didn't have to stay,' the woman retorted smugly. 'No one was twisting your arm.'

Debra's shoulders slumped listlessly. 'Anything better cost even more.'

'It was good enough for you not to pay your rent for the last three weeks, though, wasn't it?' Mrs Jenkins bent forward, her small black eyes shining maliciously. 'But don't think just because I've got another tenant that it lets you off the hook, miss, because it doesn't. I'm impounding all your property until I'm paid every last cent of what you owe me. So now what have you got to say for yourself?' she taunted.

'I—I . . .' Debra couldn't believe it was all happening. She had set off that morning with nothing more than an enjoyable day at the Show in mind, but since then her whole world seemed to have been turned topsy-turvy.

'How much?' Saxon entered the conversation again, his voice ominously harsh, one hand going to his hip pocket.

'No!' Debra reached out to stop him as she realised his intent. 'I don't want...'

'What you want doesn't concern me in the slightest...as I'm sure you'll discover before very much longer!' he rasped as he shook her fingers away roughly and brought forth a folded leather wallet. 'How much?' he demanded again of the woman before them.

Mrs Jenkins was only too pleased to tell him, but added with relish, 'She still can't have her room back, though.'

Saxon counted out and thrust a bundle of notes towards her which she grasped eagerly. 'I doubt anyone in their right mind would want it back,' he derided contemptuously. 'But now I'll have Miss Armitage's luggage, if you please. All of it!' pointedly.

'Wait here,' they were ordered with a sniff before she made her way down the hall. When she returned it was with a case in each hand which were dropped carelessly on to the top step. 'Good riddance, I say! She's brought me and my poor husband nothing but trouble ever since she came here.'

'And just what did she mean by that?' Saxon enquired grimly as soon as the reverberations from the slammed door had died away.

Debra heaved one of the cases down on to the pavement. 'Her *poor* husband,' she said in acid accents, 'is a beer-guzzling lecher who considers all female tenants to be fair game.'

'So why *didn't* you move?'

'To where? The fire instead of the frying pan?' she rounded on him hotly. 'There hasn't been one bedsitter I've rented yet that didn't have some drawback. At least with this place being old it had solid doors and strong locks. I made certain he didn't get the opportunity to cause me too much worry.'

'So where are you going to stay now until we leave?' he asked, joining her on the pavement with her other case.

The fire died out of her swiftly, leaving her expression clouded with doubt. 'The Y.W.C.A. or somewhere similar, I suppose,' she shrugged, biting at her lip.

'Don't you have any money at all?'

'Only the twenty dollars I left in my room this morning.'

'Well, at a guess, I'd say you can kiss that good-bye,' he snorted cynically. 'That old harridan wouldn't have missed a trick when she was clearing out your room.'

'Oh, but surely she wouldn't . . .' She stopped with a despairing sigh. Oh, yes, Mrs Jenkins would take it if the chance presented itself. 'It looks as if it will just have to be one of the Missions, then, doesn't it?' she proposed with a valiant half laugh.

'No family anywhere in Brisbane?'

'No family anywhere . . . period,' she grimaced dolefully.

Saxon ran a hand savagely through his hair and gave a smothered groan of irritation as he walked over to the car and pulled open the door. 'Get in,' he commanded, returning for her cases which he tossed on to the back seat.

'I'm sorry to be causing you such inconvenience,' Debra murmured apologetically, eyes downcast, after they had been driving for a few moments. 'Do you know where the Mission is?'

'No!'

At that flat denial her eyes flickered up to his coldly set profile in puzzlement. 'Then where—where are we going?' she asked hesitantly.

'Back to the hotel.'

'W-what for?'

'What the hell do you think for?' His words snapped out with the crack of a whip. 'To book you into a room, of course!'

'But you know I haven't the money to stay there,' she protested almost tearfully.

'Then let's say I figure it's the best way I know of protecting the investment I've already been forced into making in you,' he bit out corrosively.

His meaning was all too clear and she stared at him incredulously, furiously. 'You think I might just disappear now that I've had my debts cleared for me?' she gasped.

'Too bloody right I wouldn't put it past you to vanish into thin air immediately my back was turned! I don't trust you one little inch, sweetheart!' There was nothing at all endearing in the term.

'Then why pay my back rent at all?' she flared, smarting under his denigrating opinion. 'Surely that was your best solution for getting rid of me altogether.'

'What, and have you ringing Eleanor in the morning to tell her the pitiful tale so she could offer to pay it for you...with no strings attached!' He laughed mirthlessly. 'Uh-uh! I much prefer it this way, with *me* calling the tune.'

'It will take me ages to pay it all back.' Debra could see her indebtedness to him looming for months ahead.

'Won't it?' he agreed with gibing mockery. 'However I did warn you that I wouldn't be making things easy for you. If you've already found you can't take it and want to cry quits, I'm quite amenable.'

'In other words, if I tell Eleanor I've decided against taking the job, then I don't have to reimburse you, is that it?'

'Just about.'

Debra held her breath and counted to ten in an effort to control her mounting fury. 'Then you really have misread my character, haven't you, Mr McAllister?' she stormed. 'I asked for that position because I needed it—I still do—and I can assure you I'm not about to be deprived of it by some arrogant damned male who thinks he only has to wave a few of his measly dollars under my nose to have me doing exactly as he wants! Oh, no, boss,' she used the word deliberately, 'you'll have to do better than that. You can't *buy* my resignation.'

Surprisingly, the retaliation she expected didn't eventuate. Instead, one corner of his mouth twisted obliquely and he taunted, 'You have no objection to said arrogant damned male buying your services, though, I take it?'

'Not at all,' she shrugged, her temper abating somewhat. 'My services are for sale...my self-respect isn't.'

'You mean, after tonight's efforts you still have some?' he quizzed with acrid scepticism.

Debra might have known that half bantering mood was only momentary! 'Why not? I'm sure you have, even after your attempted bribe!'

'Not a bribe, Miss Armitage, an offer of severance pay,' he corrected with cool dryness.

'Made out of the kindness of your heart, I suppose?' she gibed.

'You could say that,' he agreed. 'I figured that if it
saved my stepmother some future regrets then it would
have been worth it.'

'And yet the reason you gave for taking me back to
the hotel was that you didn't trust me not to disappear before I'd repaid what I owe you. Now you're
offering it to me on a platter.' She shook her head in
confusion. 'I don't follow your reasoning.'

'Then allow me to explain the fine difference.'
Again that lazy curve to his lips took her unawares,
setting her heart thumping in an uneven rhythm. 'It's
my prerogative to *give* the money away, sweetheart,
but I'm sure as hell not having you *take* it without my
say-so! As I said, I mean to be the one dictating the
shots where you're concerned, and that includes the
circumstances surrounding the termination of your
employment with the Wyeera Grazing Company.' He
shot her an unbearably goading look. '*Now* do you
understand my reasoning?'

She nodded with what she hoped would appear as
unconcerned insouciance, but if it hadn't been for the
fact that she needed work so desperately and that she
knew Eleanor was on her side, Debra suspected she
would have been seriously considering calling the
whole thing off. The challenge she had issued so recklessly was already beginning to rebound with a ven-
geance!

'You're positive you wouldn't like to reconsider my
offer?' Saxon enquired persuasively, almost as if he
could sense her doubts.

It was just the type of remark she needed to have her
sticking to her guns and dismissing her previous

qualms. 'No, thank you, Mr McAllister, although I do appreciate your generosity,' she smiled with honeyed sweetness. 'I know what it must have cost you to make such a magnanimous gesture.'

The lights from the oncoming cars threw his glacial blue eyes into bold relief in the darkened interior of the vehicle, and she couldn't quite control an inward tremor of nervousness as he warned. 'In that case, perhaps you'd better tread a little more warily, Miss Armitage. I wouldn't like you to forget that it's my home ground where you'll be living.'

Determined that he shouldn't see just how that knowledge affected her, Debra forcibly kept her smile in place. 'But if I do I'm sure you'll be only too pleased to remind me, won't you, boss?' she quipped pertly.

'You'd better believe it!'

She did. And as she followed him into the hotel a few minutes later there was only one thought sustaining her. Thank God for Eleanor! For without that woman's moderating influence she had no doubt her time spent working for Saxon McAllister would have been extremely uncomfortable, to say the least!

CHAPTER THREE

THEY LEFT Brisbane's Archerfield Aerodrome four days later with Saxon at the controls of his Beechcraft Sundowner and on a heading of west by northwest. It was the first time Debra had been in a plane—there had never been the money nor a reason for her to fly before—and she found the extended panorama provided below her not only beautiful but interesting as well, especially the further west they travelled.

As they passed over Brisbane the scene consisted mainly of suburban homes, each set within its own boundary fence, and a large majority of them equipped with swimming pools, if those brilliant patches of blue in back gardens were anything to judge by. Then the outer perimeters of the city came into view, the buildings set further apart now, the fences marking off acres instead of perches. And so it continued. The size of the properties progressively becoming larger and larger as they moved into the inland. Over the Downs the paddocks were measured in their hundreds of acres, a little further out in their thousands, until at last it just wasn't possible to make out any boundaries at all and the homesteads were very few and far between as they began to fly over the myriad creek and river-veined landscape of the Channel country.

An area often described as a Garden of Eden and which could turn off huge numbers of prime cattle in good seasons, it could also be a harsh and forbidding region, as many early explorers had discovered to their cost. But despite its capriciousness, and for those prepared to come to grips with it, it was very profitable breeding and fattening country.

Passing through a gap between two tree-capped ridges Wyeera homestead suddenly appeared almost directly below them and, banking steeply, Saxon soon had them approaching the red dirt landing strip which had been cleared from the surrounding scrub. As they landed the buildings were promptly lost to sight behind intervening banks of trees, but before the aircraft had rolled to a halt and they had unbuckled their seatbelts a large red Range-Rover had made its appearance from the direction of the homestead, a young man of some twenty-odd years at the wheel who proved to be Saxon's senior jackaroo.

The house itself, when it finally returned to view after their half-mile drive, was large and comfortable-looking rather than elaborate, the verandah rails and supports almost submerged beneath flowering creepers, a screened structure running the length of the twin-hipped roof.

'What's that?' Debra asked of Eleanor in a low voice, indicating the decking with a frown.

'Oh, that used to be our sleep-out for those unbearably hot summer nights, in the days before air-conditioning,' the older woman smiled. 'Prue still likes to use it as such sometimes when she's staying with us, and it's very pleasant sitting up there on a summer's evening. If there's any breeze coming off the plains at all you'll catch it up there.'

'Mmm, I imagine you would,' she conceded, intrigued with the innovation. 'And with the screen to keep all the insects away...'

'You don't care for insects, Miss Armitage?' The quietly spoken but irritatingly mocking enquiry came from Saxon as he half turned in the front seat to eye her over his shoulder.

'Not when they propose sharing my meals, drinks, or my bed, Mr McAllister, no, I don't particularly care for them,' she returned drily.

'Nor do I, dear, they can be so terribly annoying,' inserted Eleanor, stepping into the breech, as she had done on a number of occasions since the previous Saturday. Even though, for the most part, her stepson seemed reluctant to involve her in any of his clashes with their newest employee, sometimes it was unavoidable.

Saxon merely twisted his lips wryly at the hasty defence and, as the vehicle came to a stop before the central steps leading into the homestead, alighted and opened the rear door so the others could follow suit.

'It's good to be home,' Eleanor sighed contentedly and, as the two girls came to stand beside her, continued, 'Let's go in and have some tea, shall we? I'm sure Sherry will have a pot ready for us.'

Sherry turned out to be Mrs Sherrington, the housekeeper, a white-haired, trim woman of much the same age as Eleanor and who also had been widowed for some years. As far as Debra could make out, she and her husband had come to Wyeera only a short time after Saxon's father had remarried, and had been a permanent and well respected resident ever since.

In the end it was only Eleanor and Debra who enjoyed the welcome brew on the shaded verandah, Prue having decided to accompany the housekeeper back to the kitchen for her own special treat, and Saxon offering his excuses and saying he wanted to catch up on what had been happening on the property during his absence.

Their cups filled, Eleanor leant back in her padded chair and eyed her companion with a faintly anxious furrowing of her brow. 'I'm sorry Saxon has developed this penchant of his for—er—baiting you, Debra. I do hope it's not going to spoil your time here on Wyeera for you.'

Debra would have been more inclined to call her stepson's behaviour out-and-out harassment, but as she didn't want to put even deeper creases in the kind-hearted woman's forehead she made light of it with a laugh and a casual hunching of her shoulders.

'No, of course it won't, I don't let it worry me enough to do that,' she lied glibly. 'I guess it's only natural that he's still somewhat suspicious of my motives in asking you for the position, but I expect that will fade in time,' adding a silently grimaced, 'Joke!' for her own benefit.

'I thought he would have been over it by now,' Eleanor mused thoughtfully. 'Although I suppose my giving you that advance on your wages without telling him didn't seem to help matters, did it? Goodness knows why, but he just refused to believe the idea hadn't been yours.'

'I know,' Debra gulped, recalling Saxon's absolutely arctic fury when he had discovered what his stepmother had done. Of course she had already surmised what would happen—one of the reasons she had tried to dissuade Eleanor from making the advance—but the other woman had insisted once she had been informed—by her stepson, not Debra—of the events which had taken place after his escorting her home that Saturday night.

In fact, all in all it hadn't been a particularly promising first four days as far as Debra was concerned. Saxon McAllister had shown not even the slightest inkling that he was beginning to revise his opinion of her, and if it hadn't been for Eleanor and Prue's presence on Monday night at the Show she was certain the evening would have been purgatory from start to finish. As it was, he had still subtly managed to make her feel uncomfortable for accompanying them and she had been extremely thankful when they had finally returned to the hotel.

'Ah, well, I suppose all we can do is wait for his good sense to prevail once he gets to know you better,' Eleanor went on with an encouraging smile. 'As soon as he sees how well you fit in he'll change his ideas, I'm sure.'

Debra returned her smile noncommittally. It was very nice of Eleanor to be so confident she *would* fit in, but not even a round peg could slip into a round hole if someone was continually attempting to hammer it out again! She decided to tactfully change the subject.

'When will I actually be starting work, Eleanor? Tomorrow?' she asked.

A rueful smile crossed the other woman's features. 'To tell the truth, I haven't really given it a thought. Hasn't Saxon mentioned anything to you about it?'

'Not yet.'

'Then I expect he will at dinner this evening. We'll leave any decision till then, shall we?'

'If you like.' Debra was agreeable. Eleanor might have done the hiring, but as Saxon had so rightly implied, he was obviously the one in control on the property.

After that they talked desultorily on a variety of topics until they had finished their tea and then Eleanor had shown the younger girl to her room so that she might settle in before dinner as it was already well into the afternoon.

It was a lovely room, Debra noted pleasurably, once Eleanor had departed and she had an opportunity to look at it properly. Rectangular rather than square, it was tastefully furnished in tones of cream and willow green, the ruffled curtains at the windows of the same material as the flounced bedspread, the highly polished parquetry floor giving off a mirror shine. If she'd known she could exchange her depressing bed-sitter for a room like this, she smiled to herself wryly, she might have thought of looking in the country papers for work long before now. But until she had met the McAllisters it just hadn't occurred to her.

A half hour was all the time she needed to see her cases unpacked and her clothes neatly put away in wardrobe and dresser, and wondering what to do with herself from then until dinner, she was on the point of going for a walk when a knock on her door announced Prue's arrival.

'Grandma's having a rest, so she sent me along to see if you'd like me to show you around.' Her head tilted enquiringly. 'Would you?'

'Yes, very much,' Debra smiled down into the animated little face watching her so expectantly. 'As a matter of fact, I was just thinking of going exploring when you arrived. It will be much better to have someone with me who knows where everything is.'

'That's what Grandma said,' Prue confided as they began walking down the hall. 'What would you like to see first?'

'I don't mind, it's all new to me,' admitted Debra wryly.

'You mean, you've never been on a cattle station before... *ever*?'

'No, never. I haven't met anyone who owned one before.'

'I've been to lots,' her young guide divulged proudly. 'Grandma and Saxon often take me when they go visiting.'

'You've stayed on Wyeera quite a few times, then, I gather,' deduced Debra with a grin as they made their way down the front steps and into the garden.

'Oh, yes, Mummy and Daddy often have to go away on trips.' Prue stopped when they came to a flight of steps at the side of the house, turning to ask, 'Do you want to see the sleep-out?' and promptly added the warning, 'It'll still be very hot up there.'

Debra shrugged fatalistically. 'I don't mind, if you don't.'

'Come on, then!' Prue was halfway to the first landing before she had finished speaking, taking the steps two at a time, while Debra followed at a more natural speed.

She found it was unexpectedly high by the time she reached the top, and as her companion had foretold, still scorchingly hot with the sun's rays being reflected back from the silver-glossed decking so that one collected the heat both coming and going. Even worse than that she soon discovered, however, was the glare, and she immediately headed for the surrounding railings in an effort to avoid it by looking out over the far-reaching countryside. The view so gained more than made up for any discomfort, she decided, and while she allowed her gaze to roam over it unhindered, Prue knowledgeably pointed out the various landmarks for her.

A quick check of the decoratively grouped tubs and pots filled with gaily flowering cacti, and the banana loungers and chairs beneath a striped awning, were all she could manage afterwards before suggesting they adjourn to the ground once more. Her shirt already clinging to her back and clustered drops of perspiration had long since made their appearance at her temples.

'What did you think of it?' asked Prue brightly when they were back in the garden. 'Did you like it?'

Debra swept her long hair back from her face and laughed ruefully. 'I think I'd probably prefer it at night.'

'Well, maybe you'd like Grandma's water house better,' Prue now offered, shrugging her shoulders lightly and seemingly unaffected by the heat herself.

'Water house?' queried Debra.

'Mmm, you'll see. It's this way.'

The water house, as Prue had called it, was in actual fact a shade or bush house made of bark over a wire frame with water trickling continuously down the walls to create the humid atmosphere the outback didn't possess for the most dazzling display of orchids and tropical flowers Debra had ever seen.

'Oh, aren't they beautiful!' she exclaimed as she closed the door behind them, and feeling herself immediately assailed by a steamy heat this time. 'Did Eleanor grow them all herself?'

'Yes, she's the President of the Garden Club in town,' Prue nodded. 'Orchids are her favourites.'

'They'd be mine too if I could grow them like this,' vowed Debra as she bent to inspect an enormous cluster of perfect gold specimens.

Prue stopped beside a pot overflowing with arching stems lined with three-inch flowers of the deepest cerise. 'I like the Cooktown Orchid best. It's Queensland's floral emblem, you know.'

'Yes, and it's really lovely, isn't it?' Debra sighed and glanced about her again. 'Although, to be honest, I'd be hard pressed to say which I thought was the most beautiful, they're all so gorgeous. This one, for instance,' pointing to another pot, 'you could almost mistake its flowers for pansies.'

'I think that's what it's called . . . a Pansy Orchid.'

'That seems appropriate, it's a very close likeness.' Then, after moving on a few steps, 'Do you know what any of these others are called?'

A wrinkling of her nose and Prue shook her head. 'Not really. Grandma's told me lots of their names, but I forget most of them. Oh, I remember this one, though, because it looks like its name,' she explained, rushing ahead to a mahogany, white and gold variety. 'It's a Slipper Orchid.'

Debra stooped to survey it more closely and found her attention riveted to the blooms behind it. Almost nine inches wide, their brilliant orange petals overlapping, they exuded an unbelievably lovely perfume.

'You don't happen to remember *their* name, I suppose?' she just had to ask.

'Epiphyllum...Orchid Cactus,' supplied a male voice from the doorway, and had her spinning round to face its owner with her instincts immediately on the defensive.

'Thank you,' she acknowledged the information tautly, but when he showed no sign of either moving or speaking again, was forced into questioning, 'Did you—um—want me for something?'

Saxon flexed one shoulder negligently, his thumbs hooking into the leather belt of the fawn drills he had changed into since she had seen him last. 'I just thought you might have been interested to see the office,' he drawled. 'But of course, if you haven't the time...'

The sentence was allowed to fade away, but the insinuation couldn't have been plainer to Debra. She was there to work, not to act like a guest!

'Naturally I have the time, Mr McAllister,' she answered quietly, a little selfconsciously. 'It's just that when Prue asked if I'd like her to show me around, I didn't realise...'

'That you might be expected to actually do some work once in a while?' he interrupted ironically.

'No, that isn't what I meant at all!' she protested resentfully. And to the child still waiting beside her, 'Thank you for what you've shown me so far, Prue. Perhaps we can finish our tour another day, okay?'

'Sure,' Prue acquiesced easily as they began walking towards the door. 'Maybe we can do it on Saturday or Sunday.'

'It's a date.'

'Provided, of course, Debra's not working on the weekend,' Saxon reminded his niece drily as she passed him on her way out.

'Not both days she won't have to, will she?' Prue promptly turned to entreat.

He smiled down at her tolerantly. 'We'll see, little one, but there's a tremendous amount of paper work which has been mounting up while we've been away.'

'Just a couple of hours,' she wheedled, undaunted.

'Maybe on Sunday,' was as far as he would relent, but Prue seemed satisfied with the result, for she threw her arms around him in a brief hug and then, with a cheery, 'I'll see you,' for both of them, she was off and running back to the house.

As soon as she had gone the smile disappeared from Saxon's face and his eyes flicked back to Debra. 'We work when there's work to be done here, not according to whatever day of the week it happens to be,' he advised shortly. 'Just because the calendar says it's Saturday or Sunday it doesn't mean we can forget about the livestock for two days.'

'I didn't suppose it did,' she defended herself swiftly. 'I just thought that, working in the office...'

'You'd have a nice easy job with a lot of spare time on your hands?'

'No!' she flared, her violet eyes darkening dramatically. 'I just hadn't expected my hours to be so closely aligned with yours, that's all!'

'Then there wouldn't be much point in my employing a secretary if she wasn't available when I wanted her, would there?' he retorted sarcastically.

Debra inhaled a deep breath but refrained from answering. No matter what she said he would manage to find fault with it somehow, and she moved out into the sunshine again with her chin edging higher in mute rebellion. Saxon closed the door of the shade house and caught up with her as she stormed across the lawn towards the homestead. From the corner of her eye she could see his shapely mouth beginning to curve humorously, and the thought that he found the situation amusing was infuriating.

'What's the rush?' he mocked.

The hunching of her slender shoulders might have given the appearance of indifference, but she still couldn't keep the snap out of her voice as she gibed, 'I wouldn't like to be accused of taking my time in order to avoid doing some work!'

'Did anyone say they were expected you to *do* any work today?'

'Not in so many words, but...'

'Then I suggest you don't put two and two together and make five, Miss Armitage.' The advice was goadingly given. 'Believe me, I'll let you know plainly enough when I want you to work.'

'Yes, Mr McAllister,' she acknowledged with doubtful submissiveness, and had the pleasure of seeing some of the glittering amusement in his eyes being replaced by suspicion.

The office was situated at the back of the house, overlooking the horse paddock and the countryside beyond. It was quite a large, though functional room, the furniture typical of a business area, the equipment modern in design, and the walls adorned with certificates and ribbons as well as pictures of Wyeera's prizewinning Brahman stud cattle.

Briefly, Saxon began explaining her duties and where everything was kept, but one piece of equipment, to which her eyes strayed apprehensively every now and then, he didn't mention at all. Deliberately, she suspected. Located on a table of its own, it looked something like a typewriter, except that it had a screen attached which rather resembled a small T.V. set. So far, what he had detailed didn't appear likely to cause her too many worries—the work would definitely be different from what she had been used to, but it certainly wasn't insurmountable. That machine, however, could put everything into an entirely different perspective, she surmised, and she continued to eye it askance.

'And this, of course,' at long last he got around to indicating the device, and she didn't know whether to feel glad or sorry, 'is our computer. Or, more correctly, micro-computer. It's invaluable for keeping our stud records and accounts up to date.'

'I see.' Debra swallowed heavily, her worst imaginings confirmed. 'And who—er—uses the computer?'

'You or I, naturally! Noreen, your predecessor, had more or less full charge of it.'

Lucky Noreen! she grimaced sardonically. Obviously, that girl had known how to use the damned thing! Up until now she had only seen them in shop windows, and even then she hadn't paid much attention. Now she was wishing she had!

'I presume you can operate a computer? Eleanor did tell you that was an essential part of your duties?' Saxon's voice broke in on her despondent musings brusquely, his eyes narrowing as a betraying flush of colour crept into her smooth cheeks and her violet gaze dropped a few inches.

'N-no,' she whispered throatily, nervously.

With a stifled epithet he reefed open the stationary cupboard door, retrieved a manual with a photo of the machine on the front cover from within, and thumped it down on to the desk with barely controlled savagery.

'Then I recommend you learn to operate one very quickly, sweetheart, because come Monday you'll be expected to extract information from those records and forward it to the printers for inclusion in our forthcoming sales brochure. And I don't want any foul-ups, understand?' he rapped out grimly.

Debra nodded rapidly, the tip of her tongue sweeping across lips which had suddenly become dry. 'May I take this to my room to study it?' she asked shakily, picking up the book.

'You'd do better to study it in here, in conjunction with the machine,' curtly.

'I suppose so,' she conceded in a troubled voice.

'I'll leave you to it, then.' He started for the doorway, a lithe swing to his stride. 'Take heart, they reckon even a child can master them with only a reasonable amount of practice.'

The slightly patronising gibe sliced through her anxiety with a biting thrust and had her muttering acidly after his retreating figure, 'Which, no doubt, accounts for *your* being able to use it!'

His about-face was so swiftly executed that Debra couldn't believe her eyes. She hadn't meant him to hear her caustic remark!

'Would you care to repeat that?' he demanded stonily as he stalked back into the room.

As quickly as it had arisen her burst of rebellion now vanished and, backing away, she shook her head uneasily. 'I—I'm sorry,' she offered contritely, her pulse racing at his nearness when he leant one hand on the filing cabinet behind her and bent towards her.

For an interminable time he didn't speak as his gaze locked with her wide and wary one, and then, when he did, it was in a totally unanticipated tone, almost as if he had completely changed what he intended to say.

'Sweetheart, a challenge is one thing, but to tempt Providence is a different matter entirely.' One long forefinger slowly traced the line of her jaw from ear to chin with demoralising effect. 'So how about you concentrate on that book and forget about trying to provoke me, hmm?'

Debra wished she could move away. She felt horribly vulnerable with him standing so close. But with the cabinet behind her and a desk by her side there was nowhere to go.

'Well, you shouldn't have goaded me first,' she reproached, albeit a little breathlessly, but feeling she had to assert herself somehow.

His white teeth gleamed in a lazy smile. 'If you don't like the conditions, Miss Armitage, you can always resign,' he drawled.

And give him such an easy victory? He had to be kidding! But at least his suggestion gave her the courage to push past him with assumed nonchalance, her whole demeanour one of amused disdain.

'Oh, no, I'm not that easily routed, Mr McAllister! In fact, from what I've seen so far, I think the conditions here will suit me admirably—with one or two exceptions, of course—but then no position is perfect in every respect, is it?' she smiled mockingly.

'And you're likely to become very much less so the longer you remain!' His retaliation was swift, his intention painfully obvious.

With a shrug she dismissed it as carelessly as possible. 'Perhaps.'

'Definitely!' he corrected adamantly, and took his departure with an unhurried arrogance.

BY DINNER time Debra felt she had become, if not proficient in their use, then at least familiar with some of the more basic commands and statements required to operate the computer. There were a few chapters she skipped, reserving them in her mind for later study, which detailed functions she guessed—hoped—wouldn't be of paramount importance at the moment, and preferring to take more time over those explaining the methods employed for the keeping of data records and inventory systems.

Even so, she would still have been the first to admit that there was a long, long way to go before she could claim any sort of competency, and almost as soon as their evening meal had been concluded she made her excuses in order that she might return to the office.

Eleanor apparently thought she intended to retire for the night. 'You're tired after our journey today, are you?' she asked in a kindly manner. 'I find flying makes me quite sleepy too.'

Unconsciously, Debra's gaze slid towards the man at the head of the table, met a pair of electrifying blue eyes which held a decided taunt, and abruptly reversed direction.

'Yes, well, I would like to be fresh to start work tomorrow,' she evaded, reluctant to reveal where she was going in case it reminded Saxon yet again of his stepmother's somewhat impetuous method of employing her.

'Oh, that's right, we were going to discuss when you should start at dinner, weren't we?'

'Don't worry about it, Eleanor, Miss Armitage and I have already settled that question,' her stepson interposed smoothly.

'*Miss* Armitage, Saxon?' She looked down the table with a frown. 'Surely you're both not intending to continue addressing each other so formally now that we're home?'

The blond streaks in his hair glinted brightly as he moved his head in a slight downward movement. 'Then if you prefer it...Debra.' His expression became mocking as he made his acknowledgment.

'Saxon.' She promptly aped his sardonic bearing in return.

'That's much better,' applauded Eleanor with a pleased smile, apparently oblivious to the glimmering undercurrents—or perhaps purposely ignoring them. And to Debra, 'You run along, my dear, if you want to, and we'll see you in the morning, after you've had a good night's rest.'

Keeping up the pretence, Debra bade them goodnight and then made her way back to the office where she settled down again in front of the computer. Slowly the minutes, then the hours, ticked past and the longer she remained there the more frustrated she became. She was doing something wrong, that she knew, but what? Even the machine kept throwing the word up at her. Either that or 'How?' And try as she might she just couldn't find where she was making her mistakes.

It didn't help that she was getting tired either, or was close to tears at being foiled by a machine, but she was determined she wouldn't leave it until she'd had at least one success in programming and adding to an indexed file. Sighing with despair for the umpteenth time, she rubbed the tips of her fingers across her creased brow and prepared to start at the beginning of the chapter again. Maybe if she took it step by step right from the start she would discover where she was going wrong.

So busy concentrating was she that it wasn't until the video displayed yet another querying sign, at which she muttered some withering remarks, and heard someone make a faintly taunting sound of reproof behind her, that she realised she had company. And unwanted company at that!

'I only said you had to be able to operate the computer by Monday... not tomorrow,' Saxon advised—but not without some evidence of amusement in his tone, she noted with a grimace—as he peered over her shoulder to see the printing on the screen more clearly. 'You do realise it's after twelve, I suppose?'

Refusing to turn and look at him, he was far too close for her to do that with any sort of composure, Debra kept her eyes riveted to the screen. 'Goodness, but it's amazing how time flies when you're having fun, isn't it?' she quipped through gritted teeth. She was surprised it was only after twelve, it felt more like after three!

'You're finding the instructions quite simple to follow, then? No problems?'

On top of her setbacks of the evening the mocking enquiry was just too much and unbidden tears flooded her eyes. 'No problems,' she denied huskily.

As if she needed it pointed out to her, Saxon indicated the video unit. 'The computer doesn't appear to agree with you.'

Debra clenched her hands in her lap, still trying to blink the betraying wetness from her dusky lashes. 'They're not infallible,' she murmured evasively.

'You don't think the operator could have something to do with it?'

It was the smile she could see reflected on the screen which finally forced her into facing him. It goaded insupportably! 'All right, all right!' she blazed. 'So I'm not having much success! Now I suppose you're going to make some gloating remark and say it's no more than I deserve!'

'No, I was going to ask if you needed help, if you must know.'

That stopped her dead in her tracks and she eyed him doubtfully, mistily. 'Are you offering any?' she queried tentatively.

'If you want it.' His lips curved upwards wryly.

She nodded quickly, before he had a chance to remember he'd planned to make things harder for her, not easier. 'I certainly seem to need something,' she confessed a little selfconsciously.

Saxon pulled a chair closer and straddled it. 'Mmm, they can be confusing if you're not sure of what you're doing,' he smiled lazily.

Debra averted her gaze in confusion. Why he was deigning to be helpful she had no idea, but the sudden change in his manner was having a calamitous effect upon her senses. When he looked at her like that her defences were about as substantial as a wet tissue!

'Now, how about you showing me where you're getting this problem you're supposedly not having?'

His drily voiced suggestion broke in on her musings and brought her attention back to her immediate difficulties with a start.

'Oh—er—it's somewhere in here, I think,' she stammered, and pointed to the troublesome section outlined in the manual. 'I can get so far and then it keeps tossing up a "What?" or a "How?" at me.'

'Well, a "What?" means it doesn't understand what you want it to do, whereas a "How?" means it understands what you want but that you haven't explained how you want it done. So let's take it from the beginning and see if we can find where you're going wrong, hmm?'

All too willing to agree, Debra surreptitiously brushed the back of her hand across her eyes in order to dispose of the last of her involuntary tears, and started feeding the programme into the machine for yet another time. Line by line they went through it together and finally, after repeating the whole exercise two or three times, she was able to manage it on her own.

'You really mean that a missed full stop or a misplaced semi-colon can throw the whole programme out?' she asked slightly incredulously after her last successful run-through.

Saxon didn't immediately reply as his eyes ranged from her to the book and back again, ironically. 'Somehow I get the feeling you haven't read everything in that book that you should have done.'

'Well, it was so thick,' she grimaced excusingly, not looking at him. She was too conscious of the heavily muscled and tanned forearms resting on the back of the chair beside her as it was. 'I—I tried to pick out those chapters I thought would be most appropriate for your type of records.'

'And thereby missed some of the most fundamental and important instructions.'

There was nothing to be gained by denying it and Debra didn't even attempt to. Instead she shot him a brief look of enquiry. 'Why *did* you help me, anyway? You said you were going to make things as difficult as possible for me.'

'Except that, in this particular instance, I considered my peace of mind to be more convenient than your discomfort,' he divulged drily.

'I don't follow you.'

Saxon rose lithely to his feet but continued resting his hands on the back of the chair as he leant towards her, his expression sardonic. 'Let loose among those records while still incompetent there was no telling what havoc you may have wrought, and on thinking the matter over I found I wasn't prepared to take the chance.'

'I see,' she murmured quietly, a little disappointedly. She had hoped he was beginning to relent in his attitude.

Perhaps some regret was evident in her tone, for now his well shaped brows lifted to their more familiar mocking slant and he taunted, 'You surely hadn't persuaded yourself I'd succumb beneath the avalanche of those crocodile tears of yours?'

She should have known he would think they had only been put on for his benefit! But rather than let him know they hadn't been feigned, she merely shrugged indifferently. 'It was worth a try,' she perjured herself with brittle lightness.

'But not quite good enough to take *me* in, sweetheart!' he retorted, an unmistakable note of contempt entering his voice. 'You forget, I know just what a hard-headed, conniving little piece you really are!'

Somehow Debra managed to smother her furious indignation beneath a fragile veneer of unconcern. 'Then I shall just have to find some other way to spike your guns, shan't I?' she proposed chaffingly. 'Who knows what worthwhile method for getting under your guard a coldly calculating little brain like the one you keep crediting me with is capable of devising. I notice you're not exactly averse to changing your attitude when it happens to suit *your* purpose.'

'Meaning?' ominously.

She swallowed hard but refused to be outstared. 'This evening...your precious records,' she reminded him ironically. 'Perhaps if I...'

Before she even had a chance to finish what she was saying her head was abruptly snapped back as a handful of her long hair was wrapped around strong fingers and pulled tight.

'Don't you try threatening me, you little vixen, or you'll wish you'd never heard of a McAllister, let alone met one!' he lowered his head to grate implacably.

Actually, a threat had been the furthest thing from her mind, and for a moment she could only stare up at him in shaken surprise. Then, as the pain from her captive hair began to register, her eyes darkened with a smouldering resentment.

'You seem to do it often enough!' she glared accusingly, and futilely attempting to break his hold. 'So why can't I?'

'Because I happen to be the injured party!'

With her hair feeling as if half of it was being dragged out by its roots, Debra wasn't quite sure how he could make that statement. 'That's a laugh!' she jeered insolently. 'I didn't think it was possible to injure case-hardened steel!'

His cold blue eyes roamed over her critically, insultingly. 'And *I* didn't think it was possible for anyone to *look* so desirable, and yet *be* such an undesirable!' he derided harshly as he released her.

'Then you obviously haven't taken a good look at yourself in the mirror of late!' she hurled back sarcastically, her breath coming in shuddering gasps, her eyes watering. Her scalp was stinging fiercely, but she wouldn't give him the satisfaction of seeing her massage it with him present.

Recovering his equanimity, Saxon flexed solid shoulders imperturbably. 'You can always leave.'

'I'll see you in hell first!' she gibed.

He laughed, a short, scornful sound. 'Don't count on it!' was his parting advice as he strode from the room.

CHAPTER FOUR

DURING THE next three days Debra worked harder than she had probably ever done before, and at the same time had been criticised—unfairly on most occasions, she believed—more often than ever before as well. Evidently Saxon was determined to be the hardest taskmaster imaginable, with the result that she hadn't seemed to have a minute to herself since arriving on the property. Oh, he'd allowed her a couple of hours off during Sunday afternoon—only because Prue had managed to cajole them out of him previously, she was positive—but for the rest of the time there had hardly been space for her to draw breath, and by Monday morning she was looking forward to the break from his ever watchful scrutiny, and needling, while she drove Prue to school in Acacia Crossing.

'Are you coming with us today, Grandma?' Prue asked as she was preparing to leave the table after breakfast.

'No, dear, not today,' Eleanor smiled, and shook her head. 'I think I'd better take the chance to look to my orchids while I have the time. I've hardly been near them since we came home.'

Prue accepted this in her stride and looked across the table, another query on her lips. 'Will you be long, Debra?'

Sensing her anxiety to be on her way Debra glanced at her watch. 'But it's only just after seven!' she exclaimed.

'It used to take Noreen almost two hours,' Prue shrugged philosophically.

And Noreen had probably been an experienced driver! Debra swallowed her mouthful of toast, had a quick drink of tea, and jumped to her feet.

'Well, you collect whatever you need, then, and...if you'll excuse me,' her glance encompassed both Eleanor and Saxon who were still seated at the table, 'we'll be off.'

'Do you know which vehicle to take?' Saxon's voice came drawling after her as she neared the doorway.

She swung about, her expression wary, and saw him also rising to his feet. 'I thought Prue would probably know,' she said.

'And you'd have no trouble driving whichever one she chose?'

Now was no time to show lack of confidence! 'I don't expect so.' She held his gaze determinedly as he approached.

He didn't appear particularly convinced, but at least he didn't comment either, merely saying to his stepmother, 'I'll be off too, Eleanor. I'll see you later.'

'Yes, dear,' she acknowledged placidly. And to Debra, 'Have a good trip, but watch out for those road-trains, won't you?'

'I will,' Debra promised, even as her thoughts turned apprehensive. How many of those powerful prime movers hauling three or four double-decker stock trailers behind them was she likely to meet on the road? Not too many she hoped!

Saxon retrieved his hat from the hallstand as he accompanied her out on to the verandah, clamping it down on his head in businesslike fashion. 'Normally, you'd take the station wagon, but there's some rolls of wire to be picked up in town this morning, so it had better be the ute. I'll show you where it's kept,' he offered casually.

'There's really no need for you to bother. Prue showed me yesterday.'

'It's no bother, that's where I'm headed too.'

Prue met them at the five-bay garage where she quickly ascertained which vehicle they were travelling in and clambered inside together with her school case. Debra checked to see the keys were in the ignition and prepared to follow suit, frowning when Saxon opened the passenger door again and slid on to the bench alongside his niece.

'Are we—er—going past where you want to go—' she enquired hesitantly.

'No, straight to it,' he advised levelly before turning to send her a deeply sardonic glance. 'You didn't really think I'd trust you to drive Prue into town on your own without first checking to see how competent a driver you were, did you?'

'I guess not,' she was forced into acceding, although she really hadn't thought about it before, and right at the moment she had other things on her mind. She was trying to discover where everything was located.

'What are you used to, a floor or column change?'

Momentarily she stopped searching in order to look at him blankly. 'I beg your pardon?'

'The gears, sweetheart,' he elucidated drily, tapping the appropriate lever. 'On the floor, or on the steering column?'

'Oh!' She flushed embarrassedly. 'On the steering column, the same as this.'

'That's something, I suppose,' he commented with a look of long-suffering.

Debra ignored him as best she could and prayed she wouldn't make a mistake as she switched the engine on and, after only two attempts, found reverse. Nonetheless, their passage out of the garage wasn't exactly sedate and she had, perforce, to slam on the brakes suddenly when she saw the homestead fence rushing to meet them. Prue giggled enjoyably as they all perked backwards on the seat, but Saxon didn't look anywhere near as amused.

'I didn't ask to see it, but I presume you *do* have a licence?' he queried stonily.

'Of course!' Luckily her forward progress was proving somewhat smoother. 'I'm not used to this model car, that's all!'

'Well, try and get used to it before we hit the highway, hmm? I'm not in the mood for a harrowing experience right now.'

'In that case, why don't you just close your eyes and let *me* do the driving?' she suggested bittersweetly.

To her utter amazement he took her at her word, easing further down on to the seat and tipping his hat forward over his eyes. 'Okay, it's all yours,' he yielded with surprising docility—although apparently not quite so complacently that he was able to resist nudging Prue and recommending in a stage whisper, 'You'd better ask if she checked whether we've got enough fuel to get us to town, otherwise we could spend most of the day stranded beside the road.'

Prue laughed, thinking it was a game, but Debra knew differently and her gaze flicked hastily down to the gauge. A second later she expelled a small sigh of relief. She would never have heard the end of it if they'd run out of gas on the way! Now it was she who nudged Prue on the arm.

'You can tell your uncle to relax,' she charged wryly. 'I wouldn't dream of inconveniencing him to such an extent.'

'Debra says...' Prue began her relay with a grin.

'I heard,' the man beside her drawled lazily.

Chancing a covert sideways glance, Debra could just make out the corner of his firmly moulded mouth as it inclined upwards in whimsical recognition of her light gibe and she looked away again swiftly, her stomach somersaulting crazily. He would be easier to dislike if he wasn't so damned attractive, she decided ruefully.

Considering the highway wasn't paved for the most part, it was still relatively comfortable driving. Some sections were worse than others, of course, but on the whole Debra found the trip less of an ordeal than she had anticipated. The ute was fortunately possessed of a smooth manoeuvrability and after the first thirty-odd miles she found she could relax as she had suggested their unexpected passenger do.

Once it became apparent her uncle didn't intend taking part in their conversation Prue kept up a steady stream of chatter which at times was quite informative from Debra's point of view when it concerned the surrounding district or personages in the area, so that by the time the signposts denoted they were approaching Acacia Crossing she was pleasantly surprised that the journey hadn't taken longer.

'I thought you said it was a two-hour trip,' she looked down at Prue quizzically. 'It's only taken us an hour and a half.'

'Mmm, but Noreen didn't used to get a move on like you did, she was always looking out for people she knew so she could stop and talk. One time I was even half an hour late for school.'

'Well, that's certainly not going to happen today. You're almost an hour early.'

'That's good.' Prue gave her approval with a wide, pleased smile. 'Now I can have as long to play as some of the others.'

'Right you are, then,' Debra grinned in return, remembering her own desire to arrive early for just such a reason. 'Where is the school?'

They had just started to pass a collection of houses at the beginning of the main street and Prue pointed ahead of them quickly. 'The last building on the left, down the end,' she said.

Debra glanced about her with interest as they continued down the now bitumened road. It wasn't a particularly large town—there was only a small scattering of shops—with the hotel, stock and station agents and bank taking pride of place in the middle of the block. But as they came abreast of them Saxon suddenly eased upright and pushed his hat back into its rightful position, and making her wonder if, indeed, he had shut his eyes at all.

'You can let me out here,' he advised, motioning towards the middle one of the 'big three' as Debra had thought of them. 'After you've dropped Prue off, you can go round to Simpson's and collect that wire, then call back, okay?'

She shrugged equably. It didn't sound too difficult. But as she pulled to a stop and he prepared to alight, she waved one hand to indicate the rest of the buildings. 'Which one's Simpson's?' she queried wryly.

Saxon gained his feet and then had to stoop to look back into the cabin of the ute. 'It's round the back of the store,' gesturing diagonally across the street. 'Prue will show you from the school, you can see it from there.'

Scant minutes later she was halting again, this time to let Prue out.

'That's where you have to go,' she was informed, and had a large ramshackle old wooden building set some way behind the main street pointed out to her.

'I see it.' Her smile was appreciatively given. 'And I'll pick you up here this afternoon when school comes out.'

'It doesn't matter if you're a bit late,' Prue put in hurriedly, her words sounding more like a hint than accommodation. 'You don't *have* to be here right on time. I can always wait at Jenny Dutton's house for you.'

'Is that what you used to do when Noreen collected you?'

'Most times. She wouldn't arrive until half past four, or even later.' Judging by her expression Noreen's tardiness *after* school hours wasn't condemned, at least not by Prue.

'Doesn't Mrs Dutton mind?' Debra was still a little doubtful, though.

Prue shook her head vigorously. 'No, she always says that once you've got eight of your own you never notice another one or two.'

'No, I guess maybe not,' Debra laughed. 'Well, as long as she doesn't mind...' She was partway to relenting. 'I'll check with your uncle on the way home, all right?'

'Sure!' Evidently that had been the right comment to make, for the little face was now wreathed in smiles. 'Saxon always lets me stay on for a while.' Then as a carrot-haired moppet called to her from the school-house steps she proffered a rushed, ''Bye, Debra, I'll see you this afternoon,' and was hurrying across the grass towards her friend.

Simpson's, Debra soon discovered after driving into one of the many loading docks, was a produce store which catered mainly for property owners and sold a variety of goods and implements as diverse as heavy machinery and flea powder. The air was redolent of chaff, mixed feeds, molasses, and a number of other equally strong but indistinguishable aromas, and she sniffed experimentally as she made her way past piled sacks of unknown substances to a glass-partitioned office where a grey-haired man looked up enquiringly on noting her presence.

One glance at the vehicle she was using, however, immediately produced a smiled, 'I know the ute, but not the face.'

'Debra Armitage,' she supplied with a laugh. 'I'm the new secretary at Wyeera.'

'Ah, taken young Noreen's place, have you? I'm Pat Beasley.' He came out of the office, a mountain of a man and as strong as an ox by the look of him, his bushy brows lifting. 'You've come for Mac's wire, I suppose?'

Mac? Oh, McAllister! It took a little time to register. 'Yes, please,' she nodded.

'Right you are, lass, we'll have it loaded for you in two shakes.'

And so it was. The huge rolls being dropped into the back of the ute as if they had weighed no more than a few pounds each, but managing to make the vehicle rock heavily each time one of them landed all the same.

On the receiving end of a cheery wave Debra was soon back behind the wheel again and heading down the street to the stock and station agents where she reverse angle parked and somewhat hesitantly entered the office. She was uncertain as to whether Saxon had meant for her to actually call for him or just to wait outside.

As she walked in she could see a young girl bending over some boxes in one corner of the reception area, but before she could speak to her a male voice sounded from one of the two inner offices.

'Come on through!' it bade. 'We're almost finished.'

Only moving forward enough so she could poke her head around the doorway, Debra smiled deprecatorily at the two men inside. 'I—it's only me.' Her glance slid to Saxon, who had just risen to his feet. 'Maybe I'd better wait for you in the ute.'

Her wrist was caught and held in a firm grip even as she took her first step backwards. 'Now that you're here it might be an idea if you met Mike. You'll probably be talking to him on the phone often enough during the next few weeks,' Saxon declared, drawing her inexorably into the room. 'Simmonds' Primary are the major agents who'll be handling the auction.'

Debra nodded her understanding, feeling rather like a recalcitrant child with her wrist still captive, and thankful when Saxon was compelled to release it during her ensuing introduction to Mike Allworth.

'And how are you liking it so far at Wyeera?' she was asked after they had exchanged greetings. 'Noreen always used to say it was one of the easiest jobs she'd ever had.'

It was almost all Debra could do to stop pulling a sardonic grimace. No doubt Noreen had received completely different treatment from what she was getting too!

'Well, it's certainly different from the last job I had,' she skirted giving a direct answer. 'But I'm sure I'll get the better of it in time.' This last for the enlightenment of her employer.

'Mmm, she's nothing if not a quick worker,' inserted Saxon ironically, and she knew he was referring to the manner in which she had gained employment and not her ability.

'Just what you need with the sales coming up, Mac.' The other man accepted his statement at face value.

'As long as she's not so fast that she gets ahead of me,' he drawled wryly.

Mike laughed and winked at Debra. 'You keep him on his toes, love,' he exhorted. 'I've noticed the paper work's been a bit on the slow side coming out of Wyeera for the last few months.'

'Well, I'll certainly do my best to keep him up to the mark,' she replied to his suggestion in joking kind, her wide-spaced eyes openly provoking as they connected with Saxon's azure gaze. 'But if someone's just naturally slow to work things out...' The sentence was allowed to trail away insinuatingly, lugubriously.

This time it was the nape of her neck which felt the warmth of Saxon's hand as she was urged towards the door in front of him. 'On your way!' he ordered, but with more dryness than annoyance in his tone, she noted with relief. 'Before either of you can cast any more aspersions.' And over his shoulder. 'We'll get moving now, Mike.'

'Okay, Mac. I'll be in touch. With you too, Debra.'

She turned her head back as much as the hand on her neck would permit. 'I'll look forward to it,' she smiled sincerely.

Once outside she slid out from under the disconcerting touch as rapidly as possible, and in an effort to disguise the nervous movement turned to ask, 'Do you want to drive?'

Saxon shrugged indifferently. 'No, you can.'

'Are there any other stops you want to make before we leave town?' she thought it best to enquire as she fastened her seatbelt a few minutes later.

'Just the Post Office. It's further down on this side.'

On looking up to acknowledge the information Debra found him surveying her with an indolent thoroughness and her gaze wavered confusedly. 'You sure made the most of your opportunity back there, didn't you?' he observed drily.

'So did you,' she half smiled, still very wary of his mood. 'But then I've never been one to look a gift horse in the mouth.'

Even before the words were completely out she knew she couldn't have chosen a worse quote to use, and his tersely clipped, 'So I've noticed!' only served to accentuate her unthinking mistake.

Damn! For a while that had been just about the closest they'd come to anything even approaching amity, and now, through a careless slip of the tongue, she had put them right back where they started. Despondently, she turned the ignition key and put the car into gear.

For most of their journey home Saxon was occupied with the mail he had collected. There seemed mountains of it to Debra—periodicals and newspapers, catalogues and brochures, and an apparently unending supply of letters. Whether this was the normal amount of mail they received, or had been brought about owing to the forthcoming sale, she didn't know, but she did take a wry guess and surmise that there would be even more work ahead of her when they reached Wyeera.

So busy had she been in casting rapid glances over the mound of assorted paper between them, however, that she didn't realise they had come upon one of the worst sections of the road until they hit the first pothole with a shuddering thump, together with quite a number of following ones before the half-mile horror stretch was left safely behind them.

'Did you manage to get them all?' Saxon took time out from the letter he was perusing to spare her a heavily sarcastic glance as they jolted their way over the last gouged cavity.

'I think so,' she retorted facetiously. 'I wouldn't want a whole morning to go past without giving you the chance to find fault with at least *something* I'd done.'

'You make the errors, sweetheart. I just point them out to you.'

'And so politely too!' she gibed. 'With all the finesse and consideration of an attacking shark!'

'You knew it wouldn't be consideration you'd be receiving from me when you insisted on taking the position, so why the complaints now? Regretting your decision at last, are you?' he taunted.

'Not my decision, your pigheadedness!' Her retaliation came promptly, recklessly. 'You need a secretary, especially at the moment, and I need the job. You'd be in a worse position if you didn't have anyone at all, and I can't see why you refuse to admit that we can both benefit from the arrangement.'

'Then it will be my pleasure to inform you why!' The abrupt corrosiveness in his tone sent shivers down her spine. 'Firstly, because nothing alters the facts! You weren't qualified for the position, and I still take strong exception to the manner in which you came by it. Secondly, and before you get carried away with thinking you're indispensable, I would just like to make it clear that since you've been here you have partially filled a gap...nothing more! Although the work for which you've been trained may be satisfactory, your shorthand leaves a lot to be desired, you're still unreliable—to say the least—with the computer, and your driving...' he shot her a look filled with stinging mockery, 'is tending to become erratic. Would you mind keeping your speed down a little until you know the road better?'

It was true her foot had been pressing down harder during his scornful diatribe, but it wasn't until she actually looked at the speedometer that Debra realised just how hard and, with a sharply indrawn breath, she eased it off again. Not that she didn't consider her foot had cause to become heavy. She felt that way all over now. Saxon's remarks had been fashioned to cause the most hurt and they had achieved their purpose extremely well!

'I s-still don't think you're being entirely f-fair,' she began, and was dismayed to hear an unmistakable tremor in her voice.

'I told you the night we met I didn't intend to be,' he countered roughly.

'So you did.' The dampness beginning to creep on to her lashes she blinked away furiously. She wasn't going to be accused of producing false tears again. 'Along with the threat to make my life hell, if I remember correctly.'

'And have I?'

'No!' she denied thickly, defiantly, although not altogether truthfully.

'Never say die, huh?' He read between the lines shrewdly.

'Not to you!'

His following smile was slow and confident. 'We'll see.'

Somehow his statement had an ominous ring to it and Debra couldn't help turning to look at him. In the sunlight her eyes were a deep shimmering violet, very beautiful, but very apprehensive. For a brief second their glances held, and then she had to turn back to the road.

'Sorry, sweetheart, it doesn't wash,' Saxon grated caustically.

'I beg your pardon?' Her forehead furrowed in bafflement.

'The wide-eyed, damsel in distress look!'

When her gaze flashed momentarily his way this time her expression of anxiety had been displaced by one of seething rebellion. 'I wouldn't waste my time even trying to appeal to your finer feelings, Saxon McAllister, because I sincerely doubt if you have any!' she disparaged vehemently.

'Not where you're concerned, at any rate!' he immediately returned with equal acrimony.

Debra bit at her lip as a dark wave of depression rolled inexorably over her. It all seemed so terribly one-sided, and her original counter-threat to make his life unbearable as well a tiny ineffectual voice crying in the wind. No matter what she said or did he immediately suspected her motives and, although he had gone to great pains to decry her performance so far, she still didn't consider her efforts to have been total failures. True, she had made some mistakes—didn't everyone in a new job?—but nowhere near as many as he liked to imply, and certainly none of any magnitude.

Engrossed as she was in her own musings, Saxon needed to repeat his instruction for her to pull over when the driver of a car approaching from the opposite direction indicated his intention to do the same, his second command being issued in a far more forceful voice and accompanied by a sarcastic, 'Or is that asking too much of your capabilities?'

Deeming it best not to reply to such a taunting gibe, she merely shrugged and eased to a stop on the gravelled shoulder of the road and sat waiting as Saxon alighted and walked to the front of the ute, where he was shortly joined by the other driver. Not that she could hear anything but a muted murmur from their conversation, but Debra guessed them to be old friends by the manner of their expressions and easy demeanour, the stranger being of approximately the same age as her employer, his features clean-cut and pleasant.

A few minutes later both men walked towards her open window and she found herself staring into a pair of deeply appreciative brown eyes as Saxon introduced her to Paul Bartlett, the son of a neighbouring property owner.

'I was just discussing the details with Mac for our cricket match next Sunday,' he relayed. 'I suppose you'll be playing for Wyeera.'

'I—I don't know,' she half smiled after her eyes had moved involuntarily to Saxon and then back again when no help had been forthcoming. 'Do the women usually play?'

'The younger ones do when it's a charity match like this one. All proceeds from the day are for the local hospital, but there's a dozen bottles of champagne for the winners.' Resting his forearms on the edge of the window, he eyed her in mock interrogation. 'Have you ever played before?'

'A little,' she admitted with a laugh. At the orphanage it had always been a case of one in, all in.

'Then that settles it, she definitely plays for Wyeera,' Saxon broke in, grinning banteringly at his friend.

'Don't be too sure!' Paul's return look was just as chafing. 'Remember, the match is on our place this year and *I'm* the one who'll be making up the teams. You already have too many good batsmen as it is.'

'But not batswomen,' came the swift counter-change.

'The teams all consist of an equal number from both sexes,' Paul advised Debra in an aside before turning to retort, 'I don't know about that! One of your stockmen's wives made mincemeat of our bowling last time.'

'Ah, but neither Joy nor Kevin will be playing this year, they're away on leave at the moment.'

'I can't say I'm sorry,' joked Paul wryly. 'The pair of them scored far too many runs for my liking.'

'The bowling's not too fast, is it?' Debra inserted a little nervously after pondering his previous remark.

His eyes twinkled as he smiled down at her. 'No, we're very gallant where the ladies are concerned. The first time you're dismissed isn't counted and we bowl underarm. Unless, of course, you start slogging us all over the paddock, in which case we may be tempted to resort to stronger measures,' he grinned.

Pearl-white teeth gleamed in acknowledgment. 'And the men, do they get two chances as well?' she asked.

'Good lord, no! It's fair dinkum when one of us is at the crease.' He looked across at Saxon and started to laugh. 'A fight to the last ditch, you might say, eh, old son?'

'And especially if it's Noonameena and Wyeera who make the final,' was the dry reply.

Noonameena being the Bartletts' property, surmised Debra. 'From which, I gather, there's more than just two teams taking part?' she directed her question towards Paul.

'Mmm, although that more or less depends on how many people arrive. We can usually manage about four teams, though, but with considerably more than the accepted number of eleven a side, of course.'

Her arched brows lifted slightly in surprise. 'In that case, wouldn't it take all day just to play one game?'

He shook his head quickly and smiled. 'Not really. You see, we put a limit on the number of runs anyone's allowed to score, we only have single innings, and there's also a restriction on the number of balls bowled. Apart from that,' his dark brown eyes danced humorously, 'not many of our players are that good that they stay at the wicket for very long, anyway.'

'I'm not surprised if you have such large fielding sides.'

'Oh, we rarely have the whole team on the field at the one time,' he discounted. 'That's the men's province in the main, while the women see to the food and drinks, etcetera. The day's intended as a social get-together rather than sports event, so if you would rather sit and talk you can, but if you want to field you can do that also.'

'In other words, everyone does their own thing,' she laughed.

'Just about,' he agreed with an answering, and admiring, smile.

'Right—well, if there's nothing else you wanted to see me about, Paul, we'd better be on our way.' Saxon successfully put an end to their conversation and began moving around the front of the vehicle. 'Debra has a considerable amount of work to do before she collects Prue this afternoon.'

'Okay, Mac.' His friend reluctantly levered himself away from the ute. 'I'll see you both on Sunday, then?'

'Uh-huh,' Saxon concurred laconically.

With a last smile and a salute to the brim of his hat Paul took his leave and headed across the road while Saxon regained his seat, and then they were mobile again.

'Does everyone call you Mac?' Debra queried interestedly, thankful for the breeze that had begun blowing through the cabin again.

'Only my friends.'

Hiding a grimace, she concentrated on the road ahead. Another snub for Miss Armitage? she asked herself wryly. It was becoming a demoralising but, no doubt from his point of view, successful habit. With a sigh she recalled another matter she had to ask him about.

'Prue mentioned she sometimes stays in town to play with one of her friends after school. I said I would check with you whether it was all right for me to pick her up later in the afternoon,' she explained.

'It is, provided you keep a sharp eye out for kangaroos on the way home,' he allowed levelly. 'As the day gets cooler they like to feed alongside the road and they have the unnerving habit of waiting until you're right beside them and then deciding they want to cross over.'

'I'll be careful,' she vowed earnestly. The responsibility for someone else's child she was discovering to be quite a sobering one.

By now Saxon had returned his attention to the mail and Debra was happy to complete the remainder of the journey in silence—and even happier when, after driving the ute down to the store shed, she found he didn't plan to accompany her back to the office but simply handed the mail to her, along with the perfunctory question, 'You're clear on what information needs to be taken from the files?'

'Yes, thank you.'

Her answer was confident, and so was she, but when she was actually at the typewriter and starting to record all the necessary details from the computer, what she suddenly realised she hadn't envisaged was just how time-consuming the work would be. For every stud animal listed for the auction there was a tremendous amount of information which needed to be gathered.

First there was the name and Lot number of the animal itself, together with its calving date, registration number, colour, and tattoo number. Then she had to extract the names of the four preceding generations in the sire's line, but luckily, only three in the dam's. Even so, it still amounted to another twenty-two animals which had to be noted each time—along with all their triple-barrelled names and five or six-figured registration numbers, of course!

When lunchtime arrived she had just about managed to memorise the reference sire's pedigree, only to discover as she turned the page of notes Saxon had left with her that the following group had come from a different parent altogether and that she would need to repeat the exercise all over again.

The one redeeming feature of her morning was that only Eleanor joined her for the midday meal in the dining room, thereby giving her the opportunity to relax a little, as well as escape from what she could well imagine would be the undeserved, but no less scathing, comments of her employer on finding how far she had progressed.

In actual fact he didn't put in an appearance at all until late in the afternoon, just as she was tidying up before leaving to fetch Prue, and she waited patiently, and just a little defiantly, as he scanned the pages of typewritten information she had completed.

Finally he replaced the papers on her desk and raised his head. 'Is that *all* you've done?' he quizzed in a condescending tone.

It was just the type of comment Debra had been expecting and she slanted her chin distinctly higher, refusing to be forced on to the defensive. 'Yes! It's very complex work.'

'Excuses... already?' His expression had a definite touch of sarcasm to it.

'No!' she denied fiercely, resentfully. 'There's nothing wrong with my typing speed, even if I do say so myself.' It was certain he never would! 'So I doubt if even my supposedly super-efficient predecessor could have done any more.'

'Not even if she only copied each reference sire's pedigree once, instead of every time?'

The implication might have been softly made, but its import rang inside Debra's head like a clanging bell of monstrous proportions, and her gaze started to waver doubtfully.

'You didn't say to do it only once,' she half accused, half protested. 'You merely said to copy out the relevant details of each animal's pedigree.'

'By which direction I assumed you would have the common sense to realise that I wouldn't be wanting a catalogue filled with repetitious information!' he gibed blisteringly. 'If you'd used your brain a little more that list could have been on its way to the printers this afternoon.'

'Then if it was so damned important that it leave today maybe you should have made your instructions a little more explicit!' she flashed, breathing hard, and stung by what she considered to be his unwarranted condemnation. If she had taken it upon herself to leave something out she was positive there would have been the devil to pay. 'Besides, surely one day isn't going to make that much difference. It will all be completed and checked by tomorrow.'

'Well, isn't that nice?' His sarcasm was almost tangible—that was, until it disappeared beneath an escalating anger. 'Especially since we only happen to get one mail a week in and out of Acacia Crossing!'

'How was I to know that?' Debra had no choice but to defend herself now. 'It might have helped if you'd told me.'

'I can't see how!' He picked up the papers from her desk and then dropped them again contemptuously. 'You obviously weren't capable of finishing it, anyway!'

'That's neither true nor fair!' she protested furiously. 'It would have been if you'd taken the trouble to explain it properly. Or don't you believe in accepting responsibility for *your* mistakes, Mr McAllister?'

Saxon's blue eyes glittered frostily at her attack. 'My only mistake, sweetheart, was in not overruling Eleanor's decision to hire you in the first place! That,' he flung a hand towards her painstaking efforts, 'isn't evidence of a mistake, but of ignorance. Your ignorance in not knowing the subject, of not being qualified to do the work, of not checking with last year's catalogue to see for yourself how much information was wanted!'

'I did try to find one!' she cried, her hands clenching at her sides, her nails digging painfully into her palms. 'But there weren't any in the filing cabinet or the cupboard.'

'So it didn't occur to you to try my desk!' he disparaged scornfully, wrenching open the bottom drawer and slapping a grey and orange booklet on to the inlaid leather centre. 'That would have been too much to expect, I suppose?'

Debra nodded, barely able to get her words past the increasing lump of indignation in her throat. 'Under the circumstances, yes, it would!' she ground out tautly. 'If you'd happened to come in while I was searching your desk, I'm sure praising me for my initiative would have been the very last thought to enter your mind.'

'Oh? What then, in your opinion, would have been my reaction?'

'To accuse me of stealing or prying, most probably!'

'Two crimes totally unknown to you, of course!'

Oh, God, what was he accusing her of now? Sudden despair overwhelmed her like a smothering blanket, enveloping all her previously outraged emotions in a cocoon of helplessness and, needing desperately to escape, she turned blindly for the door.

'I—I'll be late for Prue,' she whispered shakily, and began half running towards the verandah on trembling legs.

Before she could push open the screen door a vice-like grip on her arm halted her headlong flight and she was spun around to stand with her back to the wall.

'You're not driving anywhere!' she was informed by a terse voice.

'Why, aren't I qualified enough to do that either?' Her head drooped forward listlessly.

'At the moment, too right you're not! You're more likely to run off the road and kill yourself.'

'And naturally you wouldn't want the ute damaged in such a fashion,' she gibed bitterly.

A rough hand ensnared her chin and jerked her face upwards. 'For a remark like that I could quite cheerfully dispose of you with my own two hands!' he rasped savagely. 'But, as beautiful a corpse as you'd make, I've no wish to have it on my conscience.'

'I didn't think you had one,' she attempted to laugh, only it broke in the middle.

'Then you would be wrong, wouldn't you?'

'Again?' she grimaced.

'Again,' he endorsed drily, his attractive mouth made even more appealing by its humorous upward curve.

Confused by her own emotional reaction to his smile, Debra centred her gaze on a less disturbing area—the darkly bronzed column of his throat. 'Prue will be wondering if I've forgotten her,' she murmured evasively.

'I doubt it, knowing my niece,' he contradicted wryly. 'She's more likely to be making the most of the extra time at her disposal.'

'Maybe,' she acceded weakly, pulling out of his grasp. His touch had been having a strangely hypnotic effect on her senses. 'But I'd still better be going.'

'Uh-uh!' Saxon shook his head emphatically. 'You can give it a miss for today. I'll send one of the men in for her.'

'But it is part of my job, and—and . . .'

'You don't intend to give me the opportunity of saying you're not capable in that regard as well?' he surmised ironically.

'Partly.' Her confession was selfconsciously made. 'But mainly because I had no intention of running off the road, anyway.'

'The conditions here not tough enough for that yet, hmm?'

The pupils of her violet eyes dilated nervously. Now what was he suggesting? That there was worse to come? Just the thought of it was enough to have her moving agitatedly from one foot to the other.

'Forget it!' he snapped suddenly, dragging a hand irritably around the back of his neck. 'And forget about driving in for Prue too. *I'll* see that she's collected.'

Without giving her an opportunity to reply—for the second time—Saxon pushed out through the screen door and strode down the steps from the verandah. Debra watched him leave with a soft lip caught indecisively between her teeth. Not only were her emotions completely jumbled now, but her thoughts were as well. His behaviour had been so totally out of character, and so unexpected, that she really hadn't a clue what to make of it!

CHAPTER FIVE

'YOU REMEMBER Anthea Devenish, don't you, Debra? You met at the Show in Brisbane.'

It was the day of the cricket match at Noonameena and the petite, brown-haired and hazel-eyed girl had begun making her way over to them immediately she saw the car pull up.

'Yes, of course,' Debra smiled politely in answer to Eleanor's query. And to the newcomer, 'It's nice to see you again.'

Which wasn't strictly true since she had found the other girl's attitude rather patronising the night they had been introduced, but, for the sake of propriety, she was willing to try and be friendly.

Evidently Anthea didn't feel under any such obligation, however, for the slight flickering of her lips could hardly have been called more than a perfunctory acknowledgment of the greeting and, with only a brief word for Eleanor and a condescending pat on the head for Prue, she made it all too plain just whose company she was seeking.

'Mac! I thought you were never going to arrive!' she exclaimed, a smile certainly to the fore now as she linked her arm proprietorially with his. 'Mummy and I only came home from the city yesterday and we brought my cousin Brendan with us. He's one of the

Eldridges of Aurora Peak, you know. Do come and meet him.'

'Shortly, Anthea,' Saxon smiled back easily. 'I'll just take these things up to the homestead for Eleanor and then I'll be with you,' as he disengaged his arm from hers in order to open the luggage compartment of the car.

Debra moved forward, intending to help carry one of the hampers Sherry had carefully packed earlier that morning, but on reaching out to grip a handle found a male hand beating her to it.

'I'll take that for you,' Paul Bartlett offered cheerfully, his brown eyes telling her more adequately than words could have done that he was fully aware of the attractive picture she made in her close-fitting red slacks and white cotton top. 'We don't want to wear out your batting arm before the match even starts.'

'Thank you,' she smiled as they began heading for the house in a group, the men carrying the larger items and Prue commandeering the last small basket. 'But from that, do I assume that I'm on your team, after all?'

'No such luck, I'm afraid.' His response was accompanied by a wryly downcast expression. 'In the interests of fairness I really couldn't have put you down for any other side except Wyeera's. As it is, I've had to make up the number of females on your team with a couple of the girls from town.'

'Did you put Grandma's and my name down too?' chimed in Prue anxiously.

'I certainly did yours,' he grinned down at her, but to Eleanor's obvious relief went on to advise, 'although not your grandma's. I thought she would prefer to just watch.'

'Heavens, yes, and especially in this heat,' Eleanor added her own earnest thoughts on the matter. 'It's going to be a long hot day by the feel of it.'

Six heads nodded almost in unison in acknowledgment of that forecast, and then Anthea was calling coyly across from Saxon's other side, 'And whose team am I on...Mac's?'

Paul's mouth pulled in imperceptibly at the corners. 'Would I dare put you on any other?'

'I should hope not,' she retorted gaily, but with just the smallest hint of a bite to her voice. 'Otherwise I might refuse to play altogether!'

Everyone smiled politely at what Debra presumed was Anthea's attempted joke—even though she wouldn't have put it past the other girl to carry out her threat if Paul's answer hadn't been to her liking—and then, while the men took the hampers through to the kitchen, Eleanor began introducing Debra to those people who were making the most of their opportunity to relax in the cool comfort of the glassed-in verandah before the day's events got under way.

Not only were there families there from the surrounding district, as well as most of the population of Acacia Crossing, but some had travelled several hundred miles to participate in what had become an annual event, and there was an air of lightheartedness and festivity about the proceedings which struck an extremely responsive chord deep within Debra's system.

Perhaps because so many of them lived in such isolation and had to depend on their neighbours in times of need, they seemed like one enormous family when they came together on such occasions. A family wherein each member knew the abilities, and shortcomings, of the others, but accepted them tolerantly because, in order to survive in such an unpredictable and often hostile environment, there was no other way.

It took Paul quite some time to marshall the various teams in the paddock beyond the homestead gardens where two strips had been slashed and mown to provide the necessary wickets—the rest of the grass left ankle-high because no one deliberately destroyed more feed than they had to when it might be vital to stock in the long summer months ahead. When Saxon won the toss and decided on his team being one of those to bat first, Debra retired to the house to help set up the tables and chairs which would be necessary for lunch beneath the shady cover provided by jacaranda, bauhinia, and pepper trees.

Nevertheless, it seemed hardly any time at all before one of the score-keepers was calling, 'Debra, you're on next!' and she found herself walking out across the sun-scorched paddock again to the accompaniment of calls from her fellow team members for good luck. Something, she wryly considered she would need a considerable amount of, since her partner at the other end was none other than her boss. If anything was going to make her nervous and destroy her concentration, he would!

Not that he would purposely make things difficult for her out there in front of everyone—that wasn't his way—but during the last week she had sensed that his attitude towards her had altered in some inexplicable and undefined manner. He still found fault with most of what she did, of course, but somehow his resentment of her presence wasn't quite so noticeable any more, with the result that her own guard had relaxed with each day that passed.

And it was the lessening of those defences which was causing most of her trouble now! Instead of being able to channel all her emotions into feelings of dislike and defiance, she was discovering them to be openly responding to a virile magnetism which both dismayed and annoyed her. Dismayed, because he was coming to occupy far too large a proportion of her thoughts, and annoyed, because even if she had been searching for a beau ideal—which she certainly wasn't!—then Saxon McAllister with his so vastly different background and upbringing would be the last person she'd choose to become infatuated with.

Determinedly, she made ready to receive her first ball and, as if venting her displeasure with herself on the red missile as it bounced towards her, she swung at it forcefully, if not stylishly, and cracked it straight over the heads of the inner fieldsmen. For a moment hardly anyone moved as surprise registered on all their faces, including Debra's, to see the ball bumping across the outfield with a lone figure in furious pursuit. Then a jubilant cheer rang out from those clustered at the rails and, recovering her senses, she began racing for the wicket at the other end of the pitch.

'You keep that up and we'll have them beaten in no time,' Saxon advised hastily as they passed each other the first time.

'I think it was a fluke!' she half laughed, half panted, when they crossed again.

'Well, whatever it was, try and repeat it...often!' he urged with a laugh on their third run.

Fortunately, at least for Debra, the ball had been returned to the bowler by then, precluding their need to run again, and she wiped the back of her hand over her now perspiration-bedewed forehead as she waited while Saxon faced the next ball.

After that their scores mounted steadily until, with one last powerful sweep, Saxon reached the limit of his allowed runs and had to retire. One of Wyeera's stockmen quickly took his place, but after managing to block a couple of balls he swung wildly at the following one and sent it straight into the hands of a waiting fieldsman with nothing added to their total. The next person to share the wicket with her was Anthea.

Dainty, elegantly outfitted Anthea, who ambled out to her place as if no one had anything better to do than to wait on her convenience, and then made such a performance about finding just the right spot to stand that someone on the sidelines was impelled to threaten in an exasperated voice, 'Get on with it, or we'll start deducting points for holding up the game!'

Anthea glared in the general direction of the homestead, brushed her hair back from her face with a beautifully manicured hand, and finally took her stance. But as it happened, Debra found her a harder partner to play with than Saxon had been. Even if he had nearly run her off her feet, at least she knew when he called for her to run it was safe to do so. With Anthea exactly the opposite was the case, and after being dismissed for the first time because the other girl started moving and then changed her mind and went back, leaving Debra to be stumped, she treated all her future calls with extreme caution—and some suspicion—when, after she had nearly done the same thing a second time, Anthea purred, 'I'm so sorry. I should hate to be the one to ruin your chance of a high score.'

I'm sure you would! grimaced Debra wryly to herself, but although she tried desperately hard to avoid it, the very next time she herself called for Anthea to run the other girl absolutely refused to move at all, and before Debra could return to her own end the ball had reached her wicket first.

'Oh, dear!' Anthea managed to look suitably remorseful. 'I suppose I should have run, but really...' she fanned a delicate hand in front of her face, 'I don't think I could have made it. I'm just too out of breath.'

'That's all right,' Debra shrugged off the facetious-sounding apology evenly. It was only a game, after all, even though Anthea didn't look over-extended in the slightest. 'These things happen.'

'I'm just not much of a cricketer, I'm afraid.'

Debra merely smiled, perfunctorily, but didn't comment as she started back across the open paddock where she met Neale Stafford—Saxon's stud manager—as he came to take her place.

'Bad luck,' he commiserated, accepting the bat from her. 'We all thought you were going to make the limit.'

'The fates decreed otherwise,' she laughed over her shoulder as she kept walking.

Prue was the first to greet her and guided her to where the others were sitting and talking beneath the trees. 'Gee, you were good,' she sighed with touching admiration. 'You got twenty-five runs.'

'Did I?' Debra smiled in surprise. She had lost count after the first few. 'That just goes to show what nice easy bowling can do to improve your game, doesn't it?'

'Saxon didn't seem to think so.'

'Oh? What makes you say that?'

'Because I heard him telling Grandma that he wished he had another six like you in the team.'

Debra's eyebrows flew upwards. That didn't sound like the Saxon she knew! She was more than half expecting to be thoroughly roasted for having allowed herself to be run out so easily. Twice!

'He was probably only joking,' she suggested lightly, then turned to acknowledge with a smile Pat Beasley's approving, 'That was a real good effort, lass!' as he sat waiting his turn for one of the other teams.

'An extremely good effort,' affirmed Eleanor sincerely as Debra literally sank down on an empty seat beside her. 'Would you like a drink, dear?'

'Yes, please!' she breathed fervently, her head nodding, her eyes closed. 'I think I could drink a bucket dry right at the moment.'

The older woman leant over to catch at her arm anxiously. 'I do hope it wasn't too much for you. I noticed you weren't wearing a hat.'

About to deny there was anything amiss—except that she was boiling hot and her throat bone-dry—Debra wasn't given an opportunity to do so, because immediately on perceiving his stepmother's worried gesture Saxon had broken off his conversation with a couple some short distance away and returned to Eleanor's side to question frowningly, 'What's wrong?'

On hearing his voice Debra promptly pushed herself upright, her eyes flashing open. 'Nothing's *wrong*,' she protested drily. 'I'm just thirsty, that's all.'

'Mmm, it was rather warm out there, wasn't it?' he agreed with such a slow smile that she had to close her eyes again in order to counteract the effect it was having on her. 'What would you like to drink?'

She shook her head absently. 'I don't really care, as long as it's cold and there's plenty of it.'

'I'll get you something,' offered Prue quickly, helpfully. 'I know where they are.'

'Thank you,' Debra smiled at her appreciatively. 'That's very kind of you, Prue.'

In her absence, and while Eleanor was distracted by a passing friend, Saxon perched his lithe length on the table beside Debra, his brilliant blue eyes never wavering from her heart-shaped face.

'You played very well,' he commended softly.

Horribly selfconscious all of a sudden, she shrugged deprecatorily. 'Not well enough to stop myself being stupidly run out.'

'I rather thought that wasn't altogether your fault.'

'No?' She stared at him, amazed. Surely he wasn't making excuses on *her* account! 'Well, I suppose we all get our signals crossed at some time or another.'

'So that's what happened.' He seemed to accept her explanation readily enough. 'Weren't you calling clearly enough?'

'Apparently not.' She took the line of least resistance. There was nothing to be gained in trying to convince him his lady friend wasn't of a particularly sporting disposition.

'I got you a jug of lemon with lots of ice in it!' Prue suddenly burst back on to the scene, a glass carafe in one hand and a tumbler in the other.

'Thank you, that looks delicious,' Debra smiled as she accepted the glass the child had filled for her and drank from it slowly, savouring every last refreshing drop. 'Aren't you having any?'

'No, I'm not thirsty,' Prue shook her head swiftly. Then, as her wandering gaze roved over the crowd, 'Oh, there's Jenny. I've been looking for her all morning,' and she was off in another direction before anyone had a chance to speak.

'From the way she fits in here it's obvious she's no stranger to Wyeera, or Acacia Crossing,' Debra commented thoughtfully as she watched the small figure disappear from sight.

'No, her parents often go away on these trips. This is the second time this year she's stayed with us,' Saxon revealed tolerantly.

'You don't mind?' as her eyes flicked up to his the light shone across them, turning them to a soft shade of lilac. 'I mean, it makes a lot of extra work for you, or one of your staff, to keep taking her to and from school each day.'

'Finding it a nuisance already, are you?'

A gibing harshness seemed to have settled about him which hadn't been there a moment before and she blinked in surprise. 'No, of course not!' she defended herself quickly, and vexed that he should have chosen to put such an interpretation on her remark. 'I rather enjoy my trips into town, as a matter of fact. It's just that I thought it would be less bother if she was enrolled for the School of the Air.'

One eyebrow quirked sardonically. 'Less bother for whom?'

He was being deliberately perverse, and she didn't know why! 'Well, for Prue, for a start,' she put forward tartly. 'Those journeys must be very tiring for her.'

'Out here there's younger children who have to make longer ones... every day of the year.'

Debra clamped down on her rising temper only with difficulty. 'Maybe!' she retorted stormily. 'But I happened to have been talking about Prue. It must be hard for her to adapt to all those hours travelling whenever she comes here.'

'It's far less of a change than if she had to keep switching from a normal classroom situation to one of correspondence lessons coupled with the School of the Air at home,' he countered satirically. 'And *we* considered it was more important for the manner of her lessons to remain unchanged, rather than worry about the inconvenience it might cause one of our staff in driving her to school.'

The former point Debra was prepared to concede—now that he had finally made his way round to explaining it—but during the course of the conversation he appeared to have neatly turned her innocent enquiry into an attack on her personal willingness, and she sighed disconsolately. Obviously his attitude towards her hadn't so much changed over the last few days as it had been lying dormant!

'Oh, dear, have I missed anything?' Eleanor now turned to fix them with a querying gaze as her friend moved on. 'You are all right, Debra? The heat wasn't too much for you?'

'No, I'm fine, thank you, Eleanor,' she reassured the concerned woman quietly, although her accompanying smile wasn't quite as bright as it could have been. And hurriedly, in an effort to divert their attention elsewhere, 'Oh, look, I think Anthea's on her way back. I expect she'll be wanting something to drink as well.'

So she did, and while Saxon was away procuring a glass for her, the diminutive brunette arranged herself comfortably on a chair on Eleanor's other side.

'I really don't know why I let myself be talked into playing each year,' she immediately started to complain in long-suffering tones. 'It's not even as if I like the game.'

Debra suspected her employer provided the major incentive for the other girl's participation, but of course could hardly say so, and she left it to Eleanor to make a suitably appropriate comment. Which she did with considerable fervour.

'But it is for charity, Anthea,' she was reminded unequivocally. 'Those fees which everyone pays so they can play, and the sale of drinks and food provided by the Ladies' Auxiliary all goes for a very good cause. We raise a considerable amount of money throughout the year from days like this, and it also provides entertainment and an opportunity for everyone to gather socially, don't forget.'

Anthea didn't look as if she cared about meeting everyone socially. 'Oh, I suppose so,' she submitted less than enthusiastically, then altered her demeanour entirely when Saxon returned with another glass, which he filled and handed to her.

'Thank you so much,' she smiled up at him with such blatant eagerness that Debra had to turn away. 'Come and sit next to me so we can talk,' patting the seat beside her. 'We've hardly had a chance to say anything, except for that short time when you met Brendan. That's better,' she approved archly once he had complied with her request. 'Now, tell me how our team's going. Are we likely to win?'

For someone who only moments ago had been declaring how she disliked the game the change was quite startling, and Debra couldn't help her lips from curving wryly. Anthea was so obvious it was unbelievable! Or perhaps she just didn't care if all and sundry knew what her intentions were as long as she attained her goal. It was an obscurely dampening thought and one Debra didn't care to contemplate further, so it was with some relief, as well as genuine pleasure, that she noticed Paul and Neale Stafford walking towards them, together with Paul's sister Jeanne, who she had learnt that morning was Neale's fiancée.

'Have you all bitten the dust too?' she smiled as soon as they had pulled up chairs and seated themselves.

'Well, Neale and Paul didn't, they both scored the limit,' Jeanne relayed with a grin. 'But I'm afraid I rather let the side down somewhat.'

'Went for a duck, she did! No score at all,' Paul reproved with mock disgust.

'Mmm, I was so busy sneaking glances to see how Neale was faring in the other game that I missed the ball completely, and before I knew it my middle stump had disappeared,' his sister explained impatiently.

'You're forgetting your first effort,' he prompted drily.

'Don't be nasty!' She wrinkled her nose at him goodnaturedly and confessed, 'I was partnering Dad at the time, and he'd just belted a beauty, so I immediately set off like a mad thing. The only trouble was,' she started to laugh, 'someone caught it, and by the time I realised what was happening, the ball had been returned and I was out as well.' Amid the ensuing laughter she turned to Debra. 'How many did you score?'

'Twenty-five, according to Prue.'

'It would probably have been more, except for me,' Anthea leant across to advise, sweetly apologetic. 'But I'm sorry to say I'm just not as fast and as athletic as Debra is. I'm more at home with golf, or one of those less vigorous sports. Although,' she was quick to add, 'I *do* admire those robust girls who can stand up to the rigours of men's games and play as their equals. It's just that I'm not one of them,' she smiled with feline satisfaction.

Having been made to feel like a cross between a greyhound and the Incredible Hulk, Debra looked down at her slim, one hundred and twenty pound, five foot six length, and shook her head wryly.

'I would hardly call it competing on equal terms with the men when they're bowling underarm,' she half laughed.

'No, of course it isn't!' Surprisingly, it was Eleanor who broke into the conversation, her voice more vexed than Debra had ever heard it. 'It's utterly ridiculous to even suggest that might be the case, and I'm sure Debra would be the last person to want to compete under such conditions. I've never heard such nonsense in all my life!'

In the momentary silence which followed, Saxon's clear blue gaze locked with Debra's and she held his unfathomable glance with a slight defiance in her own. It wasn't her fault if his stepmother chose to champion his secretary instead of his lady friend!

Then he was turning to the older woman to drawl, 'Apart from the fact that I doubt very much if Anthea meant any harm by her remarks...'

Whereupon the red-faced girl at his side immediately confirmed, 'No! No, of course not!'

'I have the feeling that the chicken you're trying so hard to harbour beneath your wings, Eleanor, is more than capable of taking care of herself, should it be necessary,' he concluded with sardonic emphasis.

Although she looked considerably mollified, Eleanor apparently still wasn't altogether appeased, because she promptly sent him a frowning sideways glance and queried, 'Meaning?'

'Only that the next time *I* feel the sharp edge of her tongue won't be the first!' He subtly relieved the strained atmosphere by giving them something to laugh at. 'Believe me, if Debra considers you're out of line, she doesn't hesitate to let you know.'

'Good for you!' chuckled Jeanne delightedly, taking her cue from Saxon and keeping the talk flowing. 'We can't have these men believing they're infallible, can we?'

Debra smiled and agreed, but her eyes were wistful, and she only half heard Paul and Neale's bantering remonstrances. To defuse an awkward situation—for both his stepmother's and Anthea's sakes—Saxon had deliberately made it sound as if he was the one who came off worst in their encounters. Whereas, in actual truth, they both knew exactly the opposite was true. She had never managed to defeat him yet, and with a sinking feeling in the pit of her stomach, for the first time she really began to doubt if she ever could.

'Hey! Where have you drifted off to?'

Paul's laughing enquiry brought her back to the present sharply and had her shaking her head self-consciously on discovering herself to be the focal point for everyone's attention.

'Nowhere in particular,' she parried protectively, and urged a light smile to her lips. 'I was just day-dreaming, I guess. I'm sorry.'

'You're excused,' he pardoned her with a recipro-cating grin. 'But Eleanor was just saying it's time to head for the house and help bring out the lunches. She thought you might like to go with her.'

'Oh, yes, of course. I said I would.'

'You don't have to, if you would rather sit here for a while longer,' Eleanor assured her kindly.

'No, really, I'd like to help.' Debra was on her feet before another suggestion to the contrary could be made. At least while she was working she would be able to occupy her mind with thoughts of other things besides her employer. 'Have they nearly finished?' nodding towards the players still out in the paddock.

'They probably will have by the time we've had our lunch.' It was Neale who answered her question. 'Then they'll have theirs while we're out in the field. We don't all stop to eat at the same time because we find it takes too long.'

Which, naturally enough, made lunch an extremely casual affair, with people coming and going as they pleased, stopping for something to eat and a talk, and then either going out to the paddock again or wait-ing, relaxed, for their turn with the bat.

It also made the meal stretch over a couple of hours or more, so that by the time all the ladies present had finished clearing the tables, the next innings was well on its way to being completed.

'By the way,' Jeanne said to Debra as they, to-gether with Eleanor, resumed their seats beneath the trees, armed with some glasses and a jug of fresh orange juice this time. No one had protested when

Anthea wandered off to join some other friends now that the object of her attention was fielding. 'Our monthly supper-dance is on in town next Saturday, in case you didn't know. Neale, Paul and I usually attend and I wondered if you'd like to come too.'

'Yes, I would like to,' Debra began, and then chewed at her lip doubtfully. 'Although I—I think I'd better check with Saxon first to see if it's okay with him.'

Jeanne's blue eyes widened in astonishment. 'Whatever for?'

'Well, I—we might be too busy for me to get away, what with the sale coming up, and all.' It didn't sound a particularly feasible reason, even to Debra, but without revealing the true state which existed between Saxon and herself there wasn't much else she could say.

'But surely not on a Saturday?'

'No, I shouldn't think so,' Eleanor added her weight to the discussion with a slight frown. 'Besides, hasn't Saxon been asked to judge the Brahman section at the Stratheden Show next Friday and Saturday?' Her eyes sought Debra's for confirmation.

'I—er—don't know. He hasn't mentioned anything about it to me.' When did he ever deign to tell her anything but the barest essentials? And then usually only at the very last minute.

'Well, I'm sure it will be all right, anyway,' Eleanor smiled encouragingly. 'You go ahead and make your arrangements and I'll explain to Saxon. It's good for you to get away from the property every so often.'

'But I do that twice each school day,' Debra laughed. 'And I accompanied you to your Ladies' Auxiliary and Garden Club meetings last week.'

'So you did.' Eleanor patted her arm softly, gratefully. 'I don't know what I would have done without those notes you made for me. I'm afraid I forget so many things these days unless I write them down immediately.'

'Oops, there goes another of your opposition, Debra,' interposed Jeanne with a chuckle, seeing another batsman head back towards the homestead. 'It shouldn't be long now till we find out who's going to be in the play-off.'

'Have you any ideas which teams they're likely to be?'

The other girl shrugged and grinned. 'Your guess is as good as mine, although Wyeera were scoring pretty well early in their innings.'

'But not Noonameena?'

'Not while I was around, that's for sure!' came the laughing response. 'I was talking to Mike Allworth—you know, from Simmonds' Primary?—while we were clearing up, though, and he reckoned Acacia Crossing had also begun strongly this year, so it might be the two of you in the final. It doesn't look as if Town and Country are posing much problem for your bowlers at the moment.' She paused and held up an arresting hand. 'But back to Saturday. How about you drive over here with Neale, have dinner with us, and then we can all go in together? That's what we usually do.'

'It sounds fine to me—and thank you,' Debra smiled her gratitude. 'I might enjoy the drive to town during the day, but I'm not so sure I'd like it on my own at night.'

'Oh, there's no need to worry. Even if you did get stranded someone would come to look for you if you hadn't arrived at your destination within a reasonable time,' Jeanne imparted her information with a nonchalance born of familiarity. 'And we don't have any Min Min lights round here to make you nervous. They're further north.'

'Min Min lights?' Debra repeated dubiously.

'Mmm, haven't you heard of them?' Jeanne warmed to her subject with a gleeful impishness. 'They're very bright lights which suddenly appear out of nowhere at night, but no one knows for certain just what they are, or what causes them, because they only come *so* close and then—poof!' she snapped her fingers quickly, 'they go out...and reappear behind you!'

'You're having me on!'

'No, honestly, that's what they've been known to do,' she vowed seriously. 'People who have been stopped on the road at night say they've thought they were the headlights of another car coming towards them, only they never quite make it right to you, but go out and then reappear somewhere else. Often behind you. Apparently the Aboriginals have known about them for generations,' she went on informatively, 'but the first white person to see one—so the story goes—was a stockman coming home one night when suddenly this bright light reared up from behind a tombstone in the local cemetery—sending his horse berserk—and scaring the living daylights out of him. He promptly galloped hell for leather to the Min Min hotel, hence the name, and the damned light chased him the whole way there.'

'And no one knows what they are?' sceptically.

'There's been lots of suggestions,' Jeanne shrugged insouciantly. 'Spontaneous combustion of gases from bore-heads, natural phenomena brought about by atmospheric variations, birds with a phosphorescent substance on their wings . . . oh, all sorts of weird and wonderful ideas, but no one has yet been able to say definitely what it is because no one's been able to get close enough to find out. Some people have even tried chasing *them*, but as fast as you go forwards, they keep moving away. Then, as I said, they disappear and come to life again somewhere else.'

Still not knowing quite whether to believe her or not, Debra looked to Eleanor for corroboration.

'Yes, it's quite true,' she nodded, and smiled. 'They call the area where they occur the Boulia Triangle.'

'As long as it's not the Acacia Crossing Triangle,' Debra laughed. 'I imagine it could be quite eerie to come across something like that on a lonely road in the middle of the night.'

Subsequently, their talk turned to less puzzling subjects, although with the number of people stopping to pass the time of day and renew acquaintanceships it wasn't surprising that their conversations were inclined to be disjointed.

'Now, where was I?' questioned Jeanne humorously following one such interruption, then she pulled a wry face. 'Never mind, I don't think I'll even try to remember. It looks as if your opponents have been accounted for at last, Debra. Here comes Saxon and Neale. How did it go?' she asked of the two men as they joined them.

'Pretty good,' Neale grinned, rumpling her hair fondly as he took the seat next to her. 'We beat them by more than fifty runs.'

All too conscious of Saxon's powerful frame occupying the chair beside herself, Debra determinedly kept her face half turned in Neale's direction. 'You've made the final, then?' she asked interestedly.

'*We've* made the final,' Saxon's deeply modulated voice contradicted lazily. 'Or aren't you a part of this team any more?'

'Yes, of course I am!' Debra automatically swung round before she realised what she was doing, and her eyes flashed with sudden understanding as soon as they connected with the taunting look in his. He had said that for the sole purpose of making her face him! With a deep steadying breath she eyed him challengingly from beneath ebony lashes. She hadn't given up the battle yet! 'Unless you would rather replace me with someone else, that is,' she breathed eloquently, knowing full well he would be aware she wasn't only referring to the cricket.

'Not likely!' hooted Neale in the background. 'Right at this moment Mac wouldn't trade you for the world.'

There was no need for words. Debra just allowed the barest arching of her brows to do her questioning for her, and was rewarded by a slow, wryly curving smile which flipped her heart over with a perturbing ease.

'As the man says...what would we do without you?' he drawled.

It was a minor victory only; Debra had no illusions about that. But coming as it did after such a surplus of defeats she was more than satisfied. In public, at least, it seemed not all the advantages were his, and from now on, she decided, if it was at all possible she would be using that knowledge in order to bring a little more balance into what had been, until now, a very one-sided situation.

Presently Paul rejoined them as well, his face a study of rueful regret as he advised, 'That's the finish of us for today, I'm sorry to say.'

'We lost?' his sister quizzed.

'We were thrashed,' he amended drily, bringing smiles to the faces of his listeners. 'As unbelievable as it may seem, our bowling was even worse than our batting. They didn't even need their full innings to put us out of the game.'

'Oh, well, at least my loyalties won't be divided now. I can cheer for Neale with a clear conscience,' Jeanne advised happily. 'Besides which, I can't honestly say I'm sorry I don't have to go out there again in this heat. It is unseasonably hot today, isn't it?'

Her encompassing glance brought forth agreement, and then Saxon was rising to his feet. 'In the meantime, I guess I'd better start rounding up our people again.' His eyes were already roaming over the various groups and concentrations. 'It sounds as if it might be a long play-off.'

Which was exactly what it turned out to be, with each run being fiercely contested and, as a result, the scores being kept to a minimum. When their innings were finally completed—and having achieved a total which, although it caused no great despair among their ranks, certainly didn't give anyone reason to cheer either—Wyeera set about fielding in determined fashion. However, when Acacia Crossing's score began to inexorably close the gap, Saxon and one of the other team members returned for reinforcements, and as one headed for a particular section of the crowd, the other made for those beneath the trees.

'Come on, we need all the help we can get,' Saxon owned with a laugh as he caught hold of Debra's wrist and tugged her out of her chair. 'They're getting too close for comfort.'

Accepting his action in good part, a sweep of her hand included Eleanor and Jeanne. 'Mmm, we were only saying a while ago that we wouldn't be surprised to hear a call go out for all hands to the wheel.'

'She's being too polite,' gurgled Jeanne irrepressibly beside them. 'What we really said, was...that it looked as if the men had got themselves into a difficult position and would need the help of the fairer sex to pull them out of it...as usual.'

'Is that so?' His eyes narrowed mock-threateningly. 'Well, I'll leave Neale to take you to task for that impertinence, young lady,' he promised her tauntingly. 'But as for this one,' his attention turned to Debra and a muscular arm across her shoulders imprisoned her against his side, 'I'm sure I'll be able to devise some fitting punishment myself.'

'Such as?' she dared to ask as they left the others behind.

Saxon lowered his head confidingly, disturbingly close. 'Now that, as they say, would be telling,' he mocked. 'Suffice for you to know that...'

'What about me?'

The somewhat peevish-sounding interruption had him swinging around to face its originator with Debra still firmly pinned to his side.

'Don't you want my help too?' Anthea now enquired sharply, her expression hostile as it raked over the slim figure pressed against him.

'I wouldn't dream of asking you, Anthea,' he returned easily, pacifyingly. 'Those manicured hands of yours aren't meant for fielding a cricket ball.'

While the other girl simpered appropriate words and basked in the warmth of his obvious concern, Debra looked down at her own slender fingers and grimaced dourly. Hers weren't exactly a calloused bunch of fives either, but presumably that didn't matter!

Her gesture evidently hadn't gone unnoticed, however, for as they resumed walking Saxon smiled and disclosed wryly, 'I wanted someone I could rely on and who would at least make an attempt to stop the ball.'

'Ah, yes, my robust constitution again,' she quipped sardonically.

'Don't be such a damned fool! I didn't mean it that way, and you know it,' he retorted roughly, and abruptly spinning her loose. 'There's a lot of words I could use to describe you, sweetheart, as you should be aware by now, but...' pausing, his vivid blue eyes slid appraisingly over every shapely contour, 'I can assure you, robust certainly isn't the one which springs to mind.'

Two bright stains of colour flared into her smooth cheeks and she dropped her gaze in embarrassment. 'I wasn't fishing for compliments,' she disclaimed self-consciously.

'Did I say you were?'

'N-no, but...'

'Then let's forget about Anthea's unthinking comments, hmm?' A hand beneath her chin ensured she couldn't avoid looking at him for any longer. 'We have a cricket match to win, Miss Armitage, and, you being my secretary, I'm expecting a hundred per cent effort from you,' he teased lightly.

'Yes, sir,' she nodded, swallowing convulsively. That fascinating smile of his could hold her spell-bound so effortlessly it wasn't funny!

In the paddock Debra took her place, along with another couple of the female members of the team who had volunteered to field, and concentrated on the game. From a spectator's point of view the finish, as it crept relentlessly closer, couldn't have been more exciting. But for the players, on both teams, it was fraught with tension. Acacia Crossing were down to their last batsmen—one more out and Wyeera would win—but they were also only three runs behind, and if they succeeded in making those runs the decision would be reversed.

There wasn't one pair of eyes on Noonameena that afternoon that wasn't watching—even the children had stopped their play in order to line the fence—as one of Saxon's young stud grooms came up to bowl what everyone knew would be the last balls of the match. Debra looped her hair back behind her ears to make certain her vision wasn't impaired at an inopportune moment and waited tensely as the ball left the bowler's hand and flew towards the stocky batsman awaiting its delivery. When he merely blocked it a concerted sigh of relief went up from the fielders, and then they each went through their preparatory routines again.

The next time the bat connected with the ball with such a resounding crack that everyone immediately knew that this could be their last chance.

'For God's sake, *someone* catch it!' yelled a voice from near the wicket, and suddenly, out of a clear blue sky, Debra saw it zooming straight towards her.

With a choked gasp she instinctively put out her hands—it was either that, or collect it right in the midriff—and felt it slam into them with a force that sent her staggering two steps backward. Not until the cheers of jubilation started to ring out and the first of her team-mates raced over to congratulate her did she realise she was still holding the ball, and it was with a somewhat taut expression that she accepted their elated words of praise.

Saxon was the one who eventually drew her away from them, a knowing look on his face as he quizzed, 'How are the hands?'

Her reply was quite explicit, and not altogether facetiously uttered. 'Am I allowed to scream now, or do I have to wait until after we leave?'

'That bad?'

'I don't think they've got an unbroken bone between them,' she half laughed flippantly.

'Then perhaps you'd better let me have a look,' he suggested with a frown. 'It's quite possible you could have broken or dislocated a bone somewhere.'

She shook her head quickly, dismissively. 'No, really, I'm exaggerating, they're okay. My fingers *can* all still move.' She gave a wry grimace and owned, 'It's just that I prefer them not to right at the moment.'

'All right, we'll leave it for now,' he smiled wryly in understanding. 'But they'd better have improved by the time we go, or it will be a different story.'

'They will.' Her prediction was confident. 'In fact, they have already. See?' As she raised one slightly cupped member and viewed it with a dispassionate grin. 'It's only bright pink now instead of vermilion.'

A short laugh and Saxon was eyeing her consideringly, his head angled slightly to one side. 'You're a complex little character, aren't you, sweetheart?' he mused.

Taken completely unawares by the sudden switch in the conversation, Debra immediately became defensive and shrugged. 'I don't know what you mean.'

'No?' The peak of his brows became more noticeable. 'Well, maybe you don't at that,' he acceded ruefully before reverting to their original topic by observing, 'It looks as if there's quite a reception committee waiting for you,' seeing Eleanor and Jeanne, together with Prue—and Anthea—waiting beside the fence.

'For *us*, you mean,' she corrected drily. She knew who Anthea was waiting for, and it certainly wasn't herself!

Whether he caught her meaning and replied, Debra didn't hear, because as soon as they had passed through the gateway Prue was excitedly catching at her arm, her exclamation of admiration soon becoming submerged beneath less vociferous, but just as sincere, congratulations from the rest of Wyeera's supporters, all of which she accepted self-consciously.

'It was only one catch, after all,' she remarked wryly to Jeanne a short while later as they all began heading for the homestead verandah and the presentations. 'And an accidental one, to boot. I put up my hands to protect myself. . . catching the ball was the last thing I had in mind.'

'Oh, dear, what a thoroughly disappointing discovery, when here we all were thinking how utterly brave and sporting you'd been,' cooed Anthea from where she was walking a few paces behind them—with Saxon—and obviously referring to what she had overheard. 'It seems you've been accepting our congratulations and admiration under false pretences, Debra.' Her laugh tinkled maliciously.

Not yours, at any rate, since you haven't yet offered any, grimaced Debra to herself. By way of a reply, however, she simply hunched one shoulder in an unconcerned gesture and endorsed laconically, 'My sentiments entirely.'

'Well, I still think it was a damned good effort, no matter what the reason,' Jeanne turned back to announce loyally.

'But of course it was,' Anthea agreed in syrupy tones. 'In fact, I very much doubt if there's another woman here who could have done it at all, let alone with such—er—flair.' That laugh trilled forth once more. 'I mean to say, it's just as well not everyone prefers to remain cool and relaxed on the sidelines like languid little me, isn't it?'

Meaning that I look hot and bothered, supposed Debra sardonically, and felt like reminding the girl behind her that, originally, she hadn't been languid at all—but *piqued*—when she'd thought she was being left out of the game. But she didn't, she just sighed and kept walking. Nothing Anthea said could possibly drop her stock any lower than it already was with Saxon, so she had absolutely nothing to gain by becoming involved in any of Anthea's venomous little word-plays.

There was no formality about the presentations whatsoever once they got under way. They were strictly for enjoyment, and the winners' dozen bottles of champagne were very quickly disposed of, and not only by the team members, as were the cartons of canned beer awarded to the runners-up. All in all, it was a very pleasant, easy-going finish to what had been an extremely agreeable day for the most part, although Debra did experience one uncomfortable moment when Saxon was accepting the small cup which accompanied the win.

'You'd better marry that young secretary of yours, Mac, to ensure she's on your team for a long time to come. You would've been lost without her today!' shouted someone humorously from among the crowd.

Debra promptly flushed scarlet and bit at her lip as the ensuing laughter flowed round her. Her eyes, wide and almost purple in colour, flew unerringly to a sun-tanned face and hovered there apprehensively. How humiliating it would be if, in an effort to make certain no one else was tempted to make comments of a like nature, Saxon told them exactly how he did feel about her presence on Wyccra!

In a brief second their glances crossed, returned, held, and she released a shuddering sigh of relief. There was a mocking light in those blue depths, but no rancour—as was proved when he faced the crowd again, an answering smile on his lips.

'You're certainly right on your second count, Alan,' he was prepared to concede drily. 'But as to your first . . . well, give the girl credit for having more sense than to take on a corner country cattleman. I doubt if she'd have me.'

A tactful reply and what could have been an embarrassing situation was passed over smoothly. But as the laughing crowd began to disperse Debra turned to Eleanor with a slight frown puckering her forehead.

'Corner country?' she sought elucidation.

'Mmm, that's right, Haddon Corner. You know, where the States of Queensland and South Australia meet.'

'Oh, yes, of course.' Her smile was rueful. 'I should have realised. Perhaps while I'm out this way I should make the effort and go and see it. Is there anything much there?'

'Just a post,' supplied Eleanor so drily that they both laughed.

Now that the presentations were concluded everyone began their preparations for leaving and on one of his trips to and from the homestead, putting the equipment away, Paul stopped beside Debra with some folding chairs tucked beneath his arm.

'By the way, did Jeanne mention anything to you about the dance in town on Saturday?' he asked.

She nodded. 'Yes, she did, as a matter of fact.'

'Would you like to come?'

'Very much,' she smiled up at him engagingly. 'I'm...'

'I hope that's not *next* Saturday you're talking about, old son,' Saxon's deeply voiced insertion cut her words short and had them both looking to where he was fastening one of Eleanor's hampers for her.

'Why not?' Paul half frowned, half smiled.

'Because next Saturday Debra will be in Stratheden, with me.'

Considering that was the first time he had even mentioned it to her, it was only natural that Debra should look somewhat surprised, but then, as she covertly studied her employer's slightly mocking features, her eyes began to narrow in suspicion. Had he made that decision before, or *after*, Paul stopped to speak to her? She certainly wouldn't put it past him to be using it solely as a means of making her life less enjoyable.

It must have seemed strange to Paul too, because he promptly laughed and urged, 'Come off it, Mac! You don't need a secretary while you're away judging, and you've sure never taken one with you before.'

'Maybe not,' Saxon conceded, and without changing his expression in the slightest. 'But then they didn't need the experience. They were already conversant with the cattle business before coming to Wyeera.'

The corners of Paul's mouth turned down wryly. 'And just what experience can Debra get at Stratheden that she can't get here? Hell, you've got the biggest Brahman stud for miles around. What else does she need to know about?'

'With the sales coming up, a great many things, as you should know,' Saxon returned evenly, his composure unruffled. 'However, until now no one's had the time to teach her, so...'

'You decided on the Show at Stratheden as being a good opportunity to fill her in on the details,' Paul concluded ruefully for himself.

'Sorry, feller, but business comes before pleasure,' with a sympathetic grin.

Paul expelled a heavy breath and swung back to Debra. 'It looks as if we'll have to take a raincheck on it, I'm afraid,' he smiled. 'How about next month instead?'

'I'll make sure I'm available.'

She wasn't quite sure just how she could guarantee that, but she was determined to have a damned good try! Saxon's answers might have sounded plausible to his friend, but she still wasn't entirely convinced. There was a background to the situation that Paul didn't know about, and the more she considered it the more sceptical she became.

She was still turning it over in her mind during their journey back to the property, or at least, she was, until the arrival of low black clouds on the horizon heralded the storm which everyone had been predicting would follow such an unseasonably hot day, and her thoughts flew off at a tangent—as they had so many times before on such occasions—to dwell on memories from long ago.

CHAPTER SIX

AWAKE, DEBRA had some chance of dispelling her distressing thoughts, but asleep, she had no such control, and the images she had tried so hard to forget flooded back with insidious persistence. It was the storm which had triggered their return, and although it hadn't brought much rain it had been noisy, was still noisy, and she tossed and turned feverishly at every jarring reverberation.

In her dreams she was back on that small boat again with her parents, watching as the sudden unexpected squall turned the blue skies to black and the glass-like sea into white-capped troughs. She could see again too the look of fear on her mother's face as that freak wave appeared out of nowhere to tower over them and she made a frantic grab for her only child. Then there was nothing—only a grey blank—until Debra had woken up in hospital, crying, and complaining her head hurt.

Perspiration soaked tendrils of hair clung to her temples and she moaned softly, trying to deny the onset of the scene she knew would follow as unchangingly as night follows day.

Initially, there was that terrifying shock to be experienced of being woken from a peaceful sleep by the chilling sound of screeching metal as the roof of their car buckled beneath the weight of the fallen telegraph pole, followed by Rose Armitage's broken scream. A scream Debra had echoed in blind panic when a flare of jagged lightning illuminated the devastated interior of the vehicle and she began struggling helplessly to claw her way out.

Then, as now, there had been a strong pair of hands to restrain her, but whereas the voice which accompanied them should have been warning, 'For God's sake, lie still, little one! We can't get you out at the moment, there's live wires everywhere!' it was commanding instead, 'For God's sake, Debra, wake up!'

Abruptly her eyes flew open and she lay there unmoving as her mind registered—with the aid of the light beaming into the room from the well lit hallway—Saxon's broad shape as he sat on the edge of the bed leaning over her, his shirt completely unbuttoned as if he had been in the act of undressing, or, after having removed it, had thrown it back on again in a hurry. For a time the only sound was that made by her harsh, ragged breathing, but then a sob of reaction escaped her and she pressed her face into the pillow in an attempt to suppress the onslaught she feared might follow.

'I—I'm sorry if I disturbed y-you,' she apologised so huskily he had to bend his head even lower to hear. 'I'm all r-right now, th-thank you.'

'Are you?' His voice grated sharply in the strained silence, his hand no less rough when it forced her to face him again.

'Oh, please!' The entreaty was torn from her as she felt that suffocating lump rise into her throat again. 'Please! Can't you just leave me alone!' she cried, trying frantically to push herself upright and further away from him.

'No!' he lashed back at her furiously, his fingers digging punishingly into her arms as he dragged her to within inches of his rigidly held form. 'There's too much about you that needs explaining already. Now I want to know just what it is that has you breaking out in a cold sweat and screaming in absolute terror.'

'What's the point?' Her efforts to free herself drained the last reserves of her strength and her head drooped forward defeatedly as an uncontrollable attack of weeping overtook her. 'You wouldn't believe me, anyway. You never do!' she choked.

'Oh, hell!' Saxon slid his arms around her tightly, comfortingly, drawing her shaking figure closer to the muscular wall of his chest and cradling her head against his shoulder. 'I've been too successful in my intentions, haven't I, sweetheart?'

Debra didn't reply. Even if she had wanted to she wouldn't have been able to, for now that her tears had started they were impossible to stop. Sagging against him weakly, she could only wait for them to run their natural course, and let the hand which was stroking her hair so gently calm her troubled spirit as best it could.

'Now will you tell me what it was that frightened you so badly?' he asked softly when, after one last shivering sigh, she lay quietly against him.

She went to pull away and then changed her mind. It *was* comforting with him holding her as he was, and she liked the feel of his firm skin beneath her cheek, so why should she move?

'It was only a dream,' she murmured throatily.

'But a recurring one, hmm?'

Her long lashes flickered briefly against his shoulder. 'H-how did you know?'

'I guessed,' he disclosed deeply, his fingers massaging the nape of her neck now. 'When the storm arrived you became so edgy that I figured it must have had some special significance for you, and yet it just as obviously wasn't the storm itself. You showed no fear of that at all.' His hand continued to work its relaxing magic. 'So, when you screamed as you did in your sleep and I found you moving about so wildly, it immediately made me wonder if perhaps premonition hadn't been the underlying cause of your restlessness.' He paused and his brows drew together in a frown. 'Does this always happen when there's a storm?'

'No, not always,' she admitted with a poor attempt at a laugh. 'Mainly when there's a lot of lightning around.'

'But why?' He eased away from her in order to cup her face between his two hands. 'What happened that was so dreadful it scares you half to death when you dream about it?'

'Please don't ask me.' She stared at him miserably, begging him to understand. 'I've lived through it once tonight already, I don't want to do it again.'

The line of his jaw hardened fractionally. 'But you can't go through the rest of your life keeping something like this to yourself, and dreading every storm that might come along!'

'At least that's better than letting everyone know what a jinx I am!' she blurted defensively, and then inhaled a dismayed breath on seeing his increased interest.

'A minx, yes, but surely not a jinx!' he teased lightly.

It gave Debra the excuse she needed to retreat and she took it swiftly. 'See, I said there was no point in telling you. I knew you wouldn't believe me!'

'Uh-uh,' he vetoed, his head moving slowly from side to side. 'You don't back out of it that easily, sweetheart. I just happen to believe we make our own luck, and spellbinding though you may be at times, I can't quite bring myself to picture you as an instrument of misfortune. However...' he fixed her with a penetrating glance devoid of all humour, 'I do mean to discover *why* you choose to see yourself in such a role.'

She sighed dully. 'Because it's true, that's why. Because everyone I've ever cared about has—has...'

'Died?'

Not even by pressing her eyelids tightly closed could she prevent the tears from squeezing underneath them. 'Been killed,' she corrected tremulously.

'How?' He drew her gently back to him again.

It was obvious he wasn't going to let the matter drop until he knew the whole story and so, with her forehead buried against his chest and her fingers clutching at his open shirt for support, she told him what she had never told anyone else before.

'There was a—a boy at the orphanage t-too,' she continued jerkily afterwards. 'He was only six, but we used to pretend we r-really were brother and sister, but even he—even he...'

'Sssh!' Saxon soothed close beside her temple. 'You don't have to go on.'

'He ran out from behind the bus on his way home from school one day, right into the path of a passing car,' she concluded tonelessly.

Tipping her face up to his with a long forefinger, he laid a kiss at the corner of her trembling lips. 'You haven't exactly had a very happy life so far, have you, sweetheart?' he pondered soberly.

Debra's hands clenched harder on the material of his shirt. 'I w-wasn't asking for s-sympathy.'

'I know.' His lips found her tear-stained cheeks this time. 'But I didn't have to take it on myself to make it a damned sight more miserable for you, though, did I?' in tones of self-disgust.

'I wasn't asking for your pity either,' she denied huskily.

'I know that too,' he smiled ruefully. 'But I also know those accidents concerning your family were just that . . . accidents! You're no evil spirit, sweetheart, believe me,' he tried to impress on her earnestly.

'I might just as well be, the result's the same,' she charged dejectedly. 'Even you said I was an undesirable.'

'But for quite another reason,' he promptly reminded her in wry accents. The tips of his fingers brushed lightly against the side of her neck as he began threading them through her hair, and his shapely mouth feathered across her softly parted lips. 'I also said you looked very *des*irable, if you recall.'

Already in a highly emotional state, her senses now began to reel beneath a force she had never before experienced and she trembled as she half swayed towards him, unknowingly provocative.

'And was that for quite another reason too?' she quizzed shakily.

'No, that was because I keep getting the urge to take you to bed with me,' Saxon only just found time to reveal before his mouth closed relentlessly over hers.

It wasn't the first time he had kissed her, of course. He had arbitrarily seen to that in Brisbane. But this time was nothing like the first and as her bloodstream turned to molten fire Debra didn't fight to be free, as she had before, but responded with a willingness which both bewildered and startled her. Relinquishing her grip on his shirt at last, she smoothed her fingers savouringly, sensuously, over the sinewed flesh of his chest and shoulders to twine them within the tousled hair at the back of his head, and making no protest when he lowered her to the pillow.

Briefly, his lips left hers to scorch a mesmerising path to the vulnerable hollow at the base of her throat, then returned to claim them again with a hungry possessiveness which sent waves of desire rolling over her and left her drowning within a sea of uncontrolled emotion.

A caressing hand explored the flaring curves of hip and waist, then travelled higher to close about a tautly rounded breast. At the unaccustomed touch Debra moved against him shakenly, ripples of tingling sensation racing along her nerves, and then suddenly she was free as Saxon pulled sharply away from her and rose swiftly to his feet, all in the one lithe action.

His breathing was heavy and uneven as he raked a hand savagely through his hair. 'I'm sorry. It wasn't my intention to take advantage of your already unguarded state,' he apologised in a rough, jarring voice, and turned for the door. 'I'll see you in the morning.'

'Saxon!' Still recovering from the rush of feeling which had enveloped her, Debra called after him plaintively as she started to her knees. 'Please don't leave. I—I'm scared of going back to sleep again in case my dream returns.'

He wheeled to face her furiously, an air of rigid self-discipline emanating from him, his face in darkness with his back to the doorway. 'So what are you suggesting? That I make love to you for the rest of the night in order to keep you awake?'

She bowed her head embarrassedly, but the remembered security his arms had afforded impelled her onwards. 'Couldn't you just…hold me? Like you did before,' she whispered throatily.

'Are you being cute, or deliberately naïve?' His tone was mercilessly cutting.

'N-neither,' she faltered miserably. 'I just wanted…'

'Well, I don't! And nor do I care for being propositioned, thanks…no matter how ingenuously!' he stated with acid contempt, preparing to leave for the second time.

Propositioned! Twin flags of burning humiliation and anger vied for precedence in Debra's crimson cheeks and grabbing the only thing to hand, her pillow, she hurled it towards the closing door with all her might.

'*Get out,* you lowdown, despicable swine!' she yelled. Superfluously, since he had already departed. 'Just get out and leave me alone,' she continued in less forceful but decidedly more tearful tones. And, throwing herself face down among the rumpled sheets began to cry helplessly, 'I hate you, hate you, hate you…!'

DEBRA PUSHED her foot down harder on the accelerator and smiled as the powerful ute responded immediately. She had just dropped Prue off at school and she was in a hurry to get back to the property. There was a lot of work she had to finish before leaving for

Stratheden with Saxon the next morning and she wanted to get started on it as soon as possible.

Thinking of her employer had her lips twisting into a wry grimace and she cast her mind back ruefully over the preceding three days. If anything, Saxon's attitude seemed to have hardened since that disastrous interlude in her bedroom. The man who had originally comforted her so considerately, totally unrecognisable in the cool sardonic person who had greeted her the following day.

Whether or not he had reverted to his customary gibing manner because of what he mistakingly believed to have been her uninvited advances, she dreaded to contemplate, but conversely, due to a surfeit of pride as well as a continuing sense of mortification over the whole affair, she point-blank refused to say anything which might refute the suggestion.

In the distance a red cloud of dust approached and she watched it idly. Road-trains weren't a novelty to her any more, but they fascinated her all the same, and when the huge trailers roared towards her in a storm of flying dust and scattered stones—the sound of the horn indicating the driver recognised the ute—she acknowledged the signal with a smile and a ready wave. Everyone who used the road knew everyone else's vehicles and even she could discern some of the more regular travellers now.

Suddenly, as the last of the trailers passed her, however, there came a report as if a gun had been fired nearby, making her jump involuntarily. Then, before her widening eyes, the windshield disintegrated into a jigsaw of frosted, shattered glass, and she knew that one of those stones had been bigger and had hit harder than the rest.

Instinctively, she went for the brake—what with the dust *and* the crazy paving glass it was impossible to see where she was going—but she must have been overly zealous in her application because the ute immediately began to slew sideways on the loose surface, and before she could attempt to correct the swing she could feel it sliding over the banked shoulder of the road at a precarious angle and careering out of control down to the water-table below, where it was brought up short with a jolting crash which promptly showered half of the fractured windshield down on top of her.

For a moment she sat there too stunned to move, just thankful to be still capable of breathing, and then as she released her safety belt and shakily inched her way out of the vehicle sent up a prayer of gratitude for the inventor of the safety process which allowed glass to fragment into small pieces devoid of sharp edges. She had a couple of nicks and scratches from it tumbling down on her, but nothing compared to what it could have been if those segments had been jagged.

After thoroughly surveying the damage she sighed despondently. Although the bull-bar at the front appeared to have protected the engine satisfactorily when they had collided with the tree which had curtailed their runaway progress, the rear of the ute was still unhealthily slanted towards the top of the slope, while one of the front tires had been ripped to shreds on a small but vicious-looking tree stump on the way down. And not only that, but somewhere along the way the tail-gate had burst open and all the groceries she had picked up in town for Sherry were now scattered indiscriminately over the embankment.

So now what did she do? The angle at which the ute was balanced precluded any effort on her part to move it either up, or down, the bank, and even if she had known how to—which she didn't—she couldn't have changed the tire for the same reason. All she could do, she finally decided, was to keep an ear pricked for anyone coming along the road in order to flag them down for help, and in the meantime to recover Sherry's groceries as best she could and tidy up the mess the glass had made in the cabin.

Stopping only occasionally for a mouthful of water from the canvas bag attached to the front of the vehicle, Debra toiled on amid the uncanny silence and beneath an increasingly hot sun. Not even the tree provided any protection, for the shade was being thrown away from where she was working, and it wasn't long before trickles of perspiration began plastering her shirt to the middle of her back. A couple of times she had stopped to listen, thinking she might have heard a car approaching, but each time she guessed they must have been figments of her imagination brought on by the solitude and she had returned to what she was doing while wondering if anyone beside herself and the road-train intended using the highway that day.

It was going on for lunchtime before she could distinguish the definite rumbling of wheels in the distance heading towards town, and she scrambled up the slope with a light of relieved anticipation shining in her eyes, only to find she had a surprisingly long wait for the vehicle to come into view. Sound travelled much further than she realised in that quiet stillness.

As soon as her eyes focused upon it, though, some of her anticipation was replaced with another feeling entirely. Unless she was very much mistaken that was Wyeera's Range-Rover—probably checking to see why she hadn't returned before this—and although she was pleased to see it, she couldn't quite suppress an anxiousness as to who was driving it. Was it Saxon, or one of his men? Oh, hell, how she hoped it was the latter!

But it wasn't, there was no mistaking just who was behind the wheel as he drew up in front of her, and she started to rub the palms of her hands down the sides of her slacks nervously. Leisurely he climbed down from the seat and, pushing his hands into the back pockets of fawn drill pants, paced slowly to where she was standing.

'Well?'

As she didn't think it was an enquiry after her health, Debra shifted uncomfortably beneath his enigmatic gaze and pointed down the slope. 'I'm sorry,' she offered contritely.

With his head inclined slightly to one side Saxon inspected the scene for what felt like an interminable length of time to his warily waiting companion. 'How did it happen?' he asked at last.

Very quiet, very controlled, and *very dangerous*! Debra shivered, and explained as concisely as possible.

'Of course you do realise you could have been killed!' Nowhere near as controlled now, and she sensed the final eruption wasn't far behind. 'So what the blazes were you doing driving that fast in the first place?'

'I wasn't d-driving *that* fast,' she stammered defensively.

'No? You always skid out of control when you brake, do you?'

'Of course not! But I couldn't see when the windshield broke.'

'And if you hadn't been going like a bat out of hell you wouldn't have needed to panic into slamming on the brakes!' he countered explosively. 'What if you'd had Prue with you? Have you thought of that?'

'I don't need to! If I'd had her with me it wouldn't have happened!' she retaliated without thinking.

'Oh? And why not?'

Debra's heart sank and her eyes closed in dismay. 'Because I wouldn't have been driving that fast,' she had no option but to confess, and thereby convict herself, at least as far as he was concerned.

'Exactly!' He nodded sarcastically, then caught hold of her arm with lean biting fingers. 'Well, let's go down and see what damage you've managed to cause.' His magnetic blue eyes slanted tauntingly over her. 'It could take you years to pay off all your debts to Wyeera.'

Seething resentment gave her the strength to break loose from his grasp and she glared at him rebelliously. 'You can look at it on your own, damn you!' she blazed. 'That's all you're worried about, your precious ute. Not once have you even asked how *I* am. How do you know I wasn't knocked unconscious going down there?'

'On what?'

That took some of the steam out of her, and she fixed him with a puzzled frown. 'What do you mean...on what?'

He didn't immediately explain, but probed instead, 'You were wearing your seatbelt, weren't you?'

'Yes, but...'

'Then as the car obviously hasn't rolled, it's extremely unlikely you would have hit your head on anything,' mockingly.

All Debra's fury returned in full force and with an incensed exclamation she swung a hand wildly at him, missed, and might have fallen down the bank as she lost her footing, had not a muscular arm gripped her securely about the waist. With her back pressed tightly against his side and that iron band about her midriff she was carried, fuming and struggling, all the way to the bottom.

'A word of warning, young lady,' Saxon bent to caution before letting her go, and with just enough steel in his voice for her to heed—albeit reluctantly. 'I already feel like giving you the hiding of your life, so if I were you I wouldn't provoke me too deliberately or you might yet find yourself unable to sit for a week!'

Permitting herself one long glance of smouldering mutiny, Debra flounced resentfully over to the ute. She would dearly like to have challenged that arrogant intimidation of his, but, she frustratingly had to admit, she just wasn't reckless enough to tempt fate to such a degree. Saxon McAllister wasn't the type given to making idle threats!

On following her, he took closer stock of the damage and then exhaled heavily. 'Well, I guess the first thing is to get it back up on to the road,' he declared ironically.

'How?' The question was out before she could prevent it. She had meant to keep a haughty, disinterested silence.

'There's a winch on the front of the Range-Rover... fortunately!'

At the suggestion of sarcasm in his tone she immediately turned away again, a disgruntled expression on her face, and refused to even look—let alone offer to help—as he moved the larger vehicle into position and proceeded to couple the steel cable to the ute's tow bar.

'You can steer while I operate the winch.'

Now she had to face him. 'Steer what? That?' She pointed to the ute in no little dismay. She wasn't very keen on being a passenger while he attempted to haul it up the slope.

He nodded, a goading smile shaping his firm mouth. 'Someone has to—that flat tire will tend to make it pull continually to one side otherwise—and who better to keep it coming straight than the person who put it down there in the first place, hmm?'

Debra stifled her resentment with difficulty and gave him back a look of mock sorrowfulness. 'As long as you're not expecting too professional a performance. I've never done anything like this before.'

'Meaning I should recall the way you reversed out of the garage the first day you took Prue to school, I suppose?' he countered aggravatingly.

Nettled to find herself back on the defensive again so quickly, she immediately lifted her head higher to excuse, 'I'd never driven this make of car before then!'

Saxon's eyes gleamed sardonically, his gaze pointed as he looked at the ute. 'And you don't appear to have improved with practice either, if you don't mind my saying so.'

She did mind, of course, but as she suspected she would only be inviting more sarcasms of a like nature if she attempted a repudiation, she merely pressed her lips together vexedly and shrugged with what she hoped was suitably snubbing indifference as she slid into the driver's seat.

His instructions given, Saxon made his way up to the Range-Rover to start the winch and Debra waited, nervously expectant, to feel the cable beginning to take the strain. When it did the ute jerked slightly but refused to move, and after two more attempts she wasn't surprised to feel the tension slackened altogether, or to see her employer's lithe figure approaching down the incline. What did surprise her, however, was his action on reaching the vehicle.

Without saying a word he opened the door, placed one hand on the back of the seat for support and leant across her to survey the instrument panel. Then, with his mouth levelling in mute exasperation, he reached in and released the handbrake.

'It helps,' he turned his head to taunt acidly.

'I'm sorry, I—I forgot I'd put it on when—when I stopped,' she apologised flusteringly, and uncertain whether her nervousness was due to her own embarrassing carelessness, or to his unbalancing closeness in such a confined space. She felt at least ten degrees warmer than she had a few seconds ago.

He smiled wryly, catastrophically for Debra since she found it impossible to drag her eyes away, and chucked her irritatingly beneath the chin. 'Never mind, sweetheart, it's the type of negligence I should have anticipated from a woman driver.'

'And that's just the sort of unfounded remark *I* would expect from a male chauvinist like you!' she condemned indignantly, slapping his hand away.

'Is that so?' One eyebrow slanted whimsically upwards. 'Then perhaps you'd better take care in case I'm tempted to follow it with a typically male chauvinistic reaction as well.'

'Like what?' Her eyes dared to challenge his insolently.

When his fingers rested against her chin this time it wasn't to touch fleetingly, but to hold inescapably. 'Like this,' he advised arrogantly, and covered her lips with his own in a hard, but thoroughly proficient, kiss.

Coming as it did after almost a week of cold sarcasm the action caught Debra totally unprepared and for a moment she was trapped in a mindless limbo. But when she discovered him to be exacting a response she was far from willing to give she began struggling frantically. Futilely also, it seemed, since she wasn't allowed to go free until Saxon cared to liberate her.

'Don't you ever dare touch me again!' The blazing words burst forth angrily the minute she was able to demonstrate her feelings.

'So who's going to stop me?' His question was no less bitingly delivered and, as if to prove his point, he lowered his mouth to hers once more before she even had a chance of replying, or taking evasive action.

Whirled deeper and deeper into a maelstrom of emotion she wanted so desperately to deny, Debra hit out blindly against her tormentor who could turn her whole being upside down with such ease. Saxon promptly reciprocated by pinning her wrists to the back of the seat, effectively trapping her head between her own imprisoned hands, while his lips continued their relentless assault on her tumultuous senses unopposed.

Not until her defences had crumbled entirely and her lips parted on a wayward sigh of surrender did he finally see fit to release her, and then only slowly, after he had drawn from her the response he had imperiously been demanding.

Humiliated beyond belief by her treacherous feelings, Debra pretended to an equanimity she was far from experiencing. 'Now, if you've quite finished, do you think we could return to the immediate problem of getting the ute back on to the road?' she enquired gibingly. 'I have quite a number of things which need doing today... for Eleanor as well as yourself.'

'Whatever you say, lady!' He unexpectedly touched one finger to his temple in a teasing, laughing deference to her wishes which immediately undid all her efforts to keep her emotions under control as it sent waves of tingling awareness racing throughout her nervous system. 'Provided, of course, I receive some help from you this time.'

She might have known he would have the last word, she decided discontentedly, watching his agile progress back to the Range-Rover. He might have assented to her request that they make short work of returning to the homestead, but probably only because that coincided with his desire once he had summarily proved she wasn't capable of enforcing any orders she might give him—concerning herself, or otherwise!

With no handbrake to offer resistance, the ensuing attempt to pull the ute up to the road met with greater success, and although Debra was on tenterhooks the whole time lest she do something else wrong, they eventually made it to the top without anything else untoward happening.

'So far, so good,' commented Saxon drily after he had rewound the winch cable, then frowned as he unlocked the tail-gate of the ute and noticed for the first time the battered and partially destroyed state of some of the groceries. Pushing them aside in order to get at the spare tire he threw a querying glance over one shoulder. 'What happened to these?'

'The back opened and they fell out on the way down.'

He dropped the tire on to the ground and retrieved the jack before turning to face her, his expression sardonic in the extreme. 'Then in future, it might be an idea if you make certain you've shut it properly before you leave town, mightn't it?'

'Oh, *I* didn't shut it at all. One of the *men* at the store did,' it gave her the greatest of pleasure to be able to retort complacently. So self-satisfiedly, in fact, that she was persuaded to go a little further and taunt, 'So what have you got to say about that?'

'Nothing particularly complimentary,' he returned in repressive tones, going down on his haunches beside the ripped tire and beginning to loosen the wheel nuts. 'I dislike carelessness in any shape or form... male or female!'

Intrigued by the play of muscles beneath his drill shirt, Debra moved to stand slightly behind him. 'You being a model of meticulous attentiveness, I suppose?' she quipped daringly.

'I will be—to you—if you don't cut the riling interruptions, sweetheart,' he promised meaningfully.

She shrugged, but prudently stepped back a pace, and proceeded to make patterns in the dust with the toe of her right sandal. 'You like to goad me all the time,' she complained moodily.

He continued with what he was doing. 'Mmm, but then I'm a male chauvinist pig, remember?'

'I didn't say you were a pig,' she protested swiftly.

Now he spared her another glance and his mouth had assumed a humorous curve. 'I thought that was automatically implied along with the other.'

Debra felt her denial may have been too quickly made and decided on a hasty retreat, leaving a somewhat mumbled, 'Not always,' floating behind her as she wandered around to the far side of the Range Rover, and pretending she had suddenly lost interest in watching him work.

She wasn't at all sure herself why she should have rushed to make such a protest on his behalf, but rather than dwell on it she sank down in the shade created by the vehicle's bulk with her back propped against the wheel and deliberately occupied her mind by making mental notes of the things she would need to take with her for the two days they would be at Stratheden.

Somewhere between toothpaste and cleansing cream she guessed she must have dozed off, because the next thing she was conscious of was of being lifted to her feet to the accompaniment of a wryly drawled,

'It's a great life for some! Maybe I should have made you change the tire, seeing it was your efforts which ruined it.'

Still a little drowsy, Debra put out a hand for support and connected with a solidly powerful forearm which she clung to unthinkingly. 'I would have thought just having to replace it was enough to exempt me from doing the work as well,' she pouted.

'As if you don't know damned well you're not expected to pay for it!' All trace of laziness disappeared from Saxon's voice as he resolutely removed himself from her reach.

'But—but you said...at least, you insinuated I would have to,' she recalled perplexedly, and was startled by his abrupt change in manner as she blinked herself back to full awareness.

'Did I?' His tone was still rough. 'Well, perhaps I decided in the meantime that I would rather forgo the money so you wouldn't feel obliged to prolong your employment with us in order to repay it.'

'I see,' she acknowledged thickly, her ebony-lashed eyes dimming to an anguished purple as a despairing ache settled in the region of her heart.

It was so reminiscent of his first attempted payoff that she could only stare at him mutely. Apparently nothing at all had changed, and she had only been deceiving herself by believing that that one spark of remorse—or had it only been pity, after all?—shown during the previous Sunday's storm would have altered his desire to see the last of her.

As swiftly as it had arrived, Saxon's harshness seemed to evaporate and he rubbed a hand wearily around the back of his neck. 'Oh, for God's sake, just get in this and take it home, will you?' he sighed. 'I'll follow in the ute.'

Only her lack of experience with the Range Rover stopped her from obeying immediately. 'I—I'm more used to d-driving the ute,' she just had to point out, but tentatively.

'One wouldn't know it!' he snapped sarcastically. 'Besides which, I want to test it out to make sure nothing else has been damaged, so it would be appreciated if you would just do as you're told without wasting more time by standing here arguing about who's going to drive which vehicle!'

'Yes, *sir*!' she muttered through clenched teeth, and stormed around to the driver's side. He deliberately found fault with every word she ever uttered!

CHAPTER SEVEN

THE TWO days spent at Stratheden with Saxon might have been informative for Debra, but they could hardly have been described as pleasant. He was an able teacher, but amiable companion he was not! She didn't know why he should have been in such a particularly grim mood, but by the time Sunday morning arrived she was only too pleased to return to Wyeera where she had *some* opportunities to escape his forbidding presence.

Matters did improve to a slight degree as the following weeks slipped past into months and the sale came closer, but she had long since despaired of him ever completely accepting her as his secretary. He hadn't wanted her in the position from the very beginning and, evidently, there hadn't been a solitary thing she had said or done since that had made him want to change his mind. Some days she was convinced she was making headway, but then, almost as if he was putting a deliberate brake on himself, he would give her one of those shrewdly assessing glances of his and she would be back to square one again.

And, as if that wasn't enough, she was now positive his decision to take her with him to Stratheden had been, as she half suspected at the time, purely an excuse to prevent her from seeing Paul. Three times since he had done exactly the same thing—with differing

reasons on each occasion, of course!—but it had become more than obvious to Debra that he didn't intend for her to gain any more enjoyment from her stay
on the property than he could possibly help. Only once
had she managed an evening out without his watchful
company—Paul had taken her to a party in town—but
that had only come about because Saxon had been in
Brisbane at the time discussing the sale with his stock
and station agents' head office. Oh, he saw that she
had adequate free time, all right. The only trouble
was, he also saw to it that it never coincided with anyone else's, and certainly *never* when there was anything on in town that he wasn't planning to attend!

She had even once gone so far as to accuse him of
being unable to differentiate between employment and
imprisonment, but that had only earned her his stock
reply to any complaint she might make of always being
able to resign if she didn't like the conditions, and she
had had no choice but to let the matter drop.

Not only was she still reluctant to let him make her
resign, but she was also beginning to doubt now
whether she could resign. No matter what he thought
of her, she couldn't control her own headstrong emotions—or the direction in which they unerringly
headed—and it had taken very little soul-searching to
discover she had unwittingly, and definitely unwisely,
fallen in love with a man who not only didn't need
her—there was always tenacious Anthea to consider—but who had made it all too apparent he didn't
want her either.

She supposed she was being foolish by deliberately
refusing to leave but, right at the moment, she
couldn't bear the thought that if she did go she would
more than likely never see him again. For the time

being, at least, she preferred to suffer his barbed remarks rather than not hear his voice at all. Besides, she managed to convince herself, if she did give in her notice now he might conceivably start delving for the reason behind her sudden capitulation, and his stinging comments, should he be successful, she simply didn't dare think about.

The afternoon prior to the sale, however, an incident occurred in Acacia Crossing which had Debra pondering her decision yet again, but a trifle fearfully this time. Saxon had been involved in a car accident, and although he had neither been in the wrong, nor hurt, her old anxieties had immediately returned to plague her the moment she heard about it. Perhaps she was only being stupidly superstitious, but no matter how hard she tried, she just couldn't dispel the thought that some people *did* seem to attract, or bring, far more bad luck than others. And that was the crux of her whole problem. Was she prepared to take the chance?

It was a question which kept her awake well into the night and, judging by the untidy state of the bedclothes next morning, hadn't been out of her mind even after she had finally fallen asleep. But, by the time she went down to breakfast, she did have her answer. All things considered, no, she wasn't prepared to take that chance!

Naturally enough the talk at the table that morning concentrated on the sale, but apart from a couple of vague acknowledgments to queries directly put to her, Debra added very little to the conversation. She was mentally composing a letter of resignation. And afterwards, she still wasn't able to get to the office because it was a Friday and Prue had to be driven to school—much to her disgust at having to miss out on what she obviously considered the most exciting day of her visit.

The return trip seemed to take hours longer than normal to Debra, although in actual time spent on the road it didn't, but she did meet considerably more traffic on her way as a steady stream of prospective buyers headed for the property. Most of them, she knew from enquiries they had received during the preceding weeks, would be coming by air. In fact, two plane loads had already arrived before she left with Prue, and it wasn't difficult to surmise that after the sale ring the airstrip would probably be the most used area of Wyeera that day.

From the garages she could just make out Saxon's commanding figure as he stood talking to Neale and Mike down by the cattle yards and she hurriedly slipped across to the homestead and into the office. Maybe it was because she really didn't want to write the letter, but it took her an unreasonable amount of time to eventually settle on three suitable lines which would sever her association with Saxon McAllister for good. When it was finished she put her signature to it quickly, slipped it into an envelope and, taking the coward's way out, laid it on his desk. Once she had found the courage to write it, there just wasn't any left over to enable her to hand it to him personally.

On her way outside once more she met Jeanne and her mother crossing the verandah with their arms filled with food containers. The Ladies' Auxiliary was doing the catering again.

'I suppose you're excused kitchen duty for today?' grinned Jeanne ruefully as, with a smile, Debra stepped back to allow them to pass.

'Mmm, I think so. I'm just off to the yards now to see if I'm needed.'

'Ah well, I'll think of you out there in all that dust and heat while I'm slicing tomatoes, etcetera, in Eleanor's nice air-conditioned kitchen.'

'Thanks!' Debra laughed ruefully herself now. 'That really makes me look forward to it.'

'Pay her no mind, Debra,' Mrs Bartlett counselled over her shoulder as she disappeared down the hall. 'You know what a curse jealousy is.'

Winking at the girl beside her, Jeanne began following her parent. 'Well, it is *my* fiancé who's working down there, Mother,' she pointed out with humorous emphasis.

What Mrs Bartlett had to say in reply to that Debra couldn't hear and she continued on her way with a smile tugging at her soft lips. The Bartletts were a nice friendly family.

The usual inspection of cattle prior to sale was under way when she reached the yards, and with such a sizeable throng of men around it took her quite some time to locate Saxon in front of the bull pens inside one of the outbuildings where he and two other men were discussing the merits of one of Wyeera's finest animals. Uncertain whether to interrupt them or not, Debra hovered hesitantly near the adjoining pen for a few minutes until Neale arrived with another group, whereupon she gave a wry apology for being in the way and, taking one last look at her employer, found him holding out an arm towards her.

He was answering a question when she made it to his side, after skirting another quartet coming from the opposite direction, and couldn't help darting him a glance of wide-eyed surprise when that out-stretched arm was draped across her shoulders to pull her protectively close and shield her against the press of the ever-increasing crowd.

A swift introduction to his two companions when he had concluded what he was saying and then he was lowering his head to ask, 'What can I do for you?'

Disastrously aware of him as never before, as she was, it was all she could do to reply. 'I—er—came to ask what you wanted *me* to do,' she managed finally in something of a husky whisper.

'I'm sorry?' He bent his head even closer, his forehead furrowing. 'There's too much noise in here. I couldn't hear you.'

To make sure he heard it this time Debra went up on her toes in order to close the gap even further, but as she did so someone bumped into her from behind and caused her lips to graze across his cheek. For a split second her selfconscious gaze locked with a glittering blue one and the air was electric between them. Then, with a gulp, and a mumbled, 'I'm sorry,' she sank down to her normal height again.

'That's as may be.' Unexpectedly, white teeth gleamed in a tantalising smile. 'But you still haven't told me what you came for.'

'Oh!' She flushed embarrassedly and tore her bemused eyes away. 'It was only to—only to see what you wanted me to do.'

'Well...' His head tilted consideringly. 'You could give Mike a hand once the bidding starts. He'll probably be wanting some help with the buyers' instruction sheets to make sure they're filled in correctly, and legibly. Sometimes they can be rather difficult to read when they've been filled in against a fence post or someone else's back, and you probably know the Lot numbers as well as anyone by now.'

That was the truth! She had certainly been through them often enough since that first time she had taken all their particulars down from the computer.

'Anything else?' Her finely marked brows peaked quizzically.

His expression was dry as he looked up and down the packed walkway between the two rows of pens. 'Apart from the fact that it would appear it's impossible for you to squeeze your way out of here at the moment in order to carry out any instructions I might give, no, I don't think so.'

As much as she was inclined to agree with him regarding her chances of getting through the crowd, she still thought it preferable to at least try rather than stay where she was.

'Oh, I'll manage somehow,' she smiled blithely, and made a move to leave.

Saxon's grip tightened spontaneously. 'And I think not,' he countermanded blandly.

Unless she wanted to make herself look extremely foolish by fighting to get away it seemed she had little option but to accept his ultimatum with as much grace as possible and, with a defeated sigh, she reluctantly consented to remain where she was. No doubt he was probably only calling a truce while there were visitors around—as had always been his custom—but whether that was for her benefit, or his, she hadn't yet been able to decide.

In an attempt to distract her thoughts from such personal considerations Debra listened intently to the men's conversation as they progressed very slowly along the pens, and was privately quite proud when she realised she also had a very good idea of the points they were looking for in each beast they stopped to inspect, thanks to Saxon's expert tuition. And once, almost as much to her own surprise as theirs, she was even able to make a knowledgeable comparison between the two bloodlines they happened to be discussing at the time.

'Well, it sounds as if you've picked yourself a secretary who's got a memory for pedigrees this time, Mac,' applauded the taller of his two associates.

'Which is something that couldn't be said of your last one,' added the other.

Debra didn't say anything. She was too occupied in digesting the information that her predecessor apparently hadn't been the paragon in all respects that she had been led to believe after all.

'Oh, yes, Debra's very good when it comes to identifying the different strains.'

If she hadn't been able to feel his hand so definitely through the lightweight material of her pink slacks suit Debra would have sworn she was dreaming. Surely that wasn't Saxon *praising* something she'd done!

As a result, when their two companions moved slightly ahead, she couldn't resist sending the man beside her a glowering look and mouthing accusingly, 'I thought you said Noreen was the whizz kid of all time with the stud records!'

'And so she was... while she was working with the computer,' he admitted drily. 'Unfortunately, the minute you took her away from it she couldn't remember one bloodline from the other.'

There were quite a number of gibes she could have come back with regarding that convenient omission, but in the end she decided against all of them. With her resignation already lying on his desk there didn't seem much point in raking up old grievances, or starting new ones.

He evidently had been expecting one, though, for when it didn't eventuate he promptly slanted her a keenly measuring glance which had her rushing to divert his attention by nodding her head towards the two men ahead of them and advising, 'They're waiting for you'.

At last they made it to the end of the building and Debra could escape. But not before Saxon had managed to put a scare into her.

'Have you given Mike all the necessary vaccination certificates?' he asked.

'No, not yet.' She shook her head. 'I'll get them for him now.'

'Don't bother,' her offer was waved aside negligently. 'I'll do it myself. I want to have a word with him about them, anyway.'

'It's no bother!' She was already on her way as she said it. The last thing she wanted was for him to discover her resignation this early in the day. 'I want to get a pen and notepad from the office. I think I might have need of them if I'm going to be helping Mike.'

As it turned out, once the auction began she had never spoken a truer word. There were requests to be noted, enquiries which needed following up, and a host of other details she would never have remembered if she hadn't been able to write them down. Also, she had to check the instruction sheets as they came in after each Lot was knocked down, and often it would be a case of her having to chase after a particular buyer in order to remind, 'Excuse me, but you haven't stated what feed and bedding is required on the journey,' or, 'I'm sorry, but you haven't said where you wish your purchases consigned to. Are they to go to your home address?'

It was after one of these forays into the crowd that she found Neale beckoning to her urgently as she passed the walkway which led to the sale ring on her return to the auctioneers' stand. On either side of him stood enormous hump-backed bulls with leather halters about their heads which he was grasping firmly.

'Be a love and take this one into the ring for me,' he smiled persuasively, and held out one of the leads as she put her head between two of the rails to eye him enquiringly.

'M-m-*me*?' She stared back at him, horrified.

'He's as quiet as a lamb,' he assured her earnestly.

'But where are the men? Where's Saxon?' There had been plenty of them around when she left.

'Down the back.' He nodded behind him. 'One of the stupid...' He coughed politely and started again. 'One of the bulls has managed to lock his horns in the steel gate.'

'But surely there's *someone*!' glancing up and down the walkway hopefully.

'Just you, at the moment,' he grinned.

'Neale!' she wailed plaintively, then reluctantly climbed through the bars when she sensed no help would be forthcoming. 'What if he runs amok, or something? I always thought Brahmans weren't a particularly biddable breed.'

'I promise you, he's used to being handled. He's stud, not commercial.'

Debra eyed the young grey giant who literally towered over her askance. 'Does *he* know that?' she quipped drily.

'Would I ask you to take him if I thought he'd give you any trouble?' he countered plausibly, handing over the relevant halter into her somewhat lax fingers. Besides,' a broad grin made its appearance, 'with that many men outside the ring I'm sure he'd only have to look sideways at you to have half of them over the fence and offering to help out.'

'I wouldn't complain if they did that now,' Debra grimaced wryly before giving a tug to her charge and sighing, 'Oh, come on then, you great lump! Put your best foot forward and let's get this over and done with as soon as possible. But so help me, if you so much as breathe on me,' she squinted up at him mock threateningly, 'I'll belt you one on the nose with my notebook!'

Fortunately, there was no call for her threat to be put into practice—not that it would have been a deterrent in any case, as she well knew—although she did have to lean her shoulder into the animal a couple of times, as she had seen the men do, in order to make him turn when and where she wanted. The bidding rose quickly, as she had guessed it would as soon as the auctioneer called out his name and pedigree, but it did seem to take a long time before the final price was reached and she could return to the walkway in relief.

The men had also reappeared by then and she was met by a barrage of wide smiles as she handed over her charge with far more enthusiasm than when she had accepted him.

'A very experienced showing,' drawled Saxon as she came abreast of him, and received a very expressive grimace in return, but which was just as obviously meant for all of them.

'I'll say!' laughed one of the grooms. 'Did you hear the price he reached?'

'I heard,' with evident satisfaction.

'You don't reckon it could have been a case of them being too busy watching the handler to realise what they were bidding?' Neale grinned as he prepared to move into the ring in his turn.

'Could be,' Saxon conceded, his eyes gliding lazily over Debra. 'We'll just have to give her another one to lead around for us to find out, won't we?'

'Like fun!' she retorted explicitly, and scrambled out through the rails before she could be inveigled into anything else. 'You may all have found it amusing, but I'll have you know,' her lips swept upwards into a delightfully rueful smile, '*I* hate the lot of you!'

Their following laughter brought forth many an interested look, but Debra left it to them to do any enlightening, if they cared to, while she continued back to her seat beside Mike. Where she made certain she stayed for the rest of the morning.

Lunch was a convivial meal served smorgasbord style on the verandah, and after helping to see that the visitors were all catered for, Debra took hers with Eleanor, Mrs Bartlett, and Jeanne. Not that they were granted much time for conversation because, all too soon, everyone was resuming their places and, with a smiled apology for her companions, she prepared to do likewise.

On her way to her bedroom to renew her lipstick she met Saxon coming from the other direction, and the absolutely livid set of his features immediately informed her that he was in the foulest mood imaginable. Without having heard that anything had gone wrong she naturally wondered at the cause, and no one could have been more astonished than she was when a ruthless hand snaked out to grip her wrist painfully as their paths crossed.

'*You're* just the one I want!' he ground out explosively as, without a word of explanation, he spun about and began dragging her along behind him.

Debra's brain raced chaotically. What had she done now? Left something important out of the brochure? Put something in that she shouldn't have? Given the wrong advice to someone? She shook her head dismissively. She really couldn't think of a thing that would generate this amount of wrath!

He turned into the office and she was thrust unceremoniously into the room while he slammed the door shut with a crash she felt sure must have been heard all the way to the sale ring, and then stalked towards his desk.

'And just what the bloody hell's the meaning of this?' He slapped a hand down furiously on to her opened letter of resignation.

Dumbfounded, she could only stand and stare at him in round-eyed amazement. Jubilation, mockery, sarcasm, taunts—those she had all expected—but not *anger*! She swallowed nervously and gave a slight shrug. 'It's my resignation.'

'I'm well aware of what it is!' he lashed back savagely. 'I asked the meaning for it!'

'Isn't it enough that you've got it?' she evaded tautly.

'No! I want to know *why*!'

With every tense inch of her showing defiance she held his brilliant gaze stoutly. 'Because you've won. Why else?'

'Oh, don't give me that!' His voice changed to one of contemptuous disgust. 'Only two days ago you were reiterating your denial that I could make you leave, and as I was away for most of yesterday and hardly said more than a dozen words to you all day, kindly don't play me for a credulous idiot by expecting me to believe any of your, ''Because you've won'', myths!'

'And that's just what this is all about, isn't it?' she was goaded into taunting. 'You're just infuriated because it wasn't due to *your* efforts that I resigned!'

'Not at all,' he repudiated the suggestion tersely. 'Because until I'm satisfied with the reason, I shall simply refuse to accept it,' as he deliberately tore the typewritten page into pieces and dropped them into the waste basket.

Debra watched the last of them flutter out of sight and then put a hand dazedly to her head. 'You can't do that,' she protested.

'I just did!'

'Then I'll write out another one.'

'Don't waste your time!'

'You're just being perverse!' Her voice rose angrily.

'Am I?' A long-legged stride brought him menacingly closer. 'I would have said it was the other way around!'

'Oh, I wouldn't doubt for a minute that's what you'd say,' she gibed. 'You're so...'

A knock on the door interrupted her and it was Neale who put his head apologetically into the room in response to Saxon's acknowledgment to advise, 'Sorry, Mac, but I thought you'd want to know we're ready to start again.'

'Thanks, Neale, I'm coming.' And to Debra in a peremptory tone as he headed after his manager, 'We'll finish this later.'

'There's nothing to finish,' she contradicted with a pert lift of her chin. 'I don't have to discuss my reasons for wanting to leave with you.'

'But you will!'

'I will not!' It was a mutinous mutter rather than a confident refusal, although in either case it was doubtful if Saxon heard, because he was already making his way down the hall.

Debra continued on to her bedroom more slowly, her thoughts understandably confused. She had been preparing herself for sarcastic elation, not an irate explosion, and she just couldn't fathom why he should apparently care what had prompted her to hand in her notice. She would have thought he would have been only too happy to see her go, for whatever reason! Or maybe, no matter what he said to the contrary, it was as she had first suggested. Saxon just wasn't used to being thwarted, and the knowledge that all his efforts had failed to achieve the desired result was what had really riled him.

A theory which, unfortunately, didn't make Debra feel any better, for whenever her eyes happened to collide with his still smouldering gaze during the afternoon session of the sale, she was promptly reminded of his parting remarks and shivers of apprehension would begin trickling down her spine at the thought of what might yet be to come. Having succeeded in foiling him once, she knew without a doubt that it was going to be doubly hard to repeat the performance.

'What happened to you at lunchtime?' Mike's amused-sounding question brought her out of one of her many periods of introspection with a start.

'Oh—er—nothing in particular,' she prevaricated lightly. 'What makes you ask?'

'Only the fact that it's been perfectly obvious your mind's been anywhere but on the sale since we returned,' he enlightened her in extremely dry tones.

'I'm very sorry,' she smiled at him penitently. 'Have I missed anything?'

'Just Mac's signals to you over the last five minutes.'

She pulled a dismayed face and glanced over to where Saxon stood beside the gate leading into the ring, his exasperated expression being directed straight at her.

'Oh, hell, I'd better get over there and see what he wants. Why didn't you say something before?' she queried as she pushed out of her chair.

'I tried, in between bids,' he divulged with a laugh. 'But you ignored me too.'

'Then I guess I'd better apologise for that too.' Her smile was ruefully shaped. 'It would appear my concentration has been sadly lacking this afternoon.'

'No worries. There hasn't been anything that needed it so far.'

Except for Saxon's summons, of course, Debra mused sardonically as she made her way round to the gate.

'So you finally managed to stir yourself into coming?' he greeted her with a sarcastic inflection to his voice.

She supposed she deserved that. 'I'm sorry. I wasn't aware you wanted me until Mike told me.'

'Perhaps, if you'd been paying attention, **you** wouldn't have needed to wait for him to tell you.'

'I guess not,' she accepted his stricture with a sigh. 'But I'm here now.'

'Too late, unhappily!' he snapped.

'Oh?' Her brows drew together in a frown. 'For what?'

'For collecting Prue earlier than usual,' he informed her coldly. 'I've had to send someone else instead.'

'I don't see why!' she fired resentfully. 'I knew Prue wanted to get home as soon as possible this afternoon and, according to my calculations, I still had another ten minutes or so before I needed to leave.'

'Mmm, but by the way you were day-dreaming up there I couldn't be sure you'd remember at all.' His retort was satirically goading. 'In addition to which, Eleanor wanted a parcel of bulbs picked up from Simpson's beforehand.'

'She didn't mention anything about it to me,' suspiciously.

'No? Well, maybe she couldn't attract your attention either!'

Before Debra had a chance to deal with that gibing attack another voice came from close by, a voice dripping with false concern.

'Oh, dear, have we arrived at an inappropriate time? You don't sound very pleased with your secretary today, Mac,' Anthea smiled up at him archly.

Her companion was Paul, who Debra greeted warmly, even as she listened for Saxon's reply.

'How could I not be?' he counter-questioned smoothly, if a little ironically, in Debra's estimation.

'She paraded one of our top money-earners in the ring this morning.'

'Good on you!' Paul applauded with a grin. Anthea, as was to be expected, was far less complimentary.

'You didn't!' she exclaimed, pretending to be impressed, and then gave a coy laugh. 'Of course, I'm not big enough or strong enough to control one of those great beasts. I just wouldn't know what to do if they decided to misbehave.'

'Oh, a threatened belting with a notebook seems to work wonders,' advised Debra drily. The other girl was at it again! Apparently she was to be labelled as King Kong's stand-in this time. 'Once they've realised what damage you can do with one of those, they're no trouble at all.'

'Now you're teasing me,' Anthea protested with a girlish pout, and turned to the man beside her for confirmation, saying, 'She is, isn't she, Mac?'

'I wouldn't know.' Saxon hunched wide shoulders dispassionately, although his mouth took on an amused twist, but further than that he refused to comment, going on instead to ask, 'What brings you out here, anyway, Anthea?'

'Oh, I met Paul while I was in town, so when he said he intended coming out to see how things were progressing I invited myself along too. I thought you might offer to drive me home again afterwards,' she smiled up at him with an overweening confidence which stabbed at Debra excruciatingly.

'Not tonight, I'm sorry,' he appeared to have no hesitation in declining her blatant encouragement. 'Apart from the fact that some of these,' motioning towards the men clustered about the ring, 'won't be leaving until well into the evening, I also have other pressing matters to attend to tonight,' as his eyes clashed purposefully with Debra's above the shorter girl's head.

'That's all right, I don't mind waiting for you,' Anthea persisted. 'I'm sure Eleanor won't object to one extra for dinner.'

'You're welcome to stay for dinner, of course,' Saxon allowed courteously, but in a voice which had tightened so markedly that Debra found herself cringing inwardly on the other girl's behalf. 'And I shall be only too pleased . . .'

'I knew you'd eventually agree,' the brunette interrupted with a victorious smirk, and had at least two of her listeners staring at her in disbelief for her insensitivity.

'. . . to ensure you have someone to escort you home . . . but it will not be me!' Saxon continued as if she had never spoken. 'I will be otherwise occupied!'

Suddenly, as his words penetrated, a hectic red stain splashed over Anthea's cheeks and her eyes glittered spitefully. 'With *her*?' she went so far as to forget herself and snap.

There was no necessity for anyone to ask for clarification. They all knew exactly who she meant, and while Paul promptly uttered a disgusted snort at the outspoken accusation, Debra could only stand by stiffly and feel the tint of selfconscious colour surging into her own face.

Saxon was nowhere near as forbearing, however, as with an imperious wave of his hand he brought one of his men over. 'Miss Devenish wishes to leave, Charley,' he advised icily. 'Would you take her home in the station wagon, please?'

It was the ultimate snub. He was turning her off the property, and without even giving her the satisfaction of an answer. And Anthea, unwilling to have her pride lacerated in front of one of the stockmen as well, had no option but to accept the rebuff with as much control as possible.

As soon as she had left Debra smiled nervously and prepared to make her departure too. 'If you'll excuse me, I'd better get back and see if Mike has anything he wants me to do,' she said.

'Hey!' Paul reached out a hand to prevent her moving. 'It wasn't only to see how the sale was going that I came out here, you know.'

Indecision was written all over her face as she looked from one of them to the other, and it was Saxon who did her replying for her, his tone still a little taut. 'Sorry, old son, but you'll have to wait, I'm afraid. Debra has work to do at the moment.'

Paul laughed wryly, his eyes turning skywards. 'I know, business before pleasure!' he quoted.

Actually, Debra had so many things to think about that she wasn't unhappy to escape from both of them. Saxon, because the less she saw of him from now on the better it would be for her peace of mind, and Paul, because although she liked him, that was all she felt for him, and she didn't want to give him any ideas to the contrary.

CHAPTER EIGHT

As SAXON had prophesied, certainly not all the visitors left when the sale was concluded, and dinner was over and the evening well advanced by the time the last of them had finished partaking of their host's hospitality and departed. For Debra's part, she was sorry to see them go, conscious as she had been of a deliberating gaze resting on her the whole time they had been toasting the success of the sale, both from the sellers' and the buyers' points of view.

Now, as the final set of red tail-lights disappeared down the road to the main gate, she decided it was time to make herself scarce and, surmising her bedroom would offer no sanctuary against someone of Saxon's determination, she stayed only long enough to strip off her slacks suit and don a pair of jeans and an old cotton shirt, then headed outdoors. Perhaps, she hoped, on finding her room empty, Saxon would save his interrogation for another day. A day when she felt a little more prepared to endure it than she did right at the moment.

For the first half hour or so she wandered around aimlessly, up to the sleep-out on the roof, around Eleanor's bush houses, and then down towards the outbuildings. The air was pleasantly cool against her skin, but as she came round the corner of the cattle shed where she had found Saxon earlier that morning she caught the full force of the breeze, and to elude the cold draught she slipped inside.

It was quiet now, the dimmed light overhead showing most of the animals to be asleep, and completely unaware that within a few days they would be starting journeys—extremely long ones in some instances—to new homes. Slowly she made her way down the pens on the right-hand side, trying to recall the pedigree of each occupant as she passed, and then turned and started back up the other row. As she neared the end some sixth sense made her look towards the doorway and, with a sharply inhaled breath, she came to a standstill.

Saxon seemed to fill the opening as he stood there indolently with his hands resting on lean hips, and how long he had been there she had no way of knowing. He had changed too, she noted, from the moleskins and white shirt he had been wearing all day to slim-fitting jeans and a denim shirt which gave him such an earthy, untrammelled air that she closed her eyes in despair. Oh, God, why did he have to look so invincible, so hypnotising, so damned flagrantly male?

'You've led me quite a chase,' he drawled wryly as long easy strides shortened the distance between them.

'Oh?' She smiled weakly and pushed her hands into the pockets of her jeans in an effort to imitate his self-assuredness. 'I didn't realise you were looking for me.'

His lips twitched and then stilled. 'Well, I guess it doesn't matter now that I've found you, does it?'

'I suppose not,' she shrugged, and flattened herself against the steel rails of the pen beside her in the hope of stepping around him. 'Although it is getting late, and—and...' She stopped with a jerk as a bronzed hand slapped down on to the rail just in front of her.

'But not too late for us to complete our discussion, I trust?'

A quick duck under that restricting arm and she was edging towards the door with her back pressed against the rail. 'Discussion?' she echoed innocently.

As he kept pace with her a knowing glint appeared in the depths of his blue eyes. 'You'll never make it, you know.'

She certainly wouldn't if she didn't try! 'I don't know what you're talking about,' she parried.

'You're trying to play me for a fool again, sweetheart.' Saxon stroked one forefinger warningly across her burning cheek.

Debra began moving faster. 'Not me, boss,' she quipped flippantly.

'Yes, *you*, you little witch!' Her progress was abruptly halted by two hands descending on to the rail this time, one on either side of her, and he leant disturbingly close to propose, 'So let's go back to the beginning, shall we?'

'The beginning of what?' she desperately denied knowledge of his meaning.

'Debra!' One hand left the rail in order to span her jaw. 'Believe me, one way or another, I mean to discover why you suddenly decided to resign.'

'It's none of your business!'

'I happen to think otherwise.'

'And once again you're *wrong*!' Anger was her last resort and she used it unstintingly. 'The same as you've been wrong in every single thought you've ever had about me. You've accused me of everything unpleasant you could think of, done all you possibly could to make my life unbearable, and now you want to add browbeating to your list!' She glared at him fiercely, her breath coming in shallow gasps. 'Well, I've got news for you, Saxon McAllister! This is one time you're not having everything your own way!'

'The hell it's not!'

His lips came down on hers hard and determinedly, and against this new attack she had no defence whatsoever. Anger was of little use to her now—his actions too closely paralleled her own wayward desires—and as her heart swiftly took control from her head she melted against him uninhibitedly, her pliant form moulding itself to his rugged length and delighting in the pressure of strong arms which ensured she couldn't stray.

When it became clear she had no intention of fighting him the autocratic demands of his mouth changed to leisurely, persuasive caresses which drugged her mind to the exclusion of all else and had her ardently seeking more. With a deep-throated groan Saxon suddenly bent to swing her off her feet and into his arms, carrying her with sure steps to an empty stall used for storage, and sinking down with her among the piles of fresh clean straw.

Debra's half closed eyes were a deep, drowsy purple as he reached up to entwine slim arms about his neck and draw his head down to hers again, her gently parted lips an invitation impossible to ignore. Beneath her exploring fingers she could feel the sinewed slope of his shoulders and, remembering a night when she had been able to touch that tanned skin unobstructed, she shyly began unfastening his shirt. A convulsive shudder shook him at her first tentative contact and he gathered her ever closer, even as his lips played havoc with the pulsing nerve at the side of her throat.

Her senses were on fire and she could feel swift fingers efficiently removing the barrier of her shirt and bra, but she made no move to resist. She loved him more than he would ever know and when he made her feel like this she could deny him nothing. Nevertheless, when a work-hardened hand slid upwards to cup a firm, swelling breast she couldn't restrain the quiver of raw emotion which surged through her, a tremor which quickly became a raging flood as warm lips followed to tease an already aroused nipple into throbbing ecstasy.

For a moment she thought her heart would burst, so hard was it beating, and then in the next breath believed it had stopped altogether, from shock, when Saxon lifted his head to pin her with an impassioned blue gaze and groaned thickly,

'Dear God! When are you going to marry me?'

It was the last thing she had expected, but what she wanted most, and it was only by drawing on the very last reserves of her willpower that she managed to shake her head weakly.

'I'm not,' she whispered brokenly.

His eyes searched hers questioningly, deeply. 'In the name of heaven, why not? You must know by now how much I love you, and I'm damned sure you're not exactly uninterested in me either!'

Embarrassed by her nakedness now, Debra rolled to her knees and away from him as she hastily refastened her clothes. 'I just can't, that's all,' she choked, head downbent.

'Don't you think I'm at least entitled to know why?' A gentle hand swept her tousled hair aside in order to rest lightly against the nape of her neck.

If anything her head drooped even lower, but she didn't answer.

'Is it because you don't love me?' he probed.

Again she didn't answer and he continued. 'Then is it because you don't think I love you?'

The merest movement of her head negated that supposition and for a few seconds there was utter silence. Then, in a keenly perceptive tone, he enquired suspiciously, 'This doesn't happen to have anything to do with the reason you resigned, does it?'

He was too close for comfort and she shook her head vigorously this time, and was amazed to hear a briefly mocking laugh sound behind her. Confused, she half turned to look at him and found him beckoning to her. When she refused to comply he simply caught her about the waist and pulled her around to face him.

'As delightful as your back might be, it's your face I'm interested in seeing at the moment, sweetheart,' he advised wryly.

'So you can laugh at me again?' stiffly.

'Laugh at you? I could beat you for what you're doing to me!' His voice deepened hoarsely. 'That laugh you heard was directed at myself for having let a violet-eyed witch turn my well-ordered life into a shambles, and for being driven half out of my mind because she won't tell me why she wants to take herself out of it again!'

'Oh, Saxon.' She stared at him helplessly, tears welling into her eyes. 'It's only because I love you so much that I have to leave.'

A mirthless smile caught at his lips. 'If you'll pardon me for saying so, that may sound very touching, but it offers little comfort.'

'You don't believe me?'

'I don't know what to believe any more! You've got my thoughts almost as tangled as yours, and I'm ...' He broke off abruptly to exclaim in dawning comprehension, 'Good God Almighty! That just goes to prove what you've done to my thought processes or I would have realised long ago. I knew *I* couldn't make you resign—I think I was subconsciously counting on it, in fact—but what I didn't allow for was a superstitious little idiot who unbelievably considers herself to be some sort of jinx.' He leant forward to cup her face between his hands and query softly, 'That's it, isn't it, Debra?'

There was no call for her to agree, the answer was in her misty eyes, although she still had to convince him, 'And that's exactly why I can't stay.'

'You might just as well, because now I know the reason, wherever you go I'll be right there behind you,' he promised. 'My days of pretending I can live without you are over.'

He couldn't be serious! 'But—but what about all this?' She spread one hand expressively wide.

'Neale's a good manager.'

'It's your whole life!'

'Uh-uh!' He shook his head decisively. '*You're* my whole life.'

How could she keep fighting when everything in her wanted to surrender? 'But I'd die if something happened to you because of me,' she cried tremulously.

'I wouldn't be too keen on it myself,' he grinned drily, and bent to kiss the tears from her flushed cheeks.

'Oh, please don't joke about it,' she begged. 'It really frightens me.'

Saxon drew her trembling figure to him tenderly, his eyes the softest blue she had ever seen them. 'I know, sweetheart, I know,' he soothed. 'But that's what I'm here for, remember? To make sure nothing ever frightens you again.'

His confidence was reassuring and she did so *want* to believe. 'You think I'm being foolish, don't you?' she tilted her face ruefully up to his.

It was too good an opportunity to miss and his lips closed over hers satisfyingly. 'I think I'm very fortunate to have found someone who cares so deeply,' he breathed unevenly long moments later.

'You still haven't answered my question, though.'

He sighed and held her slightly away from him. 'What can I say? You already know my feelings with regard to luck, good or bad. Although there is one aspect of this I feel perhaps should be pointed out to you.'

'Which is?'

'That your natural parents' deaths had nothing whatsoever to do with luck! I'm afraid they brought it on themselves by failing to wear life-jackets. You survived because you were wearing one, and there's no reason to suppose they wouldn't have done so too if they'd taken the proper precautions.'

'I guess I've never really thought of it in that light before,' she mused pensively. 'Although you couldn't say that about Rose and Jack Armitage.'

'No, theirs was a case of pure bad luck,' he acceded with a shrug. 'But freak accidents do happen at times and, in this case, I rather think the blame could more appropriately be laid at Mother Nature's door than yours.'

He made it sound all so logical. 'And Jay, the boy at the orphanage?' she couldn't help asking.

Recognising her need to be convinced, he smiled wryly and reasoned, 'Darling, as distressing a fact as it may be, children have been getting themselves killed by running out on to roads from behind buses, cars, carriages, and anything else you like to name, ever since man first devised means of transport for himself, but I hardly think it's fair to suggest you were the cause of it all.'

'There's your accident yesterday too, don't forget.'

'And if all car accidents were that innocuous we would all consider ourselves fortunate!' he countered swiftly. 'You had more chance of injuring yourself when you drove over the embankment.'

'I didn't *drive* over,' she was diverted into protesting indignantly. 'It just sort of... slid over.'

'Yes, well, that's what the driver's supposed to be there for, you know. To prevent that from happening,' he teased.

She knew he was only doing it to stop her thoughts returning to less pleasant subjects, but he needn't have worried. Although he might not have yet completely laid to rest every last one of her doubts—they had been with her too long to be dismissed altogether that quickly—at least he had done the next best thing by bringing them back into perspective. Now, with her head tilting to one side, she cast him a provocative look from beneath luxuriant lashes.

'If I asked you to hold me, would you accuse me of propositioning you?' she quizzed banteringly.

'No,' he laughed in recognition of the phrase. 'But then, once again, I couldn't guarantee that's all I'd do either.'

Debra pressed closer and wound her arms adoringly about his neck. 'I'm willing to take the chance if you are,' she murmured throatily, her surrender complete.

'Oh, God yes!' His arms crushed her to him possessively, his mouth hungrily accepting all that she voluntarily offered. 'I love you so much it hurts!'

For Debra, he was her every dream come true, and had he asked it of her she would have given herself to him there and then. She had no reservations where he was concerned. But he didn't ask, he pulled reluctantly away instead.

'When *are* you going to marry me, sweetheart?' he repeated his original question fervently.

Even white teeth shone in a smile of bewitching radiance. 'Whenever you want.'

'It can't be soon enough for my liking,' he owned expressively. 'I've wanted you for a long, long time now.' A long forefinger followed the outline of her lips delicately. 'And the night of that damned storm was nearly my undoing. My God, I went in to comfort you, but if I'd stayed any longer I would have ended up raping you.'

'Not rape, my love,' she corrected softly, shyly. 'I doubt if I would have fought you at all. Except for when you accused me of making advances towards you, of course!'

'Ah, yes,' he nodded wryly. 'That was when I found I wanted nothing better than to hold you—for ever if need be—and that discovery not only made me mad with myself for letting you get under my skin, but it made me even more annoyed with you for being able to affect me so greatly.'

'Because you still believed I was conniving, and conscienceless, and all those other things you charged me with being?'

He sighed heavily, his expression remorseful. 'Partly, I'm sorry to say, but in the main because you had somehow managed to acquire the unfortunate habit—from my standpoint—of using those beautiful eyes of yours to let me know just exactly what a rotten heel I was being, whereupon I immediately wanted to strike back and hurt you all the more.'

'And succeeded quite admirably on a number of occasions,' she recalled ruefully.

'Don't remind me!' His plea was made in tones of self-disgust. 'Can you ever forgive me?'

She dimpled mischievously. 'I'll try, and especially if you continue saying nice things about me. It makes such a pleasant change.'

'Minx! I knew you were going to be trouble from the moment I first saw you, sitting there defying me before I even knew who you were,' he glowered at her mock-ferociously. 'It would have served you right if I had sacked you when I was considering it.'

'When was that?' she gasped in astonishment. He had always seemed so firm in his conviction that he could make her resign that it had never occurred to her that he might have contemplated dismissal as a means of getting rid of her.

'Your first afternoon here,' he divulged with a smile for her amazement. 'If you remember, you made a somewhat sarcastic remark as I left the office.'

'Only because you'd just done the same to me.'

'Mmm, but fair play was the last thing I had on my mind at the time, and when I walked back into the room I thought, ''To hell with waiting for her to re-sign'', and I fully intended firing you on the spot.'

'So why didn't you?' she frowned perplexedly.

'Because, my darling, that was the first time I fell victim to your eyes. They were so wide and so ner-vous, and such a glorious colour, all I could do was to stare at them, fascinated, until I'd completely forgot-ten what I damned well meant to say!' ironically.

Debra burst into delightful laughter. 'Are you sorry?' Those same violet eyes flirted with him out-rageously.

'You might be if you tempt me too far!' he vowed drily.

'Yes, Mac,' she acceded in pretended submissive-ness.

'Uh-uh!' he vetoed repressively. 'I've told you be-fore, only my friends call me that.'

Her glance turned reproachful. 'And doesn't a wife-to-be qualify as one of those?'

'*Male* friends,' he enunciated with a smile.

'But that's what Anthea calls you,' she protested.

One well shaped brow quirked sardonically. 'And did I say I liked it? I can assure you there's quite a few things Anthea says that I don't agree with.'

He wasn't the only one, but with his arms securely around her she could afford to be magnanimous. 'I felt quite sorry for her this afternoon. You were so ruthlessly blunt.'

'Was I?' He seemed unconcerned whether he had been or not. 'I thought I did extremely well in con-trolling my temper, and that she was lucky to get off as lightly as she did. Apart from the fact that there's only one female I want making overtures to me, I certainly wasn't going to permit her to vent her spite on you.'

His reasons were rewarded by a pleased smile and a sigh of utter contentment. 'Up until then I'd been under the impression she was your girl-friend,' she confessed, happily now.

'Thanks!' His arms tightened menacingly and a crooked tilt formed at the corner of his mouth. 'That really says a lot for my judgment.'

'Well, I wasn't to know,' she half laughed, half pouted. 'I mean, she used to carry on as if she was, and I certainly didn't see you doing anything to discourage her.'

'The same as you weren't exactly struggling to escape Paul?'

'There wasn't any need!' she retorted. 'You always saw to that for me.'

'Rather well too most times, I thought,' he grinned impenitently. 'You really didn't get to see much of him at all, did you?'

'No!' She wrinkled her nose at him wryly. 'But was that because you just wanted to make life less enjoyable for me, or—or...'

'Or because I was too damned jealous to let him near you? I'll give you one clue,' he volunteered huskily as he lowered his head to take possession of her lips with absorbing efficiency.

When he raised it again all thoughts of Paul had fled from Debra's mind, but there was a teasing light in her eyes as she advised, 'Er—I seem to be having a little difficulty with my translation. Do you think you could repeat that clue for me, please?'

The tender curve of his mouth was a caress in itself. 'As often as you wish, my love,' he promised.

THE AUTHOR

Kerry Allyne developed wanderlust after
emigrating with her family from England
to Australia. A long working holiday
enabled her to travel the world before
returning to Australia where she met her
husband-to-be. She now lives in
Summerland, where her family runs a
small cattle farm and an electrical
contracting business. Kerry Allyne's travel
experience adds much to the novels she
spends her days writing—when, that is,
she's not doing company accounts or
herding cattle!

A Girl
Bewitched
Marjorie Lewty

Lisa's letters to her cousin Emma were full of glowing details about the new man in her life, Trent Marston. Then Lisa suddenly decided to marry Richard Southall. What had happened?

All Emma had to do was meet Trent Marston to know. He was the callous, self-centered type who merely amused himself with women's affections. And her dear uncle had hired this man to manage the family firm!

How was Emma going to cope with working for him . . . and loving him?

CHAPTER ONE

'I'M STILL not awfully happy about letting you fly back to Heathrow on your own, Emma love.' Joe Kent, marketing manager of Fairley Brothers, of Poole, Dorset, England, shook his grey head worriedly. 'You're sure you'll be O.K.?'

Emma Fairley smiled across the yellow-topped table at him reassuringly. 'Of course I'll be O.K., Joe. Haven't you been training me for the last six weeks, all the way down from Toronto, in the art of Air Travel Without Tears? Airports are home-from-home for me now. Well—almost.'

She waved a hand airily towards the glass partition of the coffee-shop where they were sitting, beyond which the concourse of the vast international airport of Houston, Texas, U.S.A. seethed and chattered and sweltered in the warmth of early April. 'Look,' she giggled, 'what could possibly be homelier than that?'

Joe grinned back, appreciating the joke. In the last six weeks of travelling together he had come to admire Emma Fairley as well as love her—which he had done since she was born, twenty years ago. She had been a tower of strength to him when he got depressed about the business. She could always manage to find a funny side to the worst of setbacks. She was happy to take much of the paper work off his hands, which he admitted was a great relief.

But not least important, she had grown into a beautiful young woman, with her dark gold hair that was always smooth and well cared for, her slender body and long legs, and the way she had of looking at you with a calm seriousness that could change in a moment into that quirky little smile that wrinkled her small, straight nose. Oh yes, Emma Fairley was going to be a great credit to the firm. If, Joe added dismally to himself, there was going to be any firm to be a credit to.

Emma was smiling her quirky little smile now, and looking, perhaps, a little more confident than she was feeling, but she wasn't going to admit that to Joe. He had enough on his mind with the business—or lack of it—without having to bother about her.

She said, 'And anyway, look how easy it's all been made for me! You being a darling and taking most of my luggage on to Mexico with you, so that I'll only have my hand baggage to cope with. And Uncle Edward promising to have someone meet me at Heathrow! So you see—no problem!'

Her tawny brown eyes rested affectionately on Joe's slightly stooping shoulders and thinning sandy hair, and she thought what a dear he was and how she was going to miss him. She said, 'I just wish I could have finished the trip and come with you to Mexico City. I'd been looking forward to that. Nothing but this crazy idea of Lisa's that she wanted to get married all in a wild rush would have dragged me back home before our trip ended. I don't know why she couldn't have waited a week or two longer.'

'Lisa never had to wait for anything she wanted, did she?' Joe's tolerant grin removed any sting of criticism from the words.

Emma sighed. 'I suppose we have spoiled her. She's so very spoilable.'

Lisa, her young cousin—so delicately lovely, like a flower. Lisa, with her lint-fair hair and her dreamy, deep blue eyes. Lisa, so sweet, so loving, so delightfully grateful for anything you did for her. *Had* she been spoiled? No, thought Emma, loving never spoiled anyone.

'I'm glad it's young Richard Southall she's decided on finally, though,' Joe was saying. 'He's a sound lad. I was always a bit afraid Lisa might land herself in some foolish love affair that would come unstuck.'

Emma nodded soberly, marvelling not for the first time at Joe's perception. What would he say if he knew how dangerously close his fears had come to the truth? Her hand rested for a moment on her shoulder-bag, lying beside her on the table. In it were Lisa's letters to prove it.

She changed the subject quickly. 'Joe, I've had an idea. Why don't I persuade Uncle Edward to let me come back after the wedding? If I could manage to get a flight the day after, then I could join you in Mexico City for when the trade fair opens next week.'

Joe shook his sandy head firmly. 'Put that right out of your mind, love. All that travelling—you'd be completely whacked and no use to me at all,' he teased gently. 'And there's no need, my child. I've handled many a trade fair, I can cope with one more.'

'Of course you can,' Emma said, a little too quickly. Not for the world would she let him know that she had noticed how weary he had looked on the flight from New York, and while they had been not very successfully pursuing customers here in Houston. 'But I could help with the letters and the paper work. I *have* helped, haven't I?'

Joe grinned at her. 'Fishing, are we? You know darned well you've helped. You've been invaluable, and it's been a treat having you with me to cheer me up now and again.'

Their eyes met in understanding. Emma said, 'The order book isn't exactly bulging, is it? But everyone says Mexico is *the* up and coming place. I'm sure the luck will change and we'll get lots of new contacts there.'

'Well, you can bet I'll be chasing 'em up.' Joe lifted his thumbs.

She grinned back at him, reflecting the gesture. Whistling in the dark, that was what they were doing. They both knew the score—that the family firm had been slowly going downhill for years and that now nothing less than a miracle could save it. Perhaps, she thought, they were the only two people who did know. Uncle Edward, engrossed in his electronic wizardry, seemed to know little about the business side—and care even less. Or perhaps it was that he was, in some ways, still a child. Geniuses, they said, often were. Lisa took after him in that way; at eighteen she still seemed to live in a world of dreams and imagination.

The tannoy echoed through the room '—passengers for Flight P.A. 317, destination Mexico City, please—'

Joe stood up and tucked his shabby briefcase firmly under his arm. 'That's my final call, I'd better be moving.' He bent to kiss her. 'Take care, my dear, I'll be thinking of you. Wish Lisa all the best for me on Wednesday—and Richard too. Tell her how sorry I am to miss her wedding.'

Emma nodded. 'She'll be sorry too.' But Lisa wouldn't. She'd never even notice that Joe wasn't there. Her lovely young cousin could never understand or share Emma's devotion to Joe Kent, who had worked so loyally for the family firm most of his life. To Lisa, in her dreamy, romantic youthfulness, anyone over the age of forty was already in their dotage.

'Goodbye, Joe, and good luck.' She watched him weave his way between the crowded tables—a thin man, his feet dragging tiredly, and she felt a sudden catch in her throat.

It was difficult to think of Joe as getting old, but she supposed he must be nearly sixty now. He had been part of the family firm, and part of her life, for as long as she could remember and she was very, very fond of him.

When the light aircraft carrying both Emma's parents and Lisa's beautiful young mother to a conference in Italy had crashed over the Alps in a freak storm, ten years ago, it was Joe who had held Emma tightly in his arms, letting her sob out her shock and agony. Lisa, three years younger, and only just turned seven then, had been almost too young to understand what had happened. Uncle Edward had tried to comfort the two girls, but his own bewildered grief at the loss of his young wife had stunned him, and he had shut himself up in his workroom for days at a time, apparently losing himself among his charts and blueprints and his array of delicate instruments.

But Joe had understood. Had understood, too, that when the first numbing shock had passed Emma wanted to talk about her parents—about her mother, so lively and full of fun, and about her father, who was the dynamo that had kept the family firm throbbing along.

'We'll never replace him.' Joe had shaken his head sadly. 'He had a way with people. He was building up Fairley Brothers into something really big.'

'But you can do it too, Joe. You can go on where Daddy left off.' Emma had felt an odd need to encourage him.

'I'll just have to try my best,' Joe said simply.

Heaven knows he had tried his best, Emma thought now, but it looked as if his best hadn't been enough. She wondered what would happen if the firm really did go bust. Would they lose everything? Their home on the cliff overlooking the sea, in the Dorset village where she had grown up? Would that go too? Thank goodness, she thought fervently, that Lisa had made up her mind to marry Richard at long last—Richard, the boy-next-door, steady, safe. He had loved Lisa since childhood, and he would look after her and protect her from the chill winds that looked like blowing up around the family fortunes.

Emma's face softened as she sat sipping her coffee. Lisa needed someone like Richard. What a mercy she had come to her senses in time about the wild, hectic romance that started with the Trent Marston man, soon after Emma and Joe had left on their trip! Emma hadn't liked the sound of *him* at all. From Lisa's letters she recognised the type only too well, and she would be eternally glad that Lisa had cut short *that* little romance.

She glanced up at the clock. Her flight wasn't likely to be called yet, so she took out Lisa's letters from her bag. She would read them through once again and then burn them when she reached home. Once she was a married woman Lisa wouldn't want to be reminded of that foolish little fantasy.

The first letter had come soon after Emma and Joe reached Toronto, at the beginning of their trip.

'Darling, darling Emma,' Lisa had written in her schoolgirl scrawl, 'It's happened as I always told you it would! The most wonderful, heavenly man! We met yesterday when he came to see Daddy on some business or other and we only had to *look* at each other!! Oh, Em, wait until you see him, he's absolutely sensational—tall and dark with the most marvellous dark eyes that make my knees go all wobbly when he looks at me. I've dreamed about my man for so long that as soon as I saw him I just *knew*. The blissful thing is that he feels the same about me. Oh, gosh, it's unbelievable to be really in love, I'm just so glad I waited until he came. I want to give him everything and hold nothing back—when *you* fall in love you'll know what I mean. You've always laughed at me for being such a soppy, romantic idiot, haven't you, Em darling, but you see I was right—it *does* happen! I'm sitting in my room looking out over the sea and the sun's setting and I'm waiting for him to come and I'm sort of excited and scared both at once. I guess that's what love means. Goodness, there's the front door bell now and I can hear Jessie coming from the kitchen to open it. I'm all of a shake. Will write again very soon and tell you all the news, your deliriously happy, Lisa.'

The second letter arrived four days later, as they were leaving Toronto. It was shorter and even more ecstatic.

'Em darling, Just two lines to let you know I'm over the moon, swinging on a star, sliding down a rainbow. All the corny old things, and they're true!!

Trent's taking me out to dinner tonight and I'll post this on the way. Trent Marston—even his name's romantic, don't you think? Will write again to reach you in Chicago and tell you all the latest news. Trent's been here every single day. He makes a pretext that it's to see Daddy on business, but of course we both just *know*. Daddy hasn't seen what's going on between us, but he never does notice things. He's working all the time on some new gadget or other and I think Trent means to wait for a bit before we tell him about us, in case Daddy thinks it's all been too quick and I'm too young to know my own mind, but very soon it will have to come out. Must dash now and wash my hair. All my love, Your Lisa.

P.S. It sounds prissy in this day and age, but now I'm so glad I saved myself just for Trent.'

Emma folded the letters and put them back in her bag thoughtfully. The second letter was dated nearly four weeks ago. After that—nothing. She hadn't worried because she and Joe had been moving around and letters could so easily have missed them. Uncle Edward phoned once or twice, but she thought it better not to mention this new man of Lisa's. Lisa had imagined herself in love before, but the man had always turned out to have some flaw—real or imagined. Lisa had always been the romantic, the perfectionist. Everything had to be the very best for Lisa, and Emma hoped (when she went to bed at night and had time to think about it) that this man would turn out to be the right one. But she was inclined to doubt it. She didn't altogether like the sound of Trent Marston, with his expressive dark eyes that made your knees go wobbly. She had met men with that sort of look, and she steered very clear of them.

Then, a week ago, the phone call had come through from Uncle Edward, when Joe and Emma had arrived in New York.

'Splendid news, my dear,' he had told her. 'Lisa's getting herself married. They've made up their minds very suddenly, and I must say I'm very pleased about it. She says to tell you that you must come home to be her bridesmaid. The wedding's fixed for Wednesday April the fourth, that won't be giving you much time, I'm afraid, but see what you can do. It's a pity about your not being able to finish your trip with Joe, but we can't let even business spoil little Lisa's day, can we?'

Emma had been dumbfounded. Uncle Edward sounding so pleased and placid about Lisa marrying an almost complete stranger at a few weeks' notice!

'But—but—' she had gasped into the phone, 'it's such a surprise—I'd no idea. There'll be all the arrangements to make and Jessie won't be up to that. Couldn't they put it off for a week or two to give me time when I came home? There'll be so much—' Her head had been spinning.

Uncle Edward laughed. 'Lisa's made up her mind on the date and when Lisa makes up her mind nothing will stop her, as you well know. You needn't worry about the arrangements, my dear. Richard's mother has taken on that chore and she's in her element. Lisa spends all her time with her at the store, talking about clothes and so on. I leave 'em to it. She's there now.'

'*Richard's* mother?' Emma said faintly. 'She's marrying Richard?'

'Yes, of course—who else would she be marrying? And I must say I'm delighted, and between you and me, Emma dear, I'll admit to a certain relief. You know what a dreamer the child's always been, it'll be good for her to settle down early with a sensible young fellow. Now, Emma, will you put me on to Joe. There are one or two things—'

Emma folded the letters thoughtfully and put them back in her bag. She was glad, too, that Lisa was marrying Richard Southall. But a doubt nagged at her and wouldn't be silenced. Why hadn't Lisa written, and why had she let Uncle Edward do the explaining and break the news? It wouldn't be a happy thing if Lisa had decided to marry Richard on the rebound— that was never a good start to a marriage.

Oh dear, she thought, why was everything going so wrong? The near-failure of this trip with Joe, and now the worrying mystery of Lisa's sudden decision to marry Richard, when she had never before shown the least inclination to fall in love with him, as he had always been with her.

Still, she mustn't let herself get negative. Perhaps Lisa would be blissfully happy and perhaps Joe would fill up his order book in Mexico. Perhaps.

Emma put down her coffee beaker and stood up, straightening her slim shoulders, and as she made her way to the news-stand to buy magazines for the journey nobody would have guessed that the long-legged girl in the green suit, her tawny eyes clear and alert, was feeling curiously uneasy about the two most important things in her life.

'ENGLAND SEEMS SO *small* after America,' Emma observed, settling back in the passenger seat as Malcolm, the Fairleys' chauffeur, gardener and odd-job-man steered the family saloon car through London's suburbs in the gathering dusk. 'But I do think it's nice of you to come all this way to meet me.'

The big Scot grinned briefly. 'Och, Miss Emma, it's a pleasure.' Malcolm was a man of few words; his wife Jessie had plenty to spare for both of them. Malcolm and Jessie had been with the family for as long as Emma could remember, coming south reluctantly when they had been persuaded by their doctor that a warmer climate than Aberdeen's would be essential to Malcolm's recovery from a chest injury at work. The young couple had arrived in Dorset with every kind of misgiving and had stayed, all those years, to be happily part of the family.

But Malcolm remained a taciturn Scot and it was quite a speech for him when he glanced aside under bushy brows now and added, 'A man's only in the way at these times, ye know.'

'These times—oh, you mean the wedding tomorrow?'

'Aye, I do that.'

'I suppose Lisa's all excitement? And Jessie too?'

'Aye,' said Malcolm, keeping his gaze fixed ahead.

Emma settled back in her seat and closed her eyes as they joined the motorway. No use trying to find out anything from Malcolm. She would have to wait until she got home to discover exactly how things were.

As the big, powerful car swept steadily and monotonously along the fast lane Emma drifted into a half-sleep full of memories and inevitably they were all about Lisa and their growing up together. Lisa (who was delicate and missed school often) sitting up in their playroom in the tower, scribbling wild romantic stories about knights on great white horses, and noble ladies locked up in castles; Lisa, spending hour upon hour with her dressing-up box, tugging at Emma's hand—'Come on, Em, I've written a lovely play—I'm the princess and you must be the prince who comes to court me, and Teddy will have to be my grumpy old father.' Later on, Lisa at fourteen, when Emma had been working on Spanish and French for her A levels, had been deep in *Wuthering Heights*, living in that story of passionate love, her enormous blue eyes rapt, her lovely small face ecstatic.

'There must be a perfect lover for every woman,' she had assured Emma in a hushed voice. 'Two people who are fated to meet and be together all their lives. I shall wait for my perfect lover to come along.'

Emma looked down at the book in Lisa's hands. 'Cathy and Heathcliff didn't seem to get much happiness out of it,' she observed practically.

'All right, you can laugh, Em, but I know I'm right. I'm going to wait and I know he'll come.'

'How about Richard Southall?' Emma enquired. 'He's awfully keen on you.'

'Oh, Richard!' Lisa wrinkled her straight little nose. 'He's all right, I suppose, but who wants to marry the manager of a drapery store? I suppose that's what he'll be when he grows up.'

'I wouldn't mind,' said Emma. 'If he was the right man I wouldn't care what he did.'

'Oh, *you*!' Lisa had pouted. 'You just don't understand.'

Emma opened her eyes to the dark motorway, dotted with lights, red and white like a Christmas tree, and smiled a little ruefully to herself. It looked as if Lisa's Great Lover hadn't measured up, after all, and she had to settle for Richard. Oh well, it was probably a blessing; she only hoped Lisa hadn't minded too much. She couldn't bear to think of Lisa being badly hurt.

It was more than an hour later when the car finally passed through the small village and turned up a steep lane, to pull in between stone gateposts from which the gates had long since disappeared.

The old grey house was a shadowy hulk, lights pouring from every window. As she got out of the car Emma saw the dark shapes of the trees and heard the splash and hiss of waves below, and she felt a happy tug of homecoming.

Then the front door flew open. For a moment the light from the hall outlined a slender figure in dark trews and a fluffy white top, her pale hair lit from behind like a shining nimbus. Then Lisa threw herself into Emma's arms. 'Darling, darling Em, you've managed to get here! Oh, I was so terribly afraid you wouldn't!'

Emma hugged her close. 'Of course I came.' Lisa felt so small and fragile in her arms. Just a child—too young to be getting married. There was a sudden lump in her throat. They had always been so close—brought closer by tragedy—and Lisa was as dear as a younger sister to her.

They went into the house, arms entwined, and Jessie was standing in the hall, a tall, bony woman in a blue dress, with scraped-back grey hair and kind, shrewd eyes.

Emma kissed her. 'Good to be home again, Jessie.'

'Weel now, Miss Emma, and it's good to see you.' Although Jessie had long been a friend and equal she still kept to the formal mode of address. 'It's a long trip you've had. You'll be tired, no doubt. A nice cup of tea now, while you're waiting for your supper?'

'Oh, Jessie, that would be heavenly.'

Lisa turned. 'Bring it up to my room, will you, Jessie.' She was pulling Emma towards the stairs. 'I want to show Emma all my things.'

'Och now, Miss Lisa, they can wait a bit. Give your cousin a wee rest.'

'She can have a rest upstairs. Please do as I say, Jessie.' Her tone was imperious. Lisa doing her little princess act, Emma thought, amused.

But Jessie wasn't amused; she stiffened and her brows went up. She ignored Lisa and spoke pointedly to Emma. 'Would ye like something to eat with it, Miss Emma? I'll get on with supper right away now. Your uncle's still down in his workroom. He said he wasn't to be disturbed, but now you're home—'

'Oh, for goodness' sake don't disturb the mad professor, Jessie. I'll see him later.' Emma's eyes met Jessie's, sharing the old family joke, and she saw Jessie relax. 'I don't need anything much to eat, thank you, I had a meal on the plane. Just a couple of biscuits, perhaps. Bang on the gong when it's ready and I'll come down and get it.'

'Ye'll do no such thing,' said Jessie indignantly, and with a hard look in Lisa's direction she disappeared into the kitchen quarters.

'What was all that about, then?' Emma enquired. 'Have you and Jessie been getting in each other's hair?'

'Oh, she annoys me sometimes. She gets above herself.' Lisa tossed the subject aside, running lightly up the wide staircase with the carved wooden rail.

Emma followed. Lisa wasn't being deliberately sharp and unkind, of course she wasn't. Lisa was never unkind. She was probably practising her new status and authority as a married woman. Lisa had always had acting ability; if she hadn't been delicate she might have taken up the stage as a career. She wouldn't have much difficulty now in turning from the lovely, cossetted, adored daughter to the beautiful, poised, adored wife. Amusement and affection tugged at Emma's heart.

Lisa's bedroom was at the back of the house, overlooking the garden and the sea. She pushed open the door and threw out her hand dramatically, her eyes dancing. 'There—how about that, then?'

Emma drew in a breath. The room looked like a boutique when a new consignment has just arrived. There were exquisite clothes everywhere, hanging from the open doors of the wardrobe, spread on the bed, draped across chairs. Day dresses in jewel colours of fine wool, evening ones that were froths of chiffon and georgette with glittering trims, gay cotton sun-dresses, sleek trousers, sweaters and tops in softest angora and cashmere.

'I'm quite stunned, I can't take it all in.' Emma walked across to where a long dress of softest white satin, the heart-shaped neckline encrusted with tiny pearls, drifted down from a padded hanger. Beside it, on the dressing table, lay a filmy veil with tiny ornaments of pearls and orange-blossom.

Emma touched the dress gently with one finger. 'Gorgeous,' she breathed. 'It really is a dream. London? Paris?'

Lisa perched on the edge of the bed, watching her cousin's reactions with unconcealed delight. 'You're kidding,' she laughed triumphantly. 'It came from Southalls, every last bit of it. Mrs S. would have been mortally offended if I'd shopped anywhere else. She went to Bristol, to some wholesale place she buys from, and came back with a whole van-load of stuff to choose from. I've had such fun. Besides—' she pulled a mock-smug face '—it'll all be good for trade. When the local ladies find I'm shopping at Southalls they'll decide they don't need to go into Bournemouth or London for their clothes after all.'

Emma laughed. 'My word, you're getting quite a keen business head!'

'Well, I'd better, hadn't I?' said Lisa, getting up restlessly and wandering across the room. 'Richard's mother has made him manager of the store, have you heard?' She tweaked the collar of a pink organza dress and stood back to admire the result.

'That's splendid,' said Emma warmly, 'I'm sure he'll make a terrific success of it. I rather fancy being cousin to Mrs Richard Southall. Will you sell me lots of lovely clobber at cost price?'

'As much as you like, you can take your pick,' Lisa cried gaily from the far side of the long room.

Emma felt a weight falling from her. Lisa was really happy about marrying Richard, she really did love him, and it wasn't just on the rebound. No need even to mention those letters of the Trent Marston man—he was well and truly in the past. Perhaps some day Lisa would tell her about that little episode and they would laugh together over it, but until that day came she would try to forget that the letters had ever existed.

She went across the room and hugged Lisa closely. 'Sweetie, I'm so glad about everything for you. It was a bit of a shock when I heard about it, I couldn't quite take it in. It was so awfully sudden.'

If Lisa wanted to say anything about the letters, about Trent Marston, this was her chance. If she didn't, then it proved that the whole thing was just a final adolescent crush, before she grew up and saw where her real happiness lay.

Lisa drew out her arms. 'Oh, you know me. When I make my mind up that I want to do something I can't wait,' she said lightly. 'And I suddenly found out I *adored* Richard. We're going to have the most wonderful marriage there ever was. Now come and see what I've chosen for your bridesmaid's dress.'

She took Emma's hand and led her to her own bedroom next door, chattering as they went. 'I had to ask Lorna to be the other bridesmaid, of course. She's at the spotty stage, but Mrs S. took it for granted that I would want her. The snag is her hair—she's even more carroty than Richard, when you come to look at her. So I thought it had better be green. It's a bit obvious—green with red hair—but green suits *you* so well, and anyway nobody will be looking at poor Lorna, will they?'

She was giggling as they walked down the corridor, and Emma wished that the silly old superstition about green being unlucky hadn't come into her mind just at that moment.

Half an hour later, while Lisa was talking to Richard on the phone, Emma walked down the garden and ventured to push open the door of Uncle Edward's workshop.

He didn't hear the door open and she could only see the side of his face. His head was bent low over the worktop desk, the spotlight shining down on the thick, untidy fairish hair and glinting on the gold rims of his glasses. A small computer that was his constant companion stood before him, its signals flashing on and off incomprehensibly, and all around lay sheets of paper covered with complicated diagrams.

Very carefully Emma began to close the door again. You didn't disturb Uncle Edward when he was deep in thought and on the track of a new idea. But this time he heard her, and swung round in his swivel chair. 'Emma, my dear, come in.' He began to get up.

She hesitated. 'Won't I be interrupting something?'

He pulled a rueful face. 'I wish I could say that you were—I'm stuck at the moment. What I need is a break, after which all will—I hope—become clear.'

He came towards her, smiling his vague, kindly smile. Edward Fairley was forty-seven and looked older, perhaps because of the deep creases across his forehead and down his cheeks that gave him, Emma always thought, the look of a benevolent bloodhound. That wasn't such a bad picture of him, either, he was always on the track of some new idea.

He kissed her and held her at arm's length, studying her face through the thick lenses of his glasses. 'You're looking peaky,' he said. 'You haven't been overdoing things, rushing about the New World?'

She shook her head, grinning at him. They had a good relationship, and she felt that, in a way, she understood him. 'Nothing that a good night's sleep won't put right.'

Uncle Edward went back to his chair and she perched on a stool beside him. 'Tell me all your news,' he said, but she saw his glance go compulsively back towards the blinking computer.

'*My* news?' Emma hid a smile. 'I should have thought your news here is more important.'

'What—oh, Lisa's wedding.' He pulled himself back to the outside world and its doings. 'Yes,' he said heartily. 'Splendid, isn't it? I'm glad you were able to get back just in time, was it difficult?'

'It was a bit tricky,' she admitted, 'but I managed it.'

He sighed. 'You always manage, my dear Emma, I don't know what we should do without your practical good sense.' He surveyed her with a kind of surprise.

'You're glad—about Lisa?' she prompted.

'Oh yes, very glad indeed. I always hoped she would settle for Richard Southall, but you can never be sure what Lisa will come up with next. Her head's always been in the clouds,' he added with vague fondness.

Emma smiled her quirky smile. 'Like yours, only different clouds.'

'Too true, only too true. I've been a rotten father, I expect. Never managed to concentrate on the job for very long.'

'Don't be silly,' Emma told him warmly, 'you've been the very best kind of father—and uncle too. You've given us the freedom to grow up our own way.'

He looked very wry. 'Nice of you to say so, my dear, but I'm not quite convinced it's altogether true. Ah well, I'm handing over the responsibility of Lisa to Richard from now on. She'll be in good hands.'

'And the responsibility for me?' she teased.

He shook his head. 'You've never posed any problem, Emma. I've always been able to trust you to be sensible. And now, from what Joe tells me, you're going to be an asset to the firm.'

She bit her lip, not replying, and he looked up quickly. 'You're worried, aren't you? Things haven't been going too well on the trip, Joe told me on the phone.'

'Oh, don't let's talk business now, Uncle Edward. Leave it until after tomorrow.'

He didn't seem to hear. He picked up a silver pencil and ran it thoughtfully between his finger and thumb. At least he said, 'Emma, there's something I'd better tell you, if you don't know already. The firm's going swiftly downhill and if we don't do something about it soon we're sunk. All these years, since your father—left us—it seems that the lifeblood of the company has been draining away. He was the dynamic one. I've always been useless on that side of things, and Joe—well, Joe's loyal and hardworking, but he isn't your father. And he's getting tired.'

Emma blinked hard. He wasn't telling her anything new, but just hearing him say it brought a huge lump into her throat. 'I know,' she said, not looking at him. 'I thought perhaps you didn't realise; you don't come to the office very often.'

He smiled wearily. 'Oh, I realised. I don't have my nose stuck in a computer all the time, you know.'

'Just most of the time,' she murmured, trying to keep the conversation from becoming too doom-laden on the eve of a family wedding. 'Let's not talk about it just now,' she pleaded.

'There's something I must tell you—warn you about,' he said.

'Warn me?' she asked sharply.

'Yes, I think so, something you may need to adjust to.'

She waited, watching his face, seeing anxiety there. At last he said 'You know how much I value Joe, but I'm afraid the time has come to infuse some new blood into the promotional side of the business, Emma. New blood and new cash too. There will have to be changes.'

'What changes?' she asked quickly. 'If Joe's going to be pushed aside I don't think I could—'

He reached out and patted her hand. 'Ssh, my dear! Listen to what I've got to say.'

'I'm sorry, Uncle Edward, it's just that—'

He nodded. 'Yes, I know. But listen. Joe's getting tired, as I said, and I'm sure he won't be sorry to step down. He's told me so himself. You know, he never really wanted the top job, he took it on to save the situation at a very difficult time. He would have served happily under your father.' He shook his head slowly. 'But there's never been anyone to take your father's place, my dear. Until now—perhaps—now.'

Emma caught her breath. 'You're not thinking of bringing someone in from outside?' She was horrified. 'A *stranger*?'

'I know, Emma, I know. I felt the same way at first. But it's the answer, I'm sure of that. The only answer.'

'You mean you've someone particular in mind?'

He clipped the silver pencil into the pocket of his jacket and patted it. She had never seen him look so confident and pleased with himself.

'It's all settled,' he said. 'I would have liked to bring you in on the decisions, my dear, but it wasn't possible when you were at the other side of the world, and I had to act rather quickly. The bank was getting extremely nasty. So, when the opportunity came I took it.'

He was watching her face closely through his gold-rimmed glasses and his eyes were kind and understanding. 'Now, I can see this has all been a bit of a shock to you. Put it behind you until after the wedding tomorrow, then we can go into it all in detail and I can explain everything. I mean to involve you in all this from the start, Emma. You're a valued part of the firm now and this will affect you personally. I hope you'll be working quite closely with our new director in the future.'

'Who is he? Do I know him?'

'I don't imagine so. He's been away in the Far East and I only met him recently, since you went to Canada. It's all happened very quickly.' He touched her hand almost apologetically. 'He's a first-rate man, Emma. No one will ever take your father's place with me—you know that—but I get the feeling that this man will put the firm back on its feet if anyone can. He has the drive and assurance and personality to do it.'

Emma felt a sudden hot flood of anger and resentment that shook her, down to her toes. Some stranger walking in and taking her father's place! Drive and assurance and personality indeed! She could just imagine and she hated him already. She had met men like that on the trip with Joe, and drive and assurance and personality seemed to her to add up to push and conceit and arrogance. And she was going to have to accept him and work with him, instead of darling Joe!

Edward Fairley was still watching her face closely. 'Don't make any snap judgment, Emma. Wait until you've met him.'

She smiled crookedly. 'I'll have to, won't I? When do I see Wonder Man? What's his name?'

Much later, she thought perhaps that she had somehow known all along what he would say.

'His name's Marston,' Uncle Edward said. 'Trent Marston.'

Trent Marston—the man Lisa had been crazily, wildly in love with only a couple of weeks ago!

Emma was still staring blankly at Uncle Edward, her head spinning, when he added, 'And you'll probably meet him tomorrow. I told him to come along to the wedding if he could manage it.'

CHAPTER TWO

RICHARD CAME to supper. Later, he told them, he was going on to a stag party. 'A very mild and respectable one, I assure you all,' he said, his steady grey eyes twinkling round the table under his thatch of fiery red hair. 'Tomorrow I shall be at the church on time, all bright-eyed and bushy-tailed, and *not* suffering from a hangover, cross my heart.'

He turned to Lisa, sitting beside him at the big table in the dining room and smiled adoringly, squeezing her hand.

'Mind you are, then.' Lisa stretched out to the big bowl of fruit and selected a ripe peach. 'I shall wait for no man.' She lifted her chin, acting the little princess.

Lisa had been in one of her fey moods all evening—gay, laughing, brittle, vivacious. Emma, while she was helping Jessie in the kitchen before supper, had had to listen to her gloomy predictions.

'Sing before breakfast, cry before night,' she had quoted, stirring the tomato soup vigorously. 'Miss Lisa's been above herself these last few weeks—up and down, up and down. You never knew what to make of her.'

'Well, at least she'll settle down when she's married,' Emma smiled, wondering if it was true. 'Lisa' and 'settling down' didn't seem to go together.

'Aye, mebbe.' Jessie wasn't convinced either, and her tone suggested strongly that she knew more than she was saying. She had probably been witness to Lisa's brief passion for the Marston man; there wasn't much that escaped Jessie's shrewd eyes. But Emma wasn't asking. She wasn't asking Lisa either. Tomorrow Lisa would be a married woman and the time for girlish confidences would be past. All the same, Emma would dearly have liked to know whether Lisa was aware that Trent Marston was joining the firm and that he would probably turn up at the wedding tomorrow.

Coffee had been served at the table, as Richard had to leave early, and now he looked towards Emma and said, 'I suppose I should be making a move, if you'll excuse me. I'm so glad you managed to get back in time to lend Lisa your moral support, Emma, my young sister would have been very nervous if she had had to take the full bridesmaid's responsibility.' He turned to Edward Fairley. 'It was good of you, sir, to arrange for Emma to come home—I know she was on an important business trip.'

Uncle Edward smiled his vague smile. 'Emma wouldn't have missed the wedding for anything. And I fear the business trip was not turning out all that important, was it, my dear? Markets are not very booming just now.' He had not, apparently, latched on to the fact that Richard had to get away, and now—having been silent through most of the meal—he launched into a long analysis of government policy regarding export markets, most of which, Emma recognised to her amusement, were quotations from Joe.

Richard listened politely and Emma watched him across the table, liking the young man very much. She liked his style—quiet and sincere and straightforward. She even liked his looks; there was something cheerful and appealing about red hair and freckles. She hadn't seen much of him lately—she had been at college in Salisbury and later abroad, putting the finishing touches to her business training by polishing up her French and Spanish, but she remembered him well from schooldays. They had been in the sixth form together. He was a year older than Emma and something of a hero—captain of cricket, champion swimmer, and up with the first three or four on the academic side. A real all-rounder, Richard, and popular with everyone.

She remembered how it had all begun—how he had fallen for Lisa. He had called at the house one day to bring a book he had promised to lend Emma. While they were discussing economics Lisa had walked in; Lisa in palest blue, her silver-gilt hair smooth round her exquisite little face; Lisa at fifteen with her shy, vulnerable beauty. Richard had taken one look and then—it seemed to Emma—had never looked anywhere else.

He's nice, she thought now, really nice. I hope it's going to be all right.

Uncle Edward was still talking. '—I don't know how the ups and downs in the country's economy affects your business, Richard, but we have found it tough going recently, especially on the export side. However—' he glanced happily round the table '—I'm glad to say I think I have found the answer. New blood, Richard, that's what it takes.'

Richard glanced down at his watch, under cover of the table. 'Oh, yes, sir?'

'Yes indeed,' nodded Uncle Edward. 'New blood, and fortunately the very man has turned up. You'll all see him tomorrow, he'll be coming along to the wedding. Lisa, of course, has met him already, haven't you, my dear?'

Emma was watching Lisa, her throat suddenly tight, and she saw the fair head lift like that of a startled animal. There was a look in Lisa's great blue eyes that Emma had never seen there before. A look of naked fear.

Uncle Edward beamed. 'An excellent man, he'll be a real asset to the firm. Marston's the name—Trent Marston. He's been out East, starting up a company for his father, recently, and—' He broke off abruptly. 'Why, Lisa my dear, what—'

The peach Lisa was holding fell from her hand. For a moment she stared at her father, her face deadly pale, and then she sagged in her chair and slid sideways.

Richard caught her before she could fall farther. He reacted to the situation immediately, not wasting time on words. He lifted Lisa easily and carried her into the drawing room next door, where he laid her gently on the long sofa. Emma raced upstairs, carried down the duvet from her own bed and tucked it round the still form. Richard knelt beside the sofa, holding Lisa's limp white hand and murmuring reassuringly. 'It's all right, my love, it's all right. You'll be fine in a minute or two. Just take your time.'

Uncle Edward dithered somewhat ineffectively. 'Should we ring for the doctor, do you think? Her heart—'

Richard shook his head. 'I'm sure it won't be necessary, sir. Lisa was very strung up. She'll come round very soon.'

Emma admired him even more. He was a practical young man was Richard. He did what had to be done and he didn't panic or show alarm, or even surprise. Oh yes, he would be very good for Lisa.

Jessie, having heard the commotion, and put her nose round the door to sum up the situation, appeared with a cup of strong steaming tea just as Lisa was opening her eyes, and within a few minutes Lisa was sitting up, sipping her tea, smiling a faint, rueful apology to the little group around her.

'I just got too excited,' she whispered. 'I'll be perfectly okay now, Richard. You go along to your party, they'll be wondering where you've got to.'

He demurred, but she insisted with surprising determination. 'Please go, Richard, there's absolutely no need for you to stay. I shall go straight to bed and Emma will look after me, won't you, Em?' Emma felt sure that she, and only she, saw the pleading in Lisa's great, expressive eyes and caught the note of desperation in her voice.

Finally Richard agreed to leave, having insisted on carrying Lisa up to her bedroom. Emma waited for him to come down again and said goodnight to him at the front door.

'Don't worry, Richard, I'll look after her and see she gets to the church in time. As she said, she just got a bit over-excited, that's all.' Fervently she wished that *were* all, but she was horribly afraid it wasn't.

She waited until Richard's car had driven away down the drive, then she went back into the drawing room.

Uncle Edward was pouring himself a stiff whisky. He was looking rather pale; he wasn't a man to cope with this sort of crisis. 'Is there anything I can do?' he enquired, wrinkling his brow.

'Not a thing,' Emma assured him cheerfully. 'I'll cope. I'll go up to her now.'

He grinned wryly at her. 'What a comfort you are, Emma. I think I'll go down to my workroom then, and potter around for a while. Come and tell me if I can be of any use.' And to her relief, he departed.

Emma went upstairs and hesitated outside the door of Lisa's room, feeling, for some reason, that she ought to knock before she went in. How absurd—she and Lisa had always rushed in and out of each other's bedrooms without ceremony to exchange news and confidences. She didn't know if Lisa needed—or wanted—help, but Emma had to let her know it was there if she did.

She opened the door and walked in. Lisa was sitting at her dressing-table, staring at her reflection.

Emma walked over to her. 'How are you feeling, love? Better?'

Lisa shrugged, not looking at her. 'Oh, I'm okay. Richard just made a big fuss about nothing. The room was awfully hot.'

There was a strained silence. So it was going to be a cover-up, was it?

Emma said, 'Are you going to bed? Would you like a drink or anything?'

In the mirror she saw Lisa's mouth twist. 'Tea and sympathy? A nice heart-to-heart chat?'

'If you like,' Emma said steadily.

Lisa got up and walked across the room to where the wedding dress hung, its soft folds gleaming dully in the light from the bedside lamp. 'I don't think I do like, thank you,' she said in a taut, defensive voice. 'I'm a big girl now, I'm going to be a married woman to-morrow. Too late for girlish confidences, don't you think?' Her fingers moved nervously on the satin folds of the dress.

Emma watched her, frowning. Something was very wrong. Love and pity welled up inside her, but she kept her voice low and even as she said, 'Look, Lisa, I've got to say this. I had your letters about this Trent Marston man when I was in Toronto. I saw your face this evening when Uncle Edward mentioned his name.' She paused. 'If you're marrying Richard on the re-bound then it's no good for either of you. What I'm saying is that it isn't too late for you to change your mind.'

Lisa spun round, her cheeks flushed. 'Change my mind—what are you talking about? Of course I don't want to change my mind. If you're so interested I can tell you that I realised pretty soon the kind of man Trent Marston is, and that I couldn't feel anything for him but—but—' she hesitated '—but dislike and con-tempt. He's an absolute bastard!'

Lisa had never indulged in fashionably crude lan-guage, and the blunt word, spoken almost viciously, gave Emma quite a shock. Lisa was certainly growing up. But in spite of her vehement denial, there *had* been something between her and this man and he had hurt her badly. Emma's dislike of the unknown Trent Marston deepened.

But it would be foolish to make too much of it. She said lightly, 'There are plenty of that kind around, darling. Any girl can be taken in.' But particularly girls like Lisa—so young for her age, so romantic and heartbreakingly vulnerable.

Lisa's mood changed suddenly. 'Don't let's talk about him. Let's talk about tomorrow. We'll go down to the church first thing. I want you to see the flowers, they're heavenly—'

Trent Marston wasn't mentioned again that night.

'THEY'RE JOLLY late,' complained the second bridesmaid, Richard's young sister Lorna. 'I wish they'd hurry up, it's parky here.' She drew back into a corner of the church porch in a vain attempt to get out of the cool breeze that blew straight off the sea. 'Any sign of them?'

Emma put her head outside, looking up the short lane, lined with cars, that led to the church, and the wind slapped a strand of her dark gold hair across her eyes and flipped a panel of sea-green chiffon against her long, slender legs. She drew back quickly. 'Not yet, but they'll be here any moment now.'

She wished she could believe it. She had seen Lisa's ashen face and trembling hands as she fastened the tiny pearl buttons on her white satin gown, not an hour ago. She had held her briefly in her arms as Lisa suddenly gave a gulp and quavered, 'Oh, Em darling, I'm so petrified! I don't know if I can go through with it. Wedding nerves are agony.' She had bathed the great blue eyes and patted astringent lotion round them. She had finally left Lisa with Uncle Edward in the hall of the old house not ten minutes ago, looking like a beautiful frail, misty ghost.

She steadied her anxious breathing now and said again, 'They won't be long. Lisa was a bit dithery.'

'Dithery?' Lorna's rather unfortunately plain little face screwed up contemptuously. 'Good lord, not having second thoughts, is she? It's taken her long enough to make up her mind to marry poor old Richard. She's not going to leave him standing at the altar, is she?' She began to giggle.

'Shut up, Lorna,' said Emma, with the firmness of three years' seniority. 'Lisa wouldn't do a thing like that.'

'I wouldn't put it past her if she thought there was something better on offer,' said Lorna. 'She's so pretty she thinks she can get away with murder. She was in my form at school, you know, I watched her at it. Ugh, there's a spider here!' She shot out of the corner, brushing her green chiffon skirt in disgust, and dropped her posy of pink rosebuds.

Emma clicked her tongue and glanced through the arched doorway into the church. A wedding between two old local families was an occasion not to be missed, and the small Norman church was full. A discreet murmur of voices mingled with the painstaking Bach that Miss Stevens was coaxing from the wheezy little organ. The scent of freesia and narcissus filled the building and rose in waves up to the ancient roof beams. The five little boys in the front row of the choir stalls fidgeted.

In the front pew she could just see the back of Richard's neck above his stiff white collar and above that the fiery thatch of red hair, neatly slicked down. Beside him showed the fair head of Jim Bolton, his best man, who had been Emma's faithful admirer for some time. In the pew behind, the brim of Mrs Southall's large grey straw hat could be seen to dip as she glanced round with nervous expectation. The two ushers, Richard's younger twin brothers, still stood selfconsciously at their posts near the door, although all the guests must surely be installed by now.

All except one. There was no sign of Trent Marston, thank goodness. Emma would have spotted a stranger immediately. Perhaps he'd decided to give the wedding a miss. Emma had the strong feeling that he was the type of man who amused himself with a girl and then left her flat when it suited him. Perhaps, as he was going to join the family firm, he had a faint conscience about the way he had treated Lisa and had decided to keep out of her way, now that she had found a more chivalrous man. She sent up a silent prayer that he might stay away—a long way away— until Lisa was safely off on her honeymoon.

'Here they are now, I can hear the car,' Lorna's voice squeaked from behind. 'Do I look all right?'

Emma turned back into the porch. 'You look lovely.' She patted a lock of red hair back into place and straightened the pleated green chiffon collar. Then she peeped out into the short cul-de-sac lane, looking for the black family car, proudly driven by Malcolm.

What she saw instead was a silver-grey Bentley coupé. It purred to a halt, double-parking without the slightest hesitation in front of the line of cars already neatly parked. A man emerged from the driving seat and reached back for his grey top hat.

Emma's heart gave an unpleasant lurch and started to beat heavily. Oh yes, this must be Trent Marston— this tall, fabulous-looking man in superbly-fitting morning dress, his ebony-dark hair clustering thickly round his ears, who was walking with the arrogance of the devil himself up the path to the church door, between the two rows of village children and their mothers, lined up to see the fun.

He was inside the porch now and his tall form and masculine virility seemed to fill the tiny space, enclosed between its grey stone walls. Snippets of those letters of Lisa's filtered back into Emma's mind: '—the most marvellous eyes that make my knees go all wobbly when he looks at me—'

Now those dark, slumbrous eyes passed dismissively over Lorna's pink face and red hair and then turned and fixed themselves on Emma.

'I'm late, I think.' The deep, cultured voice contained no hint of apology and the wide, rather sensual mouth no hint of a smile.

Emma felt suddenly hot with anger. Oh yes, he was all she had expected—the kind of man who thought he was God and could do as he pleased with no thought for others. The kind of man she disliked intensely.

'You are indeed,' she replied crisply and with a hint of censure that she made no attempt to disguise.

He went on staring at her and the dark brows rose a fraction. She stared back and as black eyes met tawny ones it was as though lightning flashed, leaving Emma weak and amazed.

The taller of the twins appeared in the doorway, ready to do his stuff. 'Friend of the bride or groom, sir?'

'Bride,' said the newcomer, without taking his eyes from Emma's.

When he turned to follow Kenneth it was as if something physical had been wrenched away from her body. She let out a shaky breath. Phew! So that was Trent Marston. No wonder poor little Lisa had been completely bowled over! A dangerous male that, and knowing his own power. A girl would have to be much more experienced than Lisa to recognise the danger.

Her eyes went, as if pulled by some magnetic force, to where he was following Kenneth across the transverse aisle to a seat at the very far side of the church. That was a relief, he was well out of the way there and Lisa could hardly be aware of him when she walked down the centre aisle with her father. And when she was well and truly married to Richard, this Trent Marston would have no further power to hurt her.

Lorna was looking shattered. 'Who was that gorgeous hulk?' she breathed. 'I've never seen him around here before.'

'Nor me,' said Emma briefly. 'I think he must be the man who's going to work for our firm.'

'*Really?* Aren't you the lucky girl?' Lorna rolled her eyes. 'I wouldn't mind working with him. *Any* sort of work,' she giggled meaningly. 'Oh, here they are at last—' as Lisa and her father could be seen getting out of the car, to the accompaniment of 'oohs' from the assembled audience of children outside.

Emma stepped forward as Lisa came into the porch on Uncle Edward's arm, delicately, fragrantly lovely, a dream in white, with a sheaf of white rosebuds, her great blue eyes misty and far-away, everyone's vision of a beautiful bride.

Emma's eyes moved over her lovingly. Nothing to rearrange. Not a single pale-gold hair out of place, not a fold of white satin or a wisp of filmy veil. Richard's engagement ring was on the third finger of her right hand. Everything was in order. She gave Lisa's hand a little squeeze. 'You look wonderful, darling,' she whispered, and Lisa gave her a grave little smile and nodded gently.

Beside her beautiful repose Uncle Edward, unfamiliar in his morning suit, was moving from one foot
to another nervously. 'All set?' he muttered.

Lisa made a faint gesture of assent and arranged her
arm in her father's. Emma lined Lorna and herself up
behind, nodded to Kenneth, who signalled to Miss
Stevens. The muted strains of *Here Comes the Bride*
stole through the little church.

As they entered, Emma's glance went briefly across
the nave to where a man's dark head, towering above
the others, could just be glimpsed half hidden by a
pillar. Lisa, in her slow progress down the aisle, had
passed the spot from where she would be able to see
him now. Trent Marston was rapidly passing out of
her life.

The little procession reached the chancel rail, where
Richard was waiting. As Lisa took her place beside
him Emma saw the look of love and devotion on his
pleasant, square face and was deeply moved. Lisa was
safe now, and if anyone had to cope with the Trent
Marstons of this world—the selfish charmers, the
callous heartbreakers, it wouldn't be her. Emma
stepped forward, took the sheaf of white rosebuds,
and went back to her place, her heart swelling with
love and relief.

'Dearly beloved—' intoned the vicar.

Lisa's wedding had begun.

THE OLD house was looking its best for the reception.
The April afternoon sunshine poured in through the
long windows and the big, square hall was festive, with
its white-clothed buffet table groaning with sandwiches, canapés, vol-au-vents. The wedding cake
stood proudly in the middle, intricately iced and dec-

orated with silver bells. Richard's mother had made all the arrangements and a catering firm from Poole had been hired to take over the food and drink and extra china. Malcolm had brought in masses of spring flowers from the garden and greenhouse and Emma and Jessie had arranged them this morning in bowls and vases round the hall and the dining room, which was being used as an overflow for the guests.

Emma stood by the table, rearranging a small bowl of pink hyacinths, which were already perfectly arranged, and keeping an anxious eye on Lisa, standing beside Richard, with Uncle Edward and Mrs Southall lined up beyond, to receive the guests as they came in.

It was quite ridiculous to feel so horribly jittery, Emma assured herself, Lisa had been warned that Trent Marston would be coming to the wedding; she had had plenty of time to pull herself together before she had to meet him face to face. But as the guests filed in, and the kissing and handshakes and congratulations went on, Emma felt her throat constricting painfully and her fingers digging into her palms. Lisa had been dreadfully upset last night, when she had heard about the Marston man being involved with the family firm, and being invited today. If only she had talked about her feelings, Emma thought now, and not bottled them up! If only she could be sure that there wouldn't be some sort of emotional scene when he put in an appearance!

She had looked for him outside the church, while the photographs were being taken, but he seemed to have disappeared, and the silver-grey car had gone too. Perhaps he had thought better of it, and decided to give the reception a miss? Emma fervently hoped so, but she wished she knew for sure, then she could relax and enjoy things.

The first press of guests had thinned to a trickle when she saw him come in. He stood for a moment in the doorway, looking around, a dark self-assured figure, inches taller than any other man in the room, and making them look as if their morning suits had come straight off the peg, while his had been immaculately tailored in Savile Row.

Emma grabbed a pink hyacinth out of the pot and buried her nose in it, hiding her face while the scent of the flower was overpoweringly sweet in her nostrils. Her eyes were fastened on the group near the door— on Lisa's face as the man approached. It was like a close-up in a film. Everything and everyone in the room went out of focus and she only saw the two of them—Lisa's pale face flushing painfully as her eyes went up to meet the dark, sultry ones of the man standing before her. He spoke, and Lisa smiled brilliantly. Then the man bent to kiss Lisa's cheek and turned to shake Richard's hand. A few words and he had passed on to Mrs Southall and Uncle Edward, while Lisa and Richard were greeting the next guests.

Emma replaced the hyacinth and let out a long breath of relief. It was over and Lisa had been wonderful—calm and dignified. Emma felt a wave of admiration for her young cousin. She had forgotten how good an actress Lisa could be when she chose, and Lisa had risen to a difficult occasion and come through it splendidly. Surely now, she could forget about Trent Marston and be happy with Richard?

'Emma, where are you?' She heard Uncle Edward's voice. 'Ah, there you are. I want you to meet

Trent Marston, our new recruit to Fairley Brothers. Trent, this is my niece Emma Fairley.'

Trent Marston held out his hand. 'How do you do, Miss Fairley,' he said formally. There wasn't a vestige of a smile on the hard, handsome face as his sombre black eyes ran over her consideringly.

Involuntarily, Emma moved backwards, away from that insolent, almost hypnotic stare, and collided with one of the waiters, bearing a plate of sandwiches. 'Oh, I'm so sorry.' She smiled at him apologetically, but the smile left her face immediately as she turned back to the man standing before her.

It had all happened in a moment and he was still holding out his hand. It was absurd, but she felt that if he touched her she would scream. She was a straightforward girl, who liked to make her feelings plain. She wasn't the actress that Lisa was, and at this moment she felt a dislike and resentment for the man almost amounting to hate.

But she had to take his hand or risk making a stupid scene, which was unthinkable. 'How do you do, Mr Marston,' she said coolly.

His handclasp was firm and brief. Just for a second her own hand was engulfed in his and she felt the smooth dryness of his skin against her own. She almost snatched her hand away, like a child who has ventured too near the fire.

Uncle Edward beamed on them. 'I'll leave you two to get acquainted, while I go back and do my duty.' He moved away to join Mrs Southall at the end of the receiving line.

Emma stood hemmed in by the crowd of guests—talking, laughing, greeting each other—and wondered how she could get away from Trent Marston.

She felt her skin prickling at his nearness. Everyone who passed had a word for her. 'Nice to see you, Emma.' 'Doesn't Lisa look gorgeous?' 'Hear you've been abroad—was it lovely?' All the time she could see the eyes of the women on the man beside her, hear the unspoken question, Who is he?

It wasn't obligatory to introduce people at weddings and she didn't intend to draw him into the circle if she could help it. She looked around rather desperately for Jim Bolton, the best man. He was supposed to be looking after the chief bridesmaid, surely? But he was dashing in and out with the late arrivals, probably organising the parking outside the house.

Trent Marston leaned down towards her. 'You have nothing to drink, Miss Fairley.' He stopped a passing waiter and took two glasses of champagne from the tray. Just as if he were the host, Emma thought wrathfully, and not a guest—and an unwelcome one from her point of view.

'Shall we make for the verge?' he said. 'This feels rather like the central reservation of the motorway.' He glanced at the guests milling around them and put a hand at her elbow, guiding her towards the double doors into the dining-room, which was comparatively empty.

They paused beside the long polished table where the wedding presents were on display. 'I wanted a word with you, Miss Fairley,' Trent Marston said. He stood very still, looking down at her with that considering look. 'Edward tells me you are a trainee in the marketing department of the firm.' His tone suggested that he intended to end that when he sat in the seat of power.

'I've been travelling in the U.S. with Joe Kent, our marketing manager,' Emma said distantly. She thought it was particularly tactless of him to begin to talk business in the middle of a wedding reception; on the other hand she hadn't the slightest wish to enter into a more personal relationship with this arrogant individual. She disliked every single thing about him.

'I hope you had a successful trip,' he said suavely.

She met his eyes straight. 'It was disastrous,' she said. Perhaps if he really knew the state of the firm he would pull out and go away—out of all their lives.

'I rather gathered that.' The slight smile didn't reach his eyes. 'We'll have to work together to change things, won't we?' He raised his glass. 'To our better business acquaintance, Miss Fairley.'

She gripped the stem of her champagne glass. I must get away, she told herself, before I throw the contents of this glass in his face. Of all the overbearing, insolent *pigs*! She fumed inwardly at the way he subtly underlined the word 'business'.

She couldn't hide her anger now. Her tawny eyes flashed fire as she said, 'This is a wedding, Mr Marston. Sure we should be toasting the bride and groom and not be engaging in a board meeting.' She glanced through into the hall. 'Everyone has arrived now, I think they'll be cutting the cake any moment. Please excuse me.'

She put her untasted glass of champagne down and swept out of the room, her dark gold head held high, the filmy green dress swishing round her pretty legs, the heels of her silver shoes clicking smartly on the polished wood floor.

It was as well that he should recognise her hostility from the beginning, she told herself, then they would know exactly where they stood with each other.

She just wished she could have made her point without ending up by shaking as if she had a high fever, and feeling slightly sick. And she wished even more that, although she had her back to him, she did not feel those dark, sleepy eyes following her as she went.

As she crossed the hall she saw Jim Bolton, the best man, weaving his way towards her.

'Emma, sweet, forgive me, I should have been looking after you. The best man's the dogsbody around here—the jobs they find me to do!' He ogled her shamelessly. 'You look superb, lovey. Like a naiad or a dryad or something.' He had obviously been drinking to soothe his nerves even before the wedding began. 'I'll look after you now, though. Claim best man's privilege f'r a start.' Before she knew what he intended to do he had put both arms round her and kissed her—a kiss that was a little too enthusiastic and went on a little too long for the occasion.

Emma drew back. 'Hey, that's enough! And I thought the best man's privilege was to kiss the bride.'

He kept one arm tightly round her. 'Rather kiss you, Emma sweet, you're one hundred per cent more sexy.'

'You've been drinking too much,' she said severely, wriggling out of his grasp. But she smiled up into his fair, good-looking face. They had been friends for years and he proposed to her regularly, without much hope.

'Aw, what 'r weddings for?' he chuckled. 'Free drinks and free kisses.'

With a small shock Emma realised that a tall figure was standing quite close, watching the performance with interest. Trent Marston must have followed her, damn him!

She turned her back on him and encountered Mrs Southall, elegant in a silver-grey suit, and made up immaculately. 'My dear Emma, how charming you look!'

Mrs Southall was a tall, commanding woman who had managed the large store in the nearby holiday town since the death of her husband. She was in her element now, playing hostess at the wedding of her son.

'I wanted a word with you, my dear.' The grey hat dipped towards Emma confidentially. 'I do so hope you don't think I've been interfering, in making all the wedding arrangements. Of course, we realised that it should have been your job, but as it was all decided so quickly and as you weren't here—'

'Oh, please, Mrs Southall, don't think of it like that. You've done it all superbly—much better than I could have done, and Lisa's very grateful.'

Mrs Southall beamed. 'Thank you, my dear.' She looked towards Lisa and Richard. 'Don't they make a lovely couple? Lisa is so beautiful and such a sweet girl. I'm sure they'll be wonderfully happy.' She sighed gustily. 'She will be a great asset to Richard at the store. She pays for dressing, as my mother used to say. Ah, they're going to cut the cake, I see, we must gather round. I shall see you this evening at my little party?'

'Thank you, Mrs Southall.' Emma did not feel in a party-going mood, but it would have been unkind to refuse.

'Just for the young people you know. An informal supper and some dancing.' She looked round as if she were searching for someone. 'Ah, there you are, Mr Marston, I've been looking for you.' She placed a retaining hand on his sleeve and smiled up glowingly into his eyes. 'I'm giving a small party this evening at my house—I shall be so delighted if you will come along. You could perhaps bring Emma, as you're staying with Mr Fairley.'

'Oh, but—' Emma began. She hadn't realised that Uncle Edward had invited the Marston individual to stay overnight. Jessie must have prepared a room for him and forgotten to mention it. Her heart sank. She had been banking on his leaving after the reception, and the prospect of having him around filled her with something very like panic.

'Thank you, Mrs Southall, I shall be delighted, and I'll have great pleasure in giving Emma a lift.' Trent Marston was saying courteously.

'Splendid, we'll look forward to seeing you.' Mrs Southall was known as a hardheaded business woman, but now she was in quite a flutter, Emma thought disgustedly. This man just had to look at a woman with those dark, mocking eyes of his to have her purring like a bemused kitten. He was pure dynamite, no doubt about that. Her own heart had given a quick lurch as he had spoken her name just now, and it wouldn't do at all.

As Mrs Southall turned towards the group round the buffet table she said in a low voice, 'Thank you, but I expect Jim will be calling for me.'

The dark eyebrows went up a fraction. 'Jim? Is that the best man? The one who was wallowing in free kisses just recently?' He glanced across the hall. 'He'll need to sober up before he gives anyone a lift any-where.'

She turned on him angrily, but he had moved away and there was nothing she could do but fume impo-tently. She moved across to stand beside Jim while the cake-cutting ceremony and the speeches went on. In a kind of daze she heard the clapping, saw the cameras flash. Uncle Edward's speech was short, Richard's even shorter, and they both looked very glad when the ordeal was over. When Jim came to propose the bridesmaids he was inclined to ramble on in a slightly maudlin voice, an arm round each girl. He *was* rather drunk, Emma had to admit—that odious Trent Mar-ston was right. She disliked him even more.

The reception pursued the course of all receptions. The talk and laughter increased as the buffet table and champagne bottles emptied. Emma was drawn into one chattering group after another. Jim Bolton was no support at all. He had found himself a chair in the dining room and slumped into it, looking happy and stupid and willing to chat to anyone who passed, but unwilling to get up and circulate. Emma was annoyed with him; she had depended on him to stay beside her and insulate her from any further contact with Trent Marston. As it was she had to keep an eye on him and move out of the way if he seemed to be getting near.

She kept an eye on Lisa too. This was Lisa's day and she was carrying it off magnificently, always the centre of an admiring group, lavish with their compliments and praise. Richard never moved from her side. He looked the picture of happiness and his hand reached constantly for hers, his arm went round her shoulder as if he couldn't bear to be separated from his new wife. They were the perfect, blissfully happy new-

lyweds, Emma assured herself. So what had she been
worrying about?

She glanced at her watch. In ten minutes or so she
must contact Lisa and take her upstairs to change into
her going-away outfit. She and Richard were to drive
into Poole and catch the London train, staying there
overnight, ready to fly to the Seychelles tomorrow
morning.

For a moment Emma found herself alone. The swell
of talk had died down a little. One or two of the
women were looking pink and slightly exhausted.
Lorna was giggling away with two young men—
friends of her brothers—and having a high old time.
Uncle Edward was nowhere to be seen. Emma grinned
to herself as she thought that he had probably sloped
off to his study, which was conveniently along the
passage that led to the kitchens and the back stairs. He
had coped splendidly, but social occasions were definitely not his cup of tea. She would go and have a
quick word with him and then look in upon Jessie,
who was queening it over the hired waiters in the
kitchen. Jessie had attended the ceremony, in her best
lilac-coloured dress and coat, but nothing would persuade her to mix with the guests at the reception.

'Malcolm and me will be happiest in the kitchen,
Miss Emma,' she had decreed, and could not be
shifted from that decision.

Emma took a quick look round to check that she
wouldn't encounter Trent Marston, but couldn't see
him, so she stepped purposefully across the hall, under the archway and down the long passage.

It was as she reached the corner by the window alcove that she heard the study door open and some inner warning made her stop dead as a deep, hatefully

familiar voice said, 'Good, that's splendid. Then we'll discuss it later, shall we, Edward? Tonight, perhaps, when I get back from this party?'

The door closed. Footsteps approached.

It was a stupid thing to do, a blind impulse, but Emma wasn't in a mood to stop and consider. All she wanted at that moment was to avoid meeting the man and having to speak to him. She stepped into the alcove, behind the long red velvet curtain. The footsteps approached and she held her breath. Then there was a rush and a rustle passing the alcove from the opposite direction and she caught a glimpse of white satin.

Lisa's voice, trembling and breathless, came clearly. 'Trent, I had to find you—to speak to you. Why did you come? Why couldn't you have stayed away from my wedding?' The words were spilling out, agonised, pleading.

'My dear girl, why shouldn't I come?' He barely troubled to hide his impatience. 'I was invited.'

'Not by me. I just prayed and prayed that I'd never see you again in my life. After the way you treated me—'

'Oh, for God's sake don't start all that again!' He sounded harsh, utterly without feeling. 'I've had quite enough of that sort of talk. You're married now, to a decent man. Why don't you grow up, Lisa?'

'Grow up—is that all you can say? Grow up?' Her voice rose hysterically. 'After all we were to each other? I loved you—loved you as I've never loved any other man and never will—' She was almost screaming now.

Trent Marston's reply came low and vicious. 'Shut up, you stupid little fool, and pull yourself together!

Just take it that I don't love you, never did. Anything
that happened was your idea, your choice, not mine.
I don't give a damn for you, Lisa, just remember that.
Now go back to your husband and stop behaving like
a spoilt child!'

There was a gasp, a strangled sob, and then Lisa's
footsteps stumbled away along the passage towards the
back stairs. After that there was silence.

Emma's hand clutched the curtain. She was cold
with shock, her knees were shaking. At that moment
she had no power over her body at all and even if she
had tried, she lacked the control to stay squeezed behind the curtain. She stood there waiting for Trent
Marston to reach the window and see her.

He got to the spot where she stood, and stopped
dead, his dark eyes sweeping over her in a long, raking look, taking in the situation immediately. She
squirmed inside, hanging on to the red velvet curtain
like some guilty woman in a French farce.

His sensual mouth twisted. 'Well, well, doing a little snooping, were you, Miss Fairley? I trust you were
rewarded, but I assure you that I didn't seek that spot
of melodrama.'

His tone with withering, but rage and resentment
steadied her, stiffening her muscles so that she was
able to stand straight and meet his hard, contemptuous gaze.

'And I certainly didn't seek to witness it,' She was
pleased that her voice was reasonably steady although her throat was achingly tight. 'I was merely
taking evasive action to avoid meeting you.' She raised
her chin a fraction. 'I find it difficult to be polite to
you, Mr Marston.'

'Really?' The thick black brows rose a fraction. 'Then why try?'

'This happens to be my home. And the occasion should be a happy one.'

The small smile didn't reach his eyes. 'Your cousin seems to think otherwise.'

'My cousin is very young and very vulnerable,' she retorted, breathing quickly. 'She may have been foolish enough to imagine herself in love with you, but did you have to be so disgustingly brutal?'

'It was necessary to spell it out. Your cousin is a leech, Miss Fairley. She would cling on to a man with those pretty white teeth. A man must protect himself. If you call that being disgustingly brutal, so be it.' He shrugged indifferently and half turned to move away.

Emma's cool deserted her finally. The blood ran hotly into her cheeks, her tawny eyes flashed golden fire, her hands clenched. 'Oh—' she spat out '—I think you're the most odious—hateful—despicable man I've ever met! I'd like to—' Her hand went up automatically to strike out at the hard, arrogant face above her, but he caught her wrist and held it in a grip that made her wince.

'Oh no, you don't, Miss Fairley. This is no business of yours.' His voice was icy. 'Your cousin is a married woman and has a man to rush to her defence if she thinks it necessary.'

He loosened his grip and tossed her hand aside contemptuously. His eyes sent shivers down her spine. 'Two hysterical females are altogether too much for one afternoon. Please excuse me.'

He turned away and strode down the passage and disappeared from sight.

CHAPTER THREE

SHAKING WITH wrath and humiliation, Emma stood staring at the spot where Trent Marston had disappeared. Her wrist hurt where he had grasped it and she rubbed it fretfully, as if she could rub away the feeling of his skin touching hers. She wanted to rush up to her room and thump the pillows to work off the helpless frustration she felt.

But there was Lisa to be thought of. Emma turned round and walked slowly up the back stairs. Lisa would get over it in time, of course she would, but it would do no good to tell her that now. After hearing that passionate outburst she didn't know what to expect when she saw Lisa, but whatever it was, she had to calm her down. Somehow Lisa had to change into her going-away clothes; somehow she had to smile and wave through all the ritual of the confetti-throwing, the 'Just Married' signs on the car, and any other wedding jokes that Richard's young brothers were no doubt planning. Somehow she had to climb into that car looking blissful, and be whisked away to a life that was empty of the man she loved. That was quite a challenge for any eighteen-year-old girl, but for sensitive, vulnerable Lisa it could be desperate.

Lisa was standing motionless in the middle of her bedroom. As Emma opened the door she spun round, her eyes blazing.

'You heard, didn't you? You were hiding behind that curtain, spying on me. I saw your dress as I ran past, but I was too worked up to stop then. That was a dirty trick, Em, I wouldn't have believed it of you!'

Emma went further into the room. 'Now, wait a minute, love, I was *not* spying on you. You know perfectly well I wouldn't spy on you. I'd slipped in there to avoid that awful Marston man when you came hareing past. There wasn't a thing I could do. But I'm sorry I had to hear—if you want, I'll forget every word.'

Lisa stared blankly at her, then, very slowly, her great blue eyes filled with tears and she slid down on to the bed. 'It doesn't matter,' she gulped. 'Oh, Em, I'm sorry. Of course you wouldn't spy on me. It's just that I—I'm so shattered. He has such an awful effect on me.'

Emma thrust a handkerchief into her hand and she wiped her eyes and blew her nose and rushed on, choking a little. 'Oh, I hate him—I loathe him! But I only had to see him—to hear his voice—' She began to cry again, then pulled herself together with a visible effort. 'All I wanted was to forget him. When he went away I thought I'd never see him again. And now he's going to be around here all the time—part of the firm. He'll come to the house. *You'll* be working with him, Em, travelling abroad with him—'

'I certainly will not,' Emma broke in firmly. 'Not on your life! I've met men like him and I keep well away from them. No, don't worry about me, I'm quite capable of taking avoiding action. Anyway, he'll most likely be based in London, so I shan't see anything of him.'

Lisa stopped crying. 'Do you really think so?'

'Yes, I do.' Emma sensed a breakthrough and began to build on it. 'Look, love, I know it's damnably difficult, but you've got to put all this behind you. You're married to Richard and he's a dear and he adores you. You're the sun and the moon and all the stars to him, and when you go down you're going to look radiant. Everyone down there is crazy about you—the way you look, the way you behave. Such dignity! Such poise! Mrs Southall said you were just like the young Princess Grace.' She hadn't, but Emma was sure she would have done if she'd thought of it.

Lisa produced a watery little smile. 'Did she really?'

'And poor Lorna is consumed with jealousy,' Emma pressed on, hoping she wasn't overdoing it. 'She knows she hasn't much hope of getting a husband herself, poor child. She's rather plain, isn't she?'

'Yes, I *am* the first of my form to get married.' Lisa's huge eyes took on the faintest of sparkles. She fingered the skirt of the going-away outfit, laid out on the bed beside her. 'It's pretty, don't you think, Em?' she said wistfully.

The suit of softest cotton corduroy, in a delicate powdery blue with an antique silver clasp on the belt, was a smash hit and Emma said so, and went on saying so while she helped Lisa to slip out of the wedding gown and repair her make-up. By the time she was dressed and ready to go downstairs, Lisa was giving a very convincing performance of a radiant bride leaving on her honeymoon. There was just one more hurdle left to cross and Emma kept tight hold of Lisa's hand, her eyes passing anxiously over the crowd of guests for a dark head towering above all the rest. But Trent Marston was nowhere to be seen, and she breathed easily again.

Richard was waiting at the top of the steps outside the front door. He had changed too and he looked very spruce in his casual grey suit. He came forward eagerly as Lisa and Emma appeared, which was a signal for the twins and their two friends to produce guitars from somewhere and launch themselves into a somewhat ribald song which might have gone down well in a men's club but was certainly out of place at a quiet, conventional wedding in a country village.

Lisa glanced at the singers and turned away, flushing, and Richard glowered fiercely at the boys. 'That's enough of that. Pack it in—it's in bloody bad taste.'

He spoke in a low, warning voice, but Emma was standing near and heard every word. It seemed, she thought wryly, that she was destined today to overhear embarrassing exchanges.

Kenneth, the taller of the twins, looked sulky. 'For Pete's sake, Rick, can't you take a joke?'

Richard glanced at Lisa. 'Just *stop* it, will you, Ken? Lisa doesn't go for that sort of song.'

Kenneth pulled a face and obeyed, signing to the others. The music stopped. Richard moved nearer to Lisa and put a protective arm around her and murmured something in her ear.

Emma was quite impressed. She hadn't known that Richard could be so authoritative and she admired him all the more for it. He was right, too. The song was decidedly off colour for a wedding like this.

Lisa was saying her goodbyes now. She came to Emma last and put her arms around her. 'Goodbye, Em darling, you've been wonderful to me always and I love you so much.' The great blue eyes were misty. 'I *trust* you, you know that, don't you?'

She put her hand in Richard's and they ran down the steps and into the car. Showers of confetti followed them and they ducked and laughed. A moment later they were on their way, waving through the windows as they rounded the corner of the drive.

The usual anti-climax descended on the wedding party, a slackening of tension now the married couple had left. Emma's tension slackened too and she breathed a sigh of profound relief that Trent Marston had had the decency to keep away from the seeing-off ceremony. Except, of course, that it wasn't decency that had motivated him but something entirely selfish. He had already shown himself as the kind of man who will amuse himself with a girl and then toss her aside quite callously. Emma seethed inside again, remembering his brutal words to Lisa in the passage outside the study.

Uncle Edward approached, looking exhausted and relieved. 'Well, that all seemed to go off fairly well, don't you think?'

'Splendidly,' agreed Emma. 'Wasn't she lovely?'

He nodded slowly. 'So like her mother.' His eyes met Emma's. 'If only—' he added in a low voice, and she squeezed his hand, understanding.

Emma waited until the final car had driven away and then she went out to the kitchen to congratulate Jessie on her part in the festivities. The hired waiters had packed up and departed in the van, with their crates of china and glass and a good box of perks in the shape of left-overs, Jessie informed her. 'They were guid boys, they did well. I let them have a bottle of beer each, I hope Mr Edward will no' mind?'

'Of course not.' Emma sank into the basket chair opposite Jessie's, heaving a sigh. 'It was a lovely wedding and everything went splendidly. Lisa's lucky, don't you think, Jessie? Richard's a really nice boy.'

'Oh aye,' said Jessie. She folded her hands on her apron. 'Miss Lisa did the sensible thing for once. When she could'na get the one she wanted she took the next best one. I've not known her do that before,' she added.

Emma was used to Jessie's plain speaking. Like an old family nurse, she had the privilege of saying what she thought.

'You mean she had a crush on this Marston man?' Emma smiled, making it sound trivial. 'She mentioned him in her letters.'

'Did she now?' Jessie said darkly. 'I wonder what she told you?'

'Not much, really.' Emma stood up. She wasn't going to discuss Lisa with Jessie. It would seem like disloyalty. 'I'd better go up and get changed. Mrs Southall's giving a party this evening and there'll be lots of food, so don't bother about any supper for me, Jessie.'

Jessie pulled herself to her feet, a little wearily. 'I'll be taking off my finery too.' She brushed down the skirt of the lilac dress and the shrewd eyes twinkled. 'I'll be needing it again when you get married, Miss Emma.'

'Me? Oh, I shan't be getting married for ages yet. I'm choosy.' She helped herself to a tiny sausage roll from a plate of left-overs, suddenly realising that she was hungry. She had been far too tense during the reception to eat anything. 'Um, these are good. No, I'm going to be busy working for the firm. I learned a lot from Joe on our trip.'

Jessie carried her empty tea-cup to the sink. 'Aye, Joe's a guid man, but he's getting on a bit now. You'll be working with this Mr Marston, then?'

Oh lord, here it was again! Couldn't she be allowed to forget the man for a moment?

'I really don't know,' she said vaguely, turning to the door.

Jessie looked over her shoulder. 'Miss Lisa won't take kindly to it if you do,' she said flatly.

Emma couldn't let that go. 'Lisa? Why should she mind? She's married now.'

'Oh aye, she's married, but she's still just a child. She would'na like you getting together with Mr Marston, I can tell you that.'

'Getting together?' Emma almost exploded. 'What *do* you mean, Jessie?'

Jessie didn't smile often, but sometimes her face took on a wry, mischievous look, as it did now. 'Och, I don't mean anything, except that you'd make a bonny pair, the two of you.'

It was no good getting angry with Jessie. Evidently the Marston individual had been working on her, too, with his lazy dark eyes and his machismo. Better make it into a joke. It was quite an effort, but she managed to laugh. 'You'd better watch that imagination of yours, Jessie. I hardly know the man.' She couldn't resist adding, '—and I don't at all like what I do know.'

Jessie raised scanty eyebrows. 'Oh, aye?' she said, and turned back to the sink.

Outside the kitchen door Emma stood looking up and down the passage, wondering where Trent Marston was, almost holding her breath. Then she pulled herself together. She would have to encounter the man again at some time, so it was quite ridiculous to behave like some silly heroine in an adventure film, hiding behind curtains, peering round corners. She tossed back her head and marched towards the back staircase.

'Miss Fairley—' A deep voice from behind brought her up sharply with a twinge of something that felt like fear at the pit of her stomach.

'Yes?' she said, raising her eyebrows faintly.

He stood in the study doorway, one hand on the door-knob, evidently intending to go back inside. He must have been listening for her, recognising her step on the tiled floor. 'I wondered when you would like to leave for the party,' he said. 'I'm at your service, any time.'

Pompous beast, she thought. At my service indeed—that's a lie!

'I won't need to trouble you, Mr Marston,' she said coolly, avoiding his eyes. But it was almost worse to focus on the long length of his body in its well-fitting formal suit as he leaned nonchalantly against the doorpost, and imagine herself sitting beside him in the intimate closeness of his car. No, she *couldn't*!

Uncle Edward appeared behind Trent in the doorway. 'Aren't you going to the party, Emma? You're all right, are you, my dear? Not ailing? Not suffering from jet-lag?'

'No, I'm fine.' She smiled brilliantly at him. 'It's just that I'm not sure how long I'll be, so I won't bother Mr Marston. When I'm ready Malcolm can give me a lift. Or I could drive myself if the Mini's O.K.'

'No need, my dear, no need at all,' Uncle Edward assured her. 'Malcolm has taken the lad from the garage into Poole, to drive Richard's car back. And I'm afraid your Mini has gone in for servicing and re-spraying. I thought it would be a little surprise for you, when you got home.'

'Oh,' said Emma rather blankly. 'That's a lovely surprise—and how good of you to think of it.'

Edward smiled. 'As a matter of fact, my dear, I must admit that it was Malcolm who thought of it—I don't go to the garage very often.'

'Well, never mind who thought of it,' Emma pressed on gaily, aware all the time of Trent Marston's dark eyes fixed on her with cynical scrutiny, 'it was a very bright idea. The old Mini was looking decidedly the worse for wear.'

There was an awkward little silence. Emma swallowed. 'Oh well, then, I'll accept your offer, Mr Marston. At half-past seven?'

There was a touch of irony in the way he bowed and the dark eyes held an unmistakable gleam of malice. 'Delighted,' he said.

Emma fled along the passage and up to her bedroom.

Once there she sat on the bed, breathing quickly. Trent Marston got under her skin as no man had ever done before. Although he was downstairs, talking to Uncle Edward, she could still feel his presence as if he was right here in the room. She could well understand how it had been with Lisa. Poor romantic little Lisa wouldn't have had a chance with a man like that, she would have gone down like—

She sat bolt upright suddenly. Like what? What *had* happened between them? Up to this moment she had taken it for granted that what Lisa had felt for the man had been nothing more than a romantic teenage crush.

But had it? Had it been something altogether more serious? Had he seduced her? If so, that would explain a lot—Lisa's passionate outburst in the passage, her nervous fainting fit over supper last night.

She shrank from the thought. With other girls of eighteen, perhaps, it would not be so traumatic to have an affair with a man over thirty. Many of them were experienced already, as they made quite clear. But Lisa—so fastidious and delicate, such a child—no, it didn't bear thinking about. She mustn't let herself think about it. As the odious man himself had said, it was none of her business, now that Lisa was married. She would put it behind her and forget that the idea had ever occurred to her.

She got up and slid open the door of her wardrobe, debating what to wear for the party. It would be quite acceptable to keep the green bridesmaid's dress on, of course; most of the other girls would probably still be wearing their wedding gear. But she fancied something different, something that wouldn't pair her off with young Lorna, something that had been chosen by herself and not by Mrs Southall.

In the end she chose a velvet jump-suit in a beech-leaf brown that went well with her hair and her eyes and was partyish without being wispy and girlish, like the green chiffon. She took longer than usual over her make-up and chose an eyeshadow that gave a deep, almost coppery glow to her eyes, and a lipstick that provided a rich, smooth gloss. She was pleased with the final result. An up-and-coming young business woman, that was Emma Fairley. Independent. Poised. Her own girl. That horrible man would never call her an hysterical female again, not if she could help it!

He was waiting in the hall when she went downstairs at exactly half-past seven, lounging in the corner of a velvet settle, leafing through a sailing magazine. He had changed too, he looked even more spectacular in casual clothes—black cords that moulded his long legs, a dusty pink shirt and an elegant black wrapover jacket. He certainly knew how to make an impression, she thought, deciding that she'd prefer a pipe-and-tweeds man herself—if such an animal still existed.

He got up as she came down the stairs, glancing at his watch. 'On the dot,' he said. 'Are you always so punctual, Miss Fairley?'

She looked at him coldly. 'I don't claim the feminine privilege of keeping a man waiting, if that's what you mean.'

He held the front door open and she swept out before him. The low-slung silver-grey Bentley was standing in the drive. As he eased himself into the front seat beside her he said, 'That wasn't exactly what I meant. If you're going to work for me I'd like to know what to expect in the way of time-keeping.'

Fury began to stir inside her, like a smouldering volcano. 'Work for you? I wasn't aware that I was going to work *for* anybody.'

He started the car and drove slowly down the drive and along the narrow lane outside. At the turning into the main road he braked and glanced briefly at her. 'I understood from Edward that you wanted to give yourself time to learn the marketing side of the business. If so, you will certainly be working for me.' He swung the car round effortlessly. 'Perhaps your uncle hasn't had time yet to tell you about the new set-up of the firm?'

'Only that it seems you're the fairy godfather who is going to save Fairley Brothers from ruin,' she said nastily.

'And that doesn't please you?'

'No,' said Emma.

'Do you want your family firm to sink without trace, then?'

'Of course I don't,' she said crossly. 'It's the fairy godfather bit that doesn't turn me on.'

They drove in silence along the dark, hilly road. In the summer this road between the little holiday town, and the village with its Norman church and its sandy beach and sailing harbour, would be alive with traffic, but in April it was deserted. Suddenly Trent Marston asked, 'How far is this house we're making for?'

'We're nearly there,' Emma told him. 'We'll be coming into the town in two or three minutes and then the Southall house is up on the cliffs beyond.'

Abruptly he pulled the car on to the grass verge and switched off the engine and the headlights.

'It seems that there are one or two things we need to get straight while there's an opportunity,' he said. 'First, for the record, I've accepted the job of straightening things out for your firm. Your uncle has given me a free hand to do whatever is needed to get the firm on its feet again, and I believe I can do it.'

'You mean it's a takeover?'

'No.' He moved his shoulders impatiently. 'Of course it's not a takeover. Edward Fairley is the king-pin of Fairley Brothers, I'd have thought you'd know that. Without his expertise there wouldn't be a firm at all. In my opinion he's a near-genius with electronics and he's brimming over with new ideas. We plan to expand from the purely nautical navigation aids the firm is making now, into a much wider market. There's still plenty of scope for new designs in many different fields. It's the marketing side of the firm that's weak, and that's where I come in. I've got all the right contacts,' he added.

I bet you have, thought Emma. Smug, arrogant brute! But in spite of herself she felt a twinge of excitement. How lovely if Uncle Edwards's work could be given its full value and if the firm could flourish once again as it must have done when her father was alive. If only it hadn't been Trent Marston who was prepared to work the miracle. If only it had been a man she could have trusted and admired.

'And what about Joe?' she said. 'Joe Kent—our marketing manager. Does he get made redundant? Do you just step in and push out a man who has given most of his life to the firm?'

He shrugged. 'Without much success, it would seem.'

'That was exactly the reply I would have expected from you, Mr Marston,' she said icily. 'Now, may we move on, please?'

He didn't stir. 'Not just yet. There's one other thing we need to discuss.'

'I can't think of anything I want to discuss,' she said distantly. She looked out of the side window at the gorse bushes, their prickles standing out whitely in the sidelights of the car. That was how she felt sitting beside this man—prickly all over.

'We have to discuss our relationship if you're going to work for—correction, if we're going to work together.'

'Our re—' she nearly choked. 'We don't have any relationship, Mr Marston, and I'm not going to work with you!'

'Your uncle thinks otherwise,' he said smoothly, sitting back in his corner. 'He's been telling me about all the work you have put in so that you can take your place in the firm, probably rise to a directorship in a year or two. He seems to think quite highly of your capabilities.'

'That arrangement was thought of before you joined the firm, Mr. Marston,' Emma said stiffly. 'Things have altered. I accept the fact that you will be much more valuable to the firm than I could possibly be—therefore I step down. To be frank, I don't like you and I couldn't work with you. I needn't explain why, I'm sure you know.'

'Because of your cousin Lisa, you mean? Are you her nanny?' he sneered. 'Did she come snivelling to you with some pathetic story of my misdeeds?'

Emma kept her temper with a huge effort, her fingernails digging into her palms. 'As a matter of fact Lisa hardly mentioned you,' she lied. 'I disliked your attitude from the first moment I saw you. But it wasn't until I accidentally witnessed your disgusting performance outside Uncle Edward's study this afternoon that I knew my first impression had been right.' That was quite a sentence to get out. She was beginning to feel utterly exhausted by this confrontation.

'All right,' he said. 'Point made—you don't like me. I can't say that that exactly fills me with grief. But it doesn't seem a valid reason to disappoint Edward and change all the plans he has for you—and for the firm. There are plenty of business relationships where love is not lost. Sometimes it provides a cutting edge to the proceedings. I guess I like a challenge.'

She said stubbornly, 'I shan't change my mind.'

'You'd disappoint your uncle and upset his plans for the sake of a silly little girl who can't bear to be out of the limelight?'

'Oh!' she gasped. 'That's just the end, that you can say that after the way you behaved to Lisa!' Suddenly she wanted to hurt him as he had hurt Lisa. 'I don't like you and I won't work with you. Is that clear, or are you as stupid as you're callous and conceited and insufferable?'

She felt him stiffen and heard his quick intake of breath. He sat up as if she had pointed a gun at him and she winced as he took her shoulders in a grasp of steel and wrenched her round to face him.

'You little bitch,' he ground out between his teeth. 'Don't you dare speak to me like that or—' His face was so close to hers that she could feel his breath on her cheek. In the near-darkness she could see the dangerous glitter in his eyes.

'Or what?' she gasped, struggling to free herself. 'Do you include violence to a woman among your other charming habits?'

Abruptly he let her go, pushing her away from him, and sank back into his own seat. After a moment or two he said, 'All right, I'm sorry. But just don't go too far, that's all.'

'That's a warning, is it?' she mocked.

'That's a warning,' he said grimly, his hand going out to the self-starter.

As the powerful car leapt forward towards the town Emma felt trickles of fear up and down her spine. Just then she had been helpless in the grip of the most powerful emotion she had ever felt in her whole life. She had *wanted* to provoke him to anger, *wanted* to lash out against him. And it wasn't only because of the way he had treated Lisa. Love and loyalty had nothing to do with it, she had to admit. It was the man himself who released some frighteningly primitive urge in her.

She would have to watch it. She would have to watch it very carefully indeed.

They drove in silence for the rest of the way, except when Emma provided Trent with directions. Through the quiet little holiday town with its Playland still boarded up, its pier closed. Up the long, steep hill to the cliff-top where rich retired people had built their white, architect-designed homes looking over the sea. Richard had already started getting out plans for a new house for himself and Lisa. Meanwhile, Lisa had told her, they would live with 'Mother.' Emma didn't envy her. Mrs Southall was amiable enough, but accustomed to ruling over her own little empire—her store, her children. But perhaps, Emma thought, Lisa wouldn't mind. She had always been so sweet and compliant. And Mrs Southall was obviously delighted with her new daughter-in-law.

The party was already in full swing when they arrived, the opulent modern house spilling light from every window on to the lawns and flowerbeds. It was cleverly built into the slope of the ground on the cliff-top and a semi-basement with wide windows provided a long playroom, the whole width of the house. From here came the dull thud of a rockbeat, much amplified.

'Oh, lord, is it that kind of party?' groaned Trent as they got out of the car.

'Don't you dance?' Emma enquired. If he didn't then she would know exactly how to keep out of his way.

'Fortunately I escaped discomania,' he said dryly as they climbed the shallow steps to the wide front door with its ornate brass trimmings and white plaster portico.

Mrs Southall greeted them in the hall, looking elegant in a low-cut black dress, her fading fair hair pink-rinsed and immaculately coiffured, the orchid she had worn at the wedding pinned at her shoulder.

She smiled fleetingly at Emma and murmured, 'You know everyone, don't you, Emma?' and then turned a brilliant smile upon Trent. '*So* glad you could come along, Mr Marston', she cooed, linking an arm with his and turning him towards the drawing room where bridge tables could be seen laid out. 'I'm sure you won't want to rampage around with the children. Too *dreadfully* noisy! Now, I've go so many people wanting to meet you—'

She led him away, talking gaily, smiling up into his eyes. Good heavens, thought Emma, suppressing a giggle, she's the merry widow, making a bid for the handsome, eligible bachelor. She wouldn't be more than ten or eleven years older than Trent Marston; she had been much younger than her husband who had died last year.

Good luck to her, she's welcome to him, thought Emma, and escaped down the stairs to the playroom, turning for one last look at Trent's back as he walked beside Mrs Southall, his dark head bent towards her courteously. Oh yes, he would make quite a stir among the young and the not-so-young matrons in the bridge room, with his arrogant masculine charisma. Everything about him—the taut elegance of his body, the lazy grace of his movements, the challenge of those dark eyes—would set pulses leaping; send all the respectable ladies wild with improper yearnings.

I might have been taken in myself, thought Emma. I might have gone down for the count, like poor little Lisa, if he'd turned his charms on me before I knew the kind of man he really is. What a lucky escape! She was smiling to herself as she went down the last steps into the warm, cavernous darkness of the playroom.

The atmosphere came up to meet her—the heat and the noise and the shuffle of feet on the wooden floor and the jungle beat issuing from the hi-fi equipment, mercilessly amplified. Oh yes, she could get away from Trent Marston here, it would be easy to hide in the gloom, broken only by the disco lights revolving slowly, changing from red to green, to blue to yellow, shifting over the couples twisting and turning, or locked together and moving sensuously, as the mood took them.

'Here's my girl.' Jim Bolton's voice, slightly slurred, sounded in her ear. 'I've been watching for you, my lovely. Come and have a drink.'

An arm close round her waist, he led her through the maze of dancing couples to the far end of the long room, where a table was laid and cans of beer and bottles of soft drinks and Coke and a huge bowl of punch with slices of fruit and cherries and grapes floating on the top.

Jim scooped out a long glassful for each of them. 'Good show, isn't it? Ken and George rigged up the lights themselves.' He pulled her down beside him on to cushions on the floor, and Emma realised suddenly that she was feeling very tired. But when Jim put an arm round her and drew her towards him she pulled away a little.

'Ah, c'm on, sweetheart,' he urged 'Weddings put ideas into a fellow's head.' He buried his mouth in her neck, where the velvet jump-suit was scooped low.

Emma scrambled to her feet. 'Too early in the evening,' she said, realising with a sinking heart that Jim had already been drinking freely. 'Come and dance.'

She merged with the couples on the floor, and Jim, protesting, joined her. After a while she managed to lose him. As Mrs Southall had said, she knew everybody there. She was a year or two older than most of them. Lorna and the twins had gathered together their own circle of friends, whether they had been at the wedding or not. But in her velvet jump-suit, cut low and sleeveless, she looked younger than twenty. Ken, cutting in on one of his friends, grinned cheekily at her. 'Sexy, that's what you are, Emma.' His bright blue eyes moved appreciatively over her in the shifting lights. He had none of his brother Richard's seriousness; Ken was a whizz-kid.

They were all kids, Emma thought, an hour later, beginning to feel a headache coming on. She was tired and she wanted quite desperately to go home. She was dancing with Jim—or rather, they were shuffling round together, and his arms were round her waist, his cheek sagging against hers. She considered trying to sober him up, to ask him to drive her home, but it didn't seem a very good idea. The rest of them had paired off by now. She wondered if she could find a telephone and ring for a taxi, but if she ventured up into the main part of the house she would surely encounter some of Mrs Southall's guests, and that meant seeing Trent Marston again, which was the very last thing she wanted.

Jim was leaning heavily against her now. She pushed him away a little and put one hand to her throbbing head and thought longingly of slipping into a cool bed and closing her eyes.

'Mine, I think,' murmured a deep voice close above her. In one swift movement she was detached from Jim, who seemed to dissolve into the gloom, and she found herself in Trent's arms, and moving to the music.

The sheer physical shock of feeling his hard, taut body against hers after Jim Bolton's slackness left her speechless, her heart thumping. Then she pulled herself together. 'I—I thought you didn't dance,' she said idiotically.

'Did you now?' His voice was deep and soft, just above her ear, giving the words an intimacy that sent an odd shiver through her. 'Perhaps there are one or two other things about me that you got wrong.'

Emma was utterly confused. This was the man she hated, that she had been desperate to keep away from, and yet the sensations that were coursing through her as his body pressed against hers were overwhelming.

'Let's dance,' he went on huskily, his hands moving up and down her back on the softness of the velvet. 'You feel like a kitten, a beautiful strokeable kitten.'

She groped desperately for sanity. 'I have claws,' she said.

He rubbed his cheek against her hair. 'Oh, I know all about that. They scratch but don't go very deep. Now, don't talk, just enjoy the dance.'

He was a wonderful dancer, of course. She had never had a partner like him. They moved together to the languor of the beat, in perfect unison as if their two bodies were one. I must be mad, she thought wildly. I've drunk too much of that punch, it must be more potent than I thought. She ought to pull away from him, but his arm around her was like sprung steel holding her close, thigh to thigh, the soft swelling of her breast against his muscled hardness. She'd been so right about him—he was danger, he was temptation. She *had* to fight it, she had to.

Summoning every bit of will-power, she pulled away from him, stopped dancing. He still held her, loosely now. 'What's the matter?' he asked, looking down into her face.

'I—I—' Her voice refused to function. She stared up into the strong, hard face above her own and as she did so a crimson glow passed over it from the disco lights. He looks like the devil, she thought faintly.

But his voice was unexpectedly gentle as he said, 'You're tired, aren't you? You've had a hectic two days, you need a good night's sleep. Come along, I'll take you home. That's why I came to find you. I've had enough of the skittish ladies in the bridge room.'

Heaven, she thought, to get home and slide into a cool bed. But to travel back in the car beside Trent? She'd planned to ask Jim to see her home, and now, after the way she had just been feeling, that seemed even more advisable.

'But—but we can't leave so early—' she faltered.

He led her to the side of the room. 'You just watch us.'

'And—and I half promised to go home with Jim Bolton,' she said weakly. 'You know—the best man and the chief bridesmaid, it's a sort of ritual that they pair off for the rest of the day.'

She looked round for Jim and spotted him slumped on the floor near one of the hi-fi loudspeakers. He didn't seem conscious of the booming sound issuing from it. In fact, he didn't seem conscious of anything.

Trent followed her glance. 'He won't miss you,' he said dryly. 'Come along.'

At the top of the stairs they encountered Mrs Southall. 'Emma's feeling all in,' Trent told her. 'I know you'll understand if I take her off home now. All the excitement of the wedding and no doubt a spot of jet-lag too.'

Mrs Southall's light blue eyes passed over her. 'Poor Emma,' she said coolly. 'Of course you must go home straight away. But there's no need for you to rush away so soon, Trent.' She said his name coyly. 'My chauffeur will see Emma home safely.'

'Many thanks, but I'll drive her myself.' His smile and his tone were pleasant enough, but somehow he conveyed that any further argument would be quite useless. 'Have you a wrap, Emma?'

Five minutes later, after thanks and further apologies, she found herself sitting beside Trent, driving back the way they had come.

Now what? she thought nervously, watching the way his hand rested on the wheel, lightly and yet with complete control. Had he just been making an excuse to get her to himself in the seclusion of his car, to continue what he had certainly started on the dance floor? A tremor ran through her from head to foot.

They drove through the sleepy little town and up the hill on the other side into the blackness of the country road again, the headlights cleaving a dazzling white path ahead. Trent didn't say a single word until he stopped the car outside the front door of the old grey house, all in darkness except for the light from the hall window. Then he switched off the engine and turned towards her and smiled. 'Delivered safe and sound,' he said.

'Thank you,' said Emma. That smile was almost more disturbing than the touch of his hands had been.

They sat looking at each other in the dim silence inside the car. Emma felt her heart thumping against the velvet of her jump-suit.

Then, slowly, his arm came up and slid along the back of the seat and he leaned towards her. After a moment, when she could have drawn away if she had had the power to do so, his hand dropped to her shoulder, closed round her neck and he drew her slowly towards him.

Sanity left her completely and she was engulfed in an almost feverish hunger for his kiss. When his mouth closed over hers she let out a small moan and her arms went up to clasp themselves behind his dark head and draw him even nearer, while her lips and mouth responded to his with a wildness that seemed to have nothing to do with the girl she had thought she was until now.

She felt the pounding of his own heart and knew he was aroused too. For a moment his arms tightened round her, then with a little shake of his head he let her go, pushing her away gently.

'Thank you, Emma, that was nice,' he said. 'Who was it remarked that weddings are for kissing? Your friend the best man, wasn't it? Now you must get along to bed and get some sleep. I've got some things to talk over with your uncle. I see he's still working.' He jerked his head towards where lights showed in the workroom at the end of the garden. 'I'll tell him we're hitting it off very well, shall I?'

Emma had heard about blinding flashes of insight, when everything becomes clear in a second. She had one now. Of course—Trent Marston had been practising his charms on her for one reason only. He was so sure of himself that he knew she would fall for him and wouldn't be likely to say anything to Uncle Edward about the affair between Lisa and himself.

Uncle Edward, tucked away in his workroom, wouldn't have seen what was going on under his own eyes. But if he found out that Trent had hurt his beloved daughter that would alter everything. Edward Fairley was a mild man, but he would undoubtedly show Trent the door, and the firm would then proceed downhill even more rapidly.

Emma got out of the car. She was ice-cold now. As Trent slammed the door on his side and walked round to her she said calmly, 'You're keen on taking this work on for the firm, aren't you?'

She saw his eyebrows go up. 'Yes, I am. Why ask now?'

'I merely wanted to assure you that I've no intention of doing anything to stand in your way. Or of doing anything to help you either. Thank you for the lift home, Mr Marston,' she added, and turning abruptly she walked into the house and left him standing there staring after her.

CHAPTER FOUR

THE HOUSE was silent. In the hall every trace of the reception had been tidied away and the wedding might never have been. Jessie and Malcolm must have been working at it all evening and they must have already gone to bed, tired out.

Emma went out to the kitchen, switched on the light and filled the kettle. A cup of tea might restore a semblance of normality to the evening. She sat down to drink it at the big old-fashioned wooden table that Jessie refused to part with and scrubbed lovingly every day.

After the first cup of tea, sanity began to return, but she still felt more churned up inside than she had ever felt before. What had possessed her to behave as she had just done, out there in the car? Tiredness? Jet-lag? Too many glasses of punch?

No, face it, Emma, the man was devastating. He had gone through her defences like a laser beam went through—whatever laser beams *did* go through. From the first moment she set eyes on him he had given her one look and all her inside workings had begun to quiver like a jelly, she thought with bitter self-contempt. And what had just happened had been the final humiliating result.

She pulled her thoughts up short. But what actually *had* happened? She had danced with a man. He had driven her home. He had kissed her in the car. Nothing world-shattering about that—it had happened before.

Ah, but never like that! Never that wild, heady ecstasy that had made her cling to him, snuggle into his arms like the kitten he had called her. For a few moments she had been overwhelmed by a kind of madness, but not again. No, she had to admit the sheer animal magnetism of the man, and then proceed to take herself out of its field of attraction.

She knew the danger. She knew the way he treated women. She winced, hearing again the cruel bite of his voice saying, 'I don't love you, never did. I don't give a damn for you, Lisa.'

That was the kind of man he was, a man who would amuse himself with a girl and then throw her aside with callous brutality. She didn't intend to be his next victim. She would see Uncle Edward tomorrow and tell him she would prefer to spend another year on her languages—in Greece, or Germany, perhaps—before she took her place in a senior position in the firm. It shouldn't be too difficult to convince him without telling him the true reason—that Trent Marston had come close to breaking his young daughter's heart. Trent Marston seemed to be the firm's last hope. Therefore he must stay and she must go.

Not merely because she hated him and feared him, she admitted, as she dragged herself upstairs to bed. But because she was afraid of herself.

It was quite a time before she went to sleep. She kept on waking up and thinking about what had happened and what a fool she was to let herself get carried away by a man who specialised in trading on his sex-appeal. And when she did go to sleep she dreamed that she was standing naked on the bank of a fast-flowing river. Trent Marston was swimming towards her with powerful strokes, brown arms flailing the turbulent water, and calling, 'Come on, Emma darling, jump in, I'll catch you.'

She didn't need Freud to tell her what that meant. She took it as another warning.

When she finally sank into sleep she slept heavily and wakened to see Jessie standing beside the bed with a tray in her hands.

Emma shot up, pushing the hair away from her flushed face. 'Heavens, what time is it? Jessie, you shouldn't have brought my breakfast up—I'm just a lazy so-and-so.'

Jessie plonked the tray down and drew the curtains back. 'Och, no, Miss Emma, you earned a good lie-in. Flying all those thousands of miles across the sea and then all the excitement of the wedding and you having to look after Miss Lisa, and very prettily you did it too. You needed a guid long night.'

'And so did you, Jessie. You must have worked like a beaver, clearing everything up after I went out to Mrs Southall's party.'

Jessie's face creased into the nearest thing to a smile she ever allowed herself. 'You enjoyed it? I saw you go off with Mr Marston.'

Emma bent her head over the coffee pot. 'Jessie, why all the dark hints about me and Mr Marston? I assure you I don't like the man at all.'

Jessie picked up the top of a jar of cleansing cream that Emma had left lying on the dressing-table last night, and screwed it on again firmly. Her smile became even more enigmatic. 'Oh, aye?' she said on her way to the door. 'I didna think much of Malcolm when I met him, either.'

She went out on to the landing, then her head appeared round the door again. 'Mr. Edward's down in the workroom. He said to ask you to go and see him, but there was no hurry. Mr Marston went off early to the factory, so you tak' your time and enjoy your breakfast.'

Emma found she was hungry. She had drunk several glasses of punch last night and eaten nothing except a couple of biscuits with her cup of tea when she got home. Now she cracked the top off a brown egg and spread creamy Dorset butter on her toast and proceeded to enjoy herself. She was getting over last night, it couldn't have made all that much impression on her after all. What's in a kiss? she asked herself, crunching toast pleasurably.

She browsed over the subject as she ate her breakfast. She was nearly twenty-one, and she would have had to have been very stupid not to know that men found her attractive. There had been plenty of kisses in her life, and the funny thing was that every kiss was different from every other. It must be like fingerprints, she thought with a grin. No man kissed you in exactly the same way as any other man.

She drank up her coffee and went along to the bathroom for her shower. What was she thinking of—maundering on to herself about kisses at this time in the morning? A cool shower would put all that nonsense out of her head.

The odd thing was that it didn't. As she soaped her smooth body under the tepid water and dried the pinkly glowing limbs with a fleecy towel, she was still thinking about kisses—and one particular kiss at that.

As soon as she got downstairs the phone rang and it was Jim Bolton. 'Emma? What happened to you last night? You disappeared. Are you okay? Mrs Southall said you'd gone home early, you had a headache. Why didn't you say? I'd have driven you home.' He sounded half-way between huffiness and guilt.

'I was going to ask you, but you were drunk,' Emma said bluntly.

'I was *not* drunk!' he spluttered loudly. There was a sudden pause and she could see him looking round the estate agent's office where he worked to see if anyone was listening. In a lowered tone he said, 'Okay, Emma, perhaps I was a mite over the limit and I'm sorry if I let you down. We'd all had rather too much—old Richard was in a flat spin before the wedding and I had to bolster him up a bit, and then afterwards—oh well, I'm sorry if I was a clot, love. It won't happen again. Forgive me?'

She laughed. 'Of course,' she said. 'Weddings are for celebrating, aren't they?' And for kissing, she thought, with a jolt of her stomach as she heard again a deep, amused voice, felt the touch of strong fingers at the nape of her neck, smelled the clean fragrance of a man's freshly-washed hair against her cheek.

She dragged her mind back to what Jim was saying. '—lunch, can you manage it? Just to show I'm forgiven.'

'Lunch?' she echoed vaguely. 'Today?'

'Yes, today. I can get away at twelve, with any luck. I've got to take a potential customer to look over a bungalow in Worth Matravers, but after that I'm free. We'll meet at the Golden Butterfly as usual, shall we?'

Emma didn't really want to lunch with Jim, there were too many other things on her mind, but at least she would be away from the house, and any risk of encountering Trent Marston. Jim worked in Poole, and the factory and office of Fairley Brothers were in that town too. But Trent wasn't likely to lunch at the Golden Butterfly. The three-star Dolphin in the High Street would be more his style. So she agreed to meet Jim and he sounded delighted, and she had a feeling that he was going to ask her again to marry him.

She sighed as she made her way down the garden to Uncle Edward's workroom. She had told Jim 'No' so many times, but he wouldn't take it, and if there was anything she hated, it was having pressure put on, and made to feel she was letting someone down.

Uncle Edward looked up as she knocked and went into the workroom. He smiled at her and she smiled back and thought, with a sudden surge of affection, that he really was the nicest of men. His gold-rimmed glasses were perched on the end of his nose, giving him a decided look of the 'mad professor' that she and Jessie had jokingly named him. He was not yet fifty, she knew, but he looked older. Tragedy and worry and his somewhat one-pointed existence had put grey in his hair and wrinkles on his face.

'Busy?' Emma enquired, which wasn't necessary, for he was always busy.

He held up two crossed fingers, and his blue eyes shone keenly behind his glasses. 'I think I may be on to something that will make all our fortunes.'

'Great!'

'Marston thinks so too.' He nodded thoughtfully. 'You know, Emma, for a man who doesn't profess to be a boffin, that chap has a superb grasp of technology. A very bright brain indeed.'

'Yes,' said Emma, 'I'd rather gathered that.' He'd thought out his plan last night very cleverly.

Edward put down his pencil and swivelled round in his chair. 'I'm glad you're getting on with him. He seems very impressed with you. I think you'll make a very good team. When this new thing really gets cracking we're going to need all the expertise we can get.'

She drew a finger along the edge of the work-bench. 'I wanted to talk to you about that, Uncle Edward. Meeting a man like Trent has shown me that I don't have what it takes to work with him yet. As you say, he's a live wire; he'll expect more than I can give.' (And you can say that again, Emma!) 'I thought,' she went on carefully, 'that if I could have another year, perhaps, to work on my languages? I could go back to Germany and stay with Hallbachs, they'll take me any time, they said so. Then, perhaps, six months in Greece? My Spanish and French are fairly good and I can get by in Italian. But I'd like to be really confident before I take up the job. Dear old Joe isn't critical, but Mr Marston would be, I'm sure. What do you say?'

He looked disappointed. 'Are you sure, Emma? We were planning on Trent making up his marketing team straight away, and he seems keen to include you.'

Yes, she thought, and I know why—because he wants to keep things sweet between us in case I decide to tell Uncle Edward what a bastard he is in his private life. Probably the very qualities of hardness and ruthlessness that she knew he possessed would make him a success in business. Emma didn't know and she didn't propose to find out. She knew enough of her uncle to guess that he would feel the same way.

Perhaps she ought to tell him—perhaps it wasn't fair to keep him in the dark about the character of the man he seemed to be putting all his trust in. But that would mean the break-up of the firm, for sure. She couldn't take the responsibility for that.

She said, 'He's only keen to include me because I happen to be your niece. He can't have any idea of my capabilities yet, I only met him yesterday and we haven't talked business at all.'

A little sheepishly Edward Fairley said, 'I showed him a letter I had from Joe, saying quite a lot about your capabilities. Joe was most impressed with the report you compiled for him.'

'Yes,' she said, quickly changing the subject, 'and that's another thing. What about Joe? How is this new appointment going to affect him? He's so devoted to the firm and he's worked like a brick all the time we've been in the U.S. It seems—' she paused. She needed to be tactful about this— 'don't you think it seems a bit hard to bring in an outsider above him? I suppose that's what it would amount to.'

It was a moment before he replied, then he said with unusual seriousness, 'I know you think the world of Joe, Emma. So do I, and I wouldn't do anything that would hurt or distress him. But we had a long talk before you and he left on this trip and he confessed to me that he hoped it would be the last overseas commitment he was asked to undertake. He was very reluctant to upset the pattern, but he said he'd felt for some time now that he wasn't doing justice to the job. It was all getting a bit too much for him and he wished we could find someone to take on most of the promotional work and allow him to spend his time more on the routine, based in the office. I've no doubt at all that he'll be delighted when he hears about the change, and when he gets back from Mexico next week we can all put our heads together and work something out.'

He sighed and passed a hand rather wearily across his brow. 'If you only knew, Emma, how much it will mean to me to have a younger, more dynamic man in charge of that part of the business I can't handle.' He looked out through the window. 'Your father was the man—you know that—and together we could have tackled anything. I've waited a long time to find someone else.'

Emma said, holding all emotion out of her voice, 'You don't feel bad about putting another man in Father's place?'

'Not if it's Trent Marston,' he said simply. 'I just feel he's the right one.'

She bit her lip. 'Then you think I shouldn't go to Germany?'

'Oh, don't let's be hasty about it. We'll all meet and discuss it this evening. Meanwhile—' he picked up a folder— 'I wonder if you'd go along to the office with this, Emma? I promised Trent you'd take it to him there as soon as I'd finished it. He went out early this morning. Malcolm's working in the garden, so you can take the Rover. Will you do that for me?'

Her first impulse was to find some excuse, so that she wouldn't have to confront Trent Marston this morning, but she overcame the impulse rapidly. It would be childish to behave like that, and why should he have the power to affect her actions? She raised her head. 'Of course I'll go,' she said briskly. 'I'll go straight away. I was going into Poole this morning in any case—I promised to have lunch with Jim.'

Edward nodded absently. 'Oh yes? Well, enjoy yourself.' Already his attention was back on his work.

Emma went out and left him to it. The interview had certainly not been an unqualified success. But Uncle Edward hadn't definitely said 'No,' to her idea. She would work on it again this evening. Somehow she had to get herself out of Trent Marston's field of activity.

Half an hour later Emma was parking the Rover outside the Fairley Brothers premises in Poole. The factory, of which the office was a part, was in the old district of Poole, near the quay. It had originally been a boatbuilding yard, which also made and supplied other items of sailing equipment. After the war, when her grandfather died, it had gradually narrowed down to specialising in navigation instruments, which were Uncle Edward's particular field of interest. Half of the building had been sold off and was now used as a café, which was open only during the summer season.

Emma was always aware, these days, of a faint depression when she visited the factory. Now she parked the car and sat for a moment or two, looking at the outside, at the big doors that had once opened on to a thriving boatyard; at the seedy café next door, its windows boarded up against vandalism, the door covered with peeling posters.

How splendid if the whole place could be smartened up and put on its feet again! Much as she hated the idea of Trent Marston coming here and taking over, it seemed that he was their last hope.

She took the folder from the front seat and locked up the car, glancing at her watch. It was a quarter to twelve. Just time to hand over the folder and walk to the Golden Butterfly to meet Jim. That would save having to hunt somewhere to park the car in the centre of town.

As she slid open the heavy door her inside stirred uneasily at the prospect of seeing Trent Marston again, after last night. She would be very brief, very businesslike, just hand him the folder and leave.

Inside the big room, the six trained girls, whose job it was to assemble the intricate parts of the navigation instruments, bent over their work-tables. Emma paused for a moment or two for a word with a couple of the ones she knew best. They were a good, loyal work-force; Uncle Edward paid them well and they adored him—and Joe too. It was like a big happy family.

Ted Draper, the foreman, hailed Emma from across the floor. 'Hullo, Miss Emma, home again? Had a good time?' He was a hefty, tow-headed man who had a tiny, neat wife. They had produced three children, and Emma paused to ask after them.

'I've come with a folder to leave in the office,' she said. 'Is there somebody there?'

'The new boss,' said Ted, deadpan.

She studied his face and learned nothing from it. 'How's he getting along? What do you think?'

'I'll wait a bit and see,' said Ted, ever-cautious. He jerked his big head towards the girls at the work-tables. 'He's caused quite a flutter among that lot,' he said dryly.

Yes, Emma thought, he would. He'd only have to flash that dark, smouldering glance of his around to have them all working at double speed. Her dislike of the man and his tactics moved up another notch.

They talked for a moment longer about Joe. Emma said she thought he seemed rather tired when she left him and Ted nodded as if he knew all about that. Then she smiled goodbye and went through the glass door into the office.

'Good morning, Miss Fairley,' chirped the new little typist brightly. And 'Good morning, Miss Fairley, nice to see you again, have you enjoyed the tour?' offered Rose, Joe's middle-aged secretary. She'd had a colour-rinse and a new curly hair-style. She wore a frilly white blouse and a rather too-tight skirt. Her cheeks were pink and her eyes were shining. 'Mr Marston's in the private office,' she said, with what amounted to a simper.

Oh lord, you too! thought Emma in disgust, and marched into the smaller room at the far end of the office.

Trent was sitting at the big desk, surrounded by files and ledgers. He looked up when the door opened and a slow smile touched his mouth at the corners. 'Well, well, I am honoured. I was expecting Malcolm to be the courier.'

She had been prepared to feel a trifle embarrassed when they met again after that prolonged kiss in his car last night. What she hadn't been expecting was the flood of awareness that sent a tingle all through her body as she met those dark, lazy eyes with their absurdly long, curving lashes.

She put the folder on the desk. 'Uncle Edward asked me to bring this,' she said, and turned to the door again.

'Wait a bit,' Trent said quietly. 'Why the hurry?'

'I've got an appointment for lunch at twelve o'clock,' she gabbled, one hand on the door handle. 'I've only just got time to walk into town.'

He was on his feet now, standing beside her. 'My car's here, I'll run you there,' he said. 'Now, come and sit down.'

The next moment she found herself sitting opposite him across the desk. 'What do you want?' she asked in a strangled kind of voice. The way he was looking at her was sending shock waves up and down her spine.

'Just to look at you,' he said, and proceeded to do so.

She sat staring back at him, gradually feeling a sort of creeping paralysis taking over; to have someone look at you in silence, she thought helplessly, was the most agonising thing there was. She swallowed, which was an effort with a completely dry throat, and said, 'I hope you aren't thinking of buying. The goods aren't for sale.'

He laughed then. It was the first time she had heard him laugh, deep and low and velvety, like a caress, and that shook her too. Heavens, the man was dynamite!

'Relax,' he said. 'I'm not—for the moment—bidding in the sort of market you have in mind; I was merely assessing your possible usefulness in other ways. Ways that would be of benefit to the firm, of course.'

'Really?' she said with heavy sarcasm.

'Yes, really. I like your style very much, including your taste in clothes. That colour—burnt orange, would you call it?—goes particularly well with your hair and your eyes. It brings a note of cheer to a dull day.'

'Thank you very much,' said Emma. 'Is that all you have to say to me, because—'

'I can just see you,' he mused on, as if she hadn't spoken, 'drawing the crowd at a big trade exhibition, attracting potential customers to the Fairley Brothers stand. There's nothing like a pretty girl to boost business. Look at the Motor Show.'

She felt fury boiling up inside her. She clenched her fists. '*You* may see me decorating an exhibition stand, Mr Marston,' she said hotly. 'I have quite different ideas about my usefulness to the firm. Please remember that.'

He smiled with relish and she realised with vexation that she had played straight into his hands. He was the kind of man who enjoyed a fight. 'Sheathe those claws, Emma. You'd be a decoration in any place, exhibition stand or not. Don't tell me you'd rather be a collar-and-tie-and-no-make-up type of woman executive. And I'm sure your talents extend into many other fields. Many others.' He gazed up at the ceiling and then down at that part of her body, swelling prettily behind its lightweight woollen jacket, that was visible above the desk.

'Oh!' she gasped furiously. 'You're hateful and impossible!'

'Thanks,' he said coolly. He got to his feet. 'Now, as I said, I'll give you a lift into town, if you're leaving your car here. I have to see my bank manager.'

He put a hand at her elbow as they passed through the outer office and the factory workroom. All the women were aware of him as they went by—it was like a ripple passing through the room. They were probably envying her, Emma thought bitterly, pushing her way forward round a machine, so that she could disengage herself from the light hold on her arm. His touch seemed to burn through the sleeve of her jacket.

'Where can I drop you?' asked Trent as he nosed the Bentley out into the street from the factory yard.

'Oh, anywhere in the centre of the town will do,' she said hurriedly. The smell of the expensive leather and the soft cushiony feel of the upholstery inside the car were touching up memories of last night much too keenly, and she wanted to get out as soon as she could.

'Oh no, please allow me to deliver you to the door. I kept you, and I shouldn't like to think I'd made you late for your appointment.'

There was no getting the better of this man, was there? 'The Golden Butterfly,' she said briefly.

'Ah, yes, I know exactly where it is. A pleasant little restaurant.'

Something in his voice made her look up sharply. He knew it, then? Had he brought Lisa here? The words of the letter came back to her: 'I'm swinging on a star, sliding down a rainbow, Trent's taking me out to dinner tonight.'

And then he would drive Lisa home, poor little Lisa who hadn't a clue, then, about the kind of man he really was. And in the darkness he would take her in his arms and kiss her, as he had kissed Emma last night. A shudder passed through her and she couldn't get out of the car quickly enough. As soon as it stopped she almost fell out and slammed the door.

'Thanks for the lift,' she said, without looking at him, and ran into the restaurant.

As she went into the small, comfortable bar where she always met Jim the clock showed five past twelve, but Jim hadn't arrived yet. She sat down in a corner to wait. After a few minutes Jacques, the head waiter, came across to her. 'Ah, Mees Fairley, Mr Bolton 'ave just telephone. 'e is sorry he will be a leetle late and ask you please to wait. May I get you a drink while you wait? Your usual?'

He brought her favourite lime and lemon, with a dash of angostura, and beamed as he left her.

Half an hour later she was still waiting. She knew lots of people in Poole and had met and chatted with two friends, consumed another drink, and was beginning to feel very hungry, and to debate whether she should go into the restaurant and start lunch on her own.

Then the door from the street opened and Trent Marston walked in. He stood looking around him with his usual arrogant air, and Emma felt a curious tug at the pit of her stomach as his eyes lighted on her.

He came over to the table. 'Boy-friend stood you up?' he smiled.

'He's been delayed,' Emma said with as much dignity as she could manage.

He looked pointedly at his watch. 'Half an hour is much too long to keep a girl hanging around waiting for her lunch.'

'I am *not* hanging around.' She tried to freeze him, but it wasn't easy when she had to look up about half a mile to see his face. 'Jim never knows exactly when he's going to get away when he's interviewing a client about buying a house. I quite understand.' She wondered why she felt she had to justify herself or apologise for Jim.

He dropped into a seat beside her. 'Well, let's order lunch, shall we? Then if Jim-boy does put in an appearance I'll remove myself.'

He didn't wait for her to agree. He held up a finger and Jacques appeared like the genie of the lamp. This was the kind of man who can make head waiters appear out of nowhere. Money talks, Emma thought sourly.

'Miss Fairley and I will get on with lunch, Jacques.'

'Vairy good, Mr Marston.' Jacques produced large menu cards.

'Steak?' Trent enquired, looking at Emma with all the courtesy of a considerate host wishing to make a good impression on his guest. 'They do an excellent steak here.'

She shook her head. If she had to eat lunch with this man she would need something that would go down more easily than a steak. 'I'll have scampi,' she said.

She kept hoping that Jim would arrive before their lunch was served, but there was no sign of him. Trent seemed quite at ease, sipping his drink and making small talk about Poole, which town he seemed to know well, and about boats and sailing. He was in the process of buying a sea-going yacht, he mentioned, as casually as if he were talking about buying a rubber dinghy. 'You must help me to christen her when she's delivered,' he said, to which Emma didn't consider it necessary to reply.

After ten minutes Jacques reappeared. 'Your lunch is ready, sir.' He smiled broadly from one to the other of them. Evidently Jacques, too, thought Emma was doing very well for herself, lunching with Trent Marston. It was too maddening for words.

She gave a final despairing glance towards the door as she stood up. Trent followed her eyes. 'Shame!' he said dryly. 'You'll have to put up with me, I'm afraid.'

They were ushered into the restaurant, which was filling up quickly, and seated at a side table. Emma drank her tomato soup with appreciation and made no attempt to play the grateful guest and sparkle with conversation. Trent had made a point of lunching with her and he must have some reason for wanting to do so. It couldn't be that her company gave him any pleasure; not after the way she had done everything she could to discourage him.

She gave up wondering, and settled down to enjoy the food. The scampi were delicious—as golden and crisp and crunchy as scampi ought to be. Trent ordered a carafe of white wine that tasted coolly of flowers. If any other man but Trent Marston had been sitting opposite it would have been a really enjoyable occasion, but it was no good pretending that she could be completely easy in his company. In spite of the good food and the wine she felt as defensive and uncomfortable as she had ever felt in her life.

For a time they ate in silence and then Trent put down his knife and fork, sipped his wine, and said, 'The bank manager was very amiable.'

So they were going to talk business, were they? That suited her.

'Good,' she said briskly. 'That's quite a change for Fairley Brothers. I suppose the company will be heavily in your debt? You can't expand in the way you're intending to without putting in a good deal of fresh capital, can you?'

He shrugged and started on his steak again. 'No problem. The reason I'm here at all is that I find myself with a good deal of spare capital to invest.'

'So what will your position be? You're buying yourself a directorship?'

'I suppose that's the way it is.'

'I see,' said Emma coolly. So much for Uncle Edward's fond hopes of making *her* a director in the future! She couldn't see herself sitting at a boardroom table discussing business with Trent Marston. She was sure they would disagree on every possible point. The present atmosphere in the firm of 'one big happy family' would surely not survive the impact of a ruthless go-getter.

She looked across the table at him—at the handsome, hard face with its flesh drawn tight over high cheekbones, the mouth chiselled yet sensual, the brooding, liquid-dark eyes—

She swallowed, searching for words. At last she managed lamely, 'For someone who's just come into the firm you seem very dedicated, Mr Marston.'

He sat back in his chair, the arrogant half-smile touching his lips. 'I *am* very dedicated. I never take on anything that doesn't hold out a promise of success.'

'And Fairley Brothers does? You do surprise me. I don't pretend to be an expert, but I know the state our finances are in—rocky.'

'Good. If you know, then that saves me from explaining the situation.'

She lifted her eyebrows. 'I—don't understand.'

'No, obviously you don't. In fact—' his voice was touched with mockery— 'you don't understand me in the least yet, do you, Emma? Briefly, I like a challenge. I like rescue work when I come across something worth rescuing. Have you been into your uncle's workshop recently?'

'Yes, of course. Why?'

'You're aware that he's been working on some completely new technology?'

'Well, yes. He said something about a breakthrough.'

'And that's all you know?'

She began to lose her temper. 'What do you expect me to know? I'm not an electronics wizard.'

Very calmly he said, 'I didn't suggest you were. Fortunately, your uncle is—a wizard, I mean. I've met quite a few original minds working in his area, but his ideas completely shattered me.'

She stared at him. 'Is he really that good? I didn't realise.'

'He's a bloody marvel,' said Trent simply, and it didn't occur to her to question his opinion. Trent Marston knew what he was talking about.

'His ideas are spreading out into all sorts of possibilities,' he went on. He leaned forward across the table towards her. 'Like it or not, Emma, we're near the beginning of the electronic revolution—we don't know a hundredth part of it yet, only that it has to happen. And as it has to happen I believe we should go all out to make sure that the instruments and machines we make are worth making, the very best of their kind.' His dark eyes were glittering as if he were seeing a vision of the future.

Suddenly she knew what Uncle Edward meant when he said that this man was dynamic. She could still remember how her father's eyes had shone like this when he talked about what he meant to do with the family firm, how he was going to take it into the 'big time.' Only his eyes were blue and clear and candid and open—not the dark, vaguely menacing eyes of the man sitting opposite her.

But in spite of her personal opinion of Trent Marston, she couldn't help a small thrill of pleasure at his words. How wonderful to think of Fairley Brothers throbbing away again, competing in the market and not slowly drifting downhill for want of a business

brain at the head of things. To think of the loyal staff
being removed from the threat of the dole queue, and
Uncle Edward's work being recognised and valued.

If Trent Marston could accomplish the miracle, then
good luck to him. But he would have to do it without
her. She didn't believe for one moment that he would
care if she decided to opt out—just so long as she
didn't try to undermine Uncle Edward's good opinion of his—Trent's—integrity. She didn't take seriously the remarks he had made back in the office
about her appearance; he was merely flattering her for
a purpose. He would manipulate people without
thinking twice about it, if it suited him. That was what
he had been doing last night in the car.

He had just said that she didn't understand him. But
she did, and she was sure she was right. He was a man
dedicated to power and success above everything else
and he would ruthlessly discard anything and anyone
who got in his way. Similarly, he would use and manipulate anyone he thought could help him. Until—
she guessed—their usefulness was at an end, when
they would be thrown on the scrap-heap with the rest.

That was her opinion of him—she thought him despicable. But a certain fair-mindedness (or was it a
faint hope that she might be wrong?) made her say,
'You seem to have formed a high opinion of Uncle
Edward. Has he, do you think, formed an equally ac-
curate opinion of you?'

He went very still, his eyes suddenly watchful.
'What are you implying?'

Her heart began to beat uncomfortably quickly, but
she had started this and she had to go on. 'I think you
know. I wonder if he would have such a good opinion
of your character if he knew the details of the way

you'd treated his daughter, which I'm sure he doesn't.
I don't believe he has any idea of what went on between you.'

For a second she saw pure anger drain the colour
from his face. Then, almost immediately, he had control of himself again.

'I think you're right,' he said very dryly. 'I'm quite
sure he doesn't know.'

'And you wouldn't like him to know?'

'I would very much prefer,' he said, weighing his
words carefully, 'to keep the details of that small episode from him, if possible.'

She nodded, pressing her lips together contemptuously. 'Yes, I can well understand *that*. And you
thought I might tell him, didn't you? That was your
reason for staging another "small episode" with me,
last night in your car? It was all carefully thought out,
wasn't it?'

He regarded her in silence for a time, his dark eyes
brooding. Then he said, 'It wasn't the only reason. But
I admit I wanted to soften that rather harsh judgment
you seem to have of me, yes.'

'And you thought your overpowering masculine
technique would do the trick?' she lashed at him.

A gleam came into his eyes. 'I've found it the
quickest and most pleasant way to make up a quarrel.'

'Well, it didn't work with me. It didn't impress me
in the least,' she said disdainfully.

'No? I thought you seemed to be enjoying it.'

'I was tired and I'd had too much to drink on an
empty stomach,' she snapped.

Trent laughed aloud, the gleam in his eye pure amusement now. He leaned over and filled up her glass. 'I must remember that for future occasions.'

Emma was saved from trying to think of a retort to that because at that moment Jim came rushing in, barging between tables, his face pink, and worry-lines engraved between his fair eyebrows. He came straight over to Emma and leaned over her chair, without a glance at Trent.

'Sweetheart, I'm so sorry about this, but I couldn't let the chance of a sale go. The bungalow out at Worth has been on the market for months and I saw a chance of hooking this bloke.' He groaned. 'He went round everywhere about twelve times and he did everything bar digging the place up to inspect the foundations. He even lifted the carpets looking for woodworm.' He ran a hand frantically through his light brown hair.

'And is he buying?' Emma enquired brightly, pointedly turning away from Trent to express interest in Jim's business deal.

'I've got him in the office now, I'll have to dash back before he changes his mind. Forgive me, darling? You've had lunch, I see—that's splendid. I'll tell Jacques to book it up to my account.'

Trent had been leaning back in his chair, listening to this exchange with interest. Now he said quietly and incisively, 'Miss Fairley happens to be lunching with me, old man. I'm afraid you missed the boat.'

Jim goggled as he saw for the first time that Trent and Emma were together. 'Oh—I—I didn't see—'

Emma took pity on him. 'Mr Marston and I have been having a working lunch, Jim, as you'd evidently been detained. Mr Marston is our new director in the firm—did you meet him at the wedding yesterday?'

'Oh, I—' Jim gulped. 'I believe I—' He pulled himself together. 'Oh well, so long as you've had lunch. Good show, then, Em. I'll ring you. Lots of sorries, again.'

He dashed out.

Trent sipped the remains of his wine. 'Now there,' he mused, 'is a man wedded to his job. I like that.'

Emma glared at him speechlessly, longing to pick up the whole carafe and throw it in his face. But at that moment Jacques approached the table.

'Mr Fairley is on the phone, Miss Fairley. 'e ask could you come and speak to him.'

She was on her feet immediately, relieved to get away from Trent, determined to make Uncle Edward's call, whatever it was, an excuse to avoid Trent Marston's company for the rest of the day.

She picked up the receiver in the small telephone room along the passage. 'Uncle Edward?'

'Emma dear—I thought I might catch you. Listen, Emma, it's rather upsetting news, I'm afraid. I've just had a call from Mexico City, from a hospital there. Poor old Joe has been taken seriously ill. It happened last night, but they've only just found out who to contact.'

She was suddenly cold all over. 'He's not—how is he?'

'It was difficult to make out.' Uncle Edward sounded desperately worried. 'Whoever it was didn't speak very good English and you know I don't understand Spanish. I think they said it was probably his heart, but I couldn't be sure. Oh, Emma dear, what should we do?'

'I must go out to him straight away,' she said without hesitation. 'I can, can't I, Uncle? He hasn't anyone of his own.'

'Yes, of course you can, Emma. But all that flying—and booking a passage—and—oh, dear, it's all so complicated.'

'Now, don't you worry, Uncle Edward, I'll cope. I'll get out there quickly somehow. I'll come home straight away, now. All right?'

'Whatever you say, my dear,' said Uncle Edward, as she put down the phone.

Trent was standing at the far end of the passage when she emerged from the telephone room. He took one look at her face and said, 'Bad news?'

'It's Joe,' she said, not stopping. 'He's very ill in hospital in Mexico City. I've got to get to him as soon as I possibly can.'

She walked quickly through the restaurant, with Trent beside her.

At the outside door into the street she paused and turned to him. 'Thanks for the lunch,' she said briefly. 'Goodbye, Mr Marston.' She just wanted to get away. Trent Marston was the last man she wanted with her just now. He wouldn't even begin to understand her feelings for Joe. To him Joe Kent would merely be the sales manager—a cog in the wheel of the business, and a rather weak cog at that.

But he was still beside her as she hurried along the crowded pavement. 'Where are you going?' he asked.

Anywhere, away from you, she almost said. But better counsel prevailed. 'To the travel agents, to see if they can book me a flight,' she told him briefly, dodging around a fat lady with two shopping bags.

She felt his hand close over her arm, stopping her by its steely strength. 'Hold on a minute,' he said, 'I've got a better idea. I have a tame travel man in London who could probably do better for you, much more rapidly, than a local firm. Let's go back to the office and I'll do some phoning straight away.'

Emma hesitated only a moment. What he said made sense; he would probably command much better service than she could. And her need to get to Joe made her private feud with Trent Marston sink into insignificance. 'Thank you,' she said.

He hadn't waited for her to agree; already they were halfway to the car park. This was a man who moved rapidly when action was necessary.

Half an hour later, in the office, he put down the phone with a satisfied grunt. 'There you are,' he said. 'Tomorrow. I couldn't get a direct flight. It's Pan-American via Houston, but it shouldn't make all that much difference in time. Okay? It means travelling up to London tonight—can you manage that?'

'Yes, of course. And—thank you, you've been very helpful.' She hadn't really been listening to his efforts on the phone, she had been too busy thinking about dear old Joe, all alone and desperately ill in a hospital thousands of miles away. 'I'll get home now and pack.'

He got to his feet. 'We may as well drive back together. You can leave your car here for Malcolm to pick up later.'

She said, passing a hand vaguely across her forehead. 'No, please, there's no need for you to come.'

He smiled faintly. 'But I have to pack too,' he said.

'You're going back to London?' she asked mechanically.

He thrust some papers into a leather briefcase, and closed the desk drawers. 'I'm coming with you, to Mexico. Tomorrow,' he said, and led her firmly out of the office.

CHAPTER FIVE

'WELCOME TO Mexico City,' said Trent, as the limousine he had hired at the airport jolted its stop-go progress, wedged into the solid, panting chaos of traffic. 'The biggest, untidiest and most fascinating city in the world.'

Emma looked out of the car window, but could see very little over the tops of the cars that surrounded them: crumbling ancient buildings between towering modern blocks, tall trees, the domes of churches, all covered by a haze of urban smog.

She looked, but she hardly registered anything. She was desperately tired, after a flight that seemed never-ending, and she was desperately worried about Joe. It had been maddening to be stuck up in an aeroplane not able to make contact, or get news of him, for all those hours, but now that the end was in sight she felt worse than ever, with a sick stomach-turning fear of what might be waiting just ahead.

She turned to Trent, sitting back urbane and composed, as he had been on the whole of the journey, and felt a quick stab of anger that he should be so unconcerned. But of course Joe was nothing to him. It would even relieve him of a few problems if Joe—if Joe— She choked, and swallowed hard.

'Is it—is it much farther to the hospital?' The car had come to a complete halt now, in the middle of a colossal traffic jam.

She was lacing her fingers together, looking pleadingly up at him, and suddenly he leaned forward and she felt the warmth and strength of his hands covering hers. 'Relax, Emma.' His voice was so kind that she hardly recognised it. 'Don't *worry*, it won't do any good and you're tired. Joe will be having the best possible attention. We are very proud of our hospitals in Mexico.'

Surprise jerked her out of her fear about Joe. 'We?' she queried, deliberately trying to let go of her worry.

'Yes—we. In case it interests you, I happen to be one quarter Mexican myself. Spanish Mexican, I mean. We can't claim descent from the Maya or the Aztecs, or any of the other colourful tribes who were around these parts in the beginning. I often wish we could. They were fascinating.'

Emma's knowledge of Mexican history was decidedly sketchy, but she had seen TV films, read bits here and there, and she had a chilling picture in her mind of bloody sacrifices to horrifying animal gods.

'Oh, but weren't they terribly cruel and inhuman?'

Trent shrugged. 'The Spanish who conquered them in the end weren't exactly men of sweetness and light either. The Aztecs fought like tigers—but the Spaniards had the guns. That's life.'

She glanced up at the hard face of the man sitting beside her—the brown skin drawn tightly over high, proud cheekbones, the chiselled lips, the imperious tilt of the dark head. Oh yes, she could see the Spanish conquistador in him. It would explain a lot. *The Spanish had the guns.* In any sort of fight he would have the guns; he would win because he had everything it took to win; he had, to an almost ridiculous degree, what his own Spanish ancestors must have had—that superb arrogance that knew it couldn't lose.

That was why she had to get away from him and stay away. Because if it came to a fight—about business matters or—or anything else, she wasn't going to win.

She said, 'So you're partly at home here?'

'Partly. My grandfather died a few years ago, but my American grandmother is still alive and well and living in Mexico. She has relatives in the U.S. who would like her to go back there, but she refuses to move. She loves the house where she's lived all these years and her garden is her pride and joy and she likes to show it off to visitors. I must take you to meet her while we're here.'

Emma murmured something non-committal. She had to admit that she had been grateful for Trent's help on the journey, and his knowledge of this huge, confusing city was taking a load from her, but she didn't intend that her gratitude should include accepting any friendly overtures from him, outside business. Obviously, it suited him now to be friends, in order to erase from her memory that scene with Lisa that she had overheard.

'So you came along with me so that you could visit your grandmother?' said Emma. She hoped that wasn't wishful thinking. If he said Yes, then she could get away from him very soon. She could book in at the hotel where Joe had been staying, could visit Joe each day, and take things from there. At least she would be rid of Trent Marston's disturbing company, and she was sure she could manage the language problem quite satisfactorily.

His narrowed dark eyes fixed themselves on her—glinting, curious. 'And what,' he said, 'is that supposed to mean?'

'Mean? What should it mean, except what I said?' Her voice sounded squeaky. When he looked at her like that it did odd things to her breathing.

He leaned back, crossing one long leg over the other. 'Merely that I find women have a way of asking leading questions.'

'Well, that wasn't one,' she said crossly. But of course it had been, and he knew it. Damn the man, he was far too perceptive for any little ploy of hers to work. He saw through it immediately. 'I merely asked you if the reason you came with me was so that you could visit your grandmother,' she said again. 'Was it?'

She looked out of the window at the mass of completely stationary cars, but she seemed to feel Trent's gaze on the back of her head.

'No,' he said.

The single, enigmatic word, and the tone he said it in, made her swing round to face him, a question in her eyes. He hadn't travelled all this way because of Joe—he didn't know Joe. He couldn't be taking up the reins of business because there wasn't any particular business going on here—only a couple of visits planned to look round a trade exhibition in the hope of making contacts. So if he hadn't come to visit his relatives, then why *had* he come? For the first time the question occurred to her, and it surprised her that she hadn't thought of it before.

Had he come because he wanted—for some unknown reason—to be with her? And if he had, what did he expect to get out of it? Posed starkly like that, the question made her heart begin to beat heavily.

Whatever the answer, he wasn't telling her. His eyes met hers, narrowed mockingly, his mouth twitched at the corners. Oh yes, he would enjoy keeping her guessing; that was all part of the power game he was so expert in. She turned away, biting her lip in annoyance.

The big car revved up. Outside the window she saw the traffic begin to move again, apparently in all directions. Trent crossed two fingers with a grin and said, 'We should make it this time. We've only a few kilometres to go now.' And the words brought back Emma's worries about Joe, blotting out everything else.

The hospital was huge, bewildering, in line with everything else she had so far seen in Mexico, but Trent seemed to know his way around and she followed him to where a pretty, dark-skinned girl sat behind a reception desk. He, naturally, spoke perfect Spanish. Emma could follow most of it if she concentrated hard. She might possibly have got by on her own here. But again she was glad that Trent was with her. Just at first, just until she felt less worked up and could cope again.

He leaned on the polished desk, conducting his enquiries without haste. The girl smiled back at him with eyes as sloe-dark as his own as she answered his queries. She was aware of him, enjoying even this briefest encounter with a man who looked as fabulous as Trent Marston.

Finally he straightened up. *'Muchas gracias, señorita. Es usted muy agradable.'*

Again that exchange of smiles. Come on, thought Emma frantically. Come *on*! Cut out all the flowery exchange of Spanish courtesies. Her anxiety was swamping her now, she felt sick with nerves and impatience.

She grabbed Trent's arm as he led her along corridors to a waiting area with comfortable seats. 'Is he all right? How is he? Did she say?'

He pushed her gently on to a bench seat and sat down beside her, putting one arm round her shoulders. 'Ssh, Emma, just wait a bit longer. There'll be someone coming soon and then we'll know.'

His arm felt strong and comforting and suddenly she wanted to lean against him and bury her head against his shoulder. But that was weak and silly. She sat up stiffly, fixing her gaze on the tiled wall opposite.

A nurse appeared, then a young doctor. Trent stood talking to them quickly in Spanish, but Emma sat where she was. She couldn't bear to listen, even if she could have understood their rapid speech. And after one look at their grave faces she couldn't even bear to look. It was going to be the worst—she knew it was. She felt cold and heavy all through her body, as if her limbs had turned to concrete.

At last Trent slipped back on to the seat beside her and she saw that the nurse and the doctor had gone. 'Emma,' said Trent gently. She made herself look up.

'He's going to be all right,' Trent said.

She stared at him with glazed eyes. She had been so sure that Joe was dead.

'You m-mean—'

'He's going to be all right,' he said again, firmly this time. 'He had a coronary attack—not too severe. Fortunately he was in the dining room of his hotel when it happened and they managed to get him in here straight away. They say he's responding well to treatment. The Sister says she will tell him that you're here, but she would much prefer you to wait until tomorrow before you see him. Unless, that is, you insist. She thinks it would be better for him not to be disturbed in any way—even pleasantly—today.'

Emma drew in a long, shaky breath. 'Whatever's best for Joe—' She began to shiver. 'I thought—I thought—' Tears welled up and ran slowly down her cheeks and she didn't know until she tasted the salt in her mouth. 'Oh dear,' she whispered, 'I was so frightened—'

'Yes,' said Trent. 'I know you were.' His arm was round her, bracing her. 'Now, come along, you don't want to stay here. You need a good meal—you hardly pecked at anything on the plane. Then a good sleep and Emma will have her usual fighting spirit back again by the morning.' He wiped her cheeks with a folded handkerchief and yanked her to her feet. She wondered dimly if he had a sister; he would have made a nice older brother.

She had to leave everything to him. Her head was aching and she felt as if she were running a slight temperature. The air was cool outside, and she couldn't stop her teeth chattering. She stayed close to Trent while he found a taxi, which deposited them at what she vaguely realised was a very plushy hotel. After a short interlude at the reception desk they were wafted silently upwards and ushered into a suite of rooms that appeared to be almost a self-contained apartment. The uniformed boy put down Emma's slim hand-travel case at the bottom of the wide bed and departed, grinning widely as he slipped a tip into his breast-pocket.

She sank down wearily into the softness of the bed. Trent leaned over her and put a hand on her fore-head. 'Into bed with you,' he said. He opened her case and rummaged in it, finally throwing a pale blue nylon nightie towards her. 'Very chic!' he grinned. 'Now get into it.'

When she didn't obey he came and towered over her. 'Do you want me to undress you?' he growled.

'Go away,' said Emma feebly.

He looked down at her without smiling. 'Another time, perhaps?' he said, and he might have been joking or he might not. In her hazy state she wasn't sure.

This was the moment to make it quite plain to him that her gratitude for his help was not going to extend to making herself available, if that was what he had in mind. She had never had a love affair, simply because she had never been in love—although Jim Bolton, and others, had had ideas in that direction from time to time. To fall for a man like Trent Marston would be about as clever as jumping into a bonfire with fire-crackers exploding round you. You'd be lucky to get out alive, and even if you did you would be scarred for life.

But at this moment she couldn't think of any way to put it so that he would get the message plain and clear, and before she managed to speak he had disappeared through a door on the other side of the room.

He came back with a glass and two white tablets. 'Take these,' he said. 'They're only aspirins, and the water should be okay at this hotel.'

He waited until she had swallowed the tablets and then turned to the door. 'I'll go and see about food. Any special preferences?'

'I'm not hungry,' she muttered, letting her head sink on to the pillow. It was beautifully cool and smooth.

Trent walked back to the bed and stood, frowning. 'Do you feel really ill, Emma? Should I get a doctor?'

'No—please. I'm—just tired—' She closed her eyes. All of a sudden she felt completely limp as if her bones had melted. This must be jet-lag, she thought, like having gas at the dentist's when everything gets indistinct.

She knew vaguely that he pulled off the jacket of her lightweight suit, she felt his hands at the fastening of her skirt, knew that he was lifting her legs on to the bed. It seemed quite a natural thing to be happening. She closed her eyes and heaved a sigh of contentment as she sank into the softness of the bed. She heard him murmur something that sounded like 'Sleep well, sweetheart,' and she felt his lips brush lightly against her forehead, but it might not have happened. She might have been dreaming by then, for almost immediately she was asleep.

Time became eclipsed. The next thing she knew she was falling, falling, clutching at nothing, trying to cry out but making no sound. She opened her eyes, choking and gasping, to find Trent patting her cheek.

'My word, you have got yourself into a state,' he observed.

She stared at him glassily. 'I—I was having a nightmare.'

'So I gathered. I thought it wise to pull you out of it.'

Emma dragged herself up, blinking. The heavy brocade curtains were closed and the bedside light switched on. It had been daylight when she went to asleep.

'What time is it?' she said.

'Time to eat,' said Trent. 'I'm famished. I waited for you to wake up. Would you like to eat in bed, or do you feel up to getting dressed?'

'I'll get up,' she said quickly. She felt very—vulnerable, lying here with him standing beside the bed. 'Can you give me ten minutes?'

He nodded. 'Not a second more. I'll ring down and tell them to bring it up.'

As soon as he had gone and the door was firmly closed Emma slithered out of bed. Her headache had gone and her face felt cool. She decided she wasn't running a temperature. She took a quick shower in the adjoining bathroom and splashed herself from the bottle of cologne on the glass shelf. There were other bottles—after-shave, bath crystals, roll-on, talc. This must be a very expensive hotel indeed; certainly not one that she could afford to patronise. She would have to get that settled with Trent as soon as possible; just for the moment, though, she would enjoy the luxury.

She went back into the bedroom. She would have to wear again the lightweight beige suit and patterned blouse she had worn for travelling, because she hadn't any other outer clothes with her. It hadn't seemed worth the hassle of taking anything heavier than hand-baggage on the plane with her, when everything she would need was already here, in Mexico, in Joe's keeping. It would still be at his hotel, she supposed, and she would go along there later on and make arrangements about it. Perhaps she could take on the room he had so abruptly had to vacate, if it hadn't already been re-let. She had the address of the hotel written in her diary, and she was sure it would be a much more modest place than this multi-star palace she was in at the present, and more within her means.

She took clean bra and briefs from her case and looked round for her blouse. It was draped carefully on a hanger, hitched on to the knob of the closet door. The jacket of the suit was hanging over the back of one chair, the skirt over another.

Her cheeks flamed. 'Shall I undress you?' Trent had said, and he must have done just that, for she had certainly been in no state to dispose so neatly of her clothes. Hazily she remembered his hands at the waistband of her skirt and then it had seemed almost natural, nothing to worry about or resist. At least he hadn't gone to the extreme of stripping her completely and putting her into the blue nylon nightie, which still lay across the bottom of the bed.

She dressed hastily, telling herself she was stupid to let it bother her. He must have had plenty of practice in undressing girls—although in different circumstances—and it wouldn't mean a thing to him. She would put it right out of her mind.

She took her make-up box from her case and did her face carefully, steadying her hand to apply beige eyeshadow, brushing on extra mascara, combing her dark gold hair back from her face and into a loose knot in her neck. She wasn't going to face Trent looking less than her best, after the way she had gone to bits in the hospital, and afterwards. She had to show him that she wasn't usually a helpless female, ready to submit to his masculine dominance.

She stood up and walked to the door that led to the adjoining room. She would begin, she decided, by insisting on moving out of this palace of a hotel into something more within the Fairley Brothers budget, and she would simply ignore any pressure he put on her to change her mind. She paused for a moment, her fingers on the door-knob. Then, with her smooth dark gold head held well up, and determined to ignore the nervous fluttering in her stomach, she opened the door.

The room she entered was vast and shadowy, lit only by a crystal chandelier lamp pulled down low over a table at one end. The table was laid immaculately for a meal, with gleaming silver and glass, and a white-coated waiter moved silently between the table and a high trolley. A mouthwatering savoury smell issued from beneath the covered dishes he was carrying.

Trent emerged from the shadows on the far side of the room and came towards her. 'Well done, only thirty seconds late.' There was a smile in his voice. He looked devastating in dark, fitting trousers and a white silk shirt. He pulled out a chair for her at the table and sat down opposite. The waiter poured the regulation amount of sparkling wine from a cradle clinking with ice into Trent's glass. He sipped it and nodded. Both their glasses were filled.

This, thought Emma, was VIP treatment indeed: a private suite in a luxury hotel; a superb meal served in one's own room; champagne on ice. A very far cry from her recent travels with Joe, but oh, how she wished she could be back with him again at a hot-dog stand in New York, as they drank Coke and laughed together to keep their spirits up.

The waiter hovered. 'Will that be all, sir?'

'Thank you, yes, we'll look after ourselves now.' Trent dismissed the waiter with a smile; a moment later the door closed silently behind him and they were alone.

Trent lifted the lid of his soup bowl and sniffed. 'Smells good—they do you very well here, I've stayed here before. I ordered a duck thing to follow the soup, I hope that meets with your approval.'

Emma murmured something inaudible. The smell of the soup was tantalising, and the 'duck thing' sounded delicious. She just wished that Trent Marston wasn't sitting on the other side of the table, smiling at her under those long, dark lashes of his.

He lifted his glass. 'Let's drink to the success of our new venture. Fairley Brothers Mark Two. Or Fairley and Marston, what do you think?'

'I prefer the first,' she said stiffly, taking a sip of her wine.

'I see. You disapprove of the Marston touch?'

She shrugged. 'I'm not interested.' She told herself she didn't care what he called the new firm. She wouldn't let him see that he had touched her on the raw with his blithe suggestion of a new name. It had been Fairley Brothers when her father was alive and it had stayed Fairley Brothers all the years since. If his name were taken out of the firm's title now it would be like losing him all over again.

'But you *are* interested in seeing the firm revitalised?'

'Of course I am, you know that.'

'That's all I wanted to know,' he said. 'Then let's drink to Fairley Brothers, if that's the name you prefer.'

Emma glanced at him suspiciously. He was being too thoughtful, too pleasant—it didn't ring true. He was manipulating her, just to get something he wanted, and she wished she knew exactly what it was, because she didn't trust him for one moment.

She lifted her glass and drank deeply of the bubbly, delightfully cool wine and felt marginally more relaxed. She would allow herself to drink just enough to quieten her nerves but be careful not to overdo it. Not with this disturbing magnetic man sitting across the table looking at her in a way that made her heart beat unevenly.

'You look very charming, Emma.' His voice was deep and velvety; his long dark lashes brushed his cheeks. 'That colour suits you.'

She put her glass down with a sharp click. 'Thank you very much,' she said briskly. She touched the cuff of her blouse. 'As a matter of fact this suit is all I have here, I must go to Joe's hotel tomorrow and take over the rest of my clothes that I left with him when I came home for Lisa's wedding at rather short notice.' She looked levelly across the table at him. 'And I thought it would be a good idea if I took over his room as well. This hotel isn't in my price range.'

His brows went up and he didn't look seductive any longer, he looked annoyed. But he said evenly, 'What's the name of Joe's hotel? Do you know where it is?'

She rummaged in her handbag, which was lying beside her chair, and found her diary. 'I wrote it down when we made the booking. I had a room booked for myself, but that was cancelled. Yes, here it is—Hotel Redonda.'

His brows lifted even further. 'Yes, I know it, it's on Insurgentes. Clean and cheap. I think we shall stay here for the moment. I have business contacts in Mexico, and a good address is essential. One of the first rules of business is to look prosperous.'

'I'm sure you're right,' she said very coolly. 'Well, you can stay here and look prosperous and I'll take over Joe's room at—'

'Oh no, you won't,' he broke in. 'I should never be able to face your uncle if I let you stay in this wicked city on your own.'

'So *that's* why you came with me?' she heard herself say. 'Because Uncle Edward put me in your charge?'

His maddeningly enigmatic smile appeared again. 'Why are you so anxious to find out my motives for coming? Would you believe me if I told you that I'd fallen madly in love with you at first sight? That when I saw you standing in the church porch in that wispy green dress, with the organ playing in the background it put all sorts of thoughts into my mind? Such as sirens sitting on rocks, their music luring hapless sailors to their doom? Would you believe that?'

'Don't be absurd,' she said crossly.

'Well then, I'll have to think up some other reason, won't I?' Trent sighed heavily. 'Meanwhile, our food's waiting.' He leaned across the table and took the lid off her soup bowl. 'There—isn't that inviting?'

It was. Thick and creamy, with croûtons floating on the top and slivers of cucumber. It was supposed to be bad for the digestion to argue and quarrel over a meal, so Emma picked up her spoon and decided to wait until it was finished before she tackled Trent about the things that were bothering her: about staying in this too-expensive hotel; about why he had come with her; most of all about his attitude towards her and what he wanted from her, which was the most puzzling of all and the thought of which made her distinctly uneasy.

She was quite determined to clear everything up—but meanwhile the meal was superb and was there to be enjoyed. 'Tell me about Mexico,' she said.

He smiled at her, that dark, devilish smile. 'Mexico,' he said, 'is a thing to be experienced, rather than talked about. Like love,' he added.

'I don't want to talk about love,' she snapped. She choked a little as she took a sip of soup and found it highly seasoned.

'Too hot for you?' he mocked, and as she met his bland gaze with fury in her eyes, he added, 'The soup, I mean, of course.'

She said with as much dignity as she could muster, 'May we please enjoy our meal without this ridiculous conversation?'

To her disgust he burst out laughing. 'Certainly, if you wish. I was merely trying to lighten the atmosphere a little.' He started on his soup. 'Now then—Mexico. Mexico,' he intoned, 'is a land full of vivid contrasts, beautiful and exotic. The capital, Mexico City, is built upon three layers of civilisation. There are picturesque villages in many different Indian variations, there is art as good as Italy and Spain—and in my biassed opinion better—and archaeology equal to ancient Greece or Egypt. There is sightseeing and entertainment for the visitor. Also a unique culinary tradition.' He paused to drink a spoonful of soup. 'As you have just found out for yourself.'

His mouth twitched, inviting her to laugh, but she wasn't going to laugh with him. She hadn't asked him to come and she had no intention of giving in tamely to his rather too obvious gestures of friendship.

'Very funny,' she said coldly.

After that they ate in silence and Emma began to feel more and more uneasy and embarrassed. She felt a growing anger, too, that he had put her in what she looked upon as a completely false position by being so cagey and enigmatic. She couldn't believe that he had brought her here with a seduction in mind. And yet she didn't know the man at all, really, and what little she did know pointed to the fact that he was a charmer and heartbreaker. He might be the kind of man who would merely think that a girl, alone with him in a strange city, was fair game.

They had reached the coffee stage now. She glanced across at him, at the dark, hard face and the sensual mouth, and remembered how brutal he could be, how he had flayed poor Lisa with his savage words. And yet he could be kind too. He had been kind at the hospital, and when he brought her back here to the hotel. And he could be devastatingly, powerfully attractive. She began to tremble deep inside as she remembered the way he had taken her in his arms and kissed her after the party, and how she had put up no resistance. Worse, how she had kissed him back with a hunger that had shocked her. He had that much physical, masculine potency that had turned her bones to water.

She felt suddenly very young and inexperienced—and afraid.

Slowly he lifted his eyes and met hers, watching him, and she was unable to look away. 'Well?' he said slowly. 'Have you made up your mind?'

'W-what do you mean?' she stammered. 'About what?'

'About me? That's what you were puzzling about, wasn't it? Me and my sinister intentions? How I was planning that we should spend the night?'

Emma felt herself go scarlet, but she kept her head high. Now was the time to learn some more about this man. 'Can you blame me? I have inside information about how you treat women, and it doesn't exactly inspire me with confidence.'

'Oh—we're back to that, are we? You mean your cousin Lisa?'

'Exactly.'

In the short pause that followed her clipped word she didn't take her eyes from his face. Not that it told her anything; he seemed to be able to make his expression completely impassive, to order.

Then he said, 'Yes, I can very well imagine what she told you about me. But try to see it from my point of view—and I think you're fair-minded enough to do so. I see you as a modern young woman, Emma, and intelligent enough to be broad-minded about such things.'

'That's a typical male argument.' She drew down her lips contemptuously. 'I'm certainly intelligent enough to recognise it.'

He shrugged. 'But at least you're not in the least like your cousin. You're not a silly child, full of fantasies about marriages made in heaven, and waiting for the one man in the world, etc., etc.'

'Is that how you see Lisa?' she said, quietly furious.

'More or less. It wouldn't have been so bad if she stopped there. But the trouble was that all that unreleased passion had been building up while she waited for her hero to put in an appearance.' He smiled grimly. 'That was extremely dangerous.'

'Rubbish!' snapped Emma. Lisa was sweet and un-awakened certainly (though she hoped Richard would have attended to that by now). But—seething with violent passion? No, never. 'I know Lisa. I've known her all our lives. She isn't like that at all.'

'How would you know?' he said dryly. 'You're not a man.'

They stared at each other, her eyes wide and unbelieving, his darkly mocking.

Then, across the room, a telephone buzzed discreetly. Trent got up to answer it as Emma felt a dreadful stab of fear. Joe—was it Joe, was he worse?

She sprang to her feet, trembling, and then, as she heard Trent's words, sank down again into her chair. 'Who did you say? Royston? Oh yes, I know. Ask Mr Royston to wait, will you? Tell him I'll be right down.' He spoke in English, as he had done to the waiter. This must be an English-speaking hotel—American, perhaps, she registered dimly, through her relief.

Trent replaced the receiver and looked towards Emma. 'An old business acquaintance of mine—an American, living and operating in Mexico. I did some telephoning while you were sleeping earlier on—making contacts. I won't ask him up here, you're too tired to meet strangers tonight. Excuse me, please, Emma, I'll be right back.'

As soon as the door closed behind him Emma jumped up again and switched on all the lights. She must find out what sort of a hotel suite this was, and from that she could guess his intentions. Because if there was only one bedroom—

There *was* only one bedroom, the one she had been asleep in earlier. She went carefully round every door and there was no trace of another. It was evidently a double suite—the one large entertaining room, the one large bedroom, the one large double bed. She stood looking at it, with its patterned cover in vaguely Mexican colours of reds and yellows and blues, and her stomach flipped over painfully.

She put a hand on the door-frame, as if she needed support, and perhaps she did. She had tried to find out Trent Marston's intentions and she had got precisely nowhere. She was stuck here with him, in this hotel suite for two. It was late at night—she glanced at her watch and realised that she had failed to put it back during the flight. It said four minutes past five. That meant it must be about eleven o'clock here; or even twelve, she wasn't sure about the time lag. She passed a hand over her forehead, and her mind felt like cotton wool.

If Trent tried to make love to her she would refuse. And if he insisted or used force she would fight him every inch of the way. She remembered how his kiss had felt and hoped she would be capable of fighting him. Then she remembered Lisa's tears and felt tears begin to gather thickly behind her own eyes. What a horrid muddle it all was!

She stood staring at the patterned bedspread and the colours blurred and ran together before her.

'Attractive, don't you think?' Trent's voice came close to her ear.

Her breath caught in her throat and she jumped in surprise, her heart hammering. He was standing behind her, both hands on her shoulders, holding her with her back to him.

'The bedspread is native work,' he remarked. 'This is an American hotel, but they support local industry, which makes for good relations all round. Were you looking longingly at the bed, thinking of getting back into it?' His voice was teasing.

'No, I wasn't,' she said sharply, 'I've had enough sleep for the moment.' She felt a fool, standing with her back to him, unable to move.

He chuckled softly. 'I wasn't really referring to sleep,' he said. 'But I mustn't put ideas into that lovely golden head of yours, must I?'

'Oh, you—you—' she gasped. 'Let me go!' It was humiliating to be held there like a prisoner.

'Of course,' Trent murmured laughingly, and touched his cheek against her hair. 'If you insist.'

Her back was pressing against the firmness of his chest. Two thin layers of silky material was all that separated their bodies. She could feel the heat from him as if they were both naked. She should have pulled away, but she was totally unable to move.

Swiftly his hands slipped from her shoulders down to her waist, brushing against her breasts under the silk of her blouse, lingering there for a fraction of a second.

He turned her round to face him and his hands linked themselves behind her waist. 'Do you insist?' he said softly. '*Do* you, Emma?'

'Yes,' she said breathlessly. 'Yes, I do.' But she didn't move.

His face was very close to hers now and he was smiling, an odd, satisfied smile. Very slowly his mouth came down to hers, his lips moving against her own, setting up an almost painful tingling along her nerves. Then, with sudden roughness, he claimed her mouth completely in a long, deeply exciting kiss that went on and on as their bodies swayed together.

Emma felt as if she were drowning. Madness—madness—was the word that kept running through her brain. But it was ecstasy as well as madness, and the blending of the two set up such a violence of desire in her that she could do nothing but respond to him, clinging to him in a kind of frenzy, glorying in the new, delicious sensations that he was deliberately setting up in her.

Then into her rocking consciousness came again the memory of his voice, cold and vicious, saying, 'Shut up, you stupid little fool, and pull yourself together. I don't give a damn for you, Lisa, I never did.'

With a little groan she pulled herself out of his arms. 'Stop it!' she cried raggedly. 'Stop it, I'm not a vulnerable teenager for you to practise your technique on!'

He recoiled and she saw that just for a moment she had pierced his guard. 'Is that what you think I was doing?' His eyes glittered like polished jet. There was no teasing smile now, no lightness in his voice. He looked as his noble Spanish ancestors must have looked if they had suffered an insult, and she felt a sudden qualm of fear and stumbled away from him.

He came after her and gripped her wrist, not brutally, but so that she couldn't pull away. 'Tell me, Emma, is that what you thought?'

'What else can I think? You won't tell me anything. I don't understand why you felt you had to come to Mexico with me, if it isn't to visit your relatives here. I could perfectly well have managed on my own. I don't understand why you booked this suite with only one bedroom. It seems obvious that you believe I'll let you make love to me. What else can I think?' she finished rather wildly.

She shook her head in desperate confusion and a strand of silky dark gold hair escaped and fell across her temple. Trent put out a hand and very gently smoothed it back, staring into her face for a long moment. Then he said, 'Come and sit down. I didn't think that talking was necessary, but I'd forgotten that women have to have everything explained.'

He drew her back into the sitting-room and pulled her down beside him into a deep crimson velvet sofa. 'Now,' he said, 'what were your questions? Ah yes, why did I come to Mexico with you? Several reasons, one of which was to take up the job where the firm's marketing manager, your friend Joe, had unfortunately to put it down. I wanted to find out exactly what the order-book looked like. Also, I had the idea that I might be of some small service to you.' He slid her an ironic smile. 'It appears that I was mistaken.'

Emma didn't rise to that one. He was trying to make her feel ungracious and put her in the wrong.

He leaned back in the corner of the sofa, long legs crossed nonchalantly, the picture of a man completely in control of himself and events. When she didn't comment he went on wryly, 'I thought we could be—friends. As I'm to be an integral part of Fairley Brothers, and as I know the firm means a lot to you, it seemed a pity for there to be bad feeling between us.'

'And you thought that by putting on your super-macho act you could win my friendship after—after what I know about you and your winning ways?' Her tone was supremely contemptuous.

He leaned towards her and slid a hand along the back of the sofa, not touching her, but close enough

for her to sense the vibrant warmth of his fingers behind her neck, setting up an answering vibration deep
inside her. But she couldn't move away.

'I think,' he said softly, his mouth close to her hair,
'that I could make you forget you ever heard that
damned conversation at the wedding reception.'

'*No!*' She shook her head violently.

He withdrew his hand and sat back again, smiling
faintly. 'We shall see. As for your other question—I
took this suite as it was the only one they had vacant.
I shall be quite comfortable sleeping in here on this
sofa. That was my intention.'

'I don't believe you,' she said flatly. 'You were
trying to—'

'Use my wonderful technique to persuade you to
share the bed with me? Oh no, my dear Emma, you're
wrong there. That was never my intention. Although
I admit to getting a little carried away just now. You're
a very lovely and desirable young woman, you know.'

'I suppose desirable young women are two a penny
to you?' she said childishly.

He laughed and shook his head. 'Much more valuable than that. Let's say—' he looked up at the ceiling
'—two for ten new pence.'

'Oh, you're intolerable!' she burst out. If she had
been standing up she would have stamped her foot.

'So you keep on telling me,' he said mildly. 'Now,
let's put an end to this fruitless conversation and have
a drink together and talk about something we can
agree upon.'

'Such as—?' she questioned coldly.

'Business, of course.' He smiled into her eyes, and
anything less businesslike than his smile she couldn't

imagine. 'That's primarily why I'm here, didn't I mention that before?'

He got up and poured out two drinks. 'This is definitely non-alcoholic,' he said, handing her a tall glass with ice clinking in its pale green contents. 'Lime and lemon—very innocuous. So that you can't harbour any more dark suspicions about my motives.'

Emma sipped her drink; it was cool and refreshing and she felt calmer straight away. 'Before we start to talk business,' she said, 'perhaps we could ring the hospital and check on Joe's condition, and what time I may visit him tomorrow?'

'Certainly, I'll do that.' He sprang to his feet and went across to the telephone. The call came through quickly and he made his enquiries, speaking in Spanish now. Emma watched his face, turned half away from her as he sat at the writing desk. Against the background of the long crimson brocade curtains, his brown skin and black hair, with the thick, upward-sweeping brows and sharply etched features, gave him a devilish look. For all his light talk since they had arrived here, he would be a dangerous man to provoke. She had witnessed his anger once and she had no intention of being the target for it herself. But neither would she allow him to dominate her.

As she listened to him, it occurred to her that she had better let him know that she understood the language herself. It might convince him that she was quite capable of looking after herself and finding her own way around.

Trent put down the receiver and looked across to her. 'Joe's improvement is being maintained and they say you may visit tomorrow morning from eleven o'clock.'

Her face lit up. 'Oh good, that's terrific.'

He was very still, watching her. 'Yes, it is, isn't it?' he said quietly, and he sounded as if he really meant it. He was full of surprises, wasn't he? Emma thought a little ungraciously. For some reason she was peeved that he should be glad about Joe's recovery. It would be so much better if she could go on hating him—better, and safer.

'Mind if I put through a personal call while I'm here?' he asked, and she said, 'No, of course not,' and started to get up to go into the bedroom and leave him to it, but he waved her back to the sofa again.

She picked up a magazine from the low table beside the sofa, but even though she wasn't looking at him she was conscious that he was sitting forward impatiently, fingers drumming on the desk.

His call came through and he relaxed back into his chair, crossing her legs. 'Juanita? Ah—at last! Where on earth have you been all day—I've tried to get you at least three times since we arrived?' A deep chuckle. 'Yes—*we*. I have a business colleague with me. Nobody you know.' Another chuckle. 'No. A lovely lady, as a matter of fact.'

Emma had a very curious feeling. Suddenly she didn't want to hear any more. Juanita was no doubt one of the desirable young women that he priced at two for ten new pence, a dark, voluptuous Spanish beauty. She could almost see her at the other end of the line, lying among vivid cushions, cradling the telephone receiver against her smooth cheek, pouting her resentment. Trent Marston would enjoy playing off one girl against another. He really was a bastard, she thought, her anger rising.

She glared at the pictures in the magazine, seeing nothing. 'Tonight? Now?' he was saying. 'Wouldn't it be—? Yes, of course I do, you know that. Right, if you say so—I'll get a taxi and be with you in no time. *Hasta luego, querida.*'

He placed the receiver, looking very pleased with life. 'Well, that's that,' he said in a satisfied way. 'You won't mind if I leave you now?'

She lifted her eyes from the magazine. 'Of course not,' she said coolly.

He went toward the door. 'I'll be back here early and we can breakfast together, then I'll take you along to the hospital.'

She shrugged. 'Don't hurry. I can manage quite well by myself.'

'Of course you can't,' he said sharply. He hesitated and came back to stand before her. 'Promise you'll wait for me.'

Emma glanced up indifferently. 'If you wish.'

He grinned. 'At least you can be sure of having the bed to yourself,' he said. 'That will be a great relief to you.'

She made no sign of having heard him and he walked to the door again. 'Goodnight, Emma,' he said.

She looked across the room at him. *'Buenas noches, señor,'* she replied with her pretty, well-practised accent.

He checked in sudden surprise, holding the door half open as if he were about to speak, and Emma had a moment of small triumph. Two can play at the game of keeping things to themselves.

But as he closed the door behind him without speaking, her pleasure evaporated. And although she was tired, she lay alone in the big bed for a long time, chasing sleep in vain.

CHAPTER SIX

FROM A long distance away Emma was aware of a burring sound. It stopped and started again three times before she managed to throw out an arm to the bedside telephone. It seemed that she had only slept for five minutes, and it was agony to drag herself awake.

'Your seven o'clock call, madam. Good morning, it's a beautiful day,' said a feminine voice, noticeably Spanish but with an American accent.

'Oh—oh, thank you,' mumbled Emma, blindly feeling the receiver back to its stand.

She turned on to her back and lay there, her eyelids heavy, her tumbled hair spread on the white pillow like a golden aureole, fighting against the temptation to turn over and go back to sleep again, knowing there were things she had to do early this morning, while she was alone, but not quite recalling what they were.

It took an enormous effort, but eventually she dragged herself out of bed and pulled back the velvet curtains, letting the morning sunlight flood into the room. A long way below traffic was already filling the wide thoroughfare; in fact, she was dimly aware that the noise hadn't ceased all night. She looked down at the tops of cars and vans and buses, streaming in both directions, separated by an avenue of trees along the centre of the street. She must be on about the tenth or eleventh floor, she reckoned, but she remembered very

A Girl Bewitched

little about arriving yesterday, and she hadn't been out of the suite since.

In the bathroom she turned the shower to *Cool* and wakened up rapidly as the water sluiced over her body. Towelling herself, she gathered her thoughts together, remembering all that had happened, dwelling happily on the heartwarming news that Joe was making good progress and that she would see him today. That was the important thing—all that mattered, really—and it was annoying how memories of Trent Marston came creeping in all the time. Still, she knew more or less where she was with him now.

She even knew why he had insisted on coming to Mexico with her. His reason was quite plain, and it was called Juanita. It had been explicit in the tone of his voice as he said *'Hasta luego, querida,'* in that intimate way. He couldn't wait to see this Juanita, could he?

Why he couldn't have told her straight out that he had a girl-friend in Mexico she couldn't imagine. Probably he had thought she would bring up the subject of Lisa again, and however he pretended to the contrary, he must feel guilty about that.

She dressed in the beige travelling suit again and put the short jacket over her blouse. She really must go to the Hotel Redonda and pick up the rest of her luggage at the earliest possible moment. She hated having to wear the same clothes day after day.

She did her make-up carefully and brushed her hair loosely. That was another thing she must do today— get a shampoo. After tossing and turning in bed last night it looked to her far from its usual shiny self.

When she was ready she went out on to the thickly-carpeted landing. 'We'll breakfast together,' she re-

membered Trent saying before he left her last night to
go to that—that girl, Juanita. He hadn't mentioned a
time, she didn't think. Well, he could look for her
when he arrived. She certainly wasn't going to sit up
here like an obedient child in the nursery, waiting for
him to come and summon her downstairs.

She found a lift and was swished down to the
ground floor. As she had guessed, the hotel was an
enormous palace of luxury. In most of the places
where she and Joe had stayed on their tour, if you
came down early in the morning you were greeted by
trailing flexes of vacuum cleaners and sleepy maids
with dusters and armsful of bed-linen. But here—although it was only just after eight o'clock—all was
fresh and sparkling. The ankle-deep carpets were
speckless and the staff was already assembling behind
the numerous polished counters in the huge lobby,
where even the palms in their tubs looked as if they
had had a morning sponge-down.

Emma wandered round until she found what she
was looking for—a street map of the city, hanging on
a side wall. She remembered that Trent had said that
the Hotel Redonda was on Insurgentes. Was that a
street, or a square, or what? Yes, here it was, just
north of the University. But it seemed to run for miles,
right across the city. She would have to enlist the help
of a taxi-driver, as soon as she could contrive to get
away from Trent. She had a firm intention of managing on her own and not relying on him for everything.

A book-and-magazine stall was open and she
bought a guide-book of the city, which would be useful when she was finding her way about alone. She
also found out where to change her supply of bank-

notes into pesos, for her small expenses. The traveller's cheques she still possessed from her tour with Joe would meet any larger demands.

The big lobby was still comparatively empty, although a few early risers were drifting about, and travel-weary new arrivals, in ones and twos, kept appearing from the direction of the huge plate-glass doors, followed by uniformed porters carrying their luggage.

Emma sat down in a corner, in a lounge seat under a tall palm, to consult her guide-book and wait for the *cambio* counter to open at nine o'clock when she could change her money and find the most likely snack-bar in the hotel to get some breakfast.

She tried to concentrate on the guide-book, but at the back of her mind, like a storm-cloud rising, was the thought that Trent Marston would be arriving soon—coming straight from his lovely girl-friend Juanita. By this time the picture of her had become so vivid to Emma that it was almost as if she had actually seen her—seen them together all night in some satin-cushioned bed. It was no good trying to tell herself that it didn't matter a hoot to her where Trent Marston spent his nights. It seemed that the man had got under her skin to such an extent that she was aware of him even when he wasn't there.

But he *was* there. She sensed his presence before she saw him, and looked up to see him striding purposefully across the wide expanse of the lobby, threading his way between the empty tables and lounge chairs, looking disgustingly handsome in a cinnamon brown suit and a cream shirt, his black hair gleaming. Immaculately groomed, impeccably shaved. Evidently he kept a supply of clothes and toilet articles at Juanita's address, whichever that was, for he had taken nothing with him when he left the hotel last night. That figured, she thought scathingly, dredging up her dislike for him.

Then, as he got nearer, he smiled and quickened his step, and her heart gave a sickening lurch and started to thud like a road-drill. It was too ridiculous for words, she told herself vexedly. She would *not* allow him to have this impact on her. It was just his physical presence, of course; charisma was the word, she supposed. 'He makes my knees go wobbly when he just looks at me,' poor Lisa had written. Oh yes, he was a danger to woman—a man to avoid.

She just had time to compose her features into a cool mask before he reached her.

'Good morning, Emma, you're up and about early. I thought I should have to come and rout you out of bed.' He slipped into a chair beside her.

'Good morning, Mr Marston,' she said, ignoring the last bit.

'Sleep well?'

'Very well, thank you.'

He gave her a sideways look. 'Good. So did I.' He was smiling his enigmatic smile—the devil! He knew what she was thinking, of course he did. He had been deliberately devious last night; knowing all the time that he intended to spend the night with Juanita, but purposely leading her on to think he had planned a big seduction scene at the hotel. Why? Just to make her feel foolish, was the only reason she could think of. It must amuse him to draw a response from a girl and then step back. That was exactly how he had treated Lisa, she reminded herself. Well, there won't be another time with me, Mr Trent Marston!

'I was just waiting to change some sterling into pesos,' she said. 'I shall need some small change for taxis and hair-dos and so on.'

He glanced at his watch. 'A bit too early yet. Let's have breakfast first. What do you feel like—rolls and coffee, or *desayuno* with all the trimmings?' His use of the Spanish word for breakfast referred her back quite deliberately to the moment they parted last night, as did the gleam in his dark eyes.

'Rolls and coffee, please,' she said, and then— speaking as deliberately as he had done—'*Quiero bolillo y café, por favor, señor.*'

He grinned. 'Very prettily said. You will now be able to tell me how much you dislike me in two languages, instead of one.'

Once again he seemed to be challenging her to smile and relax and be friends. She glanced up at him, his mouth curved into a coaxing smile, his eyes dark and laughing, and she found herself suddenly wanting to smile back, to talk to him and find out how much they had in common, if they shared the same sense of the ridiculous. She had a feeling that he could be tremendous fun to be with, and that if things had been different he would be a fascinating companion. What utter madness—this man was her enemy still, as he had been from the beginning. It was no doubt because he had spent the night with Juanita that he was so bright and breezy and pleased with himself.

She got to her feet. 'Shall we have breakfast, then?' she said coldly.

The smile left his face and he shrugged. 'As you wish,' he said, and led the way to the nearest coffee bar.

'THE DOCTOR is with Señor Kent at present,' said the pretty nurse with the soft voice. She spoke to them both, but her eyes rested on Trent. 'If you will please wait here—'

Emma's knees were weak as she sank into the seat indicated. Now that the moment had come that she had travelled thousands of miles for, she felt very nervous indeed about what she would see when she was finally allowed to walk through that closed door before her.

Trent stood beside her, frowning slightly. 'Look, Emma, would you mind if I left you here for a short time? This man Royston, who I saw briefly at the hotel yesterday—I promised to look in at his office at the first moment I could, and this seems a good time. He might be very useful to us, he has connections all over Mexico.'

Emma nodded. 'Of course I don't mind,' she said in a surprised tone that seemed to imply that she couldn't care less where he went.

He still didn't move. 'You will want to see Joe on your own, in any case, you won't want me there. And when they turn you out will you wait here for me, if you're ready first?'

'You go ahead and see your friend,' she said, picking up a magazine. 'Go along—you don't have to look after me every second as if I were an idiot child, you know.'

A look of exasperation passed over his face. 'Sometimes I wonder whether you are,' he said, and he turned on his heel and walked away down the long corridor, without a backward look.

Joe was in a small room off the long main ward. Emma's heart was thumping as the nurse took her in to him, but once she saw his face, drawn and pallid, but with the merest trace of his familiar wry grin, she forgot herself and her nervousness and leaned over the high bed to kiss his cheek gently, the tears pricking behind her eyelids. 'Joe darling, what *have* you been getting up to, since I left you on your own? How are you feeling today?'

His eyes seemed to drink in the sight of her. 'Fine,' he said. 'I'm feeling fine, love. Better for seeing you.' He spoke carefully and slowly, without moving his head, but his voice was surprisingly strong.

'I shall come every day to see you,' she promised. 'Is there anything you want, specially?'

His eyes moved to the complicated battery of life-saving apparatus, with its tubes and flasks and dials. 'Not while they have me trussed up like an oven-ready chicken!'

Emma swallowed. Even now Joe could manage to see the funny side of things. 'They'll soon take all this gear off and then you'll be a free-range bird again, you'll see. After that, all you'll have to do is take it easy and rest for a while and you'll be as good as new.'

A little frown squeezed his brows together. 'Emma, love—'

His voice seemed weaker and she knew she mustn't stay or she would tire him. 'Yes, Joe?' She leaned over the bed.

'About the work—' he whispered '—I'm so sorry— I was hoping—'

She put a hand firmly over his limp hand. 'Listen, Joe dear, there's not a thing for you to worry about. Uncle Edward has managed to find a young man to look after things and carry on until you're ready to take over again.' (And may I be forgiven for that white lie; no one was going to take anything over from Trent Marston.) 'He's quite a bright young man—definitely promising—and he's here in Mexico with me, so I'll be able to put him in the picture.'

The frown smoothed out. 'So long as you keep a hand on the reins, Emma, and see that he toes the mark—'

'I will, I promise.' What a fantastic picture *that* presented!

The door opened and a severe-looking Sister appeared. Emma rose immediately and kissed Joe. 'I'll come and see you again very soon, Joe.'

The faintest of grins touched his mouth and he closed his eyes.

As Emma reached the door the Sister murmured, speaking in Spanish, 'Wait outside, please.' She went across to the bed.

A minute or two later she joined Emma in the corridor. 'Will you please come to my office, *señorita*. Or is it *señora*?' She sat at a desk and motioned Emma to a chair opposite.

'*Señorita,*' Emma told her. 'My name is Fairley. Mr Kent is an old and valued executive in my uncle's company. He has no relatives, and that is why I am here.' She spoke in Spanish.

'Yes, I understand. Now then—he was admitted as an emergency. I understand he is staying at an hotel in Mexico, but unfortunately the clerk on duty omitted to take all the particulars at the time and Señor Kent has not been well enough to question yet. Perhaps you can help me?'

'I think so,' said Emma. 'I have a note of the hotel where he was staying and I shall go there now to do whatever is necessary.'

'Ah—good. Also, we should like to have some personal articles for him, if you will kindly supply those. Here is a list.' She handed Emma a sheet of paper.

'Certainly, I'll get them as soon as possible and bring them in to you.' Emma stood up, hesitated for a moment and then said, 'Sister—are you able to tell me what his condition is?'

The older woman said nothing for a moment and seemed to be looking Emma over—summing up whether she was sensible enough to be trusted with medical information. Then she seemed to make up her mind. 'So far, he has made slightly better progress than is usual in such cases and I thought he seemed a little better for your visit. But, you will understand, I cannot give you any promises.' Her severe expression softened a little. 'You are fond of him, yes?'

'Oh, very fond,' Emma said warmly. 'I've loved him all my life. He's a wonderful man.'

'That is good, he will have the courage to recover, then. You are English, Señorita Fairley?' and as Emma nodded, 'You speak our language very well, it is a help.'

It was indeed a help, reflected Emma, as she made her way back to the main hall of the hospital. It gave her confidence to find herself a taxi and give the address of the Hotel Redonda to the cheery driver in the big straw hat.

She was about to step inside when she saw, to her horrified surprise, that the taxi was already occupied by three men, hefty ruffians in clothes that were anything but clean, who were obviously delighted that she should join them. They slapped each other, grinning, with repeated exclamations that she didn't understand, and the largest of them, a very tough-looking customer with leather-brown skin and long, tangled black hair, leered at her, holding out a massive, grimy paw. *'Linda señorita,'* he gloated, pulling on her hand.

Emma, alarmed, tried to pull back, but he hung on to her. The other two men joined in, shouting against each other and flashing their teeth under long moustaches, in what seemed to her a very threatening way.

'Let me go, I've changed my mind,' she tried to shout over the din, but the largest man was too strong for her and she found herself dragged in into the taxi, almost on to his knees, much to the vocal delight of his companions.

Emma was almost weeping now; pictures of kidnaps floated through her fevered imagination, of herself being borne away to some remote desert hideout, to languish for months. In desperation she stuck her head out of the taxi window, just as it was moving into the middle of the traffic, and yelled, 'Help—I want to get out!' In English. Her Spanish had deserted her at this moment of trauma.

Abruptly the door was wrenched open and Trent's voice, shouted above the rest of the din, barked, 'What the bloody hell's going on here?' He said something in Spanish to the man who was holding her, who immediately released his grasp. Trent's arm was round Emma, painfully tight. 'Jump,' he ordered, as the taxi came to a halt in the middle of a traffic jam.

She jumped into his arms and he steered her through the mass of cars, which one and all retaliated by honking their horns madly, but somehow they made it to the side of the wide boulevard.

Emma's head was spinning wildly as Trent pushed her down on to a seat under a tree. He put an arm round her and held her gently but firmly, saying nothing, until she opened her eyes and blinked up at him dazedly.

'Well,' he said in a conversational tone, 'and what exactly were you supposed to be doing?'

She gulped and dabbed her eyes. 'They asked me at the hospital to f-fetch some things for Joe and I was going to his hotel to get them.' Suddenly she shivered violently, although the sun, beating down on the grass, was blisteringly hot. 'I—I don't know what happened. This cab came along and it seemed to be a cruising taxi, so I stopped it and then—these men were all inside and—and they frightened me, rather.'

To her annoyance Trent laughed aloud, but not unkindly. 'Silly child! You're not in England now, you know, with one-taxi-one-passenger. That was a *pesero* you hailed. They cram in as many passengers as they can at one time and take them where they want to go— mostly along the big main routes. I don't suppose for a moment the men intended to frighten you, they were just being very vocal in their admiration.' He chuckled. 'Mexican men are like that; they appreciate a pretty girl and have no inhibitions about saying so. I'm sure you weren't in any danger from them.'

'I'll take your word for that,' she said doubtfully, looking up at him. The eyes that met hers were narrowed whimsically, his hair shone like ebony in the dappled sunshine under the tree. His lips were parted slightly, showing strong, well-cared-for teeth. 'Anyway, thank you for rescuing me,' she said in a small voice. 'I was very glad to see you.'

His eyes held hers. 'And that,' he said huskily, 'is the first time you've admitted it. We're making progress.'

For a long moment their eyes were locked. Emma was acutely aware of his arm around her shoulders, of the closeness of his body to hers on the wooden seat, of the smell of the cologne he used, mingled with the dried-up grass all around them. Suddenly she was oblivious to the noise and hustle of the traffic. She felt weak with longing to rest her head against the hardness of his chest, under its silky cream shirt. She wished he hadn't been so kind and understanding. If he had bawled her out for her admittedly foolish action in rushing off on her own in a huge, unfamiliar city, she could have gone on resenting and disliking him. But now—

He stood up and held out both hands. 'Are you fit yet? Because if you are, I think we should both go along to Joe's hotel. I expect he left all the papers and notes relating to your tour together, and I'd like to get my hands on them. I've arranged to meet Roy Royston for lunch. I think we may be on to something really good there, and I want to be completely genned up so that we can begin to talk business. There'll be time to go through everything with you before lunch, if we get a move on.'

He took her hands and Emma allowed him to pull her to her feet. The shakiness had gone and for some reason she felt a sudden surge of energy. 'You mean— you really want me to help you?'

'Well, of course,' he said. 'I can't do without you, can I? So I'm afraid, Emma, you're stuck with me, like it or not. That is, if you care about Fairley Brothers' revival.'

He tucked his arm comfortably through hers as they set off across the grass in the direction of the hospital. 'I've got a taxi waiting,' he told her. 'A real taxi, the kind you find at the hotels, not one of your black-and-white-*peseros*.' He grinned down at her. 'You'll only have one quarter of a blatantly admiring Mexican to put up with this time. Think you can bear it?'

Walking close beside him in the sunlight, with the roar and scream of the traffic around them, Emma forgot about Lisa, forgot about Juanita, forgot about everything but the man beside her, his devastating masculine attraction and her entirely feminine response to it.

She gave him a little upward smile under her tawny lashes. 'I'll try,' she said, and a thrill ran through her as he squeezed her arm tight, and drew her against him.

'Partners?' he said, and for the first time she felt that it was possible. If she could believe what he said— that his only interest in her was because she was in Uncle Edward's confidence and because she and Joe had been working closely together—then she couldn't refuse. She thought fleetingly of Lisa. Lisa would be hurt and disappointed to learn that Emma had gone back on her word and was actively working with Trent Marston. But Lisa was married now; she had her own life to make with Richard. What had happened between her and Trent couldn't be allowed to put at risk the survival of the family firm because of bad feeling between one of the family and its newest recruit and probable saviour.

They had reached the hospital entrance again now, and Trent led her to a salmon-coloured car that was waiting in the taxi-rank. He opened the door for her and gave the address of the Hotel Redonda to the driver.

As they drove out of the wide gateway he turned to Emma. 'Partners?' he said again.

She nodded, with a flash of her quirky little smile. 'Partners,' she said, with a sigh. 'As you say, I've got to put up with you.'

'WE'VE GOT a little time before Royston is due to arrive,' said Trent, glancing at his watch as he spread the papers from Joe's briefcase out on the low coffee table beside the sofa in their hotel suite.

Emma said, 'I must change out of these clothes and get into something cool and fresh before I can put my mind to anything. I won't be long.'

'Okay, hurry up.' He settled himself on the sofa and picked up the top sheaf of papers.

Emma retired to the bedroom, where Trent had carried her case, and closed the door. At first the manageress of the Hotel Redonda—a swarthy, hard-faced woman with beady eyes and black hair scraped up on top of her head—had looked suspiciously at Emma when she explained what she had come for. But when Trent stepped forward, drawing out his notecase and turning one of his charismatic smiles on the woman, there was no more delay, and after that all was sweetness and light.

As the taxi-driver piled the suitcases into the cab Trent looked up at the facade of the Hotel Redonda, at the shabby, cracking plaster, the broken gold lettering, the dusty windows. He said, 'You wouldn't really have been happy here on your own, would you?'

Emma followed his look. 'I'd have got by,' she said hardily.

'Well, you don't have to,' said Trent, his hand at her arm as they got into the taxi. 'A truce has been declared, and we're both fighting on the same side now, remember?'

She looked out of the window as the taxi began to move, and suddenly the sun penetrated the thin smoggy haze that seemed always to hover over the city, and everything was bathed in a clean, clear light—the little market stalls that cropped up at random on the wide pavements; the Indian woman peddling handicrafts; the boy flashing white teeth and holding a huge bunch of coloured balloons that floated up against the pale blue sky; there was even an oldish man carrying a portable organ strapped to his back and grinding out an old-fashioned waltz tune.

Emma turned to Trent, her face alive with interest. 'What a fascinating city this is,' she said.

'A city of contrasts,' he said with a sort of warm pride in his voice. 'Not all that long ago—less than a couple of hundred years—it was a small, beautiful town of palaces and churches and noble buildings all centred round the Zocalo—that's the central square where the Cathedral is, we passed it on our way earlier—and then it started to grow and grow, more or less haphazardly. So now it's a city of surprises. I love it,' he added, 'you never know what's round the next corner.'

Emma turned her head and looked at his dark, handsome face, his eyes glittering now with pleasure. Yes, she had thought, you *would* like it. Mexico City is like you—full of surprises. Confusing. Unexpected. Vital.

Now, as she pulled off the beige suit she had worn since she arrived and opened the suitcase that Trent had dumped on the bed, she kept remembering the colourful scene they had passed through and she was gripped by a pleasant sense of excitement. Provided that Joe's condition continued to improve, it would be fascinating to spend a little time in this city that was so different from any other city she had visited in her travels with Joe. And now that she and Trent had somehow managed to put their relationship firmly on the basis of a friendly business co-operation, she didn't have to worry about that, either. She hummed one of the waltz tunes the organ-grinder had been playing and took out a dress from her case—a cotton dress in spring green with a little swingy jacket. It was mercifully uncrushed, and when she had touched up her make-up and brushed her hair she looked at herself in the mirror with the kind of satisfaction usually reserved for the times she had been going out for the evening with a new boy-friend.

But this was very different. This was the new Emma Fairley, the young businesswoman, representing her family firm, partnering the dynamic Trent Marston. Nothing at all to do with romance!

Trent got to his feet as she opened the bedroom door and his eyes passed over her with appreciation. 'My, my,' he smiled. 'Very taking—you look as crisp as a fresh lettuce leaf. Now, come along and put me in the picture.'

He put a casual arm round her shoulder, leading her to the sofa where he had been sitting. When they reached it he seemed to be about to pull her down beside him. Then he gave a wry little grin and pushed her towards a chair on the other side of the table. 'If we're going to talk business,' he said, 'I think you'd better be at a safe distance. Looking as tempting as you do at present you do terrible things to my concentration.'

Emma could have returned the compliment truthfully, for her skin was tingling where his fingers had touched it. Instead, she sat down without looking at him and said coolly, 'Shall we go through the papers, then?'

There was a short silence and still she wouldn't meet his eyes. 'Don't you enjoy being told you're desirable, then?'

'In the right time and place—yes.' She shuffled through the pile of papers busily.

Another pause. Then, 'Later, perhaps?' he said with a smile in his voice.

Emma did raise her eyes then. 'Look,' she said quite forcefully, 'you suggested a business partnership and I agreed. I didn't have a casual flirtation in mind.'

His smile disappeared and the expression in the eyes that met hers and held them made her shiver inside. 'Neither had I, Emma,' he said slowly, seriously. 'Believe me, neither did I.'

He shook his shoulders, almost as if he were shaking off something that troubled him, and picked up the top sheet from the pile of papers on the table. It was a list that she had typed out for Joe in Houston. 'I'm not quite clear about the specifications here—and here—' He pointed with a gold pencil.

Emma took the sheet and stared down at it, trying desperately to concentrate. Being Trent Marston's business partner was going to be full of pitfalls that she had to avoid. If only she could understand him—even partly! But he was like a book written in a foreign language that you were only vaguely familiar with. You read a sentence and thought you had grasped its meaning and then a couple of sentences on you realised that you'd been entirely wrong. That was the effect Trent Marston had on her. A maddening man!

But for the next hour he was all the top executive— asking questions, making notes, sitting silent for minutes at a time, deep in thought. Finally he closed the order book, looking rather grim. 'It seems rather worse than I imagined.'

Emma nodded, biting her lip. 'I know. We didn't do much good on that tour.' She studied his face and learned precisely nothing. She said, 'Are you wondering if you've backed the wrong horse?' How would she feel if he decided it was too late to save the firm, and just walked out? The cold emptiness she felt was quite shocking. She hadn't realised until that moment quite how much the new prosperity he had promised meant to her. 'Are you thinking of pulling out?'

'Pulling out?' The amazement in his face reassured her. 'Good God, no, that's the last thing I'd do. I like a challenge. If things come too easily I lose interest.' His dark eyes rested on her lazily, as if he were memorising the contours of her face. 'Haven't you noticed, Emma?'

Her inside stirred in a way she was becoming familiar with and she turned her head quickly. She would *not* gave him the satisfaction of seeing just how easily he could disturb her.

The telephone buzzed and Trent reached for it. 'Royston's here,' he told her, a moment or two later. 'Shall we go down?' He grinned. 'You can practise your sales technique on him, I'm sure he'll appreciate it.'

Emma gave him a look that was supposed to be withering and swept out before him to the lift, the

green organdie dress rustling softly against her slim
legs, her dark gold hair bouncing defiantly on her
neck.

The meeting was a success from the start. Emma
took to Roy Royston—a stocky, middle-aged man with
keen eyes and prematurely white hair above a brown,
clever face. His frank, open manner was a relief, after the puzzle that was Trent Marston.

It seemed, however, that Trent reserved his de-
viousness for her alone, for over lunch in one of the
hotel's big restaurants, nobody could have been more
straightforward and forthcoming.

When the social preliminaries were over it was a
working lunch and all the talk was of the new electronic device that Uncle Edward had been working on
and which was, apparently, almost ready to go into
production.

Emma said very little, although Roy Royston now
and again drew her into the conversation with little
questions about the history of the firm and about
Uncle Edward—questions which she could answer
clearly and with undisguised warmth and assurance.
But Trent made it clear that she had been away from
home recently and hadn't had time to catch up yet on
new developments (it amused her that he said it as if
she was poised to become an electronics expert at any
moment), so she was able to relax and watch the two
men and listen to the cut and thrust of their conversation.

And as she watched Trent she found herself reluctantly comparing the way he operated—quietly confident and enthusiastic—with Joe's much more
unobtrusive manner. Trent wasn't showy and flamboyant—quite the contrary—but he wore confidence
like a second skin, and she could see that Royston, the

older man, thought highly of his opinion. They were two of a kind, she thought, and quite outside her league.

After lunch, the talk continued over drinks and coffee until Royston took his leave to keep another appointment.

'Au revoir, Miss Fairley.' He took her hand in both his and beamed at her. 'It's been a privilege meeting you and I'll sure look forward to doing business with both of you. 'We'll meet up again, Trent, before you leave Mexico.'

Trent walked with him to the entrance to the lounge where they had taken coffee, and then came back and dropped into the seat next to Emma. 'That went well,' he said with satisfaction. 'It's a good start. I think he'll take the agency, and he supplies some of the largest companies in Mexico.' He turned and smiled at her. 'Well done, Emma.'

'I didn't do anything,' she said.

'You didn't have to. Just being there was enough for the present.'

'It wasn't enough for me,' she said rather crossly. 'If I'm to be involved with you in this new venture I'll have to learn something about it. Do you think I could—have I got the intelligence?'

He laughed aloud and covered her hands with his, giving them a hard squeeze. 'Oh, Emma, Emma, you undervalue yourself. Of course you could learn— you're not just a pretty face. We're not supposed to be scientists; we're the marketing team. Edward thinks up the ideas, and we make sure they're produced and that everyone knows about it.' His eyes were shining. 'I can teach you all I know myself in a few hours—we'll start tomorrow. We'll make a splendid team.' He tossed off the remainder of his drink. 'What's the joke?'

She was smiling to herself. 'I was just remembering what Joe said this morning, when I told him about you. He told me I was to keep a tight hold on the reins and make you toe the mark.'

'Joe sounds a perceptive sort of bloke and I think he had something there.' His gaze travelled slowly over her, lingering on the low neckline of her dress, where the pleated white collar plunged demurely to the shadowy cleft between her firm young breasts. 'But I must warn you,' he drawled, and there were little devils dancing in his eyes, 'that it may prove more difficult than Joe—or you—imagines, to make me toe the line.'

'Oh!' she gasped, the heat rising to her cheeks. 'You're deliberately misunderstanding. I wish you wouldn't—wouldn't—'

'Wouldn't what?' he enquired smoothly. 'Wouldn't pay you the odd compliment? It's inevitable, Emma, business partners or not. I'm a man and you're a woman, and that's the way it is.'

'You're infuriating,' she snapped. 'I don't know what you're trying to do, but—'

'I'd have thought it was plain enough by this time,' he smiled, 'but if you require a statement of intent, then I'm trying to make you fall in love with me.'

'Well, you won't succeed,' she flung at him. 'I wouldn't fall for you if you were the last—'

'—the last man on earth?' he cut in. 'Not very original, Emma, for a quick mind such as yours! Now come along, let's end this sparring match, stimulating though it is. I suggest we take Joe's things along to the hospital and get an up-to-date report on him. After that we'll put a call through to Edward and give him all the news.'

'I was going to write,' she began. International telephone calls were expensive and she and Joe had been economising for so long that it was second nature to avoid them. But Trent Marston wouldn't know what the word economy meant.

'You can write later,' he told her, a trifle impatiently. 'Now, let's get along. When we've been to the hospital we'll take a look in at this Trades Exhibition that you planned to visit with Joe. After that I'll treat you to a slap-up dinner to celebrate our success with Royston. Oh, and by the way, bring a coat or a wrap of some sort with you. It can get chilly in the evenings in Mexico City. We're about a mile and a half high, did you know that?'

'No, I didn't know,' she said shortly. She was smarting a little from the way he seemed to think he could give her orders, and decide what they should do, without consulting her. And even here there was no consistency about him. Sometimes he treated her as a partner and an equal, and sometimes as if she were a difficult child, who had to be either humoured or disciplined and shown who was master.

The annoying thing was that his way was usually proved to be right. What remained of the afternoon passed without a hitch. At the hospital they were told that Joe's condition was satisfactory and that she could see him again tomorrow. Later, back at the hotel, Trent put through a call to Uncle Edward and she was able to reassure him that all was going well.

After that they went by Metro across the city to the large building where the Trades Exhibition was being held, and wandered among the hundreds of stands showing everything from cabinets containing nuts and bolts, to the most intricate of modern developments in technology.

Trent missed nothing. He asked questions and chatted to the exhibitors, and examined the displays on every stand with the close scrutiny of a biologist who has just come across some new form of life. He was still brimming over with curiosity and enthusiasm when Emma's feet were aching and she was longing to sit down with a long, cool drink.

At last she could bear it no longer. 'Don't they provide seats in this place?' she moaned. 'I shall flop on the floor at any moment!'

He turned to her immediately. 'You poor sweet,' he said, and his voice was not mocking or teasing or flirtatious. It was—incredibly—tender and concerned. 'I've worn you out. What would you like to do? Shall we go back to the hotel and you can have a rest and a shower before dinner?'

'Sounds lovely,' sighed Emma, bemused by his quick change of approach. Bemused—and weakened. She wanted to go on disliking him, but he was making it difficult. Tough and tender—the mixture was a dangerous one.

Back in the hotel suite he said, 'Have a good rest while I do some telephoning. Let me know when you feel up to going out to dinner.'

Emma took a shower, put on a light wrap and lay on the bed. She wasn't sleepy; on the contrary she felt wide awake. She could hear Trent's voice in the next room, although she couldn't hear the words. She wondered if he was talking to Juanita.

And what did it matter to her if he was? Why did it give her a sick feeling inside to think of him with other women? They had agreed that they were simply business partners. They were going to work together on the exciting project of getting Fairley Brothers back on its feet again—and into the big time, if she had learned anything about Trent Marston. Already she had a good idea that he was what they call a money wizard. Just as long as it was only money that he bewitched, she thought, trying to see the funny side of this unsettled, yearning feeling she had, just listening to his deep voice on the other side of the door.

Suddenly she felt restless and couldn't lie here any longer. She got up and dressed in one of the unpretentious little cocktail dresses she had worn when she and Joe dined together at one of their modestly-priced hotels. By the time she had done her face and her hair Trent seemed to have finished his telephoning, and she went into the next room to find him stretched out on the sofa, blowing wreaths of smoke from a small cigar up towards the ceiling.

'Ready?' He swung his legs round and stood up. 'You look very nice, Emma.' It was casually said, just a run-of-the-mill compliment, and he didn't come near her or touch her as they went out together to the lift. He would still be thinking of Juanita, of course.

'The famous Zona Rosa is only a few minutes' walk away,' Trent said as they came out into the cool of the evening. 'We can take our pick of restaurants there; I've heard there are about four hundred of 'em all in quite a small area, to say nothing of the bars and shops and boutiques. The Zona Rosa is the swinging side of Mexico City. What do you fancy to eat?'

They turned into a brightly-lit street with blazing shop windows and smoothly-running cars and an air of subtle excitement, and Emma said, 'Goodness, I don't know—I leave it to you.'

'Then we'll find a nice safe American-style steak and salad,' Trent said, inspecting the signs outside the restaurants as they passed by. 'I won't suggest you go in for the fiery stuff. Anyway, unless you know the right places to go it's not easy to find really superb Mexican cooking, the kind that Mexicans give the ultimate praise to when they say it makes "suck your fingers."'

Emma gave a mock shudder. 'I can't take anything really hot,' she said, and Trent laughed. 'Some day,' he said, 'I intend to find out if Emma Fairley is really as cool as she pretends to be.'

He was fooling, of course, making the kind of remark that a man is supposed to make when he takes a girl out to dinner, but Emma felt an odd little tug deep down inside her that warned, 'Be careful.'

But as the evening wore on she found herself relaxing with Trent, feeling easy in his company for the very first time. They ate juicy steaks with crisp, colorful salads at a small, intimate restaurant, and Trent ordered a bubbly wine that tasted of flowers. Afterwards there was a mouthwatering creamy concoction of unfamiliar fruits, and *café con leche*, and as they sat back, comfortably replete, Emma forgot that the man beside her, so handsome and assured and—what was the word?—so debonair—was someone that she needed constantly to be on her guard with. She giggled at his wry remarks as if they were old friends who had known each other for years.

They went out into the street again, crowded now with strollers and window-shoppers, with beautiful people unloading into the restaurants from gleaming, fabulous cars, with all the trappings of affluence and high living.

Trent stood looking around for a moment, his face serious. 'And yet,' he mused as they turned to walk back the short distance to their hotel, 'within a stone's-throw of all this there are squalid dwellings; poor people who would live a whole day on the food we left on the table. They come streaming into the cities when they can't earn a living on the land. All the big cities are bulging at the seams. They try to get into America, too. They wade across the Rio Grande, believe it or not, and most of them are discovered and turned back by the Texan Border Patrol. I've seen it happening—it's pathetic.'

Emma was silent, walking beside him, keeping in step. Was this the big-business tycoon who lived to make money, who took his women where he found them and tossed them aside when he was tired of them? She felt as if she hadn't known him at all.

'Mexico is a wonderful country,' he went on quietly, 'and with vast natural resources. Some day she'll solve her problems, but just now one feels oneself longing to help these poor people to get going to earn their own livings, to stand on their own two feet, as the saying goes.'

Emma linked her arm with his. 'You like mending things that are not working properly, don't you?' she said.

She felt him give a little start of surprise and thought that he had forgotten all about her for the moment. Then he grinned down at her. 'Perceptive lady,' he said. 'You read me like a book.'

She shook her head. 'Never—not a single line. You're a book written in a foreign language.'

Back at the hotel they went up in the lift. Trent paused at the door of the suite, his key in the lock. 'Are you going to invite me in for a goodnight drink?'

Emma looked up into his eyes, and that was a mistake, for her stomach flipped over and her heart began to race at what she thought she saw there.

She took refuge in flippancy. 'It's your suite, not mine.'

He was standing very still, very close. She was terribly conscious of his hard, muscular man's body beneath the thin texture of his suit. 'By the way,' she gabbled, her voice two tones higher than usual, 'we haven't discussed who's paying for this luxury pad. It's way out of my price range.'

He turned the key and held the door open for her. 'It's on the firm,' he said.

He closed the door behind them. Inside, the lights were dim, the big, luxurious room smelled faintly of cigar smoke, the air-conditioning hummed very softly, like a sleepy cat.

'Let me take your coat,' Trent said, and his voice sounded strained. Emma felt his hands resting on her shoulders, and the touch of them burned all through her. Her knees were trembling. She wanted to move across the room, to laugh and say something casual and ordinary, but she couldn't move.

Trent tossed her coat over the back of a chair. He, too, seemed reluctant to move.

They looked at each other in the shaded room. Then he said, 'Emma?' in a husky voice, and held out his arms.

Like a girl in a trance, she went straight into them.

CHAPTER SEVEN

IT WAS no calculated attempt at seduction. It was an immediate, driving need for them both. Trent crushed her against him as if he were a drowning man clinging to someone who could save his life. Emma gasped for breath as she was pressed against the hard, muscular length of his body.

'Oh, Emma, my darling girl, you're so lovely—so tempting. I want you—every little bit of you—' His voice was muffled against her hair and his breath came warm and quick on her cheek. She was drowning too, and helpless to resist, as a drugged sweetness crept through her senses.

Her head tilted back as his mouth came down on hers in a long, exciting kiss, and her lips parted hungrily to his. She had never been kissed like this before, but it seemed the most natural thing in the world to wind her arms tightly round his neck, her fingers digging convulsively into the hair there, crisp and resilient to her touch. She felt warm, yielding, deliciously lost in the sensations he was arousing in her as his hands moved down her body, and she knew that she had been waiting for this ever since he kissed her that night of the wedding. Waiting and longing for it, even while she told herself she was hating him.

She gave a little moan as he picked her up easily in his arms and carried her to the sofa. For a heart-stopping moment she felt his weight on her, then he rolled away and knelt on the carpet, his face close to hers.

'I don't think,' he said in an odd, strangled voice, 'that I can stay here any longer unless you let me make love to you.' His eyes were burning into hers, the lids lowered, heavy. 'Will you, Emma?'

She lifted herself on to one elbow and stared dazedly at him, shocked into a sudden realisation of what she was doing. If Trent had said nothing, if he had taken her then and there, she knew she would have given herself to him without thought, in a white-hot turmoil of pure feeling.

But he had spoken and the spell was broken. He had given her a choice, and instinctively she drew back from the brink, her lips quivering.

'No,' she gasped, 'we must be mad! This isn't really what we want. It's just the wine and the s-surroundings.' She looked vaguely round the intimately-lit, softly-cushioned room. 'No, Trent,' she said, and she realised with a small shock that it was the first time she had spoken his name. 'Don't let's spoil everything.'

He got slowly to his feet and she could see his body trembling and knew how hard he was struggling for control. '*Would* it spoil everything?' he said.

'Oh yes, of course it would.' She sat up, pulling her dress straight with shaking hands. 'You know it would. Partners, we agreed. Business partners.'

'That doesn't rule out any other sort of partnership as well.' He moved to take her in his arms again, but she drew away. 'Of *course* it does, don't you see?'

It would complicate everything. Not for him perhaps—it would mean very little to him. But she knew now that this man had the power to shake her world into fragments if she once let him love her. He would be an obsession with her, just as he had been with Lisa. And not for the world would she let a man like Trent—a man who had behaved so heartlessly once, and would no doubt do so again if it suited him—not for the world would she let such a man come between herself and Lisa and spoil a lifetime of trust and affection.

He was staring down at her almost angrily now. 'No,' he said roughly. 'I *don't* see. I believe you want it just as much as I do.'

Emma gave a little shrug. The memory of what he had done to Lisa had acted like a douche of icy water on her. 'Possibly,' she agreed in a small, controlled voice. 'You're a very attractive man, as you well know. We both got carried away, but we can see that it doesn't happen again.'

He frowned down on her. 'Is that really what you want, Emma?'

'Yes,' she said, almost serenely. 'That's what I want. We can get on very well as business partners, I think we've proved that to-day. Let's leave it that way.'

For a long moment Trent stood quite still. Then he shrugged and walked across the room to pour himself a drink. He tossed it off with his back to her, then he half-turned, not looking at her, and said coldly, 'Right. If I'm not wanted here I'll take myself off. We'll meet again in the morning, Emma, when we can resume our *business* partnership.' His lips curled into a sneer and the friendliness that had seemed to be growing between them all day had disappeared. He was bitterly, coldly angry, she could see that. It was probably better that way, she told herself bleakly. If he hated her for rejecting him then she might be able to throw off the subtle spell he had been casting on her. He wasn't a man who would take kindly to being refused.

He walked to the door. 'Goodnight, Emma, I'll remove myself from your presence.'

The irony in his voice stung her and the words seemed to speak themselves. 'To Juanita?' she heard herself say, in a high voice that she hardly recognised.

'Who else should I go to?' he said quietly, and went out and closed the door.

TRENT WAS back next morning before Emma had finished dressing. He tapped at the bedroom door, calling out cheerfully, 'Good morning, Emma, ready for breakfast?' just as if they had parted last night on the friendliest terms. She sat before the dressing-table mirror, trying to cover up the ravages of another almost sleepless night, and felt like screaming 'Go away' at him. Instead, she managed to compose her voice and replied, 'I won't be long. Five minutes.' He had evidently decided to take her at her word and keep their relationship on a strictly business footing. Well, that was what she wanted, wasn't it? But there were so many questions that remained to be answered. For one thing she couldn't go on living in this luxury hotel, allowing him to pay the bill, even if he said it was 'on the firm'. Fairley Brothers simply couldn't rise to this sort of hotel and Trent Marston hadn't yet got complete control of the firm, so that he and nobody else could call the tune.

On the other hand she couldn't possibly leave Mexico until Joe was well and truly on the mend. She had come here to stay near Joe and that was what she was going to do. So—she and Mr Trent Marston must have a talk and get things sorted out, she resolved, plastering on far too much eyeshadow and removing it inexpertly with a tissue soaked in lotion.

She glared at herself in the mirror. 'You look a wreck,' she told herself, wondering when she was going to get a good night's sleep. Last night, after Trent had left, had been a disaster. She had sat for ages in front of a blood-and-thunder film on the TV, not taking in any of it, trying to forget the scene that had just taken place between Trent and herself. Trying not to think of him with Juanita; trying to pretend she didn't care. When, finally, she had gone to bed it was to lie sleepless for hours, wallowing in a confusion of thoughts and feelings that horrified and disturbed her.

'Five minutes up,' came Trent's voice cheerfully. 'I'm coming in.'

The door opened and he appeared, looking as well-groomed and pleased with himself as he had looked the previous morning. If he and Juanita had spent a riotous night, Emma thought sourly, then he showed remarkably little evidence of it.

Emma was wearing a little green suit this morning, one that had stood her in good stead on her travels with Joe. It had white revers and a short, swingy top, and she had always felt pleasantly like a brisk young business woman in it. She didn't feel in the least brisk this morning, but Trent looked her over approvingly as he stood leaning against the doorpost. '*Very* nice,' he grinned. 'Most appropriate. I approve of my new business partner's taste in dress.'

'Thank you,' she said coolly, getting to her feet with a sidelong glance in the mirror to check on her eyeshadow.

As they went out to the lift Trent said, 'When we've had breakfast I'd like you to come back up here, if you will, please, and pack your things. I think it's time we moved on.'

She flicked a suspicious glance at him as the lift sucked them downwards. 'Move on? Where to?'

He raised dark brows. 'I'm not thinking of abducting you, if that's what's worrying you. I can take a firm "No" from a girl as gracefully as the next man, I hope.'

'Oh, I'm sure you can,' she said airily. 'I expect you have a long list of names in your little book, lined up in reserve.'

He burst out laughing, swinging the lift gates closed as they reached the ground floor. 'Does that bother you? You wouldn't by any chance be jealous?'

'Jealous? Of you? You're joking, of course.'

'No, I suppose you wouldn't,' he murmured thoughtfully as they walked across the thick carpet to the snack-bar where they had breakfasted yesterday. 'One is only jealous when one is in love—or so they tell me. Now I,' he continued conversationally, pulling out one of the red leather chairs for her, 'could be very, very jealous of you, Emma. So you can draw your own conclusions.' He pushed the chair in again with a little jerk as she sat down. 'What do you fancy for breakfast this morning? Coffee and rolls again? Or something more substantial?'

The abrupt change of subject told her that he was out to tease and bait her this morning, and the awful thing was that she had no defence ready. She hadn't expected him to behave like this after what had happened last night. She had thought he would be distant and cold. She supposed it was all part of this maddening man's technique. He took a malicious delight in surprising people.

'Just coffee and rolls, please,' she said. 'And I'd like my coffee black.'

He gave her a mocking smile as he turned away to the counter. 'Did madam have a bad night, then?'

The coffee was a life-saver. After the first few sips of the rich, dark, aromatic-smelling liquid Emma felt almost herself again, and ready to cope. 'You haven't told me where you propose to take me to,' she said.

'To my grandmother's home, up in Las Lomas, the hills beyond Chapultepec. My grandmother is looking forward to meeting you and she'll be delighted to put you up so that you can have a base here, and visit the hospital easily and frequently, as I'm sure you want to. For myself, I'll have to return to England in a day or two and I wouldn't like the idea of you staying alone in a hotel, Emma. I'm sure your uncle wouldn't either.'

'I should be—' she began. She wanted to tell him that she resented being packaged and moved around and having her mind made up for her, but it would have seemed childish and petulant if he really were concerned for her well-being and safety. It was the kind of thoughtfulness she would have recognised in Joe, but she had to admit that it was a surprise to find it in Trent Marston.

He was watching her face closely. 'Please don't refuse, Emma. My grandmother really would like to meet you. At all events, we'll go up to her house after we've called at the hospital, and then you can see how the two of you get along. Agreed?'

He really was being provokingly thoughtful. 'Thank you,' she said, and added politely, 'It's very kind of your grandmother.'

'Oh, she *is* kind, and very easy to get along with. Not like her grandson. I'm sure you'll find her a pleasant change after a few days of my company.' His mouth twisted ironically and there was a slight, challenging twinkle in his black eyes, which Emma chose to ignore as she managed to choke down, with difficulty, the remainder of her roll. Sharing a meal with Trent Marston was a hazardous occupation.

AT THE hospital, later that morning, it was wonderful to find Joe so much better. 'I'll be back on the job in no time at all,' he declared. 'Meanwhile, how about bringing this young fellow who's filling the gap to have a heart-to-heart with me? I'd like to meet him.'

Emma's own heart sank. Trent was going to be a surprise to Joe, and not altogether a pleasant one. And it was her fault; she had deliberately misled Joe, she knew that. She just couldn't confront Joe with Trent Marston, the man who was all set up to take his job over—worse than that, to establish himself as Joe's boss, if she knew anything about Trent.

She stalled. 'Of course I'll bring him along,' she said, 'as soon as they tell me here you're fit to talk business. No, Joe dear, you're definitely *not* ready yet.' She squeezed his hand reassuringly. 'Very soon, I promise.'

She stayed a little longer today, arranging the flowers that she and Trent had bought on the way, telling Joe about the Trade Fair she had visited yesterday and about the meeting with Roy Royston. 'We met him at the Exhibition,' she said, prevaricating a little. 'Mr Marston happened to know him and he may be quite useful to us.' She talked on a little longer in an optimistic vein and finally left Joe looking quite cheerful, promising to come back again next day.

Trent was waiting in the corridor when she came out of the ward. 'This time,' he said darkly, 'I'm not risking you diving into a taxi to escape from me.'

'I wasn't—' she began, but he cut short her half-hearted protest with a disbelieving chuckle.

'Don't give me that, Emma, you know darned well you were. You've been trying to escape from me since the first moment you saw me—in the porch of the church in Dorset. And quite soon you're going to have to admit it. Also,' he added smoothly, as they came into the sunshine outside the hospital doors, 'you're going to have to admit that you can't escape from me—not ever.'

Emma gasped. The sublime conceit of the man! It stood out a mile, even when he was fooling.

But once again he gave her no chance to make a come-back, if indeed she could have thought of one. He said, 'We travel in style this time. I phoned my grandmother while you were with Joe, and she's sending her car to collect us. Ah, here it is now.'

An enormous, oldish black limousine, driven by a smiling Mexican in a flapping checked shirt and a shady straw hat, was pulling up outside the hospital entrance. He jumped out and threw open the car door and his grin became even wider as Trent thumped him on the shoulder in the friendliest way, saying, '*Hola*, Conrado, *cómo está usted*?'

The big Mexican gabbled away in Spanish, to which Trent listened, nodding and putting in a question now and again. It was, Emma gathered, all about Conrado's family, of which there seemed to be a very large number. Eventually Trent took her hand and drew her forward. 'This is Conrado, Emma, a very good friend of mine. Señorita Fairley speaks Spanish, Conrado,' he added, 'so you'd better watch what you say in her presence.'

Conrado roared with laughter and shook Emma's hand and they all piled into the big car, Emma traveling in the front seat between the two men. It was difficult, in the circumstances, for her to remain remote and dignified and she was urgently conscious of Trent's thigh pressing against hers, but to move away would only have confirmed his conceited boast that he had power over her, so she turned her attention to Conrado, smiling at his remarks, most of which were about a character called Matilde, who seemed to be attached to the household of Trent's grandmother in some unspecified way, and whose cooking drew forth the utmost scorn from Conrado. Matilde's *tacos de pollo* were, according to Conrado, only fit to be thrown to the pigs. He made a guttural noise in this throat and raised his eyes to heaven, narrowly missing hitting a boy on a bicycle.

Trent said sharply. 'Watch it, *amigo*,' and the Mexican looked sheepish and muttered, '*Lo siento,* Señor Trent,' and after that was silent.

Trent leaned his head to Emma's, waving a hand towards the passing scene as the car drove through a vast area of beautiful woodland. 'This is our famous Chapultepec Park,' he told her, 'of which we are justly proud.'

The road passed close to magnificent buildings, standing in green glades, with some of the most glorious trees Emma had ever seen. Far in the distance she glimpsed a lake, with islands and fountains, and there were fascinating paths leading mysteriously away into thickly wooded copses.

'What a heavenly spot,' she said, smiling spontaneously at Trent, forgetting to be on the defensive.

He grinned. 'There's a zoo as well,' he said, and that sounded so ridiculous that they both began to laugh.

Presently the road began to wind upwards into the hills, and eventually Conrado steered the car between high gateposts, topped with fabulous stone animals, and up a winding drive between bushes starred with yellow flowers.

When finally they pulled up at the house and got out of the car Emma stood lost in pure delight. 'This is simply lovely!' she breathed. 'I've never seen anything so beautiful.'

The house was obviously a copy of an American ranch-style dwelling long and low and white, with rows of windows catching the sunlight, and seeming to wink a welcome. Most of the houses—or rather, residences—that Emma had glimpsed on their drive through the wooded hills had been enormous, some of them even looking like Colonial-style mansions, and she had expected this one to be the same: rather intimidating. But it was nothing of the sort, it was a friendly house.

And the tall, white-haired woman who came from somewhere behind the house when she heard the car looked friendly too, in her blue cotton dress with a gardening apron tied round her.

She didn't wait for introductions. She pulled off her gardening gloves and took Emma's hands in hers. 'You're Emma Fairley and you're very welcome. Trent has told me a lot about you.' She looked over to her grandson, smiling fondly, and Emma could see the likeness between them: the same thin, intelligent face with its good bone structure; the same keen, observant glance; the same air of—what was it?—breeding perhaps.

She felt at home with this attractive elderly woman straight away. 'Thank you, *señora*,' she smiled. 'I hope he hasn't told you anything too bad about me.'

'All good, my child, all very complimentary.' The dark eyes in the wrinkled, sunburned face twinkled, and she looked more like Trent than ever—Trent when he was in one of his teasing moods.

She led the way towards the house, talking energetically in her warm southern drawl, enquiring after Joe's progress, asking if they would like to have lunch straight away, or later. 'And you mustn't call me "*señora*", please, Emma. You must call me Juanita—everyone around here does.'

Emma caught her breath, stumbled, and would have fallen if Trent hadn't grabbed her arm to steady her. She couldn't take it in at once.

This was Juanita!—Trent's *grandmother*! Her brain spun wildly. He had known very well what she had thought, and he deliberately had not enlightened her. She threw him a glance of pure, smouldering resentment and shook off his restraining hand.

'Okay?' he enquired softly mocking. She drew in a hissing breath and drew quickly away from him, saying nothing. She was so angry that she wasn't capable of taking in much of the inside of the house, as they entered by way of a wooden veranda and a long window. She was only conscious of an atmosphere of comfort and space and light.

'May we have lunch straight away, please, Juanita?' Trent said. 'If it won't put Matilde out, that is. Is she in a good mood this morning?'

'Excellent,' smiled his grandmother. 'She's wildly curious to see Emma, though she wouldn't admit it for the world.' She took Emma's arm. 'Now, come along, my dear, I'll show you your room. Conrado will bring your bag.'

She led Emma along several passages and up a short flight of stairs. 'This is a winding sort of house,' she smiled over her shoulder, 'but you'll soon find your way around. Now, this is your room, I do hope you'll like it. Put Miss Fairley's case here, please, Conrado,' as the big Mexican appeared with Emma's case.

When he had departed Trent's grandmother put her hand on Emma's shoulder. 'I'm so very glad to have you with me, Emma, and I do hope you'll be happy here.' Her voice was warm and her eyes were kind.

Emma felt her own eyes prick with tears. After all that had happened in the last few days she felt she had found sanctuary in this lovely house. 'I'm sure I shall, and thank you so much,' she said quietly.

The elderly woman moved towards the door. 'I'll leave you to settle in, then,' she said. 'Come down when you're ready and we'll have lunch. Trent seems to be in a hurry to eat—I seem to remember he said he has an appointment this afternoon, so perhaps we can get rid of him and then you and I can have a lovely talk and get to know each other.'

She remained standing beside the door, her eyes fixed on Emma's face. 'I can see why Trent is so attracted to you, Emma. You're a little like his mother, she has the same dark gold hair and funny little smile.'

She nodded, went out, and closed the door gently behind her.

Emma sank down on the soft bed. So Trent had told his grandmother he was attracted to her, had he? And why, exactly, had he done that? She passed a hand wearily across her forehead. She would have to give up trying to guess the man's motives; they were completely unfathomable. Perhaps Juanita (she must get used to calling her that, although it seemed strange at first) perhaps Juanita could throw some light on the way her grandson's cryptic mind worked.

Emma sighed as she stood up and began to explore the large, pleasant bedroom with its adjoining small bathroom, trying to concentrate on what she was looking at, but she scarcely took it in at all, for her thoughts were churning round and round, centred on Trent. She didn't seem to be able to get him out of her mind, and yet she had reached a state of complete bewilderment where he was concerned.

There was a fascination about mystery. Was that why he filled her thoughts constantly? Why seeing him afresh gave her a curious little lurch in the pit of her stomach? Why her pulses beat wildly when he touched her?

She hoped fervently that it was merely the attraction of the unknown that was playing such havoc with her usually calm disposition. It would be appalling if she found out that she had fallen in love with the man.

She sat down at the dressing table and began to tidy her hair and check on her make-up. Whatever the answer to the riddle, it would be easier now that she was here in his grandmother's house and she wouldn't be alone with him all the time.

Juanita—Trent's grandmother! How absurd that mistake had been! But the smile that she saw reflected in the mirror wasn't one of amusement. With a kind of horror she decided that she looked quite disgustingly smug.

As Emma had hoped, everything became much easier from then on. Trent had arranged to fly back to England in two days' time, and Emma would stay on with Juanita and keep in close touch with Joe's progress. Juanita—bless her—insisted that Joe should come back to her home in the hills when he was released from hospital. The length of his stay could be decided later.

'Your grandmother is incredibly kind,' Emma said to Trent as he was driving her to the hospital on the day before he was due to leave. 'I really don't know why she should do all this for Joe and me.'

'Don't you know—*really*?' As he stopped the car outside the hospital Trent sat sideways in his seat and turned his gaze full on her. 'Juanita likes you very much, but more than that, I'm her one and only grandson and you're my girl.'

'I'm not—how could you tell her that?' Emma spluttered indignantly.

He patted her hand as if she were a fractious child. 'Let's call it wishful thinking, shall we?' he grinned, and got out of the car. 'And as for Joe,' he added as they passed through the big doors of the hospital, 'Joe is a valued member of our firm, so of course Juanita would want to help.'

To-day Trent asked to see the doctor who was looking after Joe's case. 'Señor Kent is getting on very well indeed,' the young doctor told them. 'If there are no setbacks he should be allowed out of hospital in ten to fourteen days. Then he must rest and take it easy for at least two months. Can that be arranged? It would not be safe for him to travel back to England.'

Emma left them talking and went in to see Joe. 'You're looking heaps better,' she told him, sitting down by the bed and squeezing his hand hard. 'And I see you've heard from Uncle Edward.' She indicated an envelope addressed in Uncle Edward's handwriting, which was lying on the locker. How much had Uncle Edward told Joe about Trent? she wondered nervously. Tact wasn't her uncle's strong point; he lived in a world of his own and wasn't always conscious of other people's reactions and feelings, although basically he was a very kind man.

Joe said, 'Read it yourself, love,' and she reached for the envelope.

Uncle Edward had been the soul of tact this time. He had sent a get-well card (purchased, no doubt, by Jessie at his request) with a picture of a white-sailed yacht ploughing through rough blue water. Inside he had written: 'Let go of the wheel for a while, old boy, until you're really fit again. We'll put her on automatic steering and ride out the storm. Regards always, Edward.'

Emma replaced the card on the locker, and Joe grinned his old wry grin and said, 'Must obey the captain, mustn't we?' He leaned his head back against the pillow, looking suddenly more tired. 'Is this bloke Marston with you now? If he is I'd like to take a look at him. Just for a couple of minutes.'

Emma said anxiously, 'Will they let you have more visitors?' If he didn't take to Trent—if he suspected that Trent was a climber who was out to insinuate himself into Joe's own place in the firm—if he got upset and worried, she didn't dare think what that might do to his chances of making a good recovery.

Joe saw her hesitation. 'Please, love,' he begged.

In the corridor Emma found Trent now engaged in conversation with the stern-looking sister, who wasn't looking at all stern at the moment.

Emma plunged in with, 'Sister, may Mr Kent have another visitor? I think he may be worrying about his work and as Mr Marston is taking over his job for the moment it might be helpful if they could meet.'

The Sister beamed at Trent. '*Si, si*, you may go in for just a few minutes, Señor Marston. You will make his mind easy, I am sure.' She straightened her already immaculate apron and swished away down the corridor.

Emma looked after her, compressing her lips. Another conquest for Mr Trent Marston! He bowled them over like ninepins. 'You'd better come in, then,' she said coolly.

He must have heard the reserve in her voice. He put a hand at her elbow as they went into the small ward, and gave her arm a reassuring squeeze. 'Trust me, Emma, just this once,' he whispered. 'I promise I won't say anything to upset him.'

She moved away from him as they approached the bed. She didn't want Joe to get any wrong ideas about her relationship with Trent Marston. She wanted him to make up his own mind about the man who was stepping into his job.

'You'd better not,' she returned fiercely under her breath.

She needn't have worried. From the first moment she could see that the two men liked each other. She knew Joe so well, had watched him with other men, and respected his opinions about them. It shook her that he so obviously accepted Trent immediately as a man to be trusted. She didn't know whether to be pleased or not.

They stayed only a short time before the Sister appeared at the door. Trent got to his feet. 'Time's up, it seems.' He stood looking down at the man in the bed regretfully. 'There's a whole heap of stuff I'd like to talk over with you and ask your advice about, Joe, but it will have to wait until you're fit again. Meanwhile, will you trust me to do the best I can—with Emma's help?'

Joe's tired blue eyes moved to Emma and back to Trent. 'Oh yes,' he said simply. 'I'll be happy to leave everything to the two of you.' He smiled faintly. 'I can see you'll work well together.'

Emma bent over the bed and kissed him, hiding the tears that pricked behind her eyes. She knew how much Joe had valued their partnership, but now he was handing her over without a scrap of resentment.

As the door of the ward closed behind them she murmured chokily, 'He's rather wonderful, isn't he?'

Trent linked his arm with hers. 'He's a good fellow,' he agreed. 'I hope he'll make a quick recovery and be able to get back on the job. The firm will miss him.'

LUNCH WAS set out on the veranda overlooking the garden when they got back to the house on the hills. 'Señora Juanita has lunched already,' Matilde told them, speaking in her quick, excited Spanish. 'She has gone to have a rest and says she will see you both later.'

Matilde was a gaunt, grey-haired woman with a face criss-crossed with wrinkles. She eyed Emma and Trent with avid interest out of beady black eyes as she served their lunch of chicken rolled up in tortillas and fried crisply, with tomatoes and beans and shredded lettuce, followed by an enormous dish of colourful, exotic fruits and little biscuity cakes.

'I can't think why Conrado complains of Matilde's cooking,' Emma said, after Matilde has served their coffee and left them. 'That was a gorgeous meal.' She spoke in a high, rather jerky tone, for in fact she was feeling the old tension gripping now that she was alone in the house with Trent for the first time since they arrived here.

He leaned back in his wicker chair, eyeing her with pleasure as she sipped her coffee. The veranda was shaded by a huge tree and Emma's creamy skin and the soft folds of the delphinium-blue dress she was wearing were dappled with little shadows.

'Gorgeous,' echoed Trent lazily, his eyes moving over her.

Something in his voice made her heart begin to thump. 'I suppose you'll be leaving early in the morning?' she said, not looking at him.

'I'm leaving today, as a matter of fact,' he said. 'I'm dining with friends who live quite near to the airport and they're giving me a bed for the night.'

'Oh,' said Emma, surprised at the quick feeling of disappointment she felt. She should have been relieved that Trent was leaving, but suddenly the weeks ahead seemed to stretch rather emptily. It could be, she told herself hastily, that she was going to miss the challenge he presented, rather than the man himself.

A quizzical smile touched his mouth. 'They really are just friends,' he said, eyeing her with amusement. 'A married couple, in fact, so you needn't be suspicious this time.'

'I don't know what you're talking about,' she told him coldly.

'I think you do. When I left you at the hotel you had all sorts of nasty thoughts about some girl-friend I was going to spend the night with. And all the time it was simply Juanita.'

She glared at him. 'You meant me to think that, didn't you?' she accused. 'You just wanted to make a fool of me.'

Trent shook his head, smiling. 'Not a bit of it. I wanted to see how you'd react—if it mattered at all to you. And it did, didn't it, Emma? Go on, admit it.' He leaned across the table and put his hand over hers.

'Oh,' she burst out in exasperation, dragging her hand from under his, 'you really are the—most—impossible—man! I never know whether to believe you— whether you're serious or not.'

She couldn't sit here any longer continuing this absurd conversation. She put down her coffee cup with a little clatter and stood up, walking away from him down the garden.

He came after her, of course. 'It's a pleasant afternoon for a walk,' he said smoothly. 'Suppose I show you the glories of Juanita's garden? I don't think you've seen all of it yet.'

So far, Emma had not gone beyond the terraces, and the exotic shrubs that rioted in the flower beds and spilled over on to the lawns. But now Trent put a hand at her elbow and urged her forward to a wilder part of the garden, under the dense foliage of overhanging trees that turned everything into a blue-green shade. It was cool here, and she could just hear the splash and trickle of water somewhere near.

They came out into a small clearing and before them the land fell steeply away in a tumble of rocks, ending in a narrow gorge some ten feet below. A stream cascaded down between the rocks, sending up fountains of spray that glistened in rainbow colours where the sunlight pierced the shade of the trees.

There was a wooden safety rail at the edge of the rocky decline, and Emma leaned on this, looking down to where plants and ferns sprung from between the wet, mossy rocks, and small, brightly coloured birds fluttered and clung, pecking at unseen insects.

'It's beautiful,' she breathed, forgetting everything else in her pleasure. 'Like fairyland. You expect to see Oberon appearing through the trees.'

Trent laughed. 'You can have your fairy king. I prefer the fairy queen myself.'

She was glad he was keeping everything light. It would be so much easier to part on a note of friendship and nothing more. But even as the thought occurred to her, a silence fell between them and she could think of nothing to say. She was desperately conscious of his tall, hard body close to hers and she wanted to move away, but some stronger spell kept her motionless.

She swallowed and her throat was dry, and the silence went on and on until she could bear it no longer. She half-turned, to look up at Trent, and what she saw in his face made time stand still. Then, very slowly, he reached out and stroked back her hair, cupping her face between his hands, looking down at her with a tenderness she wouldn't have believed him capable of only an hour ago.

'Emma?' he breathed. The word was a question, and like a girl in a dream she moved towards him and went into his arms.

The moment had a kind of inevitability, and she knew hazily that everything that had happened since the first moment they looked at each other had been leading up to this. His mouth came down to hers and she gave herself up to his kiss, to the fondling of his hands, with a hunger that held a primitive desperation. They clung together, their bodies moving against each other, a man and a woman sharing a mutual need and fierce pleasure.

His mouth buried itself in the softness of her neck, trailing slowly downwards as she arched her body back, and finding the deep cleft between her breasts. Her arms went up and her fingers wound themselves in the crisp hair at the back of his neck, digging into the taut muscles there, and again their mouths met, probing and searching each other in a kind of frenzy, as if they could become one person instead of two.

Suddenly she heard Trent groan and he pulled himself away from her, his arms dropping heavily to his sides. His face was haggard and he was shaking all over. 'This isn't the way I planned it,' he said roughly. 'You see what you do to me, Emma.' It sounded like an accusation.

He moved away and stood with his back to her, struggling for control. She stood rigid, suddenly afraid of what he would say next, knowing at last that this was the man she wanted with a burning, clamouring need, in spite of all that had happened. Her love had grown secretly, like a seed growing in the dark, and now had burst into flower and there was nothing she could do about it.

'Trent,' she whispered, longing for the feel of his arms around her again.

But when he turned back to her there was something in his face that frightened her. The tenderness had gone and the passion too, and all she could find there was his usual wry humour. 'It seems we do something to each other,' he said. 'Perhaps we should get back to the house, out of the way of temptation.'

She felt pain, as if he had struck a steel blade into her, but she managed to hold her head high and put an answering smile on her mouth. 'I think you're right,' she said, 'it would be a pity to complicate things, wouldn't it?'

Juanita had come downstairs and was sitting in her basket chair on the veranda, a gracious, elderly lady with her white hair beautifully coiffured and her long violet-blue dress hanging in soft folds around her chair. She greeted them happily, enquiring about the news of Joe from the hospital, and they sat and talked to her for a while before Trent got to his feet and announced that he must be leaving. 'Conrado's going to run me down into the city, if that's all right with you, Juanita.'

'Of course, my dear boy, I'm only sorry you're leaving us so soon. But glad you're leaving Emma behind to be company for me.' She gave Emma a warm, smiling glance.

There was a warning hoot from round the front of the house and Trent grinned. 'He'll never learn, will he?' He bent and kissed his grandmother. 'Goodbye for now, dear one, look after yourself,' and she held him close for a moment in a tight little hug.

Emma had a hollow feeling inside. Would he just say goodbye to her and walk away? But he paused in front of her chair, looking down at her. 'Coming to see me off?' he said steadily.

She got up and walked beside him down the steps of the veranda and along the path that skirted the side of the house. He didn't take her arm, or touch her. He simply said, 'Wish me luck, Emma. By the time we meet again maybe Fairley Brothers will have a new look. There's a lot to be done, but I'm looking forward to it.'

'Of course I wish you luck,' she told him rather woodenly. This was what she had asked for, wasn't it? To be his business partner and nothing more.

Conrado was sitting in the big black car. 'Your bag's in the back, Señor Trent,' he grinned cheerfully, leaning over to open the door.

Trent put a hand on the door. Then he bent and kissed Emma briefly on the cheek. 'Au revoir, Fairy Queen,' he smiled. 'We'll be in touch.'

He got into the seat beside Conrado, and the engine began to purr. Conrado pushed in the gear, but as the car moved forward Trent said quickly, 'Stop a minute, *amigo*.' He leant out of the open window. 'Just remember, Emma, that you've got me all wrong. You think I've been trying purposely to play the fool and mislead you. But the truth is that I've meant every word I've ever said to you. Cross my heart, my darling girl. Every single word. Think about that while we're apart, will you?'

Emma just stared at him, in stunned silence, her eyes wide. He had surprised her many times, but this was the biggest shock of all.

He held her eyes for a moment longer, as if he couldn't bear to go, and then he turned briskly and said, 'OK, *amigo,* drive on.'

The big car purred away down the drive, and Trent looked back and lifted a hand in salute as it turned the corner out of sight.

Emma stood for a long time, looking at the place where it had disappeared. Then, very slowly, she walked back to where she had left Juanita, and there was a pink glow on her cheeks and a shine in her tawny eyes; so unmistakably a girl in love that Juanita's own dark eyes twinkled knowingly.

She patted the chair beside her. 'Come and sit down, my child,' she said in her soft southern drawl, 'and let's talk about my wonderful grandson.'

CHAPTER EIGHT

IN THE days that followed there was a great deal of talk about Juanita's wonderful grandson—in fact, Trent was the principal topic of conversation between the two women, the old one and the young, who both loved him.

Juanita seemed to take it for granted that Emma would soon become one of the family, and Emma hadn't the heart to say that it was most unlikely. She assured herself of that frequently, not allowing herself to believe that Trent's remarks when he said goodbye were meant to be taken at their face value.

But when she was alone at night she dredged her memory and came up with the inescapable fact that he had said over and over again, in different ways, that he was in love with her. And what did that mean? A serious, permanent relationship, or merely a temporary affair—a convenient arrangement between business colleagues? She wished she knew.

His frequent telephone calls didn't make things any clearer. They were all about the business, his plans and hopes. He was reorganising the office and the workroom completely. 'You won't recognise it when you get back,' he told her. He was living at her home in the village. That suited both him and Edward splendidly. Edward didn't want to waste his time coming in to the office in Poole, and this way Trent could be in touch with him daily for conferences when he went back in the evening. 'Jessie's a brick,' Trent said. 'She's looking after me like a mother.'

Usually Uncle Edward came on the line finally, enquiring about her well-being and about Joe's progress. Lisa wasn't mentioned by either of them and Emma couldn't bring herself to ask any questions. The thought of Lisa, and the way Trent had treated her, was like an old wound that hadn't healed. You could forget about it sometimes and then suddenly it began to hurt and niggle.

She promised herself that she would write to Lisa; then the letter would be waiting at Lisa's new home when she got back from her honeymoon at the end of the month. Surely, by then, Lisa wouldn't care too much that Emma had been in Mexico with Trent, and that even now was staying with his family there. But in case Lisa still felt some lingering bitterness, she would reassure her that her own involvement with Trent Marston had been purely a matter of business, and that it was because of Joe's illness that they had come to Mexico together. But the longer she put off writing the letter the more impossible it became to write it. Finally she bought a greeting card with a picture of the Floating Gardens of Xochimilco on it and wrote, 'I bet you haven't got anything like this in the Seychelles! My best love to you both. Have a super time and I'm longing to see you when we all get home again. Your Emma.'

She felt a faint sense of relief when she had posted the card. It would be so much easier to explain things to Lisa when they actually met. So she pushed the niggling doubt into the background again and began to enjoy her stay.

Each day she visited Joe in the hospital—the talkative Conrado driving her there and back and amusing her with his frank comments on the way of the world, for which he hadn't anything very good to say. Señor Trent, however, could do no wrong, apparently. He was—Conrado rolled his eyes, searching for the most complimentary word—*caballeresco*, which Emma interpreted as meaning a very chivalrous gentleman. It wouldn't have fitted her own opinion of Trent only a short time ago. But now—she wasn't sure. She had seen a different side of him in Mexico.

And Juanita, with the adoring indulgence of a grandmother, was never tired of singing his praises. His strength, his kindness, his idealism, his generosity! It sounded to Emma much too good to be true, but she found herself lapping it all up eagerly, wanting to believe every word.

From Juanita she learned about Trent's parents. About his father, Juanita's only son, who owned a merchant bank and was at present working and living in Hong Kong with his English wife, Sylvia. Juanita seemed to approve of her daughter-in-law, who was, she kept on saying, quite remarkably like Emma herself. 'She'll love you too,' Juanita promised, 'I know she will.' Emma decided that that was a somewhat rash statement, but even that pleased her because it seemed to give her a stronger link with Trent.

'Robert and Sylvia would have liked Trent to follow his father into the bank,' Juanita said, 'but that was too dull a prospect for him. He needed the excitement of the business world. He loves a challenge.'

Emma heard how, in the ten years since he left Cambridge at twenty-three, Trent had saved no fewer

than three ailing firms from bankruptcy, and put them
on the road to recovery again.

'Trent's lame ducks, his father calls them,' Juanita
laughed. 'I don't think Robert quite approves, it all
seems a bit risky to him, as a banker, but Trent thrives
on it.'

'And then, when he has saved the firms—what
happens?' Emma asked. This was something she had
to know.

'Oh, he moves on, looking for another lame duck,'
his grandmother told her proudly. 'There's no holding Trent.'

No holding Trent! That about summed it up. There
was a tight constriction in Emma's throat. One day,
whatever happened between her and Trent, he would
'move on'. He wanted change, new challenges, he
wasn't a man to settle down; the thought was infi-
nitely depressing. For hours afterwards there was ice
in her veins as she determined to conquer this painful
yearning to see him, to be held close in his arms; then
he would telephone again and just hearing his voice
melted her resolution and the fever came hotly back.

Joe improved ever more rapidly as each day passed
and Emma's visits to the hospital became longer. She
told him everything that Trent had told her about the
rebuilding of the firm's fortunes and about his plans
and his contacts and Uncle Edward's new navigational instrument, which was soon to go into full production. Joe listened, and nodded, and was obviously
delighted, and Emma felt that she should be delighted too, only this agonising doubt about the future gnawed away at her all the time.

Juanita insisted on Emma going out and seeing
some of the sights of Mexico City. She herself wasn't

up to the noise and bustle, she said regretfully, but there was an old friend of theirs, a delightful Mexican gentleman, now retired, who was at the house constantly, and who drove Emma on several sightseeing trips himself, and also arranged for her to join a couple of guided tours to places of interest.

She stood in awe below the colossal pyramids at San Juan de Teotihuacán while the guide explained that the Toltecs, who built them originally, nearly two thousand years before, had later considered the place cursed and deserted it; she visited the Cathedral, built on the site of the Great Temple of the Aztecs; she saw the modern famous new library at the University, where the walls were covered by mosaics made from natural stones from all over Mexico. The theme of the murals was Mexico's heritage—Aztec and Toltec, as well as tribute to the Spaniards for what they had done for the country. There was, she was told, space for over a million volumes.

She was taken to the Basilica of Nuestra Señora de Guadalupe, a shrine built on the spot where the Virgin is said to have appeared to an Indian in the sixteenth century; and the Castle of Chapultepec, which was once the residence of the Emperor Maximilian and the Empress Charlotte.

The tourist trail was interesting, Emma found, but most of all she enjoyed the afternoons she spent alone at the Museum of Anthropology, where the whole history of Mexico was displayed. Here she wandered for hours as she was transported back into ancient civilisations of which she knew nothing and had only vaguely heard about. But this was Trent's heritage, and that gave it all a fascination quite apart from the interest of the impressive exhibits themselves. When they met again, she planned, she would have so much to discuss with him, so many questions to ask. By the time Conrado picked her up at the prearranged time outside the Museum she felt quite intoxicated by all she had seen and experienced.

Then, at last, came the day that Joe was released from hospital. Juanita had already visited him once, with Emma, and had been able to give him her invitation in person. Now he arrived and was installed in a pleasant ground-floor room overlooking the gardens, and from then on life changed for Emma. She went out less, was content to stay around the house. Juanita suggested engaging a day-nurse, but Emma demurred, saying that she could surely do all that was required for Joe. And so she did, and found that everything worked out smoothly and happily. It was as if time were suspended as the hours passed, sitting in the beautiful garden, looking after Joe and seeing that he rested most of the time and took just the prescribed amount of exercise and didn't forget to take his tablets.

In May, the weather became warmer and decidedly wetter. Hardly a day passed without a shower. Juanita was jubilant as her beloved garden burst into a blaze of colour. In June, there was almost too much rain and many days were spent indoors. Emma's Spanish became fluent as she practised on everyone in sight, including Juanita's elderly friend Luis Valesco, with whom Joe had struck up a friendship. The two men talked for hours together, with Joe yarning about his days as a young man in the R.A.F. and Señor Valesco, in his painstaking English, recounting stories of the colourful history of his own country, that had seen so much change in his lifetime.

Then, at last, came the day for Joe's final check-up at the hospital. He came away beaming. 'All clear,' he told the waiting Emma. 'I can travel at any time. I have to see my own doctor as soon as I get home, but Dr. Martinez thinks there's no reason why I shouldn't start work again in a couple of weeks, if I take it very easy.'

And so, on a misty morning in early July, Joe and Emma said goodbye to Juanita, with gratitude they could hardly find words to express. 'Don't try, my dear Emma. I've loved having you—and Joe, too.' Juanita kissed Emma and held her away, looking affectionately into her face. 'Just tell that grandson of mine to bring you back to see me very, very soon.'

Joe managed the long plane journey well, sleeping most of the time. Emma, on the other hand, was wide awake from the time of take-off. She found herself dreading the moment she would see Trent again. Her thoughts had gone round and round so often in the past weeks that she had almost begun to believe, by now, that she had dreamed those words he had spoken as he said goodbye on the day he left. Surely, if he had really been in love with her he would have followed it up, would at least have written to her, done more than merely put through the occasional telephone call, which was as much for Juanita as for her. All through the long flight her doubts became miseries and by the time they landed at Heathrow she had convinced herself that he couldn't possibly have been serious. When had she ever been able to believe what he said? Probably by now he had found himself another girl-friend—several girl-friends. She must be prepared for that. She wouldn't show him she had missed him and longed for him every moment since he left.

As they disembarked she tried to forget about Trent and concentrate on looking after Joe. When they finally came within sight of the arrivals lounge, with all the eager faces lining the long side barrier, she said, 'Keep a look-out for Malcolm. Uncle Edward said he would be sure to be here in good time.' Her eyes passed over the row of faces, searching for Malcolm's thick thatch of greying hair and craggy face. Finally, they came out into the main hall, but there was no sign of Malcolm. Emma stood uncertainly, looking around, hoping for Joe's sake that there wasn't going to be any hitch now, at the end of this long, tiring journey.

Then, coming towards her, she saw Trent, and felt a jolt in her stomach that was quite sickening. He had seen her now—she saw him give a start of recognition—and was pushing his way through the crowd towards her. At the same time she started to run towards him and they met with a head-on crash, and then she was in his arms and he was holding her tightly against him and kissing her, and all the uncertainty and questioning of the last weeks was over.

Joe came up, grinning. Trent wrung his hand without letting go of Emma. 'And how's Joe? You're looking fine. Gosh, it's great to see you both again, I've got so much to tell you.'

This was a different Trent, younger, laughing, almost boyish. Emma felt as if she were dissolving in love for him.

From then on he took charge of everything and half an hour later they were all in Trent's big car, with Joe settled comfortably at the back, nodding off to sleep again.

Trent pushed in the gear-lever. Then he turned to Emma and put a hand on her knee and said, very low, 'It's been a long wait, my darling, but we're going home now. And I've got a surprise for you.'

'That's nothing new,' she laughed, thrilling to the touch of his hand. 'You're always surprising me.'

'Wait till you see this one, though,' he said mysteriously. He let in the clutch and the car moved slowly out of the car park.

Not much more than two hours later they drew up at the door of the house by the sea. Jessie and Malcolm were out on the steps, in the gathering dusk, and even Uncle Edward had deserted his work-room for once to join the welcoming party. When the greetings were over Jessie bore Joe away to the room she had prepared for him; Malcolm took Trent's car to the garage; and Uncle Edward beamed on Trent and Emma, and invited them to his study 'for a celebratory drink'.

He knows, thought Emma. He knows and he's pleased. Oh, everything was coming beautifully right. In a haze of happiness her eyes met Trent's over the rim of her glass.

Later, she went up to her room to unpack. Trent came after her, carrying her travel bag. In her room he closed the door and held out his arms. They clung together as if they had been apart for years, and Emma felt her tears wet on Trent's hard cheek.

'It *is* true?' he said shakily at length. Somehow they had got on to the bed and she was sitting half-cradled in his arms. 'You will marry me?'

'Try to stop me,' she said, and he gave a long, long sigh and tightened his arms round her, his cheek against her hair.

'It was hell, leaving you behind in Mexico,' he said. 'I had to practically handcuff myself to the office desk to stop myself getting on the next plane back again. But I reckoned I had to give you time. I knew I'd got off on the wrong foot with you—that you thought I was an unfeeling bastard. You told me so, if you remember. So I had to leave you and hope you'd miss me as much as I missed you. Did you miss me, my love?'

'Every single minute,' she whispered, and turned into his arms again, her mouth seeking for his in a long ecstatic kiss.

From downstairs came the sound of Jessie pounding on the gong, announcing dinner. Trent lifted his head. 'Damn,' he muttered. 'Who wants food?'

Emma struggled out of his arms, straightening her dress. 'I do,' she grinned. 'I couldn't eat a thing on the plane. I was too scared at the thought of seeing you again and finding you didn't want me—that you hadn't meant what you said.'

He took both her hands and held them tightly. 'I'll never lie to you, Emma,' he said soberly. 'You do believe that now, don't you?'

'Yes,' she said slowly, looking deep into his eyes. 'Yes, I believe that.'

It wasn't until after dinner that Trent announced to Emma reluctantly that he had to catch the night train back to London. 'I've got an important meeting at nine tomorrow morning that I can't very well get out of, but I'll come straight back the very second it's over, I can promise you. Let's meet at the office at one, shall we? Then I can show you my surprise.'

Emma's Mini was back in the garage by now, resplendent in its new coat of white paint after its respray. She drove Trent to the station to catch his train.

'Only a few hours this time, my darling.' He kissed her hungrily as the train drew in to the platform. 'Love me?'

'Always.' She clung to his hand until the very last minute, and then stood watching as the train snaked out of the station, bearing him away from her.

As she walked slowly down the platform she told herself she was the luckiest girl in the world. It was quite ridiculous that she should feel suddenly as if a dark shadow had fallen across her happiness.

BACK AT home there was an unfamiliar white car parked at the front door. Who on earth had called at this time of night? One of Uncle Edward's scientist friends, probably. They had a habit of dropping in on him at all sorts of unreasonable hours.

The hall was empty, but the lights were on in the sitting room. Lisa was standing before the ashes of the log fire, hunched into a white furry jacket, her pale hair done up in an intricate fashion. She looked frail and very beautiful.

Emma ran across the room to her. 'Lisa—darling, how lovely! I've only been back a few hours—I was going to come along and see you tomorrow. How are you, and how's everything?' She put her arms round her young cousin and hugged her warmly.

Lisa drew away. 'I rang Daddy a little while ago. He said you'd just come back home—with Trent Marston.' Her pretty lips curled over his name contemptuously. 'So much for your promise not to have anything to do with him. You went straight off to

Mexico with him, didn't you? I do hope he gave you a good time.'

Emma took her hand and drew her towards the sofa. 'Darling, come and sit down and relax. It wasn't like that. I had to go to Mexico because of Joe, and Trent had to come because of the firm's business there. So of course we were together there.'

Lisa's face was stony. 'Daddy says you're going to marry him. I told him he must be mistaken, but he stuck to it. That's why I've come here now, to see you. You're not going to marry him, are you, Emma? You know the way he treated me—you couldn't marry him after that, could you?'

'Why not?' Emma said quietly. She was trying to keep this on a reasonable level. She knew of old how easily Lisa could get upset. 'I know what you think of him, but it would be me who was taking the risk, not you.' She put an arm round Lisa and felt the slight body tremble under the soft white fur of her jacket. 'Darling, I know you believe he treated you badly, and I'm sorry about that, but men are men and they don't look at things the same way that we do.'

'You can say that again!' Lisa bit the words out between her small, even teeth. 'He's conned you too, hasn't he, and you've fallen for it. I told you it would happen, but you wouldn't listen.' She stood up and began pacing nervously about the room. 'He's a swine, that man—a callous—disgusting—' The words poured out, words that Emma wouldn't have believed Lisa knew.

At last she came to a halt, looking down at Emma, her face white, intense. 'You *can't* marry him. If you love me—if you've ever loved me—you can't do this to me!'

Emma frowned. Surely Lisa wasn't just acting up? Surely she had grown out of her fantasies now she was a married woman? What she had felt for Trent must have gone very deep, deeper than Emma had suspected. Gently she said, 'I'm sorry, Lisa darling, I do love you, but I love Trent too, and I'm going to marry him.'

Lisa stumbled backwards as if she had received a physical blow. 'Then I'll have to tell you. I wasn't going to, but now I'll have to.'

Something she saw in Lisa's face made Emma feel icy cold. 'Tell me—what?'

Lisa's pretty mouth hardened. 'Why do you think I married Richard all of a sudden?' The words came tumbling out in a high, agitated rush. 'I was pregnant when we were married. I should think the baby will be about a month too early.' She stopped and added slowly, significantly, 'And whose baby do you think it is?'

There was a long silence. Somewhere out in the garden a night bird called, a high wailing cry. Emma stared ahead, seeing nothing. Her skin was crawling cold, her mouth was dry. 'No,' she muttered at last through stiff lips. 'No—no—no—'

'Yes,' said Lisa, nodding her head up and down.

'Does—does Richard know?'

'Of course he does.'

'And he doesn't mind?'

'Richard would have taken me at any price.' Lisa touched her hair, smoothing it back, and for one pathetic moment she was the old Lisa, sure of her charm, her ability to get anything she wanted.

She sank down on the sofa beside Emma and grasped her hand. 'You won't tell anyone, will you,

Emma?' Her great blue eyes were pleading. 'It would
be awful if it got around—you know how gossipy
small towns are. And Richard's mother would take it
very badly. Richard's mother thinks I'm wonderful,'
she added with a twisted little smile.

Emma felt nothing. The pain would come later. It
was like a mortal wound—you didn't feel the swordthrust into your heart at first.

Lisa bit her lip, and her eyes were swimming with
tears. 'I'm sorry, Emma darling, I didn't want to hurt
you. But you see, I had to tell you. I couldn't let you
go on, not knowing. You can't marry him now, can
you?'

Emma stood up stiffly. She felt like a very, very old
woman, with nothing more to expect of life. 'I
shouldn't think so,' she said.

She saw the quick relief on her cousin's face. Relief
and—was it a touch of triumph, too? She supposed
she couldn't begrudge Lisa that, after all she had suffered. 'I think you'd better go now, Lisa,' she said.
'I'm rather tired.'

Lisa put her arms round her and kissed her and the
soft white, perfumed fur brushed Emma's cheek. 'I'm
sorry, Em,' she said again, and went out to her waiting car.

SOMEHOW EMMA got through the night. If she could
have cried it might have been a relief, but she was beyond tears. She felt drained, empty, like a dried-up
river-bed when the river has changed its course and
flowed elsewhere. At some time, sitting by the window, staring out at the darkened garden, she realised
that her teeth were chattering and she got up and
switched on the electric fire and wrapped herself in a

dressing-gown. But she couldn't make herself get into bed.

As soon as it was light she pulled off the clothes she was wearing and got into a hot bath. It wouldn't do to get a chill; that would complicate everything. She got into trousers and a warm sweater, but she was still cold all through.

The house began to stir early. She heard Jessie go downstairs, and, later, Uncle Edward's firm tread along the landing. After a few minutes she joined him in the breakfast room.

He beamed affectionately at her. 'Good morning, Emma, you're an early bird. I thought you'd sleep off your jet-lag this morning.'

She poured herself coffee. 'I don't get jet-lag,' she said, with a small, brittle laugh. *Only heartbreak, and you can't sleep that off.*

She waited until Uncle Edward had almost finished his breakfast. Then she said brightly, 'About my going to Germany for another year—you know, we discussed it before.'

'Did we?' He looked puzzled.

'Oh, yes, don't you remember? I've been thinking a lot about it while I've been away, and I do feel that if it's all right with you it would be better for me to leave Trent to get on with organising the new company here, for the time being.' The ordinariness of her own voice surprised her.

Uncle Edward frowned. 'But I thought—' He looked keenly into her face. Then he sighed. 'Oh well, if you're quite sure that's what you really want—'

'I am,' she said firmly.

Uncle Edward didn't often look cross, but at this moment he did. 'Then you'd better get in touch with the folk you stayed with before and see what you can fix up,' he said gruffly. And still frowning, he went off to his workroom, leaving a whole cup of coffee untouched on the table.

Somehow Emma got through the morning. She helped Jessie with the cleaning, polishing tables and chairs until her arm ached and Jessie began to look suspiciously at her. After that she walked up to the headland beside the house, where there was only the odd hiker, and the sea-birds, and a few cows. The headland had always been a favourite place of Emma's and she had walked here for miles over the soft turf, with the breeze on her cheeks, watching the white, ragged cliffs below with the waves foaming and beating round them. But today she saw nothing. She plodded on, looking straight ahead, taking the familiar route that led through the wood and down to the road. The July sun was hot on her face, but she felt cold, right through to her bones.

Meet me at the office at one, Trent had said. At midday Emma changed into a green linen shirtwaister dress, got out her Mini, and drove across the car-ferry and along the familiar road to Poole.

There was a parking space at the front of the office and she stopped the car and got out. Here was Trent's big surprise, then. The whole premises had acquired a fresh new look. The café had gone, and once more the frontage was joined into one—spruced up, repainted, and with a shiny bronze plate on the door, reading:

Fairley Brothers and Marston Navigational Instruments

Like a girl in a trance, Emma slid open the heavy door and went inside. Here the same magic had been

at work. The small, cramped area had become large
and spacious again, as it had been once before, when
shiny new boats stood here.

The work-force, too, had apparently expanded.
There were about twenty girls busy at their tables. A
tall man whom she hadn't seen before was strolling
round overseeing. Surely Trent hadn't got rid of Ted
Draper? But even as the thought surfaced, Ted himself came through the door from the office—a different Ted, in a neat navy-blue suit and blue collar, his
tow-coloured hair brushed back slickly.

He walked up to her, smiling all over his face. 'Well,
Miss Emma, what about this, then? A bit of a change,
isn't it?'

'It is indeed,' Emma said weakly. 'A change for the
better, I'm sure.'

'You're dead right,' Ted told her. 'Better for me,
that's for sure, to say nothing of the wife and kids.
You're looking at the new Production Manager, Miss
Emma.'

Emma shook hands and congratulated him warmly.
She went round and spoke to the girls she knew, and
everywhere it was the same story, the same satisfied
grin. Oh yes, Trent Marston had worked a miracle, all
right. Suddenly Emma was conscious of a fierce desire to be part of the miracle, to share the satisfaction
with him, the success that was always waiting for a
man like Trent.

She thrust away the thought. There was no way that
could happen now.

She walked slowly through the door into the office.
A new-look office it was, of course. She might have
expected that Trent wouldn't be satisfied with the old,

somewhat cramped quarters. There was a corridor now, with light wooden doors leading off.

Rose, the secretary, appeared to have three girls working under her instead of one. There was a shiny new electric typewriter on her desk and two phones, as well as an intercom. She seemed to be very busy, but spared a moment to greet Emma, in a slightly self-important voice.

'This is all so new to me,' said Emma. 'Which is Mr Marston's office, Rose?'

She was conducted to a newly-furnished office at the far end of the corridor. 'I'm expecting Mr Marston back at one,' Rose told her, in her new, secretarial voice. 'Can I get you anything, Miss Fairley? A cup of coffee?'

'No, thank you, Rose, I'll just wait here for him.'

She sat down rather quickly in a comfortable leather chair, as her knees were feeling like stretched elastic. Rose hovered for a moment, nodded and went out, closing the door behind her.

Presently Emma heard a car draw up outside and recognised the sound of the engine. She heard Trent's voice as soon as he came into the office. She knew his step in the corridor, she would have known his step from any other in the whole world, she thought numbly. There was an awful lot she would have to forget, very soon.

He threw open the door and kicked it closed behind him. In a couple of steps he was standing in front of her, bending over her, pulling her up into his arms, his dark eyes brilliant.

She struggled away, pushing at his chest with both hands.

'It's all right, Emma, we're quite alone,' he chuckled. 'Sweetheart, I couldn't wait to get back to you. I've—' He paused. 'Emma? Is something the matter? You're not ill, are you?' His face was suddenly anxious.

She gathered all her strength and moved away from him, round to the other side of the desk. She met his troubled gaze and, drawing a quick breath, said flatly, 'Lisa came to see me last night, after you'd left.'

'Oh yes?' He eyed her—warily, she thought.

'She came to tell me she's pregnant.'

He actually smiled. 'Well, good for her. They should be—'

'Trent—' she broke in, in an odd, strangled voice. 'You don't understand. She was in a terrible state. Uncle Edward had told her he thought that you and I—that we were—' She choked on the words.

'Now look, darling,' said Trent with a touch of impatience, 'don't you think we've had enough of Lisa and her dramatics? Can't we give it a rest?'

Emma could hardly believe her ears. Was he going to bluff it out—pretend he didn't know anything abut it? She looked at him as if he were a stranger. 'She told me that the baby is yours.'

There was a long, frozen silence in the office. From the next room came the busy clack of a typewriter, the buzz of a telephone, but in here it was as if life were suspended, waiting.

At last Trent spoke. He said very quietly, 'You thought I was the kind of man who'd get a girl pregnant and then walk out on her? You thought she'd married Richard as a cover-up. The faithful boy-next-door, ready to step into the breach?'

She gazed dumbly at him. The iciness of his voice, the hardness of his face, terrified her.

'And what about Richard?' he went on. 'Is he supposed to know about all this?'

Suddenly it was too much. 'Stop it—!' she cried putting her hands over her ears. 'I didn't think about all that—I couldn't. I only thought that every time I looked at Lisa's baby I would—would see—' She sank down into a chair, her knees trembling violently.

Trent threw her a contemptuous look. 'A very pretty picture!' He bit out the words as if they were poison. Then he turned his back on her and walked across to the window and stood there, stiff and unyielding.

It took all Emma's strength to speak to that tall, rigid back, but somehow she forced the words out. 'Trent, try to understand. I've loved Lisa all my life. She's been as dear as a younger sister to me. We've shared everything, told each other everything. I couldn't just—' Tears flooded into her eyes. She leant her forehead on the desk, while the tears rolled slowly down her cheeks.

He turned round but did not come nearer. He said slowly, 'Emma, I've always told you the truth, although you haven't always believed me. I'm telling you the plain truth now when I say that Lisa's baby isn't mine, whatever she may have said to you. It couldn't possibly be, for the simple reason that we never slept together.'

Her head shot up. This was something she hadn't considered. 'Then why did she—'

'Look, Emma,' he cut in, and now his voice wasn't accusing, it was stern and quiet. 'This is where you have to make a choice. You have to decide who you're going to believe, Lisa or me. It's as basic as that. I can't offer you any proof—only my word. It's up to you to think about it and make up your mind.' He walked to the door and stood there. His face was haggard, the features looked as the graven features of one of his Spanish ancestors must have looked. 'Only for God's sake don't take too long about it, will you?'

She was on her feet in seconds. He was going—leaving her—and she didn't have to think it out. She added instinctively, without thinking or willing. 'Trent—don't go—' The words seemed to come from deep inside her somewhere.

He turned but kept one hand on the door. 'There's no more to say.' He bit out the words curtly. 'Arguments won't help.'

She stumbled blindly towards him, holding out her hands. 'But I don't *want* to argue, Trent. I only want to say that I believe you. Of course I believe you—I love you.'

For a moment he stood very still, staring incredulously at her, the muscles in his strong face working, and she thought he was near to tears himself. Then she was in his arms and they were clinging together, and her face was pressed hard against his, the taste of salt on her lips.

In the next office the telephone buzzed again. 'Come on,' said Trent, 'let's get out of here. Fairley Brothers and Marston can manage to get along without us for a while.'

He gripped her hand and they ran along the corridor and out through the side door and on to the quay, like two children let out of school. The breeze met them and Emma threw back her head and laughed, in a kind of frenzy of joy, and relief from the unbearable tension. Her hair was blown into a tangle and she put up her hands to it with a little squeal.

Trent bent and kissed her swiftly. 'We'll walk,' he said, and there was new energy in his voice and a kind of triumph. 'I'm going to find the best jeweller in the town and put a ring on your finger, so everyone will know you're my woman.'

They walked together, arms entwined, along the old quay towards the town. It was the height of the season and the harbour was dotted thickly with sails, white and red and brown. Emma had always loved days like this, when the breeze came strongly off the sea, but now the sunshine had a new brilliance, the choppy water a deeper blue, because Trent was beside her and everything was right between them. She didn't have to doubt him any more—she just *knew*.

They chose a shop in the town centre, and when the assistant had taken one look at Trent and discovered what he wanted, they were ushered into a back room, evidently reserved for important customers, and the manager himself arrived to set before them the velvet-lined cases of rings that flashed and glittered in the electric lighting. Emma was speechless as she tried on one after the other of the beautiful things—diamonds, sapphires, emeralds—single stones, bars, clusters, modern designs. They all looked fabulously expensive and she glanced at Trent questioningly, but he sat back in his chair, smiling, obviously unconcerned about the price.

Finally she chose a single emerald in a filigree setting of pure white gold. When the manager had gone out of the room to phone for confirmation of the cheque, Trent took the ring from its tiny case and slipped it on to Emma's finger. 'I just want to see it there,' he said softly, lifting her hand and pressing his lips against it.

Emma was living in a rainbow dream. This was the most wonderful moment of her life and she wanted it to last on and on, for ever. She smiled mistily up at Trent and held his hand against her cheek.

They came out into the sunny street again. 'Now what?' said Trent. 'I think a celebration is in order. Have you lunched? No? Then I suggest we make for that restaurant where we lunched together that first time. We'll plight our eternal troth in champagne.' He grinned down at her and squeezed her arm hard. Emma was feeling decidedly lightheaded already and she daren't think what champagne was going to do to her. In her present mood it didn't seem to matter very much.

But as they came into the small bar of the Golden Butterfly sober reality returned instantly and she gripped Trent's arm. 'Look,' she hissed. 'Over there, by the bar. Richard.'

Trent was unperturbed. 'So?' There was a faint smile on his face as he followed her gaze. 'The moment of truth is upon us.'

Richard had seen them. He slipped off his high stool and came towards them, beaming expansively and shaking them both by the hand. He was, Emma saw at once, rather more than half-way towards being drunk. He face was pink and shiny, under the thatch of flaming red hair and his blue eyes were having a certain difficulty in focussing.

'Business lunch,' he explained carefully, as they all sat down at the nearest table. 'Couple of fellows from London—just left. Well, how's life, Emma? I hear you've been swanning round Mexico.' He looked at

Trent in a puzzled kind of way, as if he couldn't quite place him.

'You met Trent at the wedding,' Emma said. 'He's coming into the firm.'

'Ah yes, of course, jolly good, jolly good!' He shook Trent's hand heartily once again.

Trent said smoothly, 'We hear we have to congratulate you and Lisa. Are you pleased?'

Richard's face went even pinker and assumed the smug satisfaction of the father-to-be. 'Stunning, isn't it? It takes a bit of getting used to—me, a father!' He giggled foolishly. 'But we're all very bucked. Mother can't wait to be a granny.'

'When's the infant arriving?' Trent asked casually.

Richard's face because suddenly rueful and confidential. He leaned across the table and spoke in an undertone. 'Strictly between ourselves—round about November. Rather naughty, I'm afraid. It'll set the local ladies counting on their fingers. But when Lisa finally decided to have me I'm afraid we both got a bit carried away. You know how it is?' He looked towards Trent for a man-to-man confirmation, and Trent grinned back and said, 'Sure. Sure,' in comfortable understanding.

'We'll have another drink on it,' Richard said, and began to struggle to his feet, but Trent was up first.

'Mine, I think. We have something to celebrate too, haven't we, Emma?'

He touched her left hand and Richard goggled at the emerald glittering there.

'Well, blow me down! Golly, this is a fair corker! Does Lisa know? She'll be chuffed to bits when I tell her.'

Emma's eyes sought Trent's and saw the amused gleam in them. What had so nearly been a tragedy was turning into a farce.

Trent bought drinks and it was all very friendly and jolly. By the time Richard left them, with more fulsome congratulations on all sides, Emma was beginning to feel as if she were floating inches above the ground.

Trent turned to her with his enigmatic smile, only now it didn't anger or confuse her. She felt that at last she was beginning to understand something of this man she loved. 'Well,' he said, 'was that proof enough for you?'

She pulled a face at him. 'I didn't need proof.'

'No, I know you didn't, bless you,' he said, very low, 'and I'll always remember that, my darling.'

Afterwards, the one thing that Emma managed to recall about the lunch that followed was the roast duckling. It was probably delicious, but she hardly tasted it. She watched the bubbles rising in her champagne glass and felt as light as a bubble herself.

They walked back to the office and picked up Trent's car. 'We'll make for home and tell them our news,' he said. 'But we'll go the long way round.'

They took the road that crossed the heath and after a mile or so they got out of the car and walked a little way along a narrow, rough path. There was nobody in sight, and no sound except for the chirping of grasshoppers and the carolling of larks high overhead. Most of the gorse was over now, but here and there little bursts of gold showed between the turfs of heather and grass. It was very peaceful.

Trent's arm was close about Emma. She looked up at him, frowning slightly, and said, 'Why do you think Lisa should want to do that to me, Trent?'

His own thoughts must have been miles away, because it was a full minute before he replied. 'Because, my love, Lisa is a spoilt child still—a child living in a fantasy world. She thinks she should be able to get anything she happens to want, and if she doesn't get it she'll do everything she can to make sure that nobody else does. Least of all, you.' He smiled down at her tenderly. 'You, who—if I can believe what Edward tells me—have done quite a bit of the spoiling.'

She thought for a while and then sighed. 'Yes, I suppose that's true. Do you think she'll grow up—when she has her own child, perhaps?'

He shrugged. 'Who can tell? But do we have to go on talking about Lisa? She doesn't really matter, she could never have hurt us in the long run, my darling girl, we've got too much going for us.'

He stopped and pulled her down beside him in a hollow of dried grass and took her face in both his hands, his dark eyes gazing into hers as if he could never get enough of what he saw there. 'I adore you, Emma,' he whispered huskily. 'I never thought I should find a girl like you. You're the most wonderful thing that ever happened to me.'

'And yet you went away and left me for weeks.'

'That was pure hell,' he muttered, 'but it had to be done. You kept on saying you hated me.'

'I had to keep on saying it,' she confessed, 'in case I told you I was falling fathoms deep in love with you. I think you bewitched me, but I never imagined you were serious about me.'

He groaned. 'Serious! I was besotted. I put poor Juanita through the third degree on the phone, to find out if there was any bloke out there trying anything on with you.'

She said demurely, 'There was Luis Valesco. He—'

'What?' he roared, sitting up straight.

'He must have been around seventy,' she added, as if he hadn't interrupted.

He sank down beside her, pulling her roughly into his arms. 'Enough of this,' he said, and there was a touch of the old arrogant Trent in his voice now. 'You're my woman from now on, and I've waited too long already. When will you marry me?'

She pretended to consider, but the sight of his dark face so close above hers was making her heart plunge wildly.

'Let me see—how about tomorrow?'

He gave a shout of laughter and tightened his arms round her. 'I don't know if I can wait that long.'

His hands went to the front zip of her linen dress. The zip stuck half-way and with trembling hands she finished the job for him, everything in her aching for his kisses. She put her arms around his neck and drew his head down, shuddering with delight at the touch of his lips on her swelling breast.

His mouth inched its way up her neck as his hands began to move over her body, lovingly, caressingly. He kissed her chin and muttered thickly, 'But it's going to be worth waiting for, don't you think, my love?'

'Yes—oh yes!' His face above hers was blotting out the sun. She closed her eyes and the whole world was engulfed in a great wave of love and longing.

'Yes,' she managed to gasp again just before his lips closed over hers.

THE AUTHOR

Marjorie Lewty is a born romantic. "It's all in the way you look at the world," she suggests. "Maybe if I hadn't been lucky enough to find love myself—in my parents, my husband, my children—I might have viewed the world with cynicism." As it is, she writes about "what is surely the most important and exciting part of growing up, and that is falling in love." She and her family live in Leamington, a pleasant town full of beautiful parks and old Georgian homes.

King
Kielder
Margaret Rome

Could she really marry Colt Kielder? The very idea was repulsive to Rowan, but when her brother unexpectedly sold their home, Falstone Castle, to hated Scotsman Colt Kielder, Rowan had to do *something* to retain her rightful heritage.

"Some battles are fought with dirk and sword; others with cunning and guile," old Nanny advised her. So Rowan decided to accept the challenge.

But marriage to Colt became a different sort of challenge than she'd bargained for....

CHAPTER ONE

WHEN SHE reached the Kielder Stone, a huge boulder through which ran the boundary line marking the division on the Border where England officially ceased and Scotland began, Rowan reined in her mount and sat motionless, staring down from a high vantage point over acres of forest land, an unbroken vista of conifer green that had remained undisturbed for decades—until recently.

Teeth bit sharply into a trembling bottom lip as she fought against a misery of tears. The battle had been staunchly fought, but victory had gone to the enemy, yet not even in solitude was she prepared to betray the proud traditions of a family that had survived generations of strife, bloodshed, and the bitter animosity of Scottish neighbours—thieving villains who had stolen across the border to steal sheep and cattle, to plunder the homes and even to kidnap the daughters of hated English Borderers.

Historians had attempted to prove that the blame had not been entirely one-sided, that there had been as many English reivers as there had been Scottish, and that during an era when the frontier territory had been dominated by dirk and sword—an arena where antagonists could meet—when blackmail, arson, robbery and murder had been tolerated as normal, no householder of either nationality had dared to wander unarmed, to sleep without keeping one eye open, or to leave house, family or stock unguarded.

Over the years Rowan had conditioned her mind into accepting that not all Scots were black-hearted villains intent upon treachery, but recently she had been forcibly converted to her brother Nigel's vehemently expressed opinion that Border Scots were inculcated with a resentment of their English neighbours that was almost paranoic, that because of countless defeats both physical and political, they felt compelled to assuage a deep feeling of inferiority by launching devious, underhanded attacks upon a more affluent English society.

She winced when a harsh staccato noise rent the air, and bent to comfort the startled mare whose head had jerked in panic.

"Easy, Cello," she murmured, stroking soothing hands along the length of a tautly arched neck, "that was the sound of progress you heard, a sound we shall be forced to live with for the better part of a decade now that Colt Kielder and his associates have won their case. Industry is desperate for more water, you see," numbly she intoned arguments that had been tossed back and forth between area authorities, conservationists and local residents during a tedious, months-long inquiry, "also rising living standards have brought increased domestic demands in all parts of the region, which is why, because we happen to live in the most isolated and sparsely populated part of England, it has been decided that our quality of life is of little consequence, that families must be uprooted, roads and houses flooded, wildlife destroyed and animals made homeless in order to make way for a monster reservoir!"

As if mocking her agony, deriding the long bitter struggle she and her sympathisers had put up in an attempt to preserve the peace and tranquillity of the countryside they loved, a screeching cacophony of sound rose up from the valley where a huge tunnelling machine had begun an experimental probe to discover the type of rock strata likely to be encountered once the despoiling of nature was actually under way, and with an outraged sweep of powerful wings a rare peregrine falcon rose from a massive, untidy nest built of sticks, rubbish, rags and paper to demonstrate his displeasure by angrily beating the air.

Smothering a cry of regret, Rowan jerked upon the reins, wheeling Cello around so that she no longer had to face the noble falcon of war, the almost extinct airborne vision of grace that made the skies more beautiful. With hands loosely clasping the reins she allowed the mare to pick her own way down the fellside and slumped dejectedly in the saddle, her sadly brooding eyes lacking for the first time ever the sparkle of appreciation that usually ignited at the sight of a rippling lake overshadowed by darkly frowning fells, by windswept moorland and dense tracts of fir tree forest.

She was nearing home, cantering slowly along a main road slicing straight through the heart of dense woodland, when the sound of an approaching car jerked her shoulders erect, set her senses quivering. Nigel had often accused her of being "fey", as acute as a witch in the art of premonition, and his notion was justified when she caught sight of a Land Rover being driven by the man whose presence her tense limbs and angry rise of colour had been quick to signal.

As if Cello, too, was sensitive to his awesome personality she trembled to a standstill when the Land Rover braked to a halt and its motor was cut, plunging them once more into a green-shrouded chasm of silence.

"Good morning, Lady Rowan!" Colt Kielder had the gall to smile as he eased his long, rangy frame out of the driving seat and strode towards her as if actually anticipating a welcome.

She was fiercely glad of having the advantage of being on horseback, so that for once she had no need to tilt her head in order to combat the challenge of steely grey eyes which, even in the midst of stormy dispute, had never been allowed to flicker with temper but had remained a cool, enigmatic contradiction to his shock of copper-red hair.

"That's a matter of opinion, Mr Kielder," she managed to respond stiffly.

"Mister...?" She was incensed by the humourless quirk of his lips, by the relaxed, arrogant manner in which he seemed to take charge of every situation. "As children, on the rare occasions when you and your brother were allowed to mix with village children, it was always impressed upon me that you were to be addressed as Lady Rowan and Lord Nigel respectively, but neither of you appeared to have any reservations about calling me Colt, so why the sudden formality? In what way has the situation changed?"

"You dare to ask me that!" She shot bolt upright in the saddle, her fingers itching to make contact with the teak-tanned face leathered with hard living that was hovering a tantalising slap-reach away. Conscious that her inbred attitude of dignity was in danger of slipping, she stalled for time by lifting a hand to push back from her brow a wing of hair black as the plumage of the raven that was doomed to be ousted from its natural habitat, deprived of security and freedom at the instigation of a man as insensitive and uncaring as his reiving Scottish ancestors. Lashes swept dark as bruises against flushed cheeks, her soft mouth trembled, yet somehow she managed to keep her voice steady when she husked:

"I think I could more easily have forgiven a stranger for disrupting the privacy of our home, for despoiling the beauty of our countryside with bulldozers and earthdiggers, noisy lorries, and a shanty town of workmen's caravans. But you were one of us! Granted your family pulled up roots and emigrated to America when you were twelve years old, nevertheless, exactly like Nigel and myself, you were *born* here!"

"*Exactly* like, Lady Rowan...?" His suspicion of transatlantic accent became more pronounced, nothing grating or abrasive enough to eliminate a natural Scottish burr, more like the muted harshness of sound made when the gentle waters of a burn tumble unexpectedly over a bed of gravel. "I'm afraid the similarity escapes me, for while you and your brother grew up in the rarified atmosphere of Falstone Castle, cosseted from the realities of life by a retinue of servants, my home was a farmworker's cottage on your father's estate, a tied house from which we were evicted because my father had the temerity to speak out strongly against some new method of farming that offended him greatly. Yes, we emigrated," he nodded, "but not from choice. It broke my father's heart when he was forced to leave the countryside he loved because no other employer in the area would give work to a man who had been dismissed from his previous job without a reference."

"Oh...!" Her gasp throbbed with contrition. "I'm so sorry, I had no idea..."

"Of course you hadn't," he agreed with surprising magnanimity, "you couldn't have been more than six years old at the time. But even if you had been old enough to understand, your inbred sense of superiority would have prevented you from finding fault with your father who, in common with many landed gentry of his time, was an absentee landlord, content to leave the running of his estate to a manager who did not hesitate to employ his authority to dismiss a man on the slightest pretext as a weapon of persecution."

Her proud head drooped, shamed by the sort of indictment which twenty years previously must have cost Colt Kielder's father his job. She had no recollection of her mother, who had died without making any impression upon her infant mind, and only fleeting memories of the father who, after the death of his wife, had seemed to consider his children a burden to be shifted on to any available shoulders—governesses, schoolteachers, servants—while he took up permanent residence in London and salved his no doubt uneasy conscience by paying short annual visits to the family home. His eventual death had left her less moved than the passing of an ancient gander that had been her constant companion all during childhood...

"As a boy," Colt Kielder seemed to achieve insight into her thoughts, "I could never decide whether you and your brother—the Earl of Falstone—were more deserving of envy or pity."

The bracketing of the word pity with the proud Falstone name inspired sufficient anger to tilt her chin.

"You've gained the reputation of being an astute businessman, Mr Kielder, a brilliant engineer who formed a small company and then set out to woo lucrative contracts from Middle Eastern oil sheiks, earning a name for ruthless efficiency and at the same time amassing a considerable fortune. Nevertheless, the fact that you're now head of a large international construction company has not earned you the right to patronise your... your..."

"Betters...?" he suggested mildly when she hesitated, seeking a diplomatic alternative.

"If you insist," she flashed, employing hauteur to conceal a twinge of shame. "Though you may have gained materially, you seem in the process to have forfeited all sense of decency, to have cut the ties of loyalty that have bound you since birth to this region and to people who were once foolish enough to regard you as one of themselves."

When he stepped back a pace she congratulated herself upon having probed a sensitive nerve, until a glance over his impassive features quickly dispelled this notion.

"Believe it or not," he drawled laconically, "the welfare of the inhabitants of this area was one of the motives that influenced my decision to tender for the contract to build the dam. No one knows better than I the frustration men feel when they're tied to jobs they dislike or to employers with whom they're incompatible, simply because there's no alternative source of employment in the area. Also, no other contractor would have felt the same determination as myself to ensure that the countryside is restored as far as possible to its original state once the dam has been completed. All decisions appertaining to the location of the dam were taken by area authorities who are immune to outside influences, but often instructions that have to be implemented by contractors are open to interpretation, consequently, I deliberately tendered low, hoping to manoeuvre myself into a position where I could make sure that the least possible upset is caused while work is in progress; see to it that every complaint receives a fair hearing, and to do everything in my power to ensure that householders whose homes are to be flooded receive adequate compensation."

"How very altruistic!" Rowan flared, her normally gentle nature inflamed by the hypocrisy of the man she felt certain was enjoying the anger he had caused to a member of a family whose position of privilege he had always resented. "Would you mind telling me how you intend to compensate the otter for being deprived of his holt, or the badger of his sett? Why don't you be honest and admit that you would never have returned to your old home, would have turned your back forever on a region whose best known landmark bears your name, if there had been nothing personal to be gained?"

She felt sickened and unaccountably disappointed by his narrow-eyed start of surprise, by the quirk of annoyance fleeting across a stern mouth that seemed to indicate a stabbing conscience.

"I'm right, aren't I...?" she accused, wide-eyed and motionless as the doe whose head had just appeared peeping through trunks of fir trees fringing the forest road.

He hesitated, then squared his shoulders, standing tall and implacable as the Kielder Stone.

"Yes, I did have a personal reason for returning home," he frowned, "but it's no secret—indeed, I've imagined that by this time it would have become common knowledge. My advice to you, Lady Rowan," he continued with a look of pity that caused her a stirring of panic, "is to seek an immediate showdown with your brother; it appears to me that he's kept his own counsel long enough."

Kept his own counsel! Persistent as Cello's hooves, the warning drummed into her mind as she sped homeward, leaving Colt Kielder without so much as a cursory goodbye in her anxiety to confront her brother, to wheedle out of him what she suspected might be the latest of a long line of indiscretions. Her frown deepened when Cello veered to canter up the stable drive reaching to the rear of Falstone Castle as she was struck more forcibly than usual by signs of dilapidation and neglect. Massive iron gates inscribed with the motto: *Nil Conscire Sibe*—Having No Remorse—leant drunkenly against crumbling stone pillars; the roof of a once imposing lodge had tiles askew, allowing access to inquisitive pigeons; a shrubbery resembling an unpruned jungle of suckers, dead branches and fallen leaves. Making a mental resolution to begin attacking the flourishing clumps of weeds as soon as possible, she slung the saddle from Cello's back, gave her a good rub down, then saw her comfortably stabled before entering the rear of the castle by way of a huge, old-fashioned kitchen.

At the sound of footsteps upon the stone-flagged floor an elderly woman wearing an ancient ankle-length dress beneath a spotlessly white apron turned round to greet her.

"My, but you're looking bonny today, bairn!" Sharp eyes set black as currants into a face wrinkled as a walnut, glistened with pride as they roved Rowan's flushed cheeks and wild-blue eyes. "I knew the ride would do you good," she turned to resume her task of kneading a pile of dough, "there's nothing helps a body's looks more than fresh air and exercise."

"Nanny," Rowan blurted, ignoring the maxim she had heard repeated regularly and monotonously over the years by the old servant who had exerted the only stable influence she had ever known, "do you know the whereabouts of my brother? I'm anxious to have a word with him."

"Then you'd better keep your wits about you," Nanny sniffed. "He's out at the moment, went roaring down the drive in that nasty red sports car of his about half an hour ago, but he'll be back shortly—he's ordered an early lunch before setting off for London."

"What, *again*? But he's only just returned!"

"It puzzles me why he doesn't stay there permanently," Nanny retorted with the assurance of an old retainer, "because whenever he does come home he mooches around the house with a face as long as a fiddle, hankering after bright lights and entertainment, just as your father did."

"I hope you don't encourage this extravagance, Nanny," Rowan chewed her lip. "Father could afford to live in London, but I'm certain Nigel can't, because it's as much as I can do to persuade him to pay the household bills."

"What a comedown!" Mournfully, Nanny shook her head. "To think that not so many years ago there were twenty household servants in this castle, not to mention gardeners, grooms and stable boys—and everyone kept to his proper place. Not like nowadays," she pummelled aggravated fists into the lump of dough, "when the son of a Scot—a farm labourer who worked on this very estate—is allowed leave to pretend that Jack's as good as his master!"

Rowan did not pretend to misunderstand. "Social barriers disappeared many years ago, Nanny," she reproved gently, "equal opportunities have put a good education within reach of all. I can find nothing likeable about Colt Kielder as a person, but one has to acknowledge that the man, as well as being clever, is a determined hardheaded business tycoon. And while we're on the subject," she ventured timidly, knowing the old woman's depth of partisanship for her race, "don't you think it's rather silly of you to continue adding fuel to feuds that have roots buried hundreds of years in the past? We're living in the twentieth century, for decades English and Scottish Borderers have lived peaceably side by side, so well integrated—even marriage—that it would be difficult to find one family of either nationality who could boast a completely pure strain."

"Integrated!" Nanny swung round to scoff. "As Colt Kielder's father was integrated! He was a proud man who, every time he lifted his eyes towards the Kielder Stone, was reminded that once his clan had been the most powerful and respected of all the Scottish Border clans; a man who found it difficult to bend his knee, one whose bitterness at having been reduced to accepting a job as a servant on the estate of an En-

glish earl was well known to his wife and no doubt to his son. I'm aware that mixed marriages that once were forbidden by law are accepted today as normal, nevertheless, old rancours still linger, under a thin skimming of unity the cracks are still there. Why else," she challenged fiercely, "do you suppose that within one Border village two separate accents can still be heard; why does even the smallest community support both an English church and a Scottish chapel, and why do half the regulars of local pubs leave the celebrating of Christmas to the English and save all their energies for Hogmanay? Mark my words well, bairn," Nanny fixed her with the glittering stare of the fanatic, "that man has returned to these parts determined to revenge his father's humiliation and to restore the status of a family whose sons are reputed to be gifted with a giant's strength and magic armour! Take care that you're not deceived, by Colt Kielder, whose ancestors' boast is recorded in border ballads:

In my plume is set the holly green And the leaves of the rowan tree

In spite of the derisory grimace she had directed towards Nanny before leaving her to her own devices, Rowan felt a shiver chasing down her spine as she stepped out of the kitchen regions into a flagged hall with a staircase of stone and arrow-slit windows through which sunrays were slanting upon woven wallhangings depicting tableaux in which English lances lined the Border, provoking Scots to come over to engage in one of the violent skirmishes for which the reivers had been famous; and creeping, shadowy figures—identifiable as Scots by their cocky bonnets—making their stealthy way along night-darkened fells in the direction of cattle herded into pens at the back of a farmhouse where an unsuspecting family slept.

Tattered battle standards and family portraits lined the rest of the walls of a castle built solid as a fortress, able to withstand the ravages caused by blazing arrows, so that during the three occasions when the interior had been gutted by fire the blackened shell had remained intact and had immediately been refurbished by the reigning earl. But now, centuries after the last battle cry had been heard, time and the elements were managing to achieve what the reivers had failed to do—eroding stonework that crumbled at a touch; obliterating portraits with layers of grime; rotting oak panelling to the texture of sponge; reducing once magnificent hangings to shreds—tattered as Falstone pride.

As Nanny had refused help to prepare the lunch and housework held little appeal, Rowan made her way to a shed housing an assortment of gardening tools, deciding that expending her energy upon the weed-choked shrubbery might help to take her mind off Colt Kielder's worrying warning. Although his remark had been obliquely phrased its meaning had been clear. Nigel was keeping her in the dark about something—but what? All sorts of possibilities presented themselves as she trundled a wheelbarrow down the drive, but one by one she discounted them as being too commonplace to be kept secret. If ever Nigel had gambling debts and money was tight the household bills were the first to suffer; if he had at last found someone among his crowd of girl-friends whom he wished to marry—fear clawed her throat as she wondered how she could cope if any new mistress of Falstone should turn out to be unfriendly—she would have known intuitively, because her brother was always full of high spirits whenever he fell in love. Lately he had been moody and irascible. She sighed, then turned her attention upon waist-high weeds, determined to clear her mind of useless conjecture.

By the time Nigel's car turned into the driveway the shrubbery was looking almost respectable, but her face was streaked from contact with dusty leaves, and her hair dishevelled, stuck with pieces of broken twig. Brakes squealed a protest when he caught sight of her, his fastidious nose turning up in disgust when he stepped out of the car to question disdainfully:

"What are you up to, for heaven's sake? Must you embarrass me by taking over the gardener's duties?"

"We have no gardener," she reminded him gently. "You said we could no longer afford to employ him, remember?"

He looked momentarily abashed but quickly recovered his composure. "So I did," he agreed airily. "Nevertheless, there's still no need for you to get into such a disgusting mess. Pretty soon—" With a sharp snap of teeth he broke off and swiftly changed the subject. "Get into the car and I'll run you up to the house. I must hurry, I have an appointment in London this evening."

Once again Rowan felt a fluttering of fear, a premonition that something unpleasant was hovering in the background. Her brother had always been able to dominate her, to quell with a look, but this time she meant to have her say.

"There's something I must discuss with you before you leave."

Warily, he eyed her stubborn bottom lip, the glint of determination in usually serene eyes. "I suppose you've heard rumours?" Awkwardly, he shifted his feet and dropped his eyes, reminding her of the schoolboy who had never voluntarily owned up to any misdeed.

"Rumours about what?" she queried stonily. "Are you suggesting that there's some important family matter about which outsiders are better informed than I am?"

"I don't intend to stand about any longer than I need in this damned chilly air. Get inside the car." When he swung away in a temper, unable to meet her eyes, Rowan's heart seemed to freeze, rendering mind and senses numb while she was driven up to the house and then ushered inside the hall with the terse instruction, "Have a quick wash and brush-up, in five minutes I'll join you for lunch."

Mechanically she went up to her room, grateful that shock had lent her an outward appearance of calm and rendered her unable to think, for she knew that if she did she would begin to cry. She had no illusions about her brother who, over the years, had proved himself to be weak, vain, and outrageously selfish. Yet at times he could be affectionate and kind. Certainly, he had never gone deliberately out of his way to hurt her.

Cushioned by this thought, she made her way down to the dining-room and was even able to muster a smile when Nigel turned from the window at the sound of her approach.

"Shall we eat first and talk later?"

Numbly, she nodded, knowing that food would choke her, yet, in the manner of one who appreciates that a state of limbo has to be endured before the pleasures of heaven or the agonies of hell, she toyed her way through broth, lamb cutlets, and one of Nanny's unnameable puddings. By the time the table had been cleared she felt the peak of her endurance had been reached.

"Coffee...?" With a shaking hand she lifted the coffee pot in response to Nigel's nod, then remained poised, frozen with shock, when he blurted:

"I've sold Falstone Castle—I *had* to," he appealed desperately, "there was simply no other way I could clear my debts!"

Rowan stared, transfixed with horror, at the thin, aristocratic features of the man who had inherited an ancient title, a descendant of men who had not hesitated to spill their blood in defence of their land, who had fought to the death to protect their home and to retain their children's rightful inheritance.

"You've done *what*...?" Her horrified whisper seemed to bounce from the walls of the silent room, even the expressions on family portraits looked shocked, painted eyes fixed upon the shamefaced custodian of their ancient title.

"For heaven's sake, Rowan, there's no need to look like that, it's not exactly the end of the world!" Blustering with temper, he rose to his feet and shoved aside his chair. "It'll do you good to get away from this Godforsaken place—you've never left it, not even for a day. Personally, I shall feel eternally grateful to Father for insisting upon my being educated at boarding school and for following that up with a two-year commission in his old regiment, because it was during such times that I discovered a world of laughter and enjoyment, a world in which people live, not merely exist!" Suddenly he changed tack and opted for a more coaxing attitude in an attempt to disperse her uncanny stillness, the deathly pallor of a profile that seemed etched from marble.

"You'll enjoy London, Rowan. I'll sell my flat, then once we've found a house in a decent neighbourhood we'll join the jet set for a year-long holiday—sunbathing in Barbados; skiing in St Moritz; shopping in Paris. We'll take in the Cannes Film Festival, then after Wimbledon we'll make for Monte Carlo where with a bit of luck we could be invited to join a yacht for a cruise of the Greek Islands. I promise you, Rowan," he waxed enthusiastic, "that in a year from now you won't care a damn about Colt Kielder lording it over Falstone Castle!"

"Colt Kielder...!" She dropped into a chair as her knees buckled under her. "Are you telling me that you've actually sold our home to that...that *Scot*?"

"Oh, spare me the histrionics!" Conscience, guilt, or perhaps a mixture of both ignited his explosive temper. "*Yes,* I've sold out to Colt Kielder, I don't give a damn about his nationality, all I care about is the fact that as a multi-millionaire he can afford to meet my price."

He started towards her, alarmed by her look of pain, and stared down at the face of a stranger, a pinched, stricken profile with a fixed look bearing none of the fond tolerance he was used to receiving from his gentle, unworldly young sister.

"*Traitor...!*" Her sibilant condemnation startled him rigid and for the first time the enormity of what he had done seemed to impinge upon his conscience. "For weeks you must have plotted behind my back, sharing meals, sharing the same roof, yet giving not the least hint of your intention. I'll never forgive you this betrayal, Nigel!'' she choked on a rush of tears. ''Even Scottish reivers, barbarians though they were, earned themselves the reputation of being honourable enough—whenever they were forced to break bread with their enemies—to place a black boar's head upon the table as a warning that treachery was imminent!''

CHAPTER TWO

CELLO SEEMED attuned to Rowan's mood as dolefully the mare picked her way towards the valley. Tenant farmers had to be told of the estate's change of ownership; retired servants who had spent a lifetime in the service of the Earls of Falstone had to be informed as tactfully as possible that permanent security of tenure could no longer be guaranteed to the occupants of grace and favour cottages. For days Rowan had baulked at the task ahead, then had been shamed by the realisation that she was falling prey to the same cowardly impulse as her brother, who had dodged unpleasantness until the last possible moment, thereby leaving her vulnerable to the hints of a hateful usurper.

She could have opted for the easy way out, could have faded into the background and allowed Nigel to carry out his intention of sending each of his tenants stiff, formal letters containing the bare outlines of their changed circumstances, but to Rowan most of them were not merely tenants but friends, and friendship imposed upon her a duty to ensure that the news was broken as gently as possible.

Sadly she made her way towards Beck Farm, the home of Tom and Beth Graham and their pretty teen-aged daughter Dale, cringing from the thought of taking worry and unhappiness into a household whose welcome was always warm. A strange new sound disturbed the countryside as she headed Cello away from their usual route which was no longer safe for horses and riders. Day by day the main road through the forest—narrow, winding, with deep ditches running either side, fashioned in the days when a pony and trap was the ideal way to enjoy an exceptionally lovely drive with glimpses of a stream tumbling down the fellside and erupting into a thousand tiny cascades as it was confronted by huge stones and boulders stuck fast in the river bed—was becoming choked and churned up by a heavy volume of traffic, huge-wheeled monsters glaring bright yellow against a backdrop of sober forest green; a trailing convoy of earth-diggers; concrete mixers; tunnelling machines; lorries laden with mile upon mile of steel pipe, tools and an unending variety of equipment; caravans intent upon swelling the temporary town that had already grown larger than the village, and private cars packed with tough-looking, horn-tooting men whose enthusiastic race to join in the rape of the valley had been curbed to an irritating crawl.

Mercifully, however, as she rode deep into the forest to make her daily check upon its inhabitants, everything appeared to be as normal—wild goats and deer placidly grazing; red squirrels scurrying about their business; blue and brown hares patently disinterested; red grouse, duck, ravens, woodpeckers, goldcrests; kestrels, skylarks, whinchats, nightjars, dippers, wagtails, snipe and even a rarely-sighted heron all seemed complacently unaware of the atmosphere of destruction threatening their surroundings.

Immediately Cello's hooves began clattering over the cobbled yard, Beth Graham erupted from the farmhouse beaming a smile of welcome.

"The tea's brewed, Lady Rowan. A feeling in my bones told me that you'd be visiting us today."

"Then I haven't chosen an inconvenient time?" Rowan slid from the saddle and looped Cello's bridle over a convenient post.

"Bless you, no!" assured the motherly woman, who ought to have been favoured with a large brood of children to spoil instead of just one solitary chick and every lonely youngster she could scoop within her orbit. "As I was saying to Tom only last evening, the mere sight of you brings me comfort, a reminder that if ever we're in trouble you'll always be at hand to sort it out. We're simple folk, as you well know—good farmers," she claimed without false modesty, "but babes in the wood when it comes to dealing with people of high authority. Remember how we fretted ourselves silly for weeks, wondering if our farm was to be among those to be submerged by dam water," she chuckled, ushering Rowan into a spotlessly clean kitchen, "and how you were able, in a matter of hours, to set our minds at rest?"

"That was more good luck than good management," Rowan confessed, sinking down into a chair and watching appreciatively while Beth poured steaming amber liquid into her cup. "On my way home that day I just happened to bump into Colt Kielder, and when I mentioned your worry he promptly supplied the good news that your fears were unfounded."

"But only at your request," Beth defended stoutly. "It appears to me that men involved in affairs of business become so absorbed in the mechanics of their project, especially one as big as the dam, that they're apt to overlook the fears—real or imaginary—of insignificant people such as Tom and myself who suddenly find themselves slap in the middle of the path of progress. I don't know what would happen to us if we didn't have you to rely on!''

Suddenly, the freshly-baked scones and creamy, home-churned butter lost all their appeal. Rowan pushed aside her plate, knowing she could not emulate Nigel's ability to eat, apparently unconcerned, while debating how best to confess to an act of treachery.

Seemingly oblivious to her distress, Beth prattled happily on, turning a knife in Rowan's wound. ''Tom and I have come to the conclusion that the building of the dam might not be such a bad thing after all. You remember my mentioning that our Dale has been pestering us since she left school to be allowed to stay with my sister in Newcastle while she looks for a typing job?''

Mechanically, Rowan nodded.

''Well, that problem has now been solved,'' Beth glowed triumphantly. ''Mr Kielder is in need of a junior in his site office and he's very kindly offered Dale the job.''

The mere mention of Colt Kielder's name inflicted intolerable pain; the gratitude Beth was displaying struck Rowan as the ultimate in disloyalty. She jumped to her feet to exclaim in a voice as grating as the sound made by the legs of her chair as they scraped across the sandstone floor:

''Then it's just as well that you approve of Colt Kielder, because shortly he's to become your landlord—the new owner of Falstone Castle and its estate!''

''But, Lady Rowan...!'' she heard Beth gasp as she ran towards the door, ''does that mean that *you* are thinking of leaving us? *No,* you can't be,'' she wailed, ''we need you here!''

By the time she had reached Black Dyke Rowan had had time to reflect and to feel ashamed of her unreasonable attitude. Resolving to apologise to Beth as soon as possible, she tethered Cello to a gatepost and went in search of Tom Graham, determined that this time she would keep her emotions under control, would not allow the mention of Colt Kielder's name to upset the dignity that was expected of a Falstone.

She found him in a barn and was not in the least surprised when, after she had greeted him by name, he merely grunted acknowledgement of her presence and continued forking bales of hay. He was yet another of the Border Scots whose forebears had somehow managed to stray across the Border, settling down and working among English neighbours without ever becoming part of the community.

She began without preamble, expecting no sign of regret at the news of the imminent departure of the Falstones, yet unprepared for the uncharacteristic expression of pleasure that transformed his features.

''I've come to tell you that you're soon to have a change of landlord, Tom. Falstone Castle and the estate have been sold to Colt Kielder.''

Cold eyes flickered with a spiteful gleam. ''My, but that's good news!''

She flinched from the deliberate snub and in spite of her vow to remain calm an indignant rejoinder spilled past her lips.

"It puzzles me why any Scot should choose to live on the English side of the Border!"

"Me, too," he glared, setting his shoulders in the stance of an adversary.

"Then why...?" she faltered, nonplussed.

"When my family settled here this land belonged to Scotland," he glared fiercely, "and in spite of what's written in the Statute Book in my eyes it will always remain so. For centuries ownership was disputed between England and Scotland, so much so that it earned the title of the Debateable Land, and since neither side would admit to responsibility for clashes between English and Scots settlers it came to be regarded as outlaw country, a place where the rich and powerful came to grab as much land as they could."

"Are you implying that my family—" Rowan began angrily.

"I'm implying nothing," he interrupted with a scowl. "The truth of what I've said is recorded in our family Bible, together with the threat that a curse will fall upon any member of a Scottish family who gives ground to the thieving English! For years I've been greatly angered at having been forced to pay rent to a foreign landlord," he hissed, eyeing her with a gleam of fanaticism, "but thank God the tide has turned once more in favour of Scotland and once again a Kielder is to be king—and every reigning monarch has need of a castle!"

More shaken than she had ever felt in her life before, Rowan backed out of his presence, appalled by an antagonism that she had never dreamt existed, by the realisation that beneath a thin veneer of civilisation lay the old resentments, rancour and bitterness that had existed between ancient Border clans.

Exhausted as if she had done battle, she heaved her slight, quivering frame into the saddle, tempted to set Cello on a course for home. But the impulse was checked as subconsciously she drew upon the courage and determination inherited from ancestors whose strength had made them great, whose motto *Having No Remorse* had been made applicable not only to their enemies but also to themselves.

Dusk was falling by the time she had finished her round of scattered cottages and trotted into the stable yard at the rear of the castle. She slid from the saddle, physically exhausted by miles of riding, emotionally drained by hours of wheedling, reassuring and cajoling, by the woeful, watering eyes of pensioners who had served her family well and who now looked to her for guidance. As mechanically she attended to Cello's comfort, their many bewildered questions echoed in her ears.

"If you leave, who will look in on us when we're taken badly?"

"Who'll write my letters to my grandson in Canada?"

"Who will we get to fill in forms and collect our pensions?"

"How will we contact the doctor...the chiropodist..."

HATING COLT Kielder, placing the entire blame for their distress upon his self-assertive shoulders, she left Cello quietly munching oats and, dispirited to the verge of tears, she slipped into the castle through the rear entrance. As she passed the kitchen she noted with relief that it was empty—Nanny's chatter would have been more than she could have borne at that stage—so she hurried towards the solitude of the library, intent upon curling up to brood inside one of the capacious, shabby armchairs.

The doorbell pealed when she was halfway across the hall. Impulsively she quickened her steps, hoping to gain the sanctuary of the library without being noticed, and had almost achieved her aim when she was shamed by Nanny's spear of acid humour.

"As you're obviously in an unsociable mood, shall I get rid of the caller, whoever he might be?"

"Yes, please, Nanny," she blushed, defensive as a reprimanded child. "I've heard enough of people's troubles for one day. Unless," she added the afterthought, "our visitor brings news of importance—I'll leave you to make your own judgment."

The wide curved back of an armchair seemed to open arms wide to receive her when she slumped into its embrace and leant her head against a wing of padded leather. She closed her eyes, revelling in an atmosphere of deep repose, until her peace was invaded by the sound of squeaking hinges when Nanny thrust open the door to announce dourly:

"The Cowt insists upon seeing you!"

Rowan shot upright, appalled by the ungracious introduction and by Nanny's ability to register dislike by making the pronouncement of a name sound offensive. Blessing the foresight that had led her to keep the old servant in ignorance of their changed circumstances, she jumped to her feet, prepared to apologise for Nanny's disgraceful show of truculence.

But Colt Kielder looked quite unabashed as he sauntered in Nanny's wake, one corner of his mouth curled upwards as if tugged by a ghost of amusement. "I'm sorry, Mr Kielder," she began stiffly, "Nanny finds it difficult to pronounce some words properly, I'm afraid."

Her breath caught as if severed, when unexpectedly he smiled. "Please don't apologise for reviving pleasant memories of the past, Lady Rowan. My mother used often to call me Cowt, which is the traditional Scottish pronunciation of our family name."

"I'm well aware of that fact!" Nanny bridled. "Cowt means 'strong'—it's no coincidence that the largest and most outstanding boulder in the district has been endowed with the name given to every first-born Kielder male."

When she flounced out of the room, Rowan shrugged, then turned her attention to her visitor, only to be further annoyed by his cool, disparaging appraisal of his surroundings.

"Every reigning monarch has need of a castle!" The reminder of Tom Graham's words prompted a spurt of uncharacteristic sarcasm.

"Well, Mr Kielder, I need hardly ask the reason behind your visit. You seem impatient to begin a survey of your new domain."

She regretted the statement the moment it was voiced—regretted the return of flinty hardness to clear grey eyes; the stiffening of facial muscles; the arrogant tilt of a head capped with hair as darkly-sheened as his mood, as fiery as hidden temper. As she could not afford to offend the man from whom she wished to beg a favour, she strove to rectify her mistake by making an immediate apology.

"Please excuse my lack of manners, Mr Kielder. I've no doubt that you called in the hope of speaking to my brother, who unfortunately has not yet returned from London. However, now that you are here, there's a personal matter I'd like to discuss with you. Won't you please take a seat?'' She fluttered nervous hands in the direction of a chair. ''May I offer you tea... or a drink, perhaps?''

''Neither, thank you, Lady Rowan.'' When he sat down the massive armchair seemed to assume Lilliputian proportions. ''As a matter of fact, I came specifically to see you.''

''To see me?'' She looked blank. ''But why...?''

''I'll explain later, once we've disposed of your problem. Fire away...!''

A blush rose to her cheeks. Made timid by a brusqueness that shredded the already tattered Falstone pride, she sank back into her chair and with lashes lowered, fingers twisting nervously in her lap, confessed in a whisper:

''I hate the idea of living in London. I want to stay here to look after Nanny—I'm all the family she has. Unfortunately,'' she husked, then swallowed hard to clear her throat, ''finding suitable accommodation is proving very difficult. People whose homes are due to be flooded are leaving the district because there are no houses available, so I was wondering whether in the circumstances...'' she hesitated, lashes quivering madly as the wings of an agitated moth, ''...you would consider allowing us to occupy the Lodge—for a suitable rent, of course?''

Bravely she lifted her head to stare wide-eyed with panic when for a cruel length of time he silently deliberated, his grey-eyed glance cooling the heat in her cheeks, his lack of response dampening her hopes and setting the final seal upon her humiliation.

Mortified, she withstood his scrutiny, a helpless butterfly impaled by the critical eye of a collector, then drooped with despair when instead of relieving her misery he mused obliquely:

"Destiny must be on my side. Wasn't it Shakespeare who wrote: 'There's a divinity that shapes our ends, Rough-hew them how we will?'" When her only response was mute bewilderment, he enlightened her, "I sought this meeting in order to put to you a proposition which I suspect might supply the solution to your problems as well as my own. Interior decorating is hardly my strong point, and when I move in here," his glance slewed around the room, "I shall need the help of someone possessing discrimination and impeccable taste in order to ensure that any curtains, carpets, or furniture beyond repair are replaced by items perfectly attuned to their surroundings. Also, as I intend to do a certain amount of entertaining I shall need a hostess as well as a secretary to cope with any problems arising from the estate and its many elderly tenants. In short, Lady Rowan, I'd like the castle to be run as smoothly and efficiently as I run my business, a place that I can come home to and relax without having to face any extra burden of responsibility."

Rowan felt a stirring of hope—was he about to offer her employment?

In spite of her desire to have the situation clarified, curiosity prompted her to pry:

"What attracted you to Falstone Castle in the first place—surely a smaller establishment would have been more convenient for a man in your position?"

Dusk was crowding the ancient room, filling it with shadows that veiled his eyes and set his profile into a mould that appeared dark and brooding.

"It may surprise you to learn that for me this place is full of reminders of my childhood," he astonished her by saying, "of days when my mother who was employed as a sewing maid used to smuggle me up the back stairs so that she could keep an eye on me while she darned and patched the household linen, sewed buttons on shirts, and carried out invisible repairs on your own childish frills and flounces."

As if the memory had touched a painful nerve, he rose to his feet and began prowling around the room. When he hesitated in front of the window Rowan saw a muscle twitching in his cheek as he fingered heavy velvet curtains that had hidden in their folds repairs that had been skilfully executed many years previously.

"One of the greatest ironies of life must be the way monuments are erected to fools while others less famous but of greater worth are denied even a modest inscription on a tombstone."

"Your mother is dead?" she ventured timidly, sensing a turmoil of regret behind an expressionless exterior.

"Both my parents lost their lives in a flood that sent houses bobbing like matchboxes upon a swollen river." His cool, matter-of-fact tone took her completely by surprise. "It happened two years after our arrival in America. I was staying with a school friend at the time, and returned the following day to discover that I had no home, no parents, not even the slightest possession to remember them by."

He must have recognised pity in her choked gasp, a small cry of distress for a young boy left stranded in a country full of alien faces, left to forage for himself in early adolescence, a time when the help and encouragement of loving parents is imperative. Suddenly his tough insensitivity seemed understandable—even for-

King Kielder 433

givable—in a boy who had suddenly had to become a man when a man was needed.

"Don't overburden your tender heart on my account, Lady Rowan." To her chagrin he sounded lightly amused. "The grounding I received as a boy living in temporary accommodation sited wherever dams, factories or power stations happened to be being built later proved invaluable. Having personal knowledge of the art of survival when constructing concrete jungles has helped me to understand the stresses that occur when men are herded together, living in primitive conditions, has enabled me to appreciate their points of view whenever work has been disrupted by conflict between workers and management. It has also taught me that in order to earn a man's respect a boss has to be capable of carrying out any task he expects his workers to do, to be able to roll up his sleeves and pitch in whenever an extra pair of hands would come in useful. The Earls of Falstone would have done well to have learnt a similar lesson," he mocked. "It might have enabled them to hang on to their inheritance."

Rowan stiffened, resentful of this mild criticism of her family, yet too honest to deny the truth of his words. "Both my father's and brother's management of the estate may be open to criticism," she admitted coldly, "but there is a lesson you could learn from them, for it appears to me that in your fight to achieve riches you've overlooked the importance of knowing how to relax. But perhaps you haven't yet achieved your ultimate aim, Mr Kielder," she lifted her head to direct a faintly contemptuous stare. "Money may have bought you a castle, but you're probably in the process of discovering that money can't buy prestige or love.''

She trembled into silence, wondering if she had gone too far, comparing the uncanny stillness pervading the atmosphere with the sudden cessation of birdsong in the forest, the freezing of all animal movement that always preceded the boom of an explosion in the valley below.

His voice was controlled, yet her sensitive nerves warned of danger, the sort of eruption that can be expected when volcanic lava is rumbling beneath a cap of ice. ''I find relaxation boring, I'd far rather be outside mixing in from the touchlines, in the areas that interest me. Neither prestige nor love is included in my catalogue of interests.''

''And yet you're not an aimless person, Mr Kielder,'' she tilted bravely. ''Like every other ambitious man you must have some goal. To what do you attribute the drive mechanism behind your dramatic rise to power?''

''To revenge, I suppose,'' he admitted with a trace of transatlantic drawl. ''Specifically, revenge upon the English Establishment, a bunch of toffee-nosed snobs, bastions of the so-called upper class, who attempt to perpetuate the beliefs that they are a separate entity by spelling their names differently and by pronouncing their vowels in a way that suggests they're attempting to speak with a mouthful of plums!''

Her sensitive nature recoiled from a look of disparagement that seemed to indicate that he considered her a fully paid up member of this exclusive club.

''Then presumably,'' she croaked, ''as you appear to have lumped all members of the nobility into one despised race, the guests you plan to entertain will be mainly business men?''

"Then you presume wrongly," he contradicted smoothly. "With the help of your brother, whose co-operation with my plan was one of the conditions imposed when I agreed to relieve him of his debts, I intend to become accepted by the establishment, to gain entry into their tight circle of snobbery, thereby exorcising an inherited resentment of flaunted superiority by proving that English imperiousness is mere propaganda put about to disguise the real truth, which is that an Englishman's loyalty and allegiance can be bought—quite cheaply."

Rowan sat rigid in her chair, feeling seared by a whiff of white-hot heat, sensing the presence of a furnace of resentment stoked up behind a cast iron door of indifference.

"Well, Lady Rowan," his impatient voice jerked her out of her trance, "what do you say, are you prepared to co-operate?"

Indignation drove her to her feet, gave her the courage to confront him face to face when she flared:

"Prepared to conform to your outrageous theory, don't you mean? No, Mr Kielder, whatever my brother may have led you to believe, I, at least, am not for sale, so you can peddle your offer of employment elsewhere!"

"Employment...?" Both his tone and expression registered utter astonishment. "Whenever I need workers I contact an employment agency. You've obviously misunderstood me, Lady Rowan. What I'm asking you to do is marry me."

CHAPTER THREE

FOR THE better part of two days Rowan had ridden
Cello along forest trails, wrestling with emotions that
were a tangle of anger, indignation, astonishment, and
an overriding sense of worry about Nanny's future. To
leave her alone without so much as a roof over her
head was unthinkable, yet it was a foregone conclusion that the old lady would refuse to leave the area in
which she had been born and where in a quiet church-
yard moss-covered headstones tilted by subsidence,
their inscriptions almost obliterated by the elements
and the passage of time, recorded the last resting
places of relatives who had defended the frontier
against marauding Scots, members of a family of
whom it had been said they *"Would rather lose their
lives and livings than break the code of the Border by
going back on their word"*. But in spite of a reluctance to upset Nanny's familiar world, the time had
eventually arrived when Rowan had decided that she
could not dodge the unpleasant task a moment longer.

When informed of the sale of the castle Nanny had
taken the news as Rowan had expected she would, first
of all biting deeply into a quivering bottom lip, then
immediately assuming the mien of a tough Borderer
used to weathering a lifetime of calamities. However,
her reaction to the news that she had turned down Colt

Kielder's impudent proposal of marriage had struck Rowan as shocking and totally unpredictable.

"Silly child!" she had snapped fiercely. "How could you be foolish enough to let slip an ideal chance to gain revenge, to make the arrogant Scot pay dearly for trying to emulate his betters!"

Rowan tried to blank from her mind the incredible conversation that had followed, but as Cello picked her way along a bridle path Nanny's words seemed sighed upon the breeze, whispered insidiously through the branches of rustling pines. For the umpteenth time she recalled her own highly indignant response.

"Are you actually suggesting that I ought to have *accepted* the man's outrageous proposal?"

And Nanny's uncompromisingly swift affirmative. "Certainly I am! Not for the first time, it's fallen to one of the female line to uphold Falstone pride, to fight to retain possession of family property. There are more ways than one of skinning a rabbit!" she had hissed the blunt Border maxim. "Some battles are fought with dirk and sword, others with cunning and guile. You owe a duty to old and needy tenants as well as to ancestors who sacrificed everything, even their lives, to ensure that the Falstones retained their rightful heritage."

"But the castle has already been sold, Nanny!" Rowan had protested. "Legal formalities have already been completed, so there's no way that I can cancel out the harm my brother has done."

She had been alarmed by the wicked, almost witchlike look that had distorted Nanny's face at the mention of Nigel's betrayal.

"Every generation spawns a weakling," she had muttered. "Whenever the runt of a litter is the first-born, the strength of the remainder must compensate for his weakness. Your brother was no match for the Cowt—the Strong Man—but by marrying Kielder you can ensure that Falstones are never ousted, that the line continued to flourish in the family home!''

Wearied by the argument that had raged unceasingly over the past two days, Rowan dismounted to allow Cello a peaceful graze while she sat on the bank of a stream and unwrapped the sandwiches she had packed in a cowardly effort to avoid being served lunch by Nanny whose continuous pressure was becoming unbearable.

But churning emotions had dispelled her appetite and after forcing down a couple of mouthfuls she broke up the remainder of the sandwiches and cast them into the stream before stretching out on the grass. With her hands clasped beneath her head she gazed blankly at a patch of blue sky just visible above the crowns of forest giants, striving to subdue quivering nerves, attempting to discover a route towards sanity that would bypass the path of duty that Nanny had insisted must be trod.

"Other Falstone women married for money whenever family fortunes were low... The motto: 'Having No Remorse' is not merely a pretty inscription, but a vow that commits every Falstone to weathering the pain caused by guilt or bitter repentance, to overcoming their reluctance to commit a wrong or to act cruelly whenever conscience conflicts with family interests..."

Persistent as water pounding against stone, Nanny's edicts drummed through Rowan's mind. Even when heavy eyelids drooped, weighted with weariness, she was haunted by dreams of a church filled with wedding guests divided into hostile camps by a narrow strip of aisle; of a bridegroom whose head was supporting a copper-red crown; of a bride slowly approaching an altar wearing a shimmering dress which, immediately her bridegroom took her hand, became transformed into a suit of glittering armour!

Lashes flew up over wide-awake eyes when she became conscious of a piercing whistle close by. Instinctively she froze, recognising the call of an otter making contact with its mate. Then the sound of splashing drew her attention towards the stream and she was treated to the rare sight of a chocolate-coloured male otter with small, bright eyes set into a flattened head sporting prominent whiskers, propelling himself underwater, employing his long, thick, tapering tail as a rudder.

"Don't move!" a voice urged softly in her ear. "If we're very lucky his wife might decide to join him—perhaps even their young."

It required tremendous effort of will to obey Colt Kielder's command. Not even the novelty of watching a rare sighting of the usually nocturnal animal that shunned people and ventured out of his riverside holt in daytime only when he thought himself unobserved could temper the shock of his presence, or the embarrassing realisation that he must have stolen up stealthily from behind and remained watching over her while she slept.

As she obeyed, stiff with resentment, a female otter appeared out of nowhere and slid down the river bank to begin a teasing flirtation with her mate in the water. Gradually, imperceptibly, Rowan's tension gave way to delight as for several enchanting minutes she watched a ballet of grace and strength as the otters postured, preened, bent, stretched, reared, dived, darted and glided, obviously revelling in the freedom of movement obtained from water, their natural element.

When, after a final dive, the pair disappeared beneath the surface, she expelled a long-held sigh of contentment—a contentment that was suddenly dispersed by a mocking reminder of Colt Kielder's presence.

"Every courtship should be as carefree and lighthearted. They've probably now departed to the privacy of their holt to mate or merely to cuddle close together and enjoy tender, affectionate exchanges."

Swiftly Rowan scrambled to her feet, unnerved by an ambience of intimacy that was intensified by his lazy, narrow-eyed appraisal of her scarlet cheeks and wide eyes reflecting awkward shyness.

"I wonder if there are any cubs?" She rushed into speech, conscious that strange, intense undercurrents were causing her to babble wildly. "Because cubs are born blind they're restricted to the holt for the first ten weeks of their lives and they call out for their mother in a very loud penetrating squeak if they think she's been absent too long. They swim instinctively, of course, but mother has to duck their fat furry bodies under water to encourage them to dive."

"Are you really unaware, Lady Rowan, or have you merely forgotten," he rocked on his heels, looking amused, "that a great deal of the first twelve years of my life was spent in this forest studying wildlife, first in the company of my father who taught me all he knew, then later alone, foraging, tracking and keeping watch."

"Also laying traps and snares, I've no doubt!"

For the life of her she could not resist the impulse to snap, feeling as sensitive to the menace of his towering frame as a chicken to a marauding fox.

She stared defiantly at the man whose tall, rangy frame clad in denim trousers and checked shirt seemed to epitomise power, whose grey eyes, when they were not guarded, could take on the hardness of bedrock, the flint-sharp core of earth left exposed on the floor of the valley where his monstrous yellow earth-gobblers had gorged layers of grass and rich topsoil. She blanched beneath the weight of a look that threatened to crush her disdain as boulders hacked from the quarry were crushed into gravel, then felt even more intimidated when he smiled, a smile that recalled out of the deep recesses of her mind a lesson learned in the schoolroom: *"Some maintain that smiling has its origin in facial gestures adopted by our primitive ancestors to prove that their teeth were at rest and not tensed for an attack upon an enemy's throat!"*

"You resent like hell my presence here, don't you, Lady Rowan?" he tilted gently. "What a pity your attitude is being copied by the rest of the locals who've been conditioned over the centuries to following where Falstones lead."

"Did you expect us to welcome your intrusion into our peaceful lives?" she flashed, her knees buckling with fright. "Can you give me one good reason why we shouldn't resent the noise caused by your armoured divisions making an assault upon our land; why we should enjoy being turned out of our homes, having our roads choked with traffic, our villages stormed every Saturday night by troupes of hooligans in search of diversion? You will never be accepted here!" Bravely, she jutted her chin. "Though our land has been invaded, we're determined never to frater-nise.''

"In other words you're set upon making life as dif-ficult as possible for all of us." Impatience lent to his words an extra sardonic steel. "As usual, what has been deemed best by the Falstones has had to be ac-cepted as being best for everyone. You wish to remain an elitist minority, wrapped within a cocoon of self-ishness and solitude that renders you immune to the pressures and needs of society. You sneer at my men, implying that they're an army of renegades bent upon rape and pillage, whereas in actual fact they're a bunch of tough guys, dedicated to their work, who accept the need to live in primitive conditions and in return expect others to tolerate their need to relax and enjoy themselves for just one night out of seven.

"I could give you many reasons why the building of the dam is essential," he growled, "the main one being a vital shortage of water in a country whose popula-tion keeps growing. The quantities of water used by industry are so huge as to be almost incomprehensi-ble. The bed you sleep in, every item on your table and in your household, needed water somewhere in the course of its production. Water is needed for drink-ing, for growing food, for washing ourselves and our belongings—we simply couldn't live without it—yet, obviously, if the Falstones had their way, housewives would once again be reduced to the backbreaking task of collecting water from rivers and wells in buckets. You, and others who think like you, seem quite pre-pared to ignore the hardships imposed by lack of wa-ter, the increasing instance of disease, providing your outlandish, mummified existence is preserved!''

"Mummified . . . !" she croaked, outraged, feeling battered by his hail of scorn. "We do have access to television, radio, and newspapers, Mr Kielder!" Her attempt to sound withering was foiled by her wobbling tone. "The fact that we're kept so well informed about the happenings in the outside world has made us all the more determined to opt out of it!"

"But at what cost?" he drawled, switching suddenly from antagonism to gentle mockery as his amused eyes slid over slim thighs encased in ancient riding breeches and the swell of curvaceous breasts obscured by a shapeless sweater. "How long is it since you wore a skirt, Lady Rowan? If I might hazard a guess, I'd say it was the day you abandoned gym-slips."

She could have fought argument with argument, fire with fire, scorn with scorn, but the softly jeering question left her gasping, pride decimated.

"It must be true what they say about women dressing solely to please men," he continued, cocking a derisory eyebrow. "Perhaps now that there's a surplus of eligible males in the area my men will have less reason to complain about the dowdy lack of appeal in the female population. As most local girls will follow wherever you lead," he maintained with a deceptive idleness that blunted the impact of his words, "it will fall to me, as your fiancé, to claim the privilege of supplying you with a decent wardrobe."

His cool assumption that she was prepared to accept his proposal had the effect of a douche of cold water upon her fiery cheeks, draining her of colour until her face looked pinched, her wide blue eyes appalled. Confident that it was ridiculous to feel so panic-stricken, assuring herself inwardly that no man could be as all-powerful, as all-conquering as he appeared, Rowan tightened her grip upon flustered nerves and attempted to spell out clearly and coldly:

"I wouldn't marry you if you were the proverbial last man in the world! While the dam is still under construction, I know I shall find it difficult to avoid your company, but believe me, Mr Kielder, I shall try exceedingly hard to ensure that I see as little of you as possible for the remainder of the time you're here!"

A spark flickered in the depths of grey eyes, then was just as suddenly extinguished. "Falstone Castle was purchased as a permanent home, not just as a temporary retreat," he reminded her almost kindly. "There'll be plenty of work for me to do here, long after the dam has been completed. As a matter of fact, its completion will mark the beginning of a scheme I have in mind to renew life and bring prosperity to the area."

"What sort of scheme...?" Surprise tilted her head erect, as if alerted by a battle cry warning of the approach of thieving Scottish reivers.

"I visualise a vast recreational area." Her heart plummeted to the soles of her small boots. "A place where facilities will be provided for sailing, waterskiing, rowing and angling, with a modern clubhouse where the hundreds who I'm certain will flock to the area each weekend can have their hunger and thirst assuaged. Bird hides will be situated in appropriate spots for those whose hobby is birdwatching, and nature reserves and wildlife sanctuaries will be created for those who enjoy less energetic pursuits. Picnic areas will be needed to cater for the needs of families with young children; nature trails to attract school parties, and later on," he paused, seemingly immune to the look of horror on his listener's face, "all cottages remaining above water level will be modernised and rented out to holidaymakers during the summer season."

"You don't mean it!" she croaked through a dry throat. "You surely don't intend to deprive our oldest tenants of their homes—some of them are in their eighties, they would be heartbroken if ever they were forced to move!"

His callous shrug struck her as appalling. "One mustn't allow sentiment to interfere with one's judgment, especially when one is planning a commercial venture as huge as the one I've just outlined," he told her in a tone totally devoid of compassion. "The welfare of family retainers must remain the responsibility of your brother and yourself—it's most certainly not mine. Once the Falstones move out of the Castle, so far as I'm concerned their commitments leave with them. As I've already pointed out, I have no intention of shouldering further responsibilities. In any case," he consoled her as a seeming afterthought, "once your tenants have been served notice to quit, the local council will feel bound to offer them alternative accommodation."

"Miles away," Rowan accused fiercely, "in a place full of strangers, out of sight and sound of everything and everybody they know and love!"

Once again, his smile brought a reminder of unpleasantness long past, of days when his outlaw ancestors had added the word "blackmail" to the English language.

"The remedy lies in your own hands, Lady Rowan," he confirmed that her thoughts had done him no injustice. "Any marriage between a Falstone and a Kielder is bound to unite families who have kept feuds simmering for centuries, must help to wipe out the vendettas and petty jealousies that are rife in the area because of traditional Anglo-Scottish antipathy."

Rowan wanted to flee, but her feet felt pinned to the ground; yearned to reward his cold-blooded attempt to blackmail with some vicious act of retribution. The ancient curse of the reivers was already forming on her lips—*May your soul go straight to the fire of hell!*—when a chill encompassed her body, suspending all speech, thought and action.

A ghostly whisper from the past seemed to fill her ears: *"Desire for revenge spans even eternity! At times the act can be accomplished with the satisfaction and speed of a swordthrust through the heart of an enemy, but at other times it must be a subtle, ingenious, meticulously-planned, carefully-executed art!"*

When she addressed Colt Kielder her voice sounded strangely disembodied—as if some cold unemotional being had sublimated her will and was forcing an incredible promise through her stiff lips.

"On your own head be it, Mr Kielder! A man who lacks honour holds a distinct advantage at the bargaining table, and so, although you're an unscrupulous rogue whom I dislike intensely, it appears that I've been left no choice but to gamble on the chance that marriage to you may turn out to be fractionally less distasteful than a lifetime spent with a tormented conscience."

CHAPTER FOUR

HAD SHE really promised to marry Colt Kielder?

As Nanny helped her to search through cedarwood chests packed with curtains, tablecloths, bedlinen and many ornate satin, taffeta, silk, cotton and lace dresses lovingly packed and preserved by Falstone wives during previous decades, Rowan was frantically asking herself if she had suffered a brainstorm, if she could perhaps extricate herself from an intolerable situation by pleading that she must have fallen victim to some kind of mental aberration and should therefore not be held responsible for her impulsive acceptance of his proposal.

"Ah, here it is!" With a groan, Nanny emerged triumphant from the depths of a chest and straightened her aching back to display a shroud of white muslin draped over one arm. "If you'll pass me the scissors I'll snip the stitches from the bottom of this bag," she prompted. "We'll soon find out if your grandmother's wedding dress is still wearable."

Without the slightest quickening of interest, she did as Nanny asked, then turned to stroll across to the dusty attic window. It was February, the month of spring flowers in some parts, but high up on the fells snowflakes were being tossed in a wind that was wailing and sighing around the ancient castle walls—like a mournful ballad, Rowan thought, gazing sightlessly over the fells and forest, streams and farmland the Falstones no longer owned—a sad dirge bemoaning a battle lost, the demise of a proud, once influential family.

"It's yellowed a bit with age." Rowan half turned when Nanny stepped towards her. "But the material seems sound enough and the embroidery is still perfect."

When she held out the dress for inspection a breath caught in Rowan's throat as she eyed a shimmering fall of satin, aged to the deep creamy shade of buttermilk, its high rounded collar and swirling hem encrusted with tiny seed pearls formed into garlands of exquisitely pale English roses. The bodice, tightly pintucked, arrowed down towards a waistband that looked too incredibly narrow to accommodate any healthy human form, and long tight sleeves that fell into points below the wristbands seemed to call out for hands so small, white and slender that instinctively she clenched her weather-tanned fists and thrust them behind her back.

"Will it fit, do you suppose, Nanny?" She pursed doubtful lips. "Grandmother Falstone appears to have been more wraith than human."

"A wraith that produced six healthy sons, went horseriding every spare hour available, entertained frequently, and ensured that the household was run like clockwork," Nanny chuckled grimly.

"And was she happy?" Rowan pondered wistfully. "Were she and Grandfather very much in love?"

"Love!" Nanny snorted with derision, displaying a hard intolerance of sentiment that was typical of her Border breed. "In those days love was considered to be the least important ingredient of a suitable marriage, the most vital qualities a man looked for in a wife were a healthy body capable of bearing sons and a hefty dowry to help maintain them.''

''And what about women?'' Rowan challenged with interest. ''What did they most hope to find in a husband?''

''Kindness, I dare say...'' Nanny hesitated as if surprised by the notion that women should be considered entitled to an opinion, ''and of course a title was a must so far as the gentry were concerned. But otherwise,'' she shrugged, ''a woman could count herself fortunate if she found herself wed to a man capable of restraining his temper and exercising discretion in his infidelities.''

''Big deal!'' Rowan scoffed. ''You make even Colt Kielder sound a good catch.''

''Compared with some of the previous Earls of Falstone, I dare say he might be,'' Nanny snapped, squaring her shoulders to ease the stiffness of rheumy bones. ''In spite of their renowned strength, Kielder men have never been known to beat their wives, so be grateful for small mercies, my girl; at least when you marry him you'll have the satisfaction of knowing you've done all in your power to right your brother's wrong. It was your bounden duty to ensure the wellbeing of your tenants—surely their happiness is reward enough without hankering after love as well!''

Rowan was still biting her lip with vexation when she strode towards the stables, trying to feel grateful for the fact that as Colt Kielder's wife she was unlikely to be beaten! She would not have felt so angry, so impotent in her arguments, had she not known that Nanny's outmoded, servile attitude towards marriage was upheld to a greater or lesser extent by most of the women in their community.

Their outlandish, mummified community!

Unwilling to admit that there might be even a grain of truth in Colt Kielder's sarcastic remark, she concentrated her mind upon the task of saddling up Cello before mounting swiftly and urging the mare to gallop off as if all the furies of hell were snapping at her heels.

Prompted by habit, she made her way towards the Kielder Stone, the high vantage point that supplied a view of silent, majestic forest, gently sloping fells and sparkling crystal water that could always be relied upon to act as a panacea for jangled nerves. She had reached to within a couple of yards of the boulder before spotting the figure of a man standing so motionless he seemed to have merged into the stone. Immediately she recognised Colt Kielder she jerked upon the reins, intending to veer Cello in the opposite direction, but recognition was mutual, and when he addressed her she felt she had no option but to pull Cello to a standstill.

"I know this stone is purported to possess magical properties so far as my family is concerned," he gave it an affectionate pat, "but I was not prepared to be pleasantly rewarded quite so quickly."

"Would you be prepared to test the legend's grimmer side, by riding widdershins three times around the stone?" she challenged coldly.

"And risk becoming the target of some unmentionable evil? No, thank you," he grinned, "I don't believe in tempting providence. Besides which, the sun is in the wrong position to allow me to ride widdershins—by which I presume you mean against the sun?''

When he held out a hand to help her from the saddle she looked the other way, pretending not to have noticed.

"You claim to be in sympathy with the modern world," she charged, "yet you appear wary of challenging the truth of the legend."

"Are you daring me to?" The amused question aroused her curiosity.

Swiftly she turned her head towards him so that blue eyes collided with determined grey. "No, you mustn't!" The plea escaped her lips without conscious volition, betraying a superstitious dread of retribution that caused his darkly burnished head to toss with astonishment.

"So you really do believe that harm would befall me were I to ignore the legend of the Kielder Stone?" For once he seemed too preoccupied to jeer.

"I...I don't know...I'm not certain," Rowan stammered, a blush of embarrassment running wild in her cheeks, "but I think you would be foolish to deliberately challenge fate."

With a speed that left her gasping he plucked her from the saddle and set her gently on the ground in front of him. With his strong grip burning into her waist, holding her steady, and his head lowering fiery as a torch towards her troubled face, he jested softly:

"Kielder men were said to wear plumes of rowan leaves in their helmets because they believed that by doing so they gained immunity to evil. With you as my talisman, Lady Rowan, I dare anything...!"

Every bone in her body seemed to melt when his bright reiver's head drew closer. Slowly, positively, he slid his hands around her waist and drew her forward until she was pinned against his powerfully pounding chest. Her young, untried lips began to tremble, anticipating the assault of a hard mouth that looked determined to the point of cruelty, then she experienced a gamut of unfamiliar emotions when a tremor weakened his tightly leashed body and she sensed intuitively—as if the message had sped straight from Eve—that his swiftly-indrawn breath, the tight grip of his hands against her waist, spelt danger—that he was tempted to anticipate the pleasures of marriage without the benefit of a clergyman's blessing!

Later, she was often to wonder what the outcome might have been had her bemused eyes not fallen as if in search of guidance upon the mass of heather-crowned sandstone with deep channels stained red— legend swore with the blood of bygone Kielder victims.

Uttering a gasp of self-loathing, she tore out of his embrace, sickened by the realisation that she had almost bent to the will of a member of a clan whose ability to charm was reputed to be as great as its thirst to dominate, a family that had been responsible for introducing into the English language the word "blackmail"—black rent—the illegal extraction of money from tenants and farmers in exchange for un-asked-for and unwanted protection.

"Don't touch me!" she cried out when his hands reached out to reclaim her. *"Thieving, plundering reiver...!"*

Immediately he froze, his face expressionless as a mask, a dull tinge of colour rising beneath his tan.

"For heaven's sake, Rowan," he clamped, "when will you come to terms with the fact that you're living in the twentieth century? The deeds of the reivers belong in the history books, and that's exactly where they should be allowed to remain."

"Family characteristics don't change," she accused, eyes bright with unshed tears. "How dare you treat me like a camp-follower, one who is prepared to tolerate the crude advances of a rough renegade! Must you class all women alike," she gritted, "or are you simply too insensitive to notice that some of us are different?"

Lightning flashed in cloud-grey eyes, the air fairly seemed to crackle around his fiery head as for frightening seconds he fought to harness his temper. Then suddenly tempest gave way to hail, a cold cruel shower that burst over her head, leaving her gasping.

"Yes, Rowan, you're certainly different from the majority of your sex—unique in your timid immaturity! My men have been warned that hunting and even birdwatching have been banned in certain parts of the area that are known habitats of protected species, examples of wildlife so rare they are in danger of becoming extinct. It would now appear—if your reaction to my friendly advance can be taken as a criterion—that a clause must be added to the effect that the female population of this area must also be included in the veto!"

Friendly advance! The searing imprint of his hands upon her body, the weakness of her limbs, the screaming disarray of newly-aroused senses, gave lie to the understatement.

"It's not we who are culturally retarded," she tilted. "After decades of fighting off the invasions of unscrupulous rogues, of being forced to take part in bloody and bitter battles in defence of our property, civilisation was welcomed with open arms. Whereas the aims of yourself and your gang of intruders appear to be identical with those of deliberately-destructive, coarse-mannered, pillaging reivers. It's a very long time,'' she concluded shakily, "since families in this area were last called upon to lock up their daughters!''

Colt made no attempt to argue, did not even bother to look her way when she stumbled over to Cello and heaved her shaking limbs into the saddle. She left him standing still and forbidding as the stone that bore his name, gazing north across the Border—glorying, no doubt, she decided bitterly, in the fact that ownership of the land he was surveying could no longer be disputed because once again a Kielder was king!

A noise that intruded as a murmur gradually developed into an ear-splitting roar as she approached the rim of the valley and looked down upon miles of black earth flattened by bulldozers, dozens of yellow monsters belching poisonous smoke from their exhausts as they scoured the earth, scraping closer and closer down to the bedrock into which piles had to be driven before the actual building of the dam could begin. From her vantage point, the men appeared like a nest of yellow-helmeted worker ants, scurrying and burrowing, too intent upon progress to care about the trail of destruction left in their wake.

On impulse, she urged Cello towards a dirt road that led towards a quarry where a collection of huts had been erected. Beth Graham had mentioned that her daughter, Dale, had begun working in one of the collection of huts that had been utilised as a temporary office, and suddenly it seemed imperative that the youngster should be put on her guard, to ensure that her ingenuousness was not exploited by the gang of bare-chested roughnecks who were yelling disrespect-ful exchanges across the width of the valley in coarse Celtic accents.

When the road petered out she left Cello tethered to a nearby tree and began descending narrow steps hewn out of the face of the plateau in order to gain access to the base of the quarry. Three mechanical monsters were burrowing into loose rock, gulping stone into huge shovels, then swivelling round to deposit each load into waiting lorries. Clasping her hands to her ears to deaden the noisy din, Rowan gulped in a lung-ful of air, then held her breath as she ran unnoticed past the scene of activity towards the comparatively clean and quiet spot where the huts had been situ-ated.

When the door of the nearest hut flew open she tried to check her speed, but the impetus of her flight was so swift she stumbled and catapulted forward into the arms of the man who had stepped over the threshold.

"Whoa!" He rocked on his heels at the impact, but quickly recovered and grabbed her arms to steady her. "I'd heard mention that the folk that live hereabouts are renowned for their wildly passionate natures, still I wasn't prepared for the pleasure of having the pret-tiest girl around throwing herself straight into my arms."

"Please forgive me..." Stiffly, she stepped out of his clutches, mistrusting the amused, transatlantic drawl that immediately labelled him a Kielder ally. "I'm looking for Dale Graham," she frosted. "Per-haps you can tell me where I might find her?"

Thick eyebrows drew together in a frown—ob-viously, Colt Kielder's handsome young colleague,

dressed immaculately in a pale blue safari suit and
fringed buckskin boots, was unused to being given the
brush-off by a member of the opposite sex. "Sure I
can—she's inside." He jerked a nod in the direction of
the hut he had just left. "Let me take you to her."

"No need, as she's near I'll find her myself. But
thank you all the same, Mr...?"

"McCabe...Abraham McCabe," he supplied eagerly, "but please call me Abe."

"Thank you, *Mr* McCabe," Rowan stressed pointedly. "Now if you'll excuse me," she tried to edge past
him into the hut, "I'd like to speak to Dale, if you
don't mind?"

Good humour bounced back into his face like the
proverbial rubber ball. "Of course I don't mind! And
to prove that our company's policy of being friendly
and co-operative with the natives is no mere boast, I
insist upon escorting you to her myself."

Oblivious to her annoyance, he placed a hand under her elbow and propelled her inside the office.
"Dale, you have a visitor, Miss..." he hesitated, then
cocked an enquiring eyebrow at the girl whose pale
blonde head had lifted from a typewriter when they
entered the office.

"Lady Rowan!" she gasped, rising to her feet to
greet her with a smile of welcome. "Mother was fret-
ting only last night about the time that's elapsed since
you last visited her."

"Lady Rowan...!" Abe broke in thunderstruck.
"Why didn't you say you were Colt's intended? I sure
am delighted to meet you, ma'am—we were all convinced that the boss would be content to go on adding
numbers to his book until he was ready to draw his
pension! Telephone numbers...date book," he en-

lightened when she looked puzzled. "We all have one. Travelling guys need to know where they can pick up a chick in a hurry whenever they arrive at their various destinations!"

When a frozen silence fell, a glance at Rowan's patrician profile, stiff with disdain, and Dale's flush of embarrassment made him suddenly aware of his gaffe. "Heck, I'm sorry if I've spoken out of turn, Lady Rowan," awkwardly he poked at a crack in the linoleum with the toe of his fashionable cowboy boot, "I guess I'm just not up to consorting with royalty."

This elevation of status was too much for Rowan's sense of humour. A dimple sprang to existence at the corner of her mouth as she tried to suppress a smile, and when Abe grinned engagingly she gave up the struggle and dissolved into laughter.

"Merely a member of the lesser nobility, I'm afraid," she corrected with a gurgle, "as far removed from royalty as I hope I am from farmyard fowl."

"You're such a fool, Abe!" Dale's casual admonishment, the fond, almost flirtatious glance she shared with the young American caused Rowan's tone to sound several degrees cooler when she requested:

"If you don't mind, Mr McCabe, I'd like to speak to Dale in private."

"Surely," he grinned, "but only if you'll promise to drop the Mister and call me Abe?"

"Very well, if you must hold me to ransom...Abe," she squashed, reverting to disdain.

Overawed by an air of quiet authority inherited at birth but seldom exercised, he backed out of the room mumbling some excuse about his presence being required in the quarry. But when they were finally left alone Rowan found it difficult to put into words her concern for Dale's safety.

"Won't you please sit down, Lady Rowan?" Dale sounded defensive, almost as if she had guessed the reason behind her visit and was resentful. Without preamble, Rowan took the plunge.

"I don't think your parents can be aware of the type of personnel employed by the Kielder Company," she began tentatively. "As your home is rather isolated, I suppose news of what's happening in the valley has been slow to reach them. I'm certain, however, that once they've been told about the prevailing atmosphere they'll be quick to advise that you look for more suitable employment."

"The prevailing atmosphere is just great, Lady Rowan." Dale jumped to her feet, spilling heated words of protest. "The men working on the dam aren't paragons of virtue by any means, they curse hard, work hard and play even harder, nevertheless their conduct in my presence has been irreproachable—indeed, their attitude is so protective I'm often led to wonder whether they see me as an infant rather than a responsible seventeen-year-old. *They* won't allow me to grow up, but you must, Lady Rowan," she pleaded, her eyes liquid with the threat of tears. "I love my work—so much that I can't bear the thought of being forced to leave!"

"But are you sure that it's the work that attracts you?" Rowan swept a glance over office equipment filmed with dust, spartan furniture, and bare, comfortless walls. "Mr McCabe's forceful personality could be very appealing to an impressionable young girl," she suggested pointedly.

"I won't pretend that I don't enjoy his company," Dale tilted. "He and his fellow workers have brought new enthusiasm and a capacity for enjoyment that's been sadly lacking in this valley. Not everyone in the area agrees with your views, Lady Rowan," she dared to challenge. "My friends all agree that the building of the dam is the best thing that's happened here for decades. People will come to look at the new dam and discover that human beings exist here—that it's not merely a sanctuary for wildlife in danger of extinction!"

Rowan stared, at a loss to understand how she had managed to remain so completely out of touch with the views of a generation only slightly younger than herself. She was just about to probe deeper when Dale, embarrassed by her outburst, rushed towards the door, flinging a nervous apology across her shoulder.

"Please excuse me, I've just remembered a telephone message that ought to have been passed on to Abe."

"It's time I was leaving, anyway," Rowan told her hastily, "I've taken up enough of your time. But I would like to continue our discussion, Dale. Perhaps you could suggest a time and place that would be more convenient?"

"Would you like to be shown around the quarry before you leave, Lady Rowan?" To her annoyance, Abe loomed upon the threshold, his untimely interruption allowing Dale the opportunity she had been seeking to escape. "Would you mind wearing this?" he extended a yellow protective helmet towards her. "The boss is very strict about conforming to safety regulations."

He could have said nothing more calculated to arouse her resentment, to make her determined to gain one victory, however insignificant, over Colt Kielder and his brash young deputy. If she had refused point blank to wear the helmet he could have argued his point, but when she stepped past him, ignoring both the helmet and his request, he looked completely nonplussed.

"What is the purpose of that machine?" Provocatively, she walked across to a machine standing momentarily idle, curious about the working of an attached conveyor belt leading up to the rim of a tower.

"It's a crusher," he told her, then pleaded desperately, "Lady Rowan, would you *please* put this helmet on?"

The quarry was wrapped in silence; some of the men were sipping mugs of tea, others were leaning from the windows of their cabs chatting amicably, but the sound of grit crunching beneath the tyres of an approaching car, the squeal of brakes and the slamming of a car door had the effect of galvanising the entire workforce into action. Suddenly the crusher sprang into noisy life and the conveyor belt began moving its load of rock towards the top of the tower where it toppled over and fell with a horrible grinding noise on to huge churning blades. A loud crash sent Rowan spinning round, wide-eyed with fright, to see a heavy steel ball swinging from a chain on the end of a jib smashing large boulders into pieces.

She felt it was entirely appropriate that Colt Kielder should choose that moment to step into her line of vision. He looked coldly furious, in an obviously filthy temper.

"Why isn't Lady Rowan wearing protective head-gear?" His yell stabbed through noise being made by a complete orchestra of machinery.

"Er...she was just about to put it on...the men have just this minute recommenced working," Abe stumbled, his young brow creased with anxiety.

"You're fired!" Colt Kielder snapped, his expression flinty as the gravel spewing out of the crusher. "It's your responsibility to ensure that safety regulations are observed—there's no room in this company for any man who's proved himself incapable of carrying out orders."

"That's most unfair!"

"Gee, Colt, if you'd only give me a chance to explain...!"

"But, Mr Kielder, it wasn't Abe's fault!"

Simultaneously, Rowan, Abe, and Dale voiced a protest to Colt Kielder's unyielding figure as he stalked back to his Land Rover, then shared appalled glances when without turning his fiery head he disappeared from sight.

"Don't worry, Abe." Ridden with guilt, Rowan tried desperately to comfort the shocked youth. "When he hears my explanation he's bound to change his mind."

"I wouldn't bet on it," Dale cautioned, bleakly condemning. "Before coming to work here and seeing for myself how ruthless he can be, I used to scoff at my mother's tale about the traditional rite once said to have been performed at all Kielder christenings. Every male child," she gulped, wide eyes betraying that she was not as immune as she had professed to Border mythology, "had his right hand excluded from the ceremony in order to ensure that in time of feud his enemies would be destroyed by the strength of his unblessed hand!"

CHAPTER FIVE

IN SPITE of Nanny's arguments to the contrary Rowan felt certain, as she stepped over the threshold of the tiny woodland church and began her slow walk up the aisle towards her waiting bridegroom, that no other Falstone bride, however threatened, could have entered into marriage with the same amount of dread and resentment in her heart.

The scene was like an extension of her dream: oak pews crammed to capacity with two warring factions—puzzled locals who had looked upon her as the champion of their cause and who were now feeling that she had let them down, and a deputation of off-duty workers from the enemy camp looking uncomfortably spruce and out of place, as they returned stares of defiance across the narrow dividing aisle.

As she approached the altar steps on her brother's arm a weak ray of sunshine began moving across a stained glass window donated by some previous Falstone earl and played upon her bridegroom's head so that his burnished hair took on the appearance of a fiery crown. Then as she stood quaking by his side, waiting for the ceremony to begin, it began progressing steadily across the inscribed glass, picking out each jewel-bright word so that they felt seared upon her forehead: *Having No Remorse!*

She had remorse in plenty—remorse at having been forced to strangle her pride and go in search of the autocratic company boss to explain the circumstances that had led to Abe's dismissal and to beg him to rescind his decision.

For the first time in their acquaintance his look had been cold and distant when, after following his tracks around the perimeter of the dam, she had finally spotted the empty Land Rover and saw him a few yards distant conversing with one of the site foremen. She had dismounted and stood nervously fondling Cello's muzzle, waiting to be noticed, and had quaked in her shoes, nervous as a delinquent employee expecting a rocket from her boss, when finally he had strode towards her.

She had sensed past aggravations seething beneath a surface of politeness when he had enquired. "Do you wish to speak to me?"

"Yes, please, if it's convenient," she had gulped.

Mortified, she had watched him flick back his cuff to study his watch before conceding: "I have ten minutes to spare, if that length of time will suffice?" In response to her nod, he had then suggested, "Let's walk into the forest where the noise of machinery is not quite so persistent."

After ascending a slope topped by a belt of forest green they had plunged into a depth of silence, an interior reminiscent of the peace of a centuries-old cathedral, a place whose shell had withstood the desecration of many battles, the ravages of change, while miraculously retaining its core of serenity. A resinous incense had risen from the carpet of pine needles crushed beneath their feet while they had walked without speaking until a felled tree trunk had seemed to indicate an ideal spot to rest. Rowan had sat down, expecting Colt to join her, but instead he had propped one foot on the tree trunk while, using his knee as an armrest, he had stood lowering.

"I want to speak to you about Abe," she had begun nervously.

"In which case, you can save your breath," he had cut in sharply. "I never go back on a decision."

"Not even when you discover that the decision is an unjust one," she had burst out furiously, "that you've totally misread the circumstances leading up to it? Abe tried desperately hard to persuade me to wear a helmet, but for reasons of my own I chose to ignore his request. No doubt, in his position, you would have resorted to force, but fortunately for me your deputy is not yet fully indoctrinated with Kielder ruthlessness. The blame is entirely mine—if your ego demands some show of retribution for disregarding others, then I'm the one who should be punished."

"You would enjoy that, wouldn't you, Rowan?" he had leant to jeer, "would welcome having a little extra weight added to your self-imposed burden of martyrdom—an attitude you carry like a banner of protest against intrusion into your solitude. Believe me, you're not alone in enjoying the pleasure of a peaceful read, of a calm, reflective interval spent pondering upon nothing in particular, of a quiet ride around the countryside. But solitude should be a chosen, short-lived contrast to being surrounded by convivial company, not a retreat from the world, the sort of retirement you embrace like a nun. Everyone needs a partner in life to argue and row with, to tease and have fun with, to kiss, make up, and make love with. So why fight the inevitable, Rowan, why not try to enjoy my company instead of displaying antagonism on every conceivable occasion—even to the point of rebelling against the minor issue of wearing a protective helmet?''

She had jumped to her feet blazing resentment of his patronage, of the easy, relaxed way he had straightened his tall frame until she had had to tilt her head to glare into his expressionless face.

''You chose your simile well! If I act like a martyr it's because I feel I'm being persecuted for defending my principles. Even birds are free to choose their own mates, yet I'm being forced into marriage with a confirmed bachelor full of lust, a man determined to further his ambitions but who will most likely continue living the life of a debonair tomcat even after he's married. However, your morals—or lack of them—are of no consequence. All I want is your promise that you'll meet two further conditions.''

''Which are . . . ?'' he had questioned thinly.

''Firstly, that Abe is reinstated,'' she had quivered, ''and secondly, if you still insist upon subjecting us both to the indignity of a farcical marriage, that there'll be an absolute minimum of fuss and hypocritical rejoicing attached to the actual ceremony.''

''Do you, Rowan, take this man to be your lawful wedded husband . . . ?''

The atmosphere inside the church felt as cool as the surrounding walls when she hesitated, forcing herself to remember the well-being of elderly tenants; the future preservation of the countryside she loved; Abe's reinstatement to the job he had lost through no fault of his own, before whispering a shaken: *I will . . .''*

She suffered the rest of the ceremony in a state of limbo, as detached as a newly-departed spirit hovering above the heads of mourners at her bedside. Even her husband's kiss made little impression upon lips frozen into the semblance of a smile, and it was not until they had left the church and were being driven back to the castle that she was shocked back to reality by Nigel's breezy acceptance of a situation she was finding intolerable.

"I say, what a super car! I'd love a Silver Cloud, but the manager of my garage tells me my name's way down on the waiting list." He sounded completely devoid of conscience, immune to any feelings of guilt at having shattered the lives of all who depended upon him, then leaving her to pick up the pieces.

"No doubt you'll be returning to London as soon as possible?" In spite of her own silent condemnation, Rowan's hackles rose, recognising thinly-veiled contempt in Colt Kielder's tone when he returned Nigel's friendly overture with a comment that was tantamount to an order.

"Er... well, I had planned on staying overnight."

"But wisely changed your mind when you realised that there's really nothing to keep you here," his new brother-in-law concluded smoothly. Showing characteristic disdain for protocol, he had dismissed the chauffeur and elected to drive the car back to the castle himself, and as Rowan watched his capable hands manipulating the controls she felt dominated, as helpless as any border lass at the mercy of an abducting reiver. "You'll join us for lunch before you leave," he negligently commanded Nigel. "Because Nanny was outraged by our decision to dispense with the customary large wedding reception I'm certain she'll attempt to redress the balance by offering us something rather special."

"What about the rest of the wedding guests? Won't they be expecting some measure of hospitality?" Nigel sounded shocked.

"Their needs are being catered for at this very moment in the village hall," Colt told him briefly, "also a dance has been arranged for later this evening. My wife and I," he paused as if to savour the words, flicking a glance over Rowan's pale, wan features, "will join them for the traditional cake-cutting ceremony in order to allay any doubts that we're indifferent to the importance of the occasion. After all," his tone developed the trace of transatlantic drawl Rowan had learned to interpret as a danger signal, "in spite of having a few personal differences still to be resolved, for the sake of good community relations we must try to live up to the newlyweds' image of passionate devotion."

She flinched from an undertone of savagery, yet managed to find solace in the sight of knuckles showing white as he gripped the steering wheel—an indication that her frozen acceptance of the inevitable was edging his patience near to bedrock, a flaw in his armour that she was quick to file away in her memory, to be resurrected as a future weapon of defence.

For some unknown reason Nanny had decided to serve lunch upon a table set amid the austere splendour of the baronial hall, a place where stags' heads leered glassy-eyed from the walls, where suits of armour with grisly weapons clutched in mailed fists skulked in shadows being cast by flames leaping out of the heart of spluttering logs piled into the centre of a stone fireplace that in days gone by had housed a spit large enough to accommodate whole roasted oxen.

With a gesture of distaste that caused her husband to frown, Rowan discarded her flimsy veil and head-dress before slipping into a seat at the foot of a table set with fine lace place-mats, highly-polished silver, odd crystal goblets and remnants of a once-impressive dinner service gleaned from the depths of dusty cup-boards in an obvious attempt to impress the new owner of Falstone.

"Hell, Nanny," Nigel muttered irritably, eyeing the steaming soup tureen she had placed in the centre of the table, "you'll have to offer something better than broth in exchange for forcing us to suffer the discom-fort of gale-force draughts blowing around our an-kles!"

"It isn't broth, it's cockie-leekie," she snapped, "made with onions and best boiling fowls. And to follow, there's poached salmon with cucumber, then venison cutlets seasoned with herbs, so I'll expect you to clean your plates!"

"All that's required to turn this meal into a real Scottish repast are oatcakes, whisky and the skirl of bagpipes," Nigel sneered, soured by Nanny's seem-ingly treacherous shift of allegiance. "You're acting like a tartan patriot, Nanny, yet I can remember an occasion when I heard you expressing regret that the law forbidding marriage across the line had ever been repealed!"

"True, but times and circumstances change," she glared. "I'm older now and too wordly-wise ever to expect law to govern nature. In any case, no true Bor-der would ever seek permission to go courting, they've always taken what they wanted and said hang the consequences. Even with their backs to the wall," her black eyes condemned, spearing his shell of hauteur, "men of true grit always refused to be routed, wouldn't give one inch of ground, much less a castle, for all the devils in hell!"

Nigel froze her with a look that held none of the tolerance and affection owing to the old woman who had devoted her life to two motherless children, who had not begrudged one minute of the time she had spent nursing them through childhood illnesses, who had sympathised with their woes, consoled them in sorrow, rejoiced in their happiness, the woman whose fanatical devotion to the Falstones and especially to the newest earl made her bitter criticism all the more surprising.

"I think you've said enough, Nanny! Since when have the opinions of servants been either welcomed or tolerated in this household?" Nigel withered caustically.

Her bravado sagged beneath the weight of authority in his tone; her mouth puckered as she tried to still its trembling and a network of lines deepened so that she seemed to age suddenly before Rowan's shocked eyes. She was just about to speak up in her defence when Colt's dangerous drawl forestalled her.

"Since I took over, I expect." He put Nigel firmly in his place. Then, in case his change of circumstances still had not registered, he spelled out cruelly: "When you sold your birthright, Falstone, you forfeited all the privileges that went with it. As you appear to be suffering from the delusion that you still wield authority in this household, may I remind you that as from today you are merely a guest here and as such you will be expected to accord to Nanny the respect and deference she has earned by years of devoted service. And now," he flung down his napkin with a gesture of finality, "as you have a long journey ahead of you may I suggest you make an early start? Once the renovation of the castle has progressed far enough to allow us to accommodate guests I'll be in touch."

Rowan's cheeks burned with embarrassment and pity for her brother when awkwardly he took leave of them at the head of the castle steps, his dazed eyes glancing upwards at the crumbling masonry of crenellated walls and twin circular towers, then sliding down to linger upon once-grimacing gargoyles, their expressions now rendered pleasant by erosion, that peered down upon visitors arriving at the front entrance by way of a flight of stone steps hollowed by the footsteps of generations of callers—some friendly, others not—as if conscious for the very first time of the enormity of his loss.

"Goodbye, Rowan." When he leant to kiss her a suspicion of moisture filming his eyes made her dislike of Colt Kielder soar.

"Goodbye, Nigel dear," she gulped. Then as she returned his hug she drew him closer to whisper in his ear: "Don't blame yourself too much—we haven't been completely routed, there's still one Falstone remaining in the castle!"

"Have you forgotten already, or has it not yet registered that you're now a Kielder?" As Nigel's car disappeared down the driveway her keen-eared husband put an arm around her shoulders to lead her back into the hall. When a violent trembling seized her his expression sharpened with concern. "You're frozen—come closer to the fire."

Without protest, Rowan allowed him to urge her towards the fire leaping furnace-hot up the stone chimney and stood with her head bent, eyes downcast, while Colt massaged warmth into her frozen limbs, sliding his palms along her back, shoulders and arms until her body began pulsating with thousands of tiny nerves leaping in response to tender, almost seductive strokes.

"You wear purity like a suit of armour, Rowan," he murmured huskily, devouring her frozen beauty with eyes fired by the lick of reflected flame. "You were an unbelievably lovely bride. For the rest of my life I shall remember my first sight of you walking towards me down the aisle, your slender body trembling beneath a sheath of satin, pale as your small solemn face, with vivid blue eyes and a mouth glowing ripe and moist as rowan berries behind a veil of early morning mist. Even now, as I feel you quivering beneath my hands and see your very kissable mouth mere inches away, I'm finding it hard to believe that at last I possess the rare and distant being that has haunted my memory since childhood."

Deliberately, inexorably, his arms tightened to draw her stiff, shocked figure into a close embrace. "Once," he husked, feathering a kiss across her brow, "you challenged me to be honest and admit that I would not have returned to my birthplace had there been nothing personal to be gained." He hesitated, his eyes fastened hungrily upon soft lips quivering around a gasp of surprise, before astounding her further. "I decided then that it was too soon to admit that *you* were my motive, that the thought of returning home, in a position to claim Lady Rowan Falstone as a bride, was the goal that forced me to grit my teeth and persevere whenever the going got tough, that made all the sweat, toil, agony and despair of the intervening years worthwhile!''

Grey eyes blazed with a sudden leap of flame seconds before his mouth plunged upon hers, drinking deeper and deeper, as a wanderer lost in the desert would gorge upon the sweet, cool waters of an oasis that for once had not turned out to be a mirage.

Numbed by the shock of his brutal confession, confused by the pressure of steely limbs thrusting hard and unyielding as a blade against her satin-sheathed body, Rowan was swiftly overwhelmed, defeated by a maelstrom of emotion that forced an agonised gasp of protest past her lips—but leaping, treacherous response from her captive body.

Swords, lances and leering stags, tattered pennants, muskets and shields kaleidoscoped above her head when she was lifted into his arms and carried in triumph up the wide stone staircase and along a gallery leading to a passageway lined with many closed doors. He lifted his mouth from hers just long enough to urge:

"Tell me, which is our room?"

The request acted as a lifeline to sanity which she seized in trembling hands.

"Put me down, please, Colt."

The calmness of her tone, the ease with which she had spoken his name, lulled him into a mood of complacency. Gently he lowered her to her feet and stood smiling, waiting for her directions. Panic was the ally that helped to co-ordinate shaking limbs into a movement so swift he was caught completely off guard when she slipped inside her bedroom, slammed shut the door, then turned the key in the lock with a loud, decisive click.

"*Rowan!*" She backed away in fear from the thud of fists upon the heavy door and from the anger evident even through a barrier of solid oak. "Don't be foolish—you can't run away for ever from the responsibilities of marriage!"

"A marriage of convenience," she called back in a terrified treble, "*my* convenience, not yours! You resorted to blackmail and extortion as a means of getting a wife, you *bought* me, just as you bought my home, but believe me, Colt Kielder, a castle and a wife *in name only* were the only Falstone possessions up for sale!"

CHAPTER SIX

"WILFUL CHILD!" Nanny snapped. "You ought to know better than to pit your wits against the Cowt of Kielder, the last remaining member of a family whose pride in its ability to overcome opposition is legendary."

"I have pride, too!" Rowan turned upon the old woman whose persistent show of allegiance towards the enemy seemed little short of treachery. "Too much pride to even contemplate sharing a room, much less a bed, with a man who's made no secret of the fact that he married me simply to prove to himself that he's capable of attaining what appears to be unattainable."

"As you married *him* in order to retrieve what appeared to be irretrievable!" Nanny countered triumphantly, "so my advice to you both would be to call an armistice and settle down to making the best of a bad job. You're not the first Falstone bride to have married without love, but you appear determined to be the first to renege upon the solemn vows to love, honour and obey! Colt Kielder isn't likely to allow his line to die out, he's bound to want an heir, therefore I can see nothing but trouble ahead if you persist in refusing to move into the bridal suite, the rooms which for centuries have been reserved for the exclusive use of the master and mistress of Falstone."

Tense as a bowstring, Rowan stared out of the window, turning a defensive back against Nanny's condemning eyes while nervously she licked her tongue around suddenly dry lips, trying to weather the impact of words that had forced her to realise how incredibly naïve she had been. It had simply never occurred to her that Colt Kielder would expect more than a matrimonial façade, a wife that could be displayed like a pennant to prove his power over the superior Falstones—but Nanny's confident statement, together with his surprising assault a couple of hours ago, had lent her a glimpse into a future that promised to be far more distasteful than she could possibly have imagined. To be legally bound was bad enough, but to be physically bound, to become just another scalp added to the collection he had strung around his belt, was too humiliating to be borne.

She swung on her heel, startling Nanny with a firm, decisive order. "Put those clothes back into the wardrobe—all except the brown dress, I'll wear that this evening."

Nanny was so shocked she almost dropped the pile of clothes she was waiting to transfer into the main suite of rooms situated at the head of the passageway.

"What...that old thing!" Her scandalised eyes probed through Rowan's modest collection of garments in search of the offending article. "But you haven't worn that dress for years—you even admitted that buying it was a mistake, that the colour doesn't suit you!"

"Exactly," Rowan nodded agreement. "As my husband seems convinced that women dress solely to please men, I intend to prove him wrong."

"He won't be pleased," Nanny warned sharply.

"I'm sure he won't," Rowan smiled, bolstered by the memory of a ghostly whisper from the past instructing her upon the subtle, ingenious, meticulously-planned, carefully-executed art of extracting revenge. "King Kielder wants a wife who'll add a pearl of respectability to his stolen crown—unfortunately for him, he's about to discover that the jewel he bought is faceted with thorns!"

Trying to appear unmoved by Nanny's disapproving looks and muttered forebodings, she began preparing herself for the ordeal of facing critical tenants and bold-eyed workers in the company of her new husband. With the deliberate aim of subduing her natural beauty, she skewered wings of raven-black hair into a tightly constricting bun, then puffed a cloud of face powder over dark eyebrows and lashes so that, when the surplus had been brushed away, delicately arched wings and sooty rims were rendered inconspicuous. Leaving her bloodless lips untouched, she slipped into the drably-coloured dress with a hem that because of its immediate loss of favour had been left too long, then, suppressing a squirm of vanity, she laced on a pair of sturdy brogues that added clumsy weight to small feet and detracted from the shapeliness of slender, finely boned ankles.

Nanny's aghast look supplied sufficient proof that her efforts had been rewarded with success.

"Lord save us! You look pale as a ghost," she gasped, "a frumpish ghost that no man in his right mind would take to his bed! You're a wicked, conniving creature," she accused, but with a glint of admiration and a quirk of amusement softening the stern set of her mouth. "If the Cowt should decide this evening that his bride deserved a thrashing then I for one will bury my head beneath the bedclothes and leave you to reap your just deserts!''

''Now you're being foolish!'' Rowan scolded, feeling her heart lurch. ''I married an ambitious schemer, a ruthless, blackmailing rogue, but not, I think, a sadistic barbarian.''

Yet in spite of her brave assertion her heart was beating a tattoo of trepidation as she descended the stairs and felt the unnerving stillness of the shadow-filled hall—its gloom relieved only by one malevolent red eye of slowly dying embers—rising up to meet her. Her attention was caught by a moving patch of shadow that slowly materialised into the tall figure of a man who could have stepped from a previous century—a man wearing kilt and plaid with a weft and sett so distinctive that the tartan immediately stamped him an inhabitant of the Borders. His swordbelt and sporran, his bonnet, hose, brogues, brooches and buckles were of a quality expected of a clan chief, one of the born leaders of men whose skills were tested against the best among the sporting, hunting, and fishing members of his clan, who was expertly trained in the use of weapons, and whose word was paramount, his honour jealously guarded.

''How good of you to finally put in an appearance!''

She was startled by the discovery that the words were not mouthed by some phantom spirit but had been gritted from the lips of her impatient bridegroom, and had to struggle to associate pride of birth and loyalty to heritage with the man who, in spite of his history, seemed best suited to his image of abrasive, hardheaded business man.

"You startled me!" she choked. "For a second I thought..."

"...That you were seeing a ghost from ages past?" he countered grimly. "This outfit belonged to my father, and to his father before him; I was asked to wear it tonight as a special favour to an old and faithful friend of my family. At first I wanted to refuse, but upon reflection I decided that it would do no harm to demonstrate to Falstone followers that the clan system is still surviving strong and healthy in the Borders, and will continue to supply proof of the adage: *What is in the blood must come out!*"

His dominance was frightening, yet somehow Rowan managed to tilt scornfully: "Such sentiments sound hypocritical coming from the lips of a man who professes to despise inherited positions of privilege and authority."

"No clansman bends under the yoke of serfdom," he countered with a scorn that was damning. "In place of the feudal system favoured by the English, we Scots share a warm kinship and are honoured by the knowledge that every man is considered to be as good as his chief in battle and in peace."

Feeling suddenly chilled, Rowan stepped nearer to the fire and stretched her hands towards the glowing embers. When his breath hissed against her ear she drew back her head and saw grey eyes flashing with ferocity as he studied her appearance. Silently he began a thorough examination that scoured her cheeks red and seared a trail of contempt down to the soles of her shuffling feet.

"So...!" he deduced, displaying an insight into her thoughts that ripped her naked of assurance, "you've decided to turn our marriage into a battleground, with your husband as the enemy! So be it, sweet foe," he conceded almost kindly, "but I give you fair warning—you're in danger of handing to your enemy the means for your own destruction!" He waited for some response, but when none was forthcoming he snapped a command that jerked her shoulders erect. "Return to your room and put on your wedding dress—our guests will be expecting to see a radiant bride and, whether by the use of force or persuasion, I intend to ensure that they're not disappointed."

She found it a galling experience, having to react to his note of authority, having to take orders when she was used only to giving them, but the slight stress he had placed when referring to her bedroom had indicated that he was teetering on the edge of a further skirmish for which she felt ill prepared. So, acting upon the principle that discretion is the better part of valour, she backed out of his menacing presence and fled to her room to carry out his order.

The festivities were in full swing when they entered the village hall, its interior made almost unrecognisable by masses of out-of-season flowers which, together with a buffet table running the full length of one wall, piled high with a delectable assortment of food ranging from small dishes of potted shrimps covered in butter and spiced with mace, huge fresh, pink-fleshed salmon, herrings pickled in vinegar, cold roast turkeys and chickens, sirloins of beef, pork with crackling, boiled legs of lamb and rounds of haggis, to fruit cake and pastries, shortbread, oatcakes and a varied selection of cheeses, must have cost someone a small fortune.

The floor in the centre of the room held a crush of dancers who were evidently finding the toe-tapping music of pipes and drums, clarsach, accordion and fiddle irresistible, and watchers crowding around the dance floor were adding a happy babble of sound that was a mixture of many different accents: softly-lilting Gaelic; the harder Lowland tones, rich in feeling, strong in character; and the louder, heartier voices alien to the area coming from tough, weather-hardened men, spruced up for the occasion in checked shirts and denims, who formed Colt Kielder's army of invaders.

The sight of these men pushing and elbowing their way through the crowd in search of partners, arrogantly filching the youngest, best-looking and most impressionable girls from under the noses of less belligerent locals, aroused Rowan's simmering resentment to boiling point.

"You promised a minimum of fuss!" she flared at her unrepentant husband. "I was expecting to make a short appearance at a quiet social gathering, not this ... this ..."

"My men are citizens of the world," he reminded her, showing not the slightest trace of compunction. "In America, for instance, a gathering of this size would be classed as a modest little shindig. In any case," her nerves reacted with a leap to the return of his lazy drawl, "from where I'm standing your friends appear to be making the most of an opportunity to let their hair down. Why don't you follow their example, Rowan?" His hands clamped upon her waist, delaying their entrance by pulling her back inside the small, dark no-man's-land that separated the front entrance from the main body of the hall. "If there's any truth in the saying that matrimony ought to begin with a little aversion, then we should be set on course for a highly successful marriage," he muttered roughly, the closeness of his lips taking her breath away, "but for the next couple of hours let's try to sink our differences. Though friendship may still be a little out of our reach, we can at least pretend a state of armed neutrality!"

As his words registered, appealing to both heart and reason, tension left her and she settled suddenly still within the circle of his arms. With the sound of merriment in their ears and a host of friends waiting to greet them, his request for a truce seemed far from unreasonable. He gave her time to ponder, content to watch conflicting expressions of doubt and decision chasing across her sweetly-solemn face. Within their oasis of solitude the sound of silence seemed gradually to smother all other intrusive noises until Rowan became conscious only of the pounding of heartbeats and the hiss of a sharply-indrawn breath as Colt's mouth drew nearer, hovering over lips quivering soft and gentle as the wings of a butterfly—so easily crushed; so easily startled into panic-stricken flight.

"Rowan . . . !" he groaned in a torment of temptation. Then, displaying an uncertainty she had never before encountered in the man who had rampaged into her life, destroying her hopes, her solitude, and her peace of mind, he requested gently, "Would you mind very much if I kissed you . . . ?"

"I say, folks, they're here, our guests of honour have arrived!"

She jolted out of his arms when Abe's shout broke the spell that had almost seduced from her the shy, breathless denial for which Colt had been hoping. Closing her ears to a breathed curse consigning Abe to the fires of hell, she retreated like a startled fawn, backing straight into Abe, who was standing on the threshold, his wide grin slowly fading as he puzzled over the savage look flung his way by his obviously irate boss.

A concerted yell of welcome rose to the rafters when Colt appeared at her side and began leading his wildly blushing bride into the middle of the floor that had been swiftly cleared to accommodate a table covered with Kielder tartan on top of which had been placed a silver cake stand displaying a wedding cake iced and decorated with national symbols—the heather and thistle of Scotland entwined with English rosebuds.

Rowan fought hard to assume the attitude of cool composure expected of her position, but when Colt's hand enveloped hers, following the traditional custom of bride and bridegroom together cutting the first slice of wedding cake with a silver beribboned sword, she felt a treacherous wave of weakening, an urge to surrender to the strength emanating from a rock-hard arm holding her firmly against his side; from his tight, possessive grip upon her waist.

Her knowledge of tradition should have prepared her, the sea of smiling faces, the hands holding glasses aloft, preparing to toast the bride and groom, should have signalled a warning, but it was not until Colt's arm slid around her waist to draw her into a close embrace that she was reminded of the culminating act of ceremony.

All hell seemed to be set loose the moment his lips met hers, yells, whoops and cheers, the clashing of cymbals, the banging of drums, combined into a background of noise as shattering to her nerves as the baying of an advancing army. The impact of his kiss, thrusting as a blade into the heart of a rose, the crush of hands spanning her waist threatening to snap her lance-slim body in two, the intimate brush of lean cheeks and rough-velvet skin against her cheek, spearheaded an attack that routed all resistance, an oppressive, merciless, overpowering show of strength that forced her surrender and demonstrated her susceptibility to the devastating weapon of seduction she had never before encountered.

When finally, taking pity on her crushed mouth, Colt lifted his head to survey his victim with a gleam of triumph, her dazed blue eyes responded with a look of defeat that darkened to fear when Tom Graham's jubilant Celtic toast rang out above the babble of laughing, congratulatory voices.

"His plume is set with the holly green
And the leaves of the rowan tree
Lang life King Kielder!"

Because pride demanded a show of composure, she acceded to the wishes of their chanting guests by allowing Colt to lead her on to the empty dance floor and nerved herself to submit to the torture of his possessive embrace while they waltzed to a tune played sweet, low and unashamedly romantic.

Her relief was tremendous when, after encircling the dance floor once, they were joined by a crush of eager dancers whose laughing exchanges made it possible for her to plead in an urgent undertone:

"Please, may we leave now?"

"Would any military tactician voluntarily retreat from a position of advantage?" he teased her gently, exploiting the need not to be overheard by resting his lips against the tender curve of her ear. "If only I could believe that your request was prompted by an urge to enjoy my exclusive company! But as it is," he shrugged regretfully, "I feel reluctant to release my captive bride whose responses are no less sweet because they're forced, whose company I can claim at will, whom I can kiss in front of wedding guests without fear of having my face slapped." He illustrated his point by feathering his lips across her cheek and coolly claiming her lips, prolonging the kiss until they stood motionless, swaying in time to the music. For lingering seconds Rowan felt she was floating on air, then was jolted back to earth by a burst of ribald laughter and an acute awareness of being the object of dozens of laughing, sympathetic, amused and envious eyes.

"Well, do you still want to leave?" He held her ransom with a look that dared her to chance being alone with him, leaving her no option but to fall back on treachery as a ruse to escape from an intolerable situation.

"Yes, please..." She pretended a look of eager longing, then as if overwhelmed by shyness she cast down her lashes in a manner she guessed might be typical of an enticing young bride. The moment she heard his hissed-in breath, felt steel hard muscles tensing against her spine, she knew Colt had been fooled.

Suddenly she was released, left covered in blushing confusion while he strode on to the platform and signalled the band to stop playing.

"Friends, colleagues, ladies and gentlemen!" With the assurance of a redhaired giant he addressed the gathering of guests. "...Regretfully, we must beg leave to be excused. This has been a long though very enjoyable day and naturally my wife and I are feeling rather tired. Thank you for joining in our wedding celebrations, and I hope you'll stay so that the party can continue into the wee sma' hours of the morning."

Cheers of appreciation followed his final wave and swift descent from the platform, then Rowan barely had time to register the swing of a kilt revealing a dirk stuck into the top of tartan hose, the purposeful advance of sturdy brogues, the sparkle of a jewelled brooch and the glint of silver buttons before she was plucked off her feet and into the arms of her reiver husband and swept, a bundle of furious feminine booty, towards the exit.

She could have screamed, yelled and ranted, just as many had done before her when threatened with abduction, but she hung on grimly to her dignity, even managed to cast her profile into a mould of serenity while she submitted to being lowered into the car and sitting without protest while Colt drove back to the castle.

A huge golden moon dipped and surfaced behind banked-up cloud so that one moment the fells were sharply outlined and the next obscured by shadows.

"A hunter's moon," he indicated with a nod, displaying an uncanny ability to read her mind. "The sort of night relished by steel-bonneted reivers who needed light to find a pathway through the bogs and shadows to cloak the dirtiest of deeds. It's a consolation to know that conflict is far behind us, Rowan," he sounded deeply serious, "good to be in a position to demonstrate to any remaining doubters that English and Scots make passionate foes—and equally passionate lovers."

She could not trust herself to speak, but huddled into her wrap, using it as a shield to hide expressions of fear and uncertainty flitting across her expressive face. *Having No Remorse!* Her family motto sighed through her mind as if whispered by a vengeful spirit. *There is no shame in employing deceit as a weapon against a deceiver, but tread cautiously, a step at a time, until you are out of the morass and can challenge Kielder strength from an unassailable position!*

The castle was deserted. As only the minimum number of rooms were in use—the rest bolted and left to gather dust—Nanny was the only live-in servant and she, for reasons of her own, had decided at the last minute to spend the night at her sister's house in the village once the party was over. So when they entered the hall Rowan shivered, sensitive to an ambience of threat, an aura of past conflict lingering within the castle that had contained many battles between English and Scots within its grim walls.

"Would you like a nightcap?" When Colt put a hand beneath her elbow to lead her towards the library she jerked out of reach.

"No, thank you," she stammered, conscious of the need to keep a clear head, "if you don't mind I'll go straight up to my...our...room."

He smiled, eyeing her slim tenseness, her pale set features that looked sculpted from marble, with the resignation of a hunter used to the ways of timid creatures of the wild, a man who took time to stalk his prey and was prepared to be patient—for a little while longer.

"Rowan," he closed the gap between them and captured her startled face between cupped hands, "don't feel ashamed. Some defeats hold more triumph than victories. You displayed true bravery in acknowledging the futility of further conflict, so relax,

brave heart, I promise you will not regret your surrender.''

The conceit of the man was unbelievable! She
seethed behind the smiling mask she had donned in
order to lull him into a mood of complacency.

"I'm sure I won't," she agreed, quaking at the
knees, reminding herself that coolness was imperative
if she was to effect her escape. Trying to hide the
cringing she felt when his hand stroked a tendril of
hair from her cheek, she backed out of his clutches
and started towards the stairs.

"You know where our rooms are situated?" she
managed to choke across her shoulder.

"I do," he called after her, a thread of laughter in
his voice, "I made it my business to find out!"

The suite of rooms Nanny had prepared in spite of
orders to the contrary comprised a main bedroom
panelled from ceiling to floor in dark, carved oak,
dominated by a huge four-poster bed with drapes
pulled back to reveal smooth plump pillows edged
with lace, a heavy damask bedspread already turned
down over paler green blankets and pristine sheets
with one edge flicked back as if to offer comfort and
encouragement to a shy bride, and a dressing-room
and bathroom secreted behind two doors so symmet-
rically perfect they appeared as one with panelled
walls.

Warmth from a fire burning low in a marble fireplace attracted her like a magnet, and she bathed in its
glow as frantically she tossed her wedding-dress over
her head, then, with a disgusted look at her best cotton nightdress laid out on the bed, rummaged through
drawers and wardrobe in search of pyjamas and a serviceable dressing-gown to pull over her frozen limbs.

Conscious that speed was the very essence of success, she did not wait to tidy her discarded clothes but ran towards a stretch of panelling, fumbled with an ornate piece of carving and gasped with relief when, with a slow, reluctant groan, a section slid open to reveal six stone steps leading up to a void of darkness. With the confidence of long practice she stepped through the aperture, heeled back the panelling, then struck a match taken from a box left on a ledge next to an ancient but serviceable oil lamp. Seconds later, with the lamp casting elongated shadows upon bare stone walls, she gained the safety of her hiding place, the secret room just large enough to accommodate a table, two chairs and a shelf full of books, that she and Nigel had considered their bolthole, a place used whenever they had felt the need to ponder in solitude, or to escape Nanny's wrath, during childhood.

For the first hour she tried to read, but gave up the effort when the strain of listening for sounds of movement in the room below made it impossible to concentrate. Then after she had sat for an age, staring blankly, cold began seeping into her bones, numbing until her flesh felt frozen, her limbs stiffly set, forcing her to acknowledge the foolishness of attempting to spend the rest of the long night entombed within an atmosphere chilly as an ice box.

She had entered a state of frozen paralysis, a trance-like immobility of mind and body brought about by stubbornness, a determination not to give an inch even if the outcome should be wilful self-destruction, when a sound impinged upon her subconscious—the creaking of ancient woodwork, perhaps, or the squeaking of a mouse—but she was too miserable to care.

"Have you suffered enough, or shall I leave you to indulge in masochistic penance for a while longer?"

She raised her head from forearms stretched out across the table to direct a stupefied stare at the angry figure with fists thrust savagely into the pockets of a dressing-gown, glowering from the doorway.

"How...how did you know where to find me?" she husked, swallowing painfully.

"How could an adventurous schoolboy, his curiosity fired by servants' gossip, fail to discover a priest's hole whose location is common knowledge?"

"You mean..." she struggled to sit upright, wincing from the suspicion that her agony had been unnecessary, "that you've known all along that I was here? Then why...?" She stopped abruptly, wondering why the thought of his indifference should cause her extra pain.

"Because you deserved to be taught a lesson," he told her tightly, "and because nothing I could have done would have inflicted more misery than you've inflicted upon yourself!" In two strides he reached her side. Lowering his head until she felt drowned by the upheaval in grey, storm-tossed eyes, he charged thickly: "No doubt you thought you had me fooled, but in spite of my optimistic claim that we could achieve an amicable partnership, I felt your capitulation was too sudden to be completely believable. You see, Rowan, I can't help being aware of the depth of animosity you feel towards me—even so, until tonight I hadn't suspected that your hatred ran so deep you would choose to freeze to death rather than accept me as a husband!"

She moaned a protest when he stooped to lift her into his arms, but was too chilled to put up much of a fight when he carried her downstairs and into a bed-room glowing with the warmth of a stoked-up fire. The spitting of logs, the roar of flames leaping up the chimney sounded no less furious than the threat smouldered against her ear as, tightening his grip upon her numbed body, Colt directed her attention to-wards the moon sailing past an uncurtained window.

"A hunter's moon, Rowan, remember...? A moon reivers looked upon as an omen of success whenever they felt the urge to ride, rape, pillage and plunder!"

CHAPTER SEVEN

ONCE AGAIN Falstone Castle had been taken by storm, this time by an army of builders who had erected scaffolding in the downstairs rooms and were in the process of carrying out Colt's orders to replace rotting timbers, renew outdated plumbing, and discover the source of damp rising and seeping in dark patches through damask-covered walls. Every room in the castle was to be renovated, even those that had been locked and left deserted for decades, before a second wave of workers descended, experts in the art of restoring the interiors of ancient buildings to their former glory.

It had taken the dynamic new owner of Falstone less than a week to set the ball rolling, yet Rowan felt, as she sat in the breakfast room toying with a piece of toast and sipping coffee, that the banging of hammers and the rasping of saws through wood had been assaulting her ears for an eternity. Surprisingly, Nanny had proffered no complaints about the upheaval. Indeed, she sounded aggravatingly cheerful when she appeared with a tray to clear the dishes from the table.

"You'll be staying in this morning?" Suspiciously, she eyed the baggy jumper and disreputable denims which Rowan, almost as a defence mechanism, had adopted as a uniform.

"I have to ride over to the cottages." She tensed, anticipating an argument. "Old Mrs Story has sent word that she wants to see me urgently."

"To ask the chiropodist to tend to her corns, no doubt!" Nanny snorted. "Ann Story was a fusser in her teens and has grown worse with old age. You must make it known that you're far too busy to be at the beck and call of everyone." She banged the tray down on the table, to the detriment of an ancient coffee pot. "We're taking on extra household staff and Mr Kielder has arranged for you to interview some people from the village this morning."

"Then he ought to have had the courtesy to tell me first!" Rowan jumped to her feet, her blue eyes flashing.

"You're quite right," a voice drawled from the doorway. "I'm sorry, the interviews slipped my mind. Immediately I remembered, I left the site hoping to tell you in person, but obviously," he grimaced, sauntering into the room, "Nanny has beaten me to it."

Displaying a deference Rowan found galling, Nanny almost bobbed a curtsey before retreating from an atmosphere reeking with acrimony.

It had been raining heavily all morning, but Colt seemed impervious to damp that had toned his hair to a deep, rich chestnut red, or to rivulets of moisture coursing slowly down a hard jawline and a length of bronzed neck, then left glistening on a hairy chest left exposed to the elements by a partly unbuttoned shirt and a sheepskin jacket he had shrugged over broad shoulders and then left casually undone.

Startled by an impulse to berate him for a careless disregard for his own well-being, she edged nervously towards the window, hoping to conceal a blush from grey eyes used to scanning far horizons, pinpointing and assessing every movement, every slight area of activity.

"I'm afraid you'll have to carry out the interviews yourself," she told him stiffly. "I have a previous engagement."

"Then break it." She tensed, sensing his approach from the rear, and reacted as to the stab of a rapier when his hand clamped down upon her shoulder, spinning her round to face him.

"Don't touch me!" She jerked away, shocked by an attack of sharply-needled nerves. Hating his easy dominance, his ability to arouse her emotions in spite of a strong will to remain calm, she refused coldly. "Unlike yourself, once a promise has been given I never go back on my word."

"Don't you, Rowan...?" The cynical question hovered over her head, making her want to cower, timid as a mouse under threat from a bird of prey. She braced to combat the humiliation of being reminded of her marriage vows...to *love, honour, and obey... with this body I thee worship.* On that count, at least, he had little room for complaint!

Then for some reason his keen glance softened as it roved a suddenly wounded mouth that refused to be still, and he decided to be kind.

"Part of our bargain was that you would relieve me of all household responsibilities," he reminded her quietly, "to make this a place where I could come home to and relax."

She was ashamed of feeling so ridiculously grateful for his compassion in throwing her a lifeline when he could have decimated her pride at a stroke.

"The surroundings are hardly conducive to relaxation," she pointed out, her heart keeping pace with the furious pounding of hammers.

"Point taken," he agreed wryly, when the air was rent by the high-pitched whine of an electric drill, "but to a man who has known only transient shelter, the essence of a home lies in its permanence—a house at journey's end that is familiar, where he'll find a wife to humour his moods; servants to minister to his comfort, and children," he concluded meaningfully, "to set the final seal upon his happiness."

This hint of his intentions revived a painful memory, provoking the blush that was never far from her cheeks, a lingering, scorching momento of a night she would have preferred to forget. Unable to withstand his steady scrutiny, she turned her face aside.

"I suppose I could delay my business until after lunch," she conceded with difficulty, wondering why, in spite of her determination to oppose him at every turn, she should find herself continually bending to his will.

"Thank you, Rowan..." the warmth of his tone sent a tremor running up her spine, "from past experience I knew that I could depend upon you to be...generous."

When the door closed quietly behind him she slumped down on to the windowseat and gave way to the relief of tears, a tempest of contradictory emotions made up of shame and pride, fear and elation, misery and passionate, demoralising, uneducated pleasure. More than a week had past since the night she had been dragged back in time to the days of plundering reivers and had lived out the trauma of a girl abducted by an enemy motivated by anger, resentment of defeat, and a desire to see the pride of a ruling English family trampled underfoot by forcing physical union upon a youthful maiden in the hope that hated Scottish seed might flourish and grow fruitful in fertile, virgin soil, yet every moment of every passing day she felt conscious of being humbled, in the way a soldier is humbled when he loses a battle and is then condemned by his enemy to the ranks of walking wounded.

Clasped within angry arms, with his fiery breath fanning her cheek, and the pulsating heat of his hard masculine body crushing her into a nest of downy blankets, the blood had quickly melted in her frozen veins, beginning as a tingling trickle, then a surge, and finally developing into a racing torrent of new and frightening feeling. She had fought as her predecessors must have fought, with raking fingernails, snapping teeth and wildly flailing limbs, yet she had sensed from his indulgent growl of laughter that he was enjoying restraining her puny efforts. Feinting blows from her clenched fists, he had pinned her kicking legs with the weight of his body and imprisoned her wrists in a steely grip, stretching her arms out wide until the only defence left to her had been an angry tongue and contemptuously blazing eyes.

Then all at once he had seemed to tire of the skirmish and had silenced her tirade with a kiss more stunning than a blow, forceful as the waters of a dam that had seemed gradually to build up inside her before bursting with a thunderous roar, spilling an overflow of passion that had mingled with his to form a racing, boiling, pounding current that had tossed them together in a maelstrom of ecstasy before disgorging their shaking, clinging, exhausted bodies into calmer, less turbulent waters.

He had been kind in victory, rough wooing had given way to gentle consideration, to whispered assurances mingling with kisses pressed without ceasing upon her trembling, responsive lips, and with a soothing, sensitive touch of hands that had caressed her into contented stillness so that for a while they had slept with naked limbs entwined, half-drowned castaways tossed on to a peaceful shore, until the dam had filled once more to danger level, floodgates had burst open, and with joyful confidence they had welcomed a second vortex of rapturous emotion.

"Rowan, my love," Colt had charged in a shaken groan, "you have the sweet, pure breath of a child, the candid generosity of the very young—and the sensuous allure of a she-devil!"

But the mysteries of womanhood, her illogical, feminine reaction to overwhelming emotion had proved him to be unversed in the ways of women—her kind of woman—for once the storm had abated leaving them calm she had sought relief from unbearable tension by bursting into tears. He had held her loosely, wincing from the scorch of tears upon a muscled chest toughened and bronzed from exposure to the elements, then had shocked her into silence with an oath ripped savagely from a constricted throat.

"Dammit, Rowan, did you have to cry!"

Seconds later she had been left alone, staring dry-eyed through the window at a hunter's moon sailing high in the heavens, wondering if others had felt as shamed, bewildered, and bereft when abandoned by a passionate enemy.

The interviewing of applications eager to fill the posts of gardeners, kitchen helpers and general cleaners did not take long. The villagers were all well known to her, so it was simply a matter of agreeing suitable hours and rates of pay before she was free to saddle up Cello and set off to keep her appointment.

She rode at a leisurely pace, enjoying the sight of miles of wild moorland—marshy ground growing only rank grass providing rough pasturage for a few sheep—spruce-covered hills breaking up the smooth outline of the moors, and acres of conifer forest, a soft flowing monotone of dark blue-green broken by occasional patches of brighter green larch.

Avoiding high ridges that looked down upon the scarred valley, she headed Cello into the forest in search of solitude, hoping to erase some of the jumpy tension that had plagued her for days. But a glimpse of the little church in the forest sentinelled by shapely Irish yews set her pulses aching with a reminder of her wedding day, so that not even the discovery that the inhabitants of the forest were still grazing unconcerned by the daily encroaching noise of machinery was sufficiently comforting to curb tremors of nervous tension.

Consequently, she was all the more alarmed, all the more ready to erupt into anger, when deep inside the forest she picked up the sound of a tuneless whistle as she neared a clearing and saw the figure of a man squatting low over a bulging haversack.

"Why are you here?"

Abe spun round, startled by the pistol-sharp question, then immediately relaxed with an expression of relief.

"Lady Rowan," he grinned, "you gave me one hell of a...you scared the daylight out of me," he amended hastily.

She was in no mood for banter. Fastening eyes hard with suspicion upon the haversack at his feet, she demanded icily: "I insist upon knowing why you're here!"

"For a very innocuous reason, I assure you." He forked his fingers through his hair in a gesture of bewilderment. "I was merely intending to record some bird calls—it's a hobby of mine." He halted, made awkward by her unfriendly attitude. "I earmarked this spot weeks ago because of its lack of background noise and seeming isolation. As you can see," he flipped open the cover of his haversack with his foot, "I have with me a tape recorder and microphone—I trust you have no objection?"

Rowan slipped out of the saddle to examine thoroughly the contents of the haversack.

"Don't you believe me?" Abe sounded indignant, and slightly hurt. "What were you expecting to find in there, a couple of snares?"

She straightened. "I'm sorry, Mr...Abe," she tendered a strained smile, "if I appear unduly suspicious. Unfortunately, we've found it necessary over the years to keep a close watch upon known habitats of protected species of birds, nevertheless, in spite of our vigilance and what some might consider to be an unnecessary amount of secrecy, word has spread and many precious eggs have been stolen from nests by thoughtless amateur collectors."

"Blast their selfish hides!" His spontaneous outburst of disgust forged an immediate affinity. Rowan relaxed, reassured by the ferocity of his frown, then by way of an apology for suspecting him of such sacrilege, she proffered an olive branch.

"There's another reason why the protection of this clearing is so vital," she confided, leading him towards a spot beneath the trees where the ground was thick with moss and rotted pine needles. She knelt down and carefully cleared a small area of vegetation, then sat back upon her heels, inviting him to take a look.

He puzzled over what looked to him no more than a dead main stem that had various side branches with a just-visible growth of new shoots branching either side of it.

"It's an orchid—one of a nest of rare orchids known as Creeping Lady's Tresses that appear only in a few scattered locations where the habitat is suitable. You must come back and see it in July when the blooms are at their best—creamy white, short and plump, with a heavenly scent that attracts every pollinating bumble bee for miles around." His expression reflected recognition of the honour she had paid him and when she had carefully re-covered her secret store and walked back to the clearing, he found words to express his gratitude.

"Thank you for allowing me to share your secret, Lady Rowan—for allowing me to become a member of what I guess must be a very tight circle of confidants."

"Only two other people beside myself know about the orchids," she confirmed. "You must promise me, Abe, that you will never, under any circumstances, betray my trust by telling anyone else of their existence?"

"Cut my throat and hope to die!" Solemnly, he wetted a finger and traced a line across his neck from ear to ear. "Everyone back at camp treats me like an irresponsible boy—especially Colt—yet you, who can't be much older than myself, didn't hesitate to entrust me with knowledge kept even from local inhabitants. I promise you'll never have cause to regret it," he assured her, his usually devil-may-care expression replaced by a depth of earnestness. "And in return," he hesitated, blushing to the roots of his hair, "might I extract from you a promise not to mention my...er...hobby to any of my workmates? They're a tough bunch of guys," he explained with obvious embarrassment, "with hearts of gold, each and every one of them, but their interest in birds is strictly confined to the young female variety."

"Commonly known as chicks...?" She smiled, sympathetic to his need to keep secret a hobby that might give rise to derisive comment and detract from his macho image. "Of course you have my promise, but I feel certain you're being unduly sensitive; every wildcat, however ferocious, has a small grain of tabby in his composition."

"Then all I can say is that, in the case of my buddies, they keep it very well hidden," Abe countered gloomily.

"Even Colt...?" She wished she could speak his name without a catch in her voice.

"Especially Colt." He was bending to retrieve his haversack so did not notice her wince. "Any hopes we might have harboured about marriage mellowing his temper have been dispelled this past week—only yesterday he tore a strip off a guy who dubbed him King Kielder within earshot, even though he must be aware

by now that the nickname has well and truly stuck."
When he turned round to face her, with a thermos in
one hand and a packet of sandwiches in the other, the
tight set of her features must have communicated displeasure. "Heck, have I spoken out of turn again?
And just as I was about to ask you to share my
lunch!"

He looked so downcast she felt forced to relent.
"What a lovely idea, it's ages since I enjoyed a meal
al fresco."

As they sat on a fallen treetrunk demolishing with
relish generous helpings of ham sandwiched between
slices of bread baked early that morning in the camp
cookhouse, washed down with coffee made memora-
ble by a rich aroma rising in the air to mingle with the
scent of resin, Rowan felt tension seeping out of her,
could almost have convinced herself that the clock had
been turned back to the peaceful era she had enjoyed
before the invasion, had it not been for a faint sound
in the background like the rumble of distant artillery,
indicating the presence of an army bent upon destruction.

Time sped on wings as they chatted amicably, discovering more and more areas of mutual interest, es-
tablishing a rapport that dispersed Abe's awe of her
elevated position and helped her to recognise him as a
kindred spirit, youthful, willing to undertake responsibilities, yet basically uncertain.

Which probably accounted for the ease with which,
in response to her enquiry about his job, he displayed
irritation.

"I'll always be grateful to Colt for taking me on his
payroll, but after five years you'd imagine he'd stop
treating me as a probationer, show me a little trust, so

that I could prove my worth and dispel the reminder that initially he took me on only as a favour to my sister."

"Your sister?" she prompted, conscious of a sudden return of tension.

"Diane," he enlightened moodily, completely absorbed in his own misery. "She's a fashion model—working in London at the moment—but when she first met up with Colt she was just an amateur striving to achieve recognition in the States. His influence helped to get her career off the ground. But as ever since the death of our parents she's reacted towards me like a broody hen, Colt relieved her of all responsibility by offering me a post designed to provide me with a promising future."

In spite of her revulsion, her contempt of self-inflicted pain, she forced herself to probe further.

"Colt and your sister must have been very close?"

"They were," he nodded, unknowingly twisting a knife in her wound, "but Diane was never under any illusion about having a special place in his affections. I realised that she was content to be one of many, when she confided: *'Colt always needs a mountain to climb. Whenever a peak has been conquered he's content for a while, but then he becomes bored and has to lift his sights higher.'"*

Rowan shrank from the matter-of-fact statement that confirmed what she had suspected—that to Colt Kielder she represented no more than a challenge, a rare and distant peak that had to be scaled to be reduced to the ordinary. He possessed the vital attraction of power most women found irresistible, power of physique and power of achievement, yet even he, accustomed though he must have become to quick conquests, must have been surprised at the ease with which his latest target had been accomplished!

Dusk had fallen by the time she had concluded her business and returned to the castle. Without bothering to change, she made her way to the dining-room where she knew Colt would be waiting to begin his evening meal, and as she walked across a darkened hall, its walls lined with scaffolding, she felt a sense of imprisonment, a feeling of being trapped within a state of siege.

"Where the devil have you been?" He whipped around from the window, his expression clamped as a man who has kept close vigil. "I'd begun to wonder if you'd been thrown, if Cello had perhaps stumbled?"

"It's been such a lovely day, I lost all track of time." Rowan tried to sound airy as she prepared to take her seat at the table, but regretted her show of bravado when his hand fastened upon her shoulder, then froze, as if fighting an impulse to shake her.

"Have you so little concern for those who worry about your welfare? You were absent so long that even Nanny had begun to panic—and just look at you!" His disgusted glance raked from the crown of her dishevelled head to the soles of mud-caked boots. "How much longer do you intend keeping up an act of childish defiance, parading the most disreputable garments in your wardrobe in order to try my patience?"

"I've always lived too far removed from society to bother about feeding my vanity with fashion!" she retorted, daring to cast a scornful eye over an impeccable white shirt, silk Hermès tie, and a black velvet dinner jacket stroking cat-supple over muscular shoulders. "Anyway," she chanced the utmost show of temerity, "it's a mistake to appear too well dressed when aspiring to being accepted by the aristocracy! According to my brother, who's something of an expert on clothes, the "preppy" look is now all the rage in London—identical sporty T-shirts, trousers, striped blazers and jackets being worn by both sexes. Therefore it's arguable," she challenged triumphantly, twirling a full circle in order to display her boyish outfit to full advantage, "that what I'm wearing is socially unacceptable!"

Her attack ought to have totally destroyed his vanity, but there was no hint of blight in eyes narrowed with annoyance, no honed edge to the voice that rasped sharp as a saw through wood:

"You resemble a popular song that's been sung too often, a melody redolent of stables, manure, and sweaty horse blankets! But as I'm paying the piper I intend choosing both the tune *and* the composer. I have a friend whose exquisite taste and eye for colour has made her internationally famous in the fashion world—I'll telephone her tonight and test her ability to choose a wardrobe with no more than a description and a set of measurements to give clues to the intended wearer."

Obviously, he was referring to Diane! The compliment to his one-time mistress made her resentment soar.

"You can't supply my measurements, even I don't know what they are because I've never bothered to take them," she told him stiffly.

"The solution to that problem lies as near as a tape measure," he clipped. A shaft of light beamed down upon his lowering head, firing his hair torch-bright as he stressed with a menacing glitter: "I should search one out, if I were you, little warrior, for should the information I require not be forthcoming I may feel forced to resort to Braille!"

CHAPTER EIGHT

THE CONTENTS of the castle supplied a record of the
history of past inhabitants, a study of their lifestyle
that began with a few odd items of primitive, purely
functional furniture that had survived the ravages of
sixteenth-century warfare then continued to demonstrate, by way of carpets, needlework, wrought iron
and ormolu mounts, clocks and furniture, the developing style and taste of a procession of Falstone earls.

When Nigel sold his birthright the entire contents of
the castle had been included in the deal, and as Rowan supervised the removal and storage of objects in
danger of being damaged if left in the vicinity of
workmen, she was struck by the bitter thought that
although civilisation might have advanced, the attitude of one man in particular was attuned to that of
the Dark Ages when it had been common practice to
barter for a wife in the marketplace.

Rooms left uninhabited for years had been utilised
for the storage of irreplaceable items, and as she traced
a finger through dust covering a black marble top in-
set with a fantastic variety of various-coloured mar-
bles and semi-precious stones depicting leaves, flowers
and birds, Rowan became suddenly still, her senses
alerted by the ring of footsteps crossing the stone
paved hall. Only one man of her acquaintance strode
impatient as a god of war thirsting for battle!

"So this is where you've hidden yourself!" Colt towered in the doorway, grey eyes quizzing her slender, dejected figure, a pensive mouth, and drooping, raven-black head. "What are you doing?" He advanced into the room, treading wary as a cat towards a shrinking bird.

"Taking inventory of your assets, as requested," she replied, then added sarcastically: "I've listed myself under items of Swag."

When grey eyes clouded she realised that she had made the foolish mistake of underestimating the intelligence of an adversary.

"There's no denying your classical perfection," he agreed dryly, "yet you're hardly petrified enough to be likened to a carved garland of foliage—more of an Amorine, perhaps...?"

She blushed when his lips tugged upward in a smile, conscious that his mind was dwelling upon their wedding night, the night he had asserted his right to caress her naked-Cupid form, to love like a lion—before spurning naïveté as boring. This train of thought seemed confirmed when his glance fell upon a delicately sculptured torchère depicting chained Nubian slaves holding aloft glass lampshades moulded into the shape of flaming torches, an extravagant vulgarity purchased by one of the more flamboyant earls of Falstone.

"Petrified poetry," he murmured, and somehow she knew that he was not referring to the shapely nudes immortalised in marble. "Nature recognises no indecencies, yet man is bludgeoned into following laws of decorum, ceremony, and manners that decree he must do this, or he must not do that. Is it so unforgivable, Rowan," he turned on her so fiercely she stepped back alarmed, "for a man to fall victim to the promptings of his own nature? Is propriety really so important to a woman that she's unable to forgive a man who made her blush?"

"Sovereigns seldom seek forgiveness," she reminded him stiffly, "their consciences are usually salved by declaring an amnesty, an act by which kings can pardon injustices committed by themselves!" With fingernails digging deeply into her palms, she steeled herself not to read penitence in a face grown suddenly sombre, not to be deceived into thinking that his stern mouth could ever be softened by remorse.

He was near enough to touch her, close enough for passionate vibrations to breach the chasm between them so that inward quivering forced her to back away until the edge of a nearby table lent support to her trembling limbs. The distant sound of hammering merged with her heartbeats until her ears felt deafened by the din, her body rendered inert by pulses that leapt into throbbing life immediately he drew nearer.

But the threat to her shaky defences was averted when after an angry bombardment of her pale, pinched face, Colt thrust clenched fists deep into the pockets of his jacket and bit savagely:

"If that's how our marriage appears to you—an act of injustice—how do you see yourself? As a wife sacrificed on the altar of duty?"

For one wildly illogical moment she felt tempted to absolve him of guilt with a denial, by confessing that she had emerged from the sacrificial rite revitalised, with senses more acute, nerves vibrant and tingling, with a body that had been permitted a taste of paradise and left with a gnawing hunger for more. She stabbed back the impulse, but the shock of knowing

herself capable of such traitorous thoughts startled her
blue eyes wide with self-accusation.

"How do you expect me to feel?" Her forced whisper seemed to hover like smoke over his damped-down
furnace of wrath. "I've been bought, wedded, and
bedded, but you won't break my pride," her chin tilted
high as Falstone courage, "whatever further punishment you might impose, I will not be consumed by
your insatiable appetite for power!"

"So, you are to be a morsel forever sticking in my
throat, hoping, no doubt, that some day I might
choke," he drawled, looking suddenly dangerous.
"But what if I should grow tired of the indigestible
and decide to spit it out?"

"I'd prefer to be a crumb in the belly of a spar-
row," she indicted coldly, "than allow a beast to gorge
upon my carcase."

The convulsive jerk of hands thrust deep into his
pockets should have signalled an elated sense of victory, but though for once her dice had thrown up a
winning score, misery smothered every faint flicker of
satisfaction. It seemed hard to believe that Colt's
tough, rawhide skin had developed a sensitive spot, yet
after seconds of strained silence his voice when he
spoke sounded flat, his shrug seemed defeated.

"I sought you out this morning in order to broach
an idea I thought might meet with your approval." His
swift change of subject took her by surprise. When he
stooped to examine a cabinet panelled with oyster ve-
neering radiating circles of end cuts of wood displaying the natural growth rings of the tree, his expression
became hidden. "As every generation seems to have
left its cultural mark upon the castle, I wondered if
you might like to perpetuate the custom by decorat-

ing one of the rooms entirely to your own taste, using your own choice of fittings and furniture. It's been said that a person's choice of surroundings can be considered a reflection of hidden character," he straightened to direct a brief, noncommittal smile, "so it would be a shame, don't you think, if posterity were to be denied the closing chapter of Falstone family history?"

"Before the advent of King Kielder...?" Rowan almost sneered, incensed by his peremptory dismissal of her proud family line. "No doubt your reign will herald a quest for luxury in terms of comfort, an entire devotion to the type of splendour deemed a necessary status symbol to the newly-rich. Are you planning to have Gucci dogs in every alcove, a diamond-studded doorbell, and gold-plated toothpicks on the dining table? Or would you prefer a mink-lined Jacuzzi in the bathroom?"

Like a bear prodded beyond endurance, Colt rounded with a snarl to clutch her shoulders between hands powerful enough to crush.

"What I would prefer above all else, Rowan, is a truce, an intermission, a respite from constant sparring. Even warring barons of the Dark Ages agreed to stop carving each other up, burning each other's wheatfields, raping each other's women—at least on Sundays, feast days, and church holy days! I would be grateful if just once I could waken knowing that for one day at least I'll be granted a small truce, one that begins at daybreak and continues peacefully through until sundown. Must it remain a pipe dream, Rowan?" he shook her fiercely. "I've tried as hard as I know how to atone for my mistakes, to merit some sign of approval—is your purse of pardon so tight that even the small gift of leniency is more than you can afford?''

Before words had time to form on her startled lips he had gone—flung out of the room in a temper of frustration!

Miserably, she forced herself to continue with her task of taking inventory of oak chairs with carved lions displaying the rose of England; a lacquered cabinet on a silvered stand; a gaming table and matching stool; an oak sofa plushly upholstered in pink; a round satinwood table; an ornate cabinet veneered with tortoiseshell; gilt-wood mirrors; elegant clocks with fine ormolu mounts; a pair of Regency armchairs covered with olive green velvet; a walnut stool with needle-worked seat—all allegedly prizes of war taken by successive earls of Falstone, uniquely valuable items that Nigel had attempted to sell, only to discover that because of torn upholstery, chipped woodwork, cracked glass and missing handles, their value had been considerably reduced.

She blessed her forebears whose careless attitude had ensured she would not be deprived of familiar objects she had grown to love, but as she moved among relics of a more glorious past her mind was concentrated upon the present, and more exactly upon the husband who had taken her as a prize of war with the sole object of revenge against the hated English aristocracy. It seemed that now he had achieved his aim he wanted hostilities to cease, so far as he was concerned the war was over—so far as she was concerned it had only just begun!

She was still pondering over his dislike of her family, and especially of her brother Nigel, when Nanny entered the room.

"Kielder's gone." She had adopted this form of address for the master of the house, pronouncing his surname with the sort of deference usually accorded to a title. "What have you said to make him go storming out of the castle with a brow as black as thunder?"

"Or a child in a tantrum because he can't get his own way?" Rowan qualified coolly.

"Some child!" Nanny snorted, breaking into a chuckle as grating as the hinges on a long-unopened door. "He was born big as a toddler; at three he looked old enough for school, and at twelve he was already showing signs of developing into a tall, broad-shouldered man."

"You watched him growing up, then?" Rowan bit her lip, hoping Nanny had not read her note of eager surprise.

"But of course I did—and his father before him!" she retorted with a pride usually reserved for her own kith and kin. "Even when impoverished, the Kielders are not the sort of men who can be overlooked—indeed, among Scottish Borderers they've always been as highly revered as Falstones are by the English. Surely you must recall playing with him when you were a child?" Nanny shot her a surprised glance. "During the school holidays he came every day to the castle and was allowed to run loose in the grounds until his mother had finished her work."

Rowan's brow wrinkled as she concentrated hard, trying to revive memories of the distant past. With the master of the household seldom in residence discipline had grown lax, so that many of the children whose fathers worked on the estate had regarded the paths winding through overgrown shrubberies, the neglected orchards, the deserted outhouses and stables, as a huge adventure playground.

"There was one boy," she began diffidently, then with growing conviction, "whose red head always towered above the rest—he was always bullying Nigel!"

"That would be Kielder," Nanny nodded, looking suddenly shamefaced, "but though your brother always insisted that he was being bullied, I often suspected that the boot was actually on the other foot, because in spite of his superior physique, Kielder was noted for his protective manner towards those less robust than himself, especially the little ones. Whereas your brother, I'm afraid to say," her thin lips pursed, "was always inclined to take advantage of his position."

"He did throw his weight about rather," Rowan felt forced to agree.

"We'll never know the true ins and outs of the affair," Nanny continued to brood, "but after one final scrape involving all three of you, Kielder was banned from entering the castle grounds ever again. You and he were discovered all muddy and soaking wet and Nigel covered in bruises and with a black eye."

Rowan sat down suddenly when out of the depths of her subconscious shot a startling spear of recall. She had been less than five years old at the time, yet the experience had left her with a horror of dark, dank tunnels. During one of many forays of exploration that had been a favourite childhood pursuit, some of the older children had stumbled across an old, dried-up well. Years before, its head had been sealed with planks nailed across its rim, but rotted timber had yielded to the probing of a dozen pairs of hands that had uncovered a black void deep enough to encourage the childish fantasy that it was a bottomless pit, an endless tunnel boring straight through the planet.

Arguments had ensued about the advisability of testing the strength of the length of rope still coiled around an overhead beam that had once been used with a bucket attached to draw water from the well. Rowan remembered clearly that it had been Nigel, who had always taken charge whenever the redhaired boy was absent, who had insisted that she, being the smallest and lightest of them all, should be lowered down the well in order to prove his assertion that it was shallow, merely the depth of the length of rope. Even while mulling over the incident beads of sweat chilled her brow as she experienced in retrospect the trauma of being tied with rope beneath her armpits, then lowered, kicking and screaming in protest, into what had appeared to her childish mind as a black hole of eternity. Then her terrified scream when the knot had come undone, dropping her swift as a stone into a bed of evil-smelling mud.

The events that had followed had merged into a panic-stricken blur. She knew she had screamed and pleaded hysterically with faces ringed around a patch of daylight high above her head to come down and fetch her. She remembered Nigel's shaken, very frightened voice urging her not to panic as he was going to fetch help, then there had followed the sound of argument, a scuffle, and a yell of pain from Nigel, before the small spot of daylight had disappeared as a body had begun lowering down the rope towards her.

She knew now that it had been Colt who had encouraged her not to be afraid while he had tied the rope competently beneath her armpits, that it had been his voice that had urged her to remain calm while jerkily, laboriously, she had been hauled towards the surface. Which method he had used to climb out of the well she had never discovered, because from that day onwards he had been banished from the castle grounds, banned from approaching within yards of the son of the Earl of Falstone, who must have sworn to Nanny and to every other adult concerned that he was blameless, that the villain of the piece was one of the distrusted Scots, son of the hothead Kielder.

Was it any wonder Colt held a hard contempt for English justice—that for years he had bided his time, determined to wreak revenge upon both deceitful Falstones.

An hour later, in spite of the fact that a grey veil of mist was wreathing the fells and a steady drizzle of rain borne upon high winds was soaking sheep huddled for protection against drystone walls and turning trickling burns into chocolate-coloured froth racing down fellsides to disgorge into an already swollen river, she set out to keep what had become a regular tryst with Abe.

He had one whole day off each week, and without prior arrangement, without so much as a hint of verbal collusion, they had formed the habit of making their way to the clearing where the first seeds of friendship had been sown. He was awaiting her arrival with a broad grin of welcome that erupted immediately he heard the thud of Cello's hoofbeats.

"I must try to hire a mount," he confided ruefully, as he helped her down from the saddle. "I've left my car bogged down in mud at the edge of the forest—some parts of the road are so badly flooded I thought

I wasn't going to make it! Doesn't it ever do anything else but rain around here?''

"Presumably, the amount of rainfall was one of the deciding factors in the choice of location for the dam," she reminded him dryly. "We do get a lot of rain and snow and high winds, but as always, there are compensations, for when the sun begins glowing through the mist, throwing a mantle of red-gold bracken over the sloping shoulders of fells, when every leaf and blade glistens tear-bright, and the air is filled with the twittering and fluttering of birds drying off their feathers, the countryside seems newly-born, fresh, clean and sweet-smelling."

"That's how I always think of you." The words seemed jerked from his lips without volition. For a second he looked startled by his own temerity, but when she smiled, accepting the compliment as it had been meant—a genuine, non-flirtatious expression of admiration—he smiled his relief.

"D'you know what I admire most about the girls in this region," he confided as they left Cello to graze and began sauntering along the path through the forest, "their lack of coquetry, their acceptance that a guy, in spite of being a member of the opposite sex, is capable of friendship. Take Dale, for instance—I don't think I've ever felt so relaxed, so uncommitted to the chore of searching my mind for compliments, in the company of any other girl—with the exception of yourself."

"Who was it that said, 'a compliment is akin to a kiss through a veil, a compromise between giving a woman what is forbidden and denying her what is her due'?" Rowan mused. "Personally," she had no idea how sad she suddenly sounded, "I think the greatest compliment a man can pay to a woman is honesty."

"Then you must be pleased you married Colt," Abe decided cheerfully, unaware that the very mention of his name had caused her to flinch, "for he is the one contradiction I know of to the theory that an honest man is a man condemned to poverty. To some of his more recent recruits, men who haven't worked with him long enough to know him well, he sometimes appears aloof and none too approachable, rather tight-lipped about bad language and dirty jokes—imposing no bans, you understand, just making culprits feel definitely uneasy—yet even so he communicates such integrity, such a sense of justice and fair play, that every one of them, from the rawest to the toughest, is soon committed to following him to hell. Even in the boardroom where his contempt of needless courtesy, his reputation for aiming straight for the jugular, offends many who enjoy the ritual ceremonies of business deals, his friendship is prized, his character and ability so respected that directors are prepared to accept his crucial sums scribbled on the back of an envelope, before the findings of expert accountants."

"I've no need to be convinced that my husband is a man of action," she rebuked a trifle bitterly. "I know only too well how he thrives upon dealing and manipulating, upon imposing his will on others. Of course he's a driving force, but heading where . . . ? Only he knows."

"So you, too, have spotted his one weakness." When he pulled her to a halt she saw that his brow was furrowed into lines of anxiety. "Colt rarely stops working because he seems to find it impossible to delegate responsibility. The fact that I have a personal axe to grind is immaterial, management structure is so sparse he's stretched tight as an elastic band trying to keep tabs on everything. Even his social life has tended in the past to be restricted to dinner parties with top executives, and they more often than not have evolved from social chit-chat into a business discussion. We all expected—hoped—that marriage would put an end to his bad working habits, but it simply hasn't happened, he's still pushing himself too hard, almost as if," he hesitated, reluctant to give offence, then forced the grim conclusion, "he were a compulsive gambler risking his all in the hope of hitting some elusive jackpot."

In spite of her conviction that he was worrying needlessly about a human dynamo whose ego thrived upon power, Rowan felt shamed by the slight hint of criticism lurking among his words.

"I'm sorry if my conduct has fallen short of the standards expected of the wife of your boss," she replied stiffly, "but as you and your colleagues must know, my husband is a law unto himself and is therefore hardly likely to allow me to influence the habits of a lifetime."

But the imperious rebuke, far from having the effect she had intended, surprised from him a hoot of laughter.

"My dear Lady Rowan, if you can't persuade him to relax no one can!"

She found his teasing grin infuriating. "Why me?" She all but stamped her foot. "Why should I be singled out to exert pressure upon my husband?"

His grin slowly faded as he sensed bewilderment mixed with fiery indignation. "Because," he spelled out slowly and distinctly, as if anxious to enlighten a backward child, "out of the many chicks Colt has pulled, you're the only one who's managed to tempt him to the altar. I'd given up all hope of seeing the boss take a tumble, but now that he has, I'd be willing to wager a year's salary that he'll never spare a glance for any other woman!"

Fortunately, when she walked on without speaking, he seemed to mistake her embarrassed blush for the shy awkwardness of a bride too new to marriage to find such intimate remarks acceptable, so tactfully he changed the subject.

"What's on our agenda today?" His enquiry was deliberately matter-of-fact. "You've pointed out the best bird hides, shown me how to distinguish a stoat from a weasel—what about Brock the badger, how do I go about finding him?"

"It's highly unlikely that you'll ever see a badger in broad daylight," she responded with relief. "They wait until dusk before coming out to play, hunt for food, air old bedding and transport new grass, straw or bracken to their sleeping chambers."

By the time she had located a patch of alders, favoured by badgers because they were partial to the berries, and pointed out copses and hedgerows most likely to house a sett, the drizzle had developed into a downpour, so in spite of wearing gear appropriate to the weather conditions they reluctantly decided to abandon their study of nature on the tacit understanding that it would be continued the following week.

Crouched low in the saddle, her head bent to avoid the slash of rain against her cheeks, she galloped Cello homeward, slackening pace only when they began cantering up the drive towards the stable yard. She was busily absorbed in the task of rubbing down the mare when she heard the squeal of brakes, the slam of a car door, then the crunch of booted feet approaching the stable. Expectantly she paused and raised her head just as Colt's towering frame appeared in the doorway.

"I've just seen Abe." His voice sounded leashed, as if he were labouring under some kind of strain, then as his cold grey eyes raked her sodden figure he continued tightly, "By the looks of him, he appears to have spent the entire afternoon wandering in the rain."

"Oh...?" she quavered nervously, running her tongue around suddenly dry lips as she sensed seething anger, the threat of some sort of showdown. "Is that so unusual?" she shrugged, trying to appear unconcerned. "For that matter, so have I."

"I must agree that walking in the rain can hardly be classed as unusual," he replied, motionless as a wildcat poised to spring, "neither is it strange that both you and he should choose to do so at the same time and in the same location. What does lead me to suspect that the arm of coincidence is being stretched too far is the fact that on the same day last week, and also during the previous week, Abe's car was parked on the very same spot at the exact times that you chose to exercise Cello. Have you been making secret liaisons, Rowan?"

His words dropped heavily as stones into a deep pool of silence.

"Don't be ridiculous!" she croaked, alarmed by his barely controlled fury.

With the hissing breath and snapping teeth of a predator he pounced, pinning her by the shoulders with her back against a wall.

"Then prove me wrong, Rowan!" He shook her vigorously in his temper. "Tell me, what draws a dedicated Lothario to wander a lonely forest on every one of his days off?"

She stared appalled at the flint-eyed, fiery-haired demon whose iron control had never before been allowed to snap, tempted by sheer terror into betraying Abe's secret. But a reminder that Falstone honour was at stake gave her just enough courage to whisper:

"I . . . can't."

The crush of his grip became so intense she almost cried out, then pain was superseded by unbearable remorse when his powerful frame shuddered and he stepped out of reach.

"Get out of my sight, Rowan!" he commanded in a harsh, rasping voice, "while I'm still capable of resisting the temptation to wring your treacherous English neck!"

CHAPTER NINE

DURING THE previous three days there had been heavy falls of snow, but as Rowan set out to keep her weekly date with Abe all that remained were a few white patches strewn over the higher fells while the hedgerows in the valley were lined with clumps of snowdrops, their delicate heads nodding bravely in a fresh spring breeze.

Deep in thought, she guided Cello through puddles of melted snow, over humped-back bridges crossing swollen streams, then skirted the edge of the forest where every now and then she passed stacks of long-handled beaters—fire-fighting equipment serving as a reminder that even summer brought its drawbacks—on her way towards a rise looking down upon a valley turned into a rubbish dump of piled-up ballast, hard-core, granite chippings, concrete blocks, and empty plastic bags enjoying a game of hide and seek with a playful wind. But for once, the din of working machinery, the shouts of men trying to make themselves heard, the glaring yellow cranes and matching steel bonnets of Colt's army of dam builders, caused her little concern as she brooded over his puzzling reaction to her last meeting with Abe.

After his explosive burst of anger had been doused, he had left her severely alone, returning to the castle long after she had eaten a solitary dinner and leaving each morning without breakfast, before even Nanny was astir. Rowan gnawed her bottom lip, wondering why she should be finding his long absences so disturbing, puzzled by a sense of rejection, bewildered by a strange feeling inside her that she could not fathom, a tight knot of yearning that kept her senses poised, leaping to the sound of every footfall, every door slam, every voice or movement that might be his.

But the worst time of all was night when she lay wide awake straining to detect the slightest sound of movement behind the door connecting her bedroom with the comfortless dressing-room containing a single narrow bed, which, ever since their wedding night, Colt had chosen to occupy in preference to a four-poster huge enough to accommodate his large frame in comfort, spread with lavender-scented sheets, lace-trimmed pillowcases, downy blankets—and a painfully naïve wife!

Mistaking the convulsive jerk of her wrists for a tug upon the reins, Cello tossed back her head and wheeled in the direction of the forest, heading instinctively towards the path leading to the clearing where each week she was usually left to graze. But surprisingly, there was no sign of Abe, who usually arrived first and sat patiently waiting. When after an hour spent checking the bird hides and looking for signs of any untoward disturbance, he had still not put in an appearance, Rowan was forced to the conclusion that he would not be coming and dejectedly decided that rather than return to the castle echoing with the noise of busy workmen she would make her way down to the village to ensure that all was well with a few of their elderly, less isolated tenants.

The first thing that struck her as she cantered past the line of cottages, the small garage with its two meagre petrol pumps, the solitary pub tucked small as a house beneath the spreading branches of a chestnut tree, was the lack of warmth in the villagers' greetings, the brief nods and quickly-averted glances that seemed to indicate some underlying grievance. A few paces onward, a glance towards the village store disturbed her further. The tiny stone built shop with its incongruous corrugated roof, faded paintwork and wooden nameplate bearing the barely discernible description: Hardware, Drapery, Grocer, Newsagent, had had its display window removed and the aperture filled with boarding that had scrawled across its surface: Business as Usual.

With a swift premonition that the occurrence had a connection with something unpleasant, she tethered Cello to a nearby post and hurried towards the entrance. The interior of the shop was so dark she felt temporarily blinded and for a moment could not distinguish the faces belonging to a babble of angry voices, but as her sight became adjusted she managed to single out Meg Storey, the shopkeeper, standing behind the counter with arms akimbo, holding forth to an audience of six that was cramming the shop to capacity.

"What happened to your window, Meg, has there been some sort of accident?"

The miniature crowd fell silent and shuffled sideways to allow Rowan's slight figure access to the counter.

Meg bridled. "Not an accident, Lady Rowan, but deliberate vandalism, I'm certain." The usually placid woman sounded incensed. "I'm sorry to have to say so, but we consider it was a sad day for all of us when your husband brought his steel-bonneted dam builders to our valley!''

A hearty chorus of ''Ayes!'' underlined the villagers' bitter agreement with this statement.

''Vandalism? Surely not...?'' Rowan faltered. ''Tell me exactly what happened.''

''The same thing as happens every Saturday night when those crazy dam-dogs are let off the leash!'' a male voice boomed from the rear of the crush. ''They come tearing down to the village, a hundred or more at a time, fighting to get into a pub built to accommodate a dozen. Then after closing time when they've drunk themselves silly they start roistering around the village in search of girls, and when they can't find any—and parents make certain they don't!—they mark their disappointment by wrecking everything in sight!''

''Not the window...!'' Rowan questioned faintly, her eyes pleading to be contradicted.

''And the street lamp,'' Meg affirmed. ''It's been smashed to smithereens, leaving folk to grope their way to their own front doors!''

''And lighted cigarettes dropped into the letter-box!''

''And garden gates lifted off their hinges!''

''And what about the time they polluted the stream by emptying a drum of oil left on the garage forecourt!''

''And the noise of blaring horns as they race each other back to camp!''

''Don't forget old Archie's dog—for fourteen years it wandered the village streets, slow on his feet and blind as a bat, without coming to a ha'porth of harm, only to finish his days beneath the wheels of some maniac's car!''

"Stop, please!" Rowan clasped her hands over her ears to shut out the rising sound of resentment felt by villagers who seemed to be including herself among Kielder's band of culprits. "I'm terribly sorry," she gasped, backing towards the door. "I'm certain my husband has no idea...I promise you that once he's been told the disturbances will cease."

Shaking with reaction, she untethered Cello and climbed into the saddle, unnerved by a personal antipathy directed by villagers who had always treated her with respect, whom she had always considered to be her friends.

Flags of anger flew high in her cheeks as she headed Cello away from the village and began racing her in the direction of the dam, determined to search out Colt and spill out her grievances while resentment was still hot, while concern for the welfare of the villagers remained a whip to flog her flagging courage.

But after a hard, fast ride across the moor had cooled her temper instinct began counselling caution, reminding her of the need for steady nerves and a clear head when pleading her cause to a less than amenable husband. Acting upon impulse, she veered in the opposite direction, deciding that a visit to the Grahams would supply the interval of calm necessary before what might—depending upon Colt's uncertain humour—turn out to be a heated confrontation.

Dale was just about to step into her father's car when Rowan approached the farmhouse.

"Hello, Dale," she greeted her, "I didn't expect to see you home at this time of day!"

"Nor would you, as a rule," the girl sounded peculiarly sullen, "but owing to pressure of work we've had to stay late at the office these past few evenings, so the boss insisted I took the morning off. I tried to argue that it's he who needs time off, that he can't continue indefinitely working eighteen hours a day, trouble or not, but he wouldn't listen."

"Trouble...?" Rowan echoed stupidly.

"Don't you know?" Dale sent her a curious look. "The workforce was on strike until yesterday—surely you noticed the absence of sound, the lack of movement? The valley was like a deserted battlefield."

"Yes, of course," Rowan stammered, lying to save face, to prevent Dale from guessing that as well as being denied the privilege of her husband's confidences she had been too wrapped up in her own affairs to notice the cessation of activity in the valley. She was spared the embarrassment of trying to appear knowledgeable about the cause of the strike when Dale defended hotly.

"The boss was very sympathetic towards the men's views, he did everything in his power to ensure that working conditions were made as comfortable as possible during a spell of atrocious weather by providing protective clothing, agreeing to shorter shift working and extra pay to compensate for the unusually difficult conditions, but still a tiny minority, encouraged by what I'm certain are a couple of professional troublemakers, held out for more, pressing for further concessions with tongue in cheek, knowing full well that their demands were outrageous! And of course," Dale's glance grew even more unfriendly, "the situation was not improved by Abe's absence.

Had he still been here he could at least have relieved
the boss of minor responsibilities.''

Rowan felt stunned, as if kicked by a bucking mule.
''Where has Abe gone?'' she croaked. ''On holiday... on a business trip... ?''

''I have no idea, Lady Rowan,'' Dale turned her
head aside, but not before Rowan caught a glimpse of
tears. ''One day he was here and the next he had gone.
I was hoping,'' she hesitated to take a deep breath,
then rounded defiantly, ''that as you and he have become so friendly lately you might be able to tell me.''

Rowan blushed scarlet. As in all small communi-
ties, rumour raged hot as a forest fire, but even so it
had simply not occurred to her that her innocent
meetings with Abe could be giving rise to speculative
gossip—gossip that must somehow have drifted to
Colt's ears, making him justifiably angry!

A little of this anger, together with a large amount
of hauteur inherited from ancestors who had always
been counted as being beyond criticism, was reflected
in her cool rebuke.

''I consider it my duty to be approachable and
friendly towards all my husband's employees; it's
gratifying to learn that my efforts have been noted
with approval. However, my level of involvement
doesn't require me to keep tabs on employees' com-
ings and goings. Abe quite properly has gone about his
business knowing that I would neither require nor
expect to be told of his intentions.''

Without bothering to dismount, she tugged on the
reins, wheeling Cello about with the intention of re-
tracing her steps. Pride was rampant, pride of race,
pride of position, and a newly-provoked feminine
pride that was baulking at the thought of anyone

knowing that all was not well between herself and her husband.

"It's much later than I'd thought," she glanced at her watch. "Would you please convey my apologies to your mother and tell her I'll call again soon? Oh, yes," she called airily across her shoulder as Cello began cantering out of the farmyard, "and would you please tell my husband when you see him that I insist he returns home in time to have dinner with me this evening!"

As she and Cello sped towards the castle she found it hard to decide whether her heartbeats had become erratic because of anger or because of the prospect of Colt's reaction to her reckless demand for his presence. He was almost certain to read her message as a challenge—and be quick to accept!

The workmen had finished their jobs in the hall and all planks, trestles and scaffolding had been removed so that cleaners, under Nanny's supervision, could remove all traces of dust from walls and floor in preparation for the arrival of a second wave of invaders who were awaiting Colt's command to begin upon the task of restoration. As she crossed the hall, making towards the stairs, Nanny appeared bristling from the direction of the kitchen quarters, obviously having been on the alert for sounds of her arrival.

"What do you intend doing about those?" She pointed to a pile of cardboard boxes which, ever since their arrival some days earlier, had remained stacked in a corner. "I'm tired of moving them around. What's inside, for heaven's sake?"

"Clothes," Rowan replied succinctly, "most probably a useless assortment of outfits that my misguided husband arranged to have sent from London fashion houses. I believe he was motivated by an urge to uncover hidden facets, Nanny,'' she scoffed, ''the jewel in his crown is not shining half so brightly as he'd hoped!''

''A man can't be blamed for preferring a silk purse to a sow's ear!'' Nanny scathed. ''But you no doubt intend continuing with your strategy of revenge by refusing to co-operate?''

''Certainly...'' Rowan began, then suddenly changed her mind, ''...not! Give me a hand to take them upstairs, out of your way.''

When all the boxes—pale grey, featherlight, and tastefully decorated—had been deposited in her bedroom she stared at them thoughtfully. She had deliberately left them standing unopened in the hall where Colt was bound to see them in order to supply an extra bone of contention, a symbol of defiance with which she had hoped to shatter the silent armistice, so allowing the battle in which words replaced the stab of dirks to recommence. But although he could not have helped noticing the pile of boxes slowly gathering dust, he had remained uncharacteristically unresponsive. Was it, she wondered, because his anger was still seething? Or had the chauvinistic, egotistical war lord become weary of combat and conceded defeat? She frowned as an alternative thought crossed her mind. Had Abe and Dale been right in their assumption that Colt was being too far-stretched, that he was struggling with a load too heavy for any man—even the immortal Kielder?

Casting a freshly speculative eye over the pile of boxes, she was smote by conscience and made an impulsive decision. The question of Abe's sudden disappearance and the villagers' problems would have to wait. Colt's appeal for an amnesty had obviously been born of weariness—the claws of the lion had been cut, it seemed pointless to insist upon drawing his teeth!

Some time later when Nanny stepped inside a room knee-deep in tissue paper and empty boxes she gave a gasp of startled admiration. A vision of loveliness swung round to face her.

"Well, Nanny, what do you think?"

She looked long and hard at the girl whose youthful beauty had remained cocooned by a preference for old, comfortable, and strictly functional clothes. But now the chrysalis had emerged, and with the aid of a diaphanous dress swirling, light, and shimmering with intricate detail, changing quickly as a mood from snow-white to pale pink as she moved beneath the light, had developed into an incredibly beautiful butterfly.

"Child...!" her voice trembled with proud emotion, "you look as I've always wanted you to look—as I've always known you would look if ever you decided to take pains with your appearance."

"You don't think the bodice is cut too low?" Immaturity showed as her fluttering, downcast lashes doubted the modesty of gently rounded breasts plunging into a tantalisingly deep cleavage.

"Not at all." Nanny suppressed a smile of satisfaction at the thought of Kielder's reaction to a bride made to look ethereal and very desirable in a dream dress with a flattering neckline, full, wrist-length sleeves, and a deeply flounced skirt with a hand-span waistline wrapped twice by a wide sash belt. "You'll do nicely." She reverted to her usual irritable snap in case too much approval should scare the butterfly into discarding her finery. "If the rest of the outfits are as comely you should find no cause for complaint."

"They are—and I haven't!" Rowan's blue eyes sparkled with delight as they roved the selection of original, fashionable, brilliantly designed clothes made from materials ranging from pastel see-through chiffon to vibrant body-hugging jersey. "They're all so stylish, and what's more, they couldn't fit more perfectly if I'd been measured for each one!"

"Good! Now help me to clean up this mess." Nanny stooped and began gathering up tissue paper, ribbons and pins. "If you like, as I've a while to spare before dinner, I'll do your hair just as I used to do your mother's whenever she and your father were to attend a dance or some important function."

Exactly as she had expected, Rowan took fright.

"Oh, that's hardly necessary, Nanny! I might even decide to change—it's such a waste, don't you think, to wear a dress such as this just to spend an ordinary evening at home?"

Nanny straightened and for the first time that Rowan could recall pleaded quietly, "Don't do me out of my treat, it's been such a long time since I've practised my skill as a lady's maid—please, child, humour me just this once?"

Whether the exercise was prolonged deliberately Rowan could not be certain, but by the time the old servant had finished brushing and pinning glossy coils of raven-black hair into a style that left a vulnerable nape bare and displayed to perfection a young, tender neckline and smooth slope of shoulders, the crunch of tyres on the gravelled driveway gave warning of Colt's approach. With suspiciously good timing, Nanny threw down the comb and rushed towards the door.

"You look perfect! I'll leave you now, I must make sure that everything's as it should be in the kitchen!"

The advance of quick, firm footsteps along the passageway outside her room, the sound of movement from next door, then the gurglings and rumblings that erupted from ancient water pipes each time a bath was being drawn sent Rowan shivering towards a fire kept constantly replenished with logs in order to banish chill from the spacious bedroom. Now that confrontation was imminent she felt nervous, at a complete loss how to word the explanation Colt was bound to demand—so much so that when the door between their rooms was finally flung open and she swung round flustered to see him standing on the threshold, enquiring eyebrows winging, she could only manage to blurt.

"Thank you for the dresses . . . !"

"Thank you for finally deciding to accept my gift." The drawl she had been dreading was missing, and as he advanced towards her she noted signs of strain around tight-set lips, in the fine network of lines that sprang into life as his eyes narrowed warily. Breath caught in her throat when a beam from an overhead lamp struck a glint of silver in his hair, reminding her of snow sprinkled lightly over autumn-red bracken. How right Abe and Dale had been to warn her! Colt looked taut enough to snap, so finely balanced a mere speck of sand might upset his equilibrium.

"Your hair is still damp." As much to her own surprise as his she extended her hands to coax him closer to the fire. The moment their fingers touched she realised her mistake, but when she tried to pull away his grip fastened tight as the jaws of a trap around her wrists. Immediately, senses starved of contact began to writhe and purr, the blush of firelight on her cheeks deepened to a scorching inferno, then paled to the whiteness of ash beneath the shocking coldness of a stare that douched her from head to toe, missing not one silken coil of hair, one quivering eyelash, one trembling curve, one infinite quantity of milk-pure skin left exposed by what she belatedly realised was a far too revealing neckline.

"Once I was misguided enough to think you meek, Rowan," he grated rawly. "I know now that what I mistook for meekness is in reality an uncommon patience in planning a revenge that's worthwhile. But let me warn you, before you embark upon whichever devious exercise you have in mind, that our clan's battle cry still remains: *'Wha' dare meddle wi' me!'*"

As many had done before her, Rowan stiffened with alarm at the menace contained in the war cry of a clan chief who in days gone by had been feared the length and breadth of the Border.

"I don't understand," she gulped, feeling shocked as a stray in the middle of a minefield. "I realise you've put the wrong interpretation on my meetings with Abe and I'd explain fully if I could do so without breaking my word. However, as soon as I see Abe—"

"You won't be seeing Abe ever again."

His cold shock of words left her gasping. "I won't—why not...?"

"He's been banished," he astounded her by saying, looking flint-eyed and incredibly stern, "found guilty of offending against Border law that decrees a man shall not cut down the trees of other men, sow his corn or feed his cattle on others' grass, nor," roughly he pulled her into his arms until, pinned against his chest, she felt in danger of drowning in the depths of grey, storm lashed eyes, "shall he cast covetous glances in the direction of other men's wives!"

"You're a barbarian," she choked, wide-eyed with disbelief, "in wickedness a league beyond the devil!"

He silenced her by planting an explosive kiss upon her wrecked mouth, lighting a fuse that blasted her defensive barricade to smithereens. Every deprived nerve responded by leaping to the touch of hands intent upon removing every silken obstacle between them and the slim, satin-skimmed body trembling with an urgency that began as fear then dissolved into ecstasy as his hungry lips traced a path of desire along a tender line of neck and shoulder, lingering against pulsating nerves, seeking, exploring, then finally coming to rest with a groan of anguish against a creamy, delicate curve of breast.

All will to fight became submerged by an urge to surrender, to lay down her arms and submit to becoming a prisoner of love—a word that never once, not even at the pinnacle of passion, had ever escaped his plundering lips. Tossed by a cataclysm of emotion, she clung to his powerful frame as he tortured her with kisses until her mouth felt crushed, her body racked, pride shattered by the indignity of being forced to plead humbly as a prisoner before a jailor.

"No, Colt, don't...! Punish me if you must, but in any other way but this!"

But his reiver blood was up, his veneer of polish stripped, laying bare material that was raw, tough, and ill to tame—a man bent upon practising the ancient Border code applying to property and theft: *"Reivers have a persuasion that all property is common by the law of nature and is therefore liable to be appropriated by them in their necessity".*

Necessity was rife in slumbrous grey eyes when he lifted her into his arms and began carrying her towards the bed.

"Sweet simpleton!" he mocked without compassion her wide fearful eyes and tear-stained cheeks—pale as the lace-trimmed pillow beneath her head. "Even the mildest-natured beast grows savage when fed only bread and water—surely, novice nun, you must have foreseen the outcome of issuing an invitation to dine, then setting a sumptuous meal before a man who's starving!"

CHAPTER TEN

ROWAN STOPPED dead in her tracks, halted by the sight of Colt enjoying a leisurely breakfast with a newspaper propped up against the coffee pot in front of his plate.

"Good morning, Rowan," he greeted her with the ease of a friendly acquaintance, as if last night's torrid, earth-shattering encounter amid cool cotton sheets had never happened. "I've decided to take the day off to go fishing—would you care to join me?"

She glanced out of the window at puffballs of cloud chasing across an expanse of brilliant blue sky; at a garden glowing golden with sunshine, spread from terrace to driveway, along borders and under trees with a carpet of nodding daffodils.

In spite of a heart heavy with pain, steps rendered leaden with the weight of an imaginary ball and chain, her lips refused to utter the refusal that pride demanded.

Something about her young, tragic figure drove him to his feet and sent him striding towards her. The sudden jolt of her reflexes when his finger tipped up her chin could have been mistaken for revulsion. Swiftly as sun disappearing behind cloud his smile faded, his eyes grew bleak, as he grated:

"Please . . . ?"

She flinched out of reach of his lithe body, as far away as possible from muscles rippling beneath a shirt fitting sleek as a pelt, with sleeves rolled up over sinewed biceps and a collar falling open to expose a powerful neck and a wide expanse of wind-burnt chest. Denims slung low around narrow hips, cinched with a leather belt sporting a barbaric brass buckle, projected a prowling sexuality that refused to allow her respite from the memory of the sensuous moulding of her body against his, the sensation of power, the trembling weakness she had felt when satin-skinned muscles had knotted and writhed as if tormented by the tender stroke of her hands.

Huskily, keeping a spear's length between them, she conceded with the hot cheeks and trembling mouth of a coward: "Thank you, I'd like to..."

Though that part of the river they had decided to fish was situated within the castle grounds, Colt told Nanny to prepare them a packed lunch and swore her to secrecy about their movements, insisting that all telephone enquiries and even personal callers, however urgent their needs, were to be instructed to call back tomorrow as today he could not possibly be reached.

Beware the Ides of March! A superstitious shiver ran down Rowan's spine as without apparent reason she recalled that the date was the fifteenth of March, the day Julius Caesar had been warned of impending and certain danger. But when Colt smiled and offered a hand to help her over a stile she shrugged off the premonition, determined to make the most of a day stolen from spring, a precious day of truce from the warring elements of winter.

Amid an atmosphere of untalkative neutrality they reached the river and began stalking the bank in search of a likely beat. Almost immediately, Colt spotted a patch of bubbles rising to the surface of the water, indication that a shoal of hungry bream were sucking and sifting for food along the muddy bottom.

With a grunt of satisfaction he slipped a haversack from his shoulder and unearthed a tinful of ground bait—stale bread soaked, squeezed dry and then mixed with meal—which he had hopefully prepared as a lure to encourage any shoal to linger.

Rowan left him searching for a tin of worms and made her way farther downstream to a stretch of easy water shadowed by trees and bushes. Carefully she crept through a tangle of undergrowth and baited a hook with cheese paste, a delicacy to which chub were extremely partial, letting it dribble on the surface, casting towards the sun so that her shadow would not fall upon the water.

Gradually her mood of slight depression gave way to contentment as sunshine began warming the earth and the scent of resin rose to mingle with woodsmoke drifting from some far-off bonfire. Excitement bounded when a chub began sucking in her bait, but she managed to curb her movements, waiting until the sturdy fish turned down before striking.

A couple of satisfying hours later Colt appeared carrying the luncheon basket and called out the usual fisherman's enquiry: "Any luck?"

Proudly she responded with a nod, indicating a sizeable catch of chub, their scales glistening jade and silver in the sunlight.

"How have you done...?" For the first time that day she was able to meet his eyes without embarrassment.

"Just a couple of eels," he told her ruefully, betraying a reluctance to admit himself beaten.

"I suspected you were being over-generous with ground bait," she dared to tease. "Bream are shy enough without encouraging them to be too lazy to rise!" She bubbled over with laughter when his expression grew wry, experiencing a heady sense of triumph at the knowledge that for once she had managed to outdo King Kielder.

"Bighead!" he accused so disgustedly that she burst out laughing, then when after a second's pause he joined in she felt a swift stab of pleasure, a certainty that this bright golden day was destined to be one of the happiest of her life.

With healthy appetites they attacked the meat and potato pasties, crusty rolls wrapped around thick slices of ham, crisp apples and chunks of crumbly cheese that Nanny had deemed a fitting accompaniment to a healthy outdoor pursuit. Then as they sipped white wine that Colt had chilled to perfection by embedding the bottle up to its neck in the gravelled riverbed, she gradually felt able to relax her guard, to talk freely and warmly about small inconsequential things.

"I do hope today marks the beginning of a long settled spell," she mused, lying back replete, using her hands as a pillow beneath her head. Unaware that her words could have been misinterpreted as a wish for a lull in their stormy relationship, she sighed with contentment and allowed her lazy lids to droop, so missing his sharpened glance, his sudden jerk to attention. "It very often happens that during a warm spell at this time of year half a clutch or more of precious eggs are laid, then along comes the night frost to kill any hope of the eggs being hatched. Even heavy rain is a hazard to early lambs who have no lanoline on their coats and need at least a week in dry conditions for their fleece to become waterproofed.''

As if anxious to reassure her, a feathered Romeo perched on the branch of a nearby tree began serenading his Juliet, a sweet penetrating trill that filled the air with a message of springtime, an anthem made poignant by a vital resurgence of the urge to mate. Her heart began racing as she listened, conscious of Colt's fixed stare, sensing that if only she dared to look she would discover his grey eyes transmitting the same trilling, vibrant message sent by every male lusting after his mate.

When the tension threatened to become unbearable and a deep pink blush was beginning to betray her awareness of his magnetism, she made a cowardly effort to break the spell by jerking upright to enquire brightly:

"I do hope you saved your eels for Nanny, she reckons they make a very tasty pie."

Her tactic was deliberately devious, prompted by a suspicion that without his being aware of it, he had probably been inculcated during childhood with a deep-rooted prejudice against the eating of eels that was characteristic of all Scots. She had to force back a smile when his shudder of repugnance told her that her shot in the dark had landed on target.

"Which only strengthens my suspicion that you English are very far from particular in your feeding," he responded with evident disgust.

"Nonsense!" Her lurking smile sprang into full existence. "I think it's a shame that Scots allow prejudice to prevent them from taking advantage of the most plentiful and nutritious fish in our waters. I'm even willing to bet," she nodded sagely, "that most of you at some time or another have eaten an excellent 'filleted sole' without being aware that you were actually eating eel."

"I dispute that." Much to her relief, his response was crisp, the heat of his tone well below danger level. "The serpent is the symbol of the devil, and all Scots feel that the eel, being like a serpent, is a creature of evil influence and so must always remain taboo."

"In case they should be accused of cannibalism?" The impudent retort left her lips without thought, and to her dismay seemed to change in flight from a light tease to a heavily poisoned barb. When his expression darkened she regretted the impulse that had revived all the resentment he had shown last evening after her hissed accusation: *"In wickedness, you're a league beyond the devil!"*

"Whether it's true or false, what is said about a man often influences his actions," he warned her grimly, rising to his feet. "We'd better take a walk in case I should feel tempted to exercise the devil's prerogative to seek slaves and claim obedience. I think you will agree that our route should avoid highly evocative place names such as Murder's Rack, Hell Cauldron, Kielder's Edge and Thrust Pick!"

Feeling utterly miserable and close to tears, she followed in his wake along a path leading away from the river bank, so overgrown she often found it necessary to edge sideways through bramble thickets that scratched her face and ran thorny fingers through her hair, to pant up steep inclines then to be precipitated down muddy slopes before she had time to draw breath. A dozen times she was on the verge of giving up, deciding she was foolish trying to keep up with his deliberately punishing pace, but she doggedly persisted, following his progress through woodland with unexpected streams, uneven contours and endless variety of mosses, ferns, plants and trees that contrasted like a shambles against the orderly, strictly regimented fir tree forest.

She had no way of knowing whether it was by accident or design that he discovered the well, but when she finally caught up and saw him peering down a circular, stone-rimmed aperture she felt a surge of hysteria as strong as she had felt on the day many years before when as a terrified child she had believed the well was destined to become her grave.

"Colt, be careful, please come away...!" Her strangled shout jerked him back from the rim to stare in long-drawn-out silence at a face white with shock, eyes dark with newly-resurrected horror.

"So you do remember," he challenged softly, "and all this time I've been thinking you'd forgotten."

"I could never forget!" She expelled a long, shuddering breath. "Nightmares keep fresh in my mind the horror of being enclosed within dark walls running with damp, slippery with slime, of lying covered in reeking mud, knowing that any minute I might slip and plunge for ever down a bottomless pit. It was only recently that Nanny told me that you were my rescuer, the one who saved me from the water kelpies!"

She knew she was babbling hysterically, giving way to cowardice, when a feverish ague attacked every limb and she had to clutch at a tree trunk to support knees buckling beneath her.

"Stop it, Rowan!" He reacted just in time to save her from falling. As he snatched her close, encircling her trembling body within the comforting circle of his arms, she fell quiet, reassured by the feel of powerful shoulders beneath her fretful hands.

"Fool that I am," he condemned himself roughly, "I should never have brought you here, yet I felt so certain that the well would have been filled in years ago—as it ought to have been, as it will be," he decided, "no later than tomorrow!"

She weakened to the stroke of his chin against her cheek, to a rough-velvet voice urging tenderly: "But before that happens, I want you to try to overcome your fear that has its roots not so much in a nasty experience as in the vague warnings issued to us when we were children by elders who ought to have known better."

"Always spit three times into the spring before drawing water, otherwise you will be dragged into the well by the water kelpies!"

"Remember how terrified we all were at the very mention of the kelpies," he mused lightly, trying to ease her tension. "They were credited with powers of speech, but if the gift of a coin were to be thrown into the well the kelpies were miraculously propitiated to the point of granting a wish. Your subconscious must have retained your childish fear of those tales," he told her gently, "but I promise that the fear can be exorcised by walking up to the well and examining it thoroughly."

"I won't go near the well! I can't . . . !"

"You must," he insisted, "if only to prove to yourself how little need you have to be scared—it's merely a hole in the ground, Rowan, and a fairly shallow one at that. Also," he stressed grimly, "there's no brother Nigel lurking in the background waiting to use you as a sacrifice to his monumental conceit."

Reluctant to show cowardice in the face of such logic, Rowan allowed him to lead her towards the well and held on tightly to his hand while she nerved herself to peer over the edge into the bottomless pit of iniquity that had plagued her dreams since childhood.

"I can see the bottom!" she gasped. Feeling a strengthening sense of shame at her own timidity, she whirled round to confess, shamefaced: "I've always believed the well to be bottomless, that I'd fallen on to a ledge . . . !"

Solemnly, his eyes alight with laughter, Colt sighed. "There goes my cherished image of bravery! You *were* only five years old at the time, yet you displayed all the enchantment of Eve when you rewarded my rescue act with a ravishing kiss and a promise to love me for ever."

"I did . . ." she faltered, blushing with the shyness of the child he remembered.

"Yes, Rowan," he assured her in tone to match an expression grown suddenly grave, "you certainly did."

She had to disperse the ambience of intimacy that was playing riot with her emotions, to prove to him and to herself that she would never voluntarily give in to desire writhing like a snake between them, that the only way she could be taken was by force.

"You mustn't allow the memory of a childish outburst to embarrass you," she told him, striving to sound lightly amused. "I vaguely remember that even as a boy you showed signs of the ruthless, overbearing man you were later to become, a man whose dedication to the accumulation of power left him no time for the frivolous occupation of loving and being loved!''

He recoiled as if from a blow, the weariness and strain of the past few days reappearing in a face that for most of the day had looked carefree and relaxed.

"That is unjustified criticism," he countered, tight-lipped, "simply another example of English unfairness."

Impetuously, and completely without reason, she reacted in the manner of a child who, because she has seen a cherished object marred, decides to wreck it entirely. Bitter words spilled from her lips as every past grievance pushed and shoved to the forefront of her mind, anxious to claim its turn. "By your own admission you returned to this place nursing resentment like a festering sore in order to exact revenge against a family you had been taught from infancy to hate. Were you not ruthless in your determination to blackmail me into marriage and overbearingly patronising to my brother once you became master of his estate? You bought yourself a bride, not to love and to cherish, but simply to display a superior Falstone as one of your worldly goods. Even your mistress, Diane," she stormed, his lack of return fire giving her confidence, "has admitted to Abe that you're incapable of fidelity, that once a woman has been taken she's discarded, reduced to being filed as a telephone number in your book of conquests!"

This jibe penetrated his tough hide. Ferocious hands grasped her shoulders as he gazed down, temper rearing, at her suddenly aghast face.

"How dare you discuss me with Abe!" He shook her fiercely. "In spite of the alliance you and he have formed, the secrets you share, I'd imagined that you possessed sufficient loyalty to avoid discussing your husband with an employee!"

"Why should a tyrant expect loyalty from a slave?" she spat, incapable of restraining bolting resentment that was rushing her headlong towards disaster. The peace of the woodland had flown, the clearing had turned into an arena containing clashing antagonists employing the cut and thrust of words in place of dirk and sword. "King Kielder may reign, but for how long?" she jibed. "His subjects are on the verge of rebellion against indignities inflicted by his army of rowdies; his second-in-command has been banished because of groundless suspicion; and though the King has managed to buy possession of lands and castle, he's unable to purchase the allegiance that's the prerogative of the rightful heir, my brother Nigel, Earl of Falstone!"

"An incorrigible snob," he thrust back, "a penniless parasite who's spent the last few years of his life draped across bars imbibing dry Martinis, clinging to the fringes of White's Club, Lloyds, the Polo Club, losing what little cash he had to spare over the green baize tables of gambling dens—a man ever-conscious of his social position, yet ever ready to shrug off the consequent responsibilities! I couldn't agree more with your supposition that a boy is a reflection of the man he's to become, for your brother has developed exactly along the lines of the character I observed years ago—a braggart, an egotistical bully who felt no qualms about putting his sister's life at risk for the sake of proving a point, but who became hoist by his own petard when he was shown up as a coward, too concerned for the safety of his own skin to even attempt a rescue. Do you really believe your brother capable of exciting admiration or respect?'' he blasted, looking ready to choke the truth past her mutinous lips. ''My mother used to call you a 'croodlin' doo','' his voice softened, ''a motherless dove left abandoned in a nest of vultures. Surely, Rowan, you must by now have recognised your brother as a rotten staff that none may lean on without risking a fall?''

She jerked out of his slackened grip, family pride outraged. Though Nigel had proved beyond doubt that he was deserving of condemnation, some inner devil lit a sparkle of indignation in her wide blue eyes, poured angry scorn into her indictment.

''If that's so, then why were you so eager to step into his shoes, to emulate his role even to the point of forcing a promise from him that he would coax his friends into accepting your hospitality immediately the castle has been renovated into a condition suited to your elevated status?''

''That plan was evolved solely for your benefit.'' Smartly, Colt rejected the mantle of social climber. ''For too many years you've been left abandoned to isolation, cut off from parties, social chit-chat, from gaining experience in the art of conversation, denied the opportunity of learning how to dress, how to apply make-up, how to behave in a manner fitting to your position. My aim was to redress that wrong!''

Humiliated beyond belief by this sudden insight into his mind, this glimpse of the socially inadequate, rawly-naïve, shabbily dressed picture she presented before his eyes, Rowan lashed out in her pain:

"Undoubtedly there's truth in the rumour that every Kielder's right hand belongs to the devil! When you were christened," she condemned low and emphatically, "some over-zealous relative must have contrived to exclude your heart as well as your hand from the baptism!"

She gained no sense of comfort from his recoil, or from lines of weariness etched deep as newly-inflicted scars upon his expressionless face. Defeat was an anathema to the proud Kielder, yet though his lance-straight body remained still, not a muscle twitched, she sensed defeat in his cold, unemotional decree.

"I had expected much of today, Rowan—obviously too much. But if business life has taught me anything, it's that there's a time to press on and a time to cut one's losses. For the first time in my life I'm being forced to face failure, to concede victory to superior forces." A hush fell over the clearing, birds fell silent, not a leaf stirred, no movement disturbed the winter-crisped bracken that housed countless small creatures, so that his apology fell flat and unfeeling into the breath-held air.

"I'm sorry I parted you and Abe. Because I'm responsible for the completion of the dam I can't do the gentlemanly thing and remove myself from your vicinity. What I can do is send a message to Abe telling him to return immediately. If he responds quickly—as I've no doubt he will—you two should be reunited some time tomorrow."

CHAPTER ELEVEN

"KIELDER'S GONE!" Nanny's voice was harshly condemnatory. "He's packed most of his things and left instructions that any mail should be forwarded to his office on the site. What's gone wrong, what foolishness have you been up to, bairn?"

As a result of a sleepless night caused by thoughts in a turmoil, by emotions twisting and writhing like a bucketful of eels, Rowan's face looked pinched with misery, her heart heavy with a sense of loss even greater than the anguish she had been caused by her brother's treachery. In the manner of a suffering animal seeking solitude in which to lick its wounds, she tried to escape Nanny's probing by making towards the door, but Nanny had no intention of being foiled from having her say.

Twitching the cover over the huge bed on which only one pillow was ever indented, only a minute area of bedsheet was ever crumpled, she sighed.

"The opportunity God sends is wasted on a sleeper! When will you waken up to the realities of life, child, and be grateful for your blessings?"

The indictment stung. Rowan did not feel blessed, more like cursed. "As I'm so blind to my blessings, Nanny, perhaps you'd be good enough to enumerate them?"

Nanny faced her with arms akimbo, ready to bris-
tle, but changed her mind when a glance at Rowan's
face betrayed confusion and deep unhappiness.

"You've managed to keep the home you couldn't
bear to part with," she pointed out gently, "you have
the comfort of knowing that elderly tenants will never
be evicted from their homes; you have health, wealth,
and," she hesitated for barely a second, "a husband
who loves you."

Rowan's laughter rang hollow as she swung away
from Nanny's far-seeing eyes and walked across to the
window to stare at a view of fells and woodland shimmering through a haze of tears.

"You used to be perceptive as a witch," she choked,
"and a loyal friend to my family, but your strange allegiance to Kielder has distorted your vision, Nanny,
for I fear that you now see only what you want to see.
You can't pretend to have forgotten that he bought
me, the castle and its estate, purely as an act of revenge."

"I must admit that at first I was fooled, just as you
were, into thinking so, but not for long."

The old woman's tone of complacency sent Rowan
swinging round, bewildered. "What are you suggesting?"

"I'm not merely suggesting," Nanny snapped with
a return to her usual no-nonsense manner, "I'm offering a conclusion from the evidence of my own eyes!
I've seen the way Kielder looks at you when he thinks
he's unobserved, the way...the way a pauper might
look at a banquet, or with the wistful, yearning look
of a boy staring through a toy shop window knowing
he can look but never touch. Ask yourself," she almost snorted, "what use has a man like Kielder, who's

become accustomed to living well, for a rambling, draughty castle lacking every modern convenience? Though you were the last to hear of it, your brother made no secret of his intention to sell. Kielder bought this castle to prevent it from falling into strange hands, because he wanted to make you happy—and I'm willing to wager that he married you for exactly the same reason!"

After Nanny had slipped quietly out of the room Rowan slumped down upon the bed, her stunned mind hovering between derisive rejection and a surprising eagerness to believe the astonishing conclusion. She strove to be sensible, to marshal her arguments as a general would marshal his troops.

Colt had never once been unkind—but he had often shown impatience, even occasional fury.

Nanny was correct in her assumption that he was in some ways a sybarite, one who accepted luxury almost as a divine right—yet fable had it that sybarites had expected everyone to dance to their tune, so much so that even their horses had been trained to dance to the pipe.

Colt was a roistering reiver, a swinge-buckler, always ready and eager for a fight—yet though his sword and buckler had swashed and swinged with a great show of strength, she had emerged from each battle unhurt. All but twice...

She flinched from recalling the two nights she had spent in his arms, but forced herself to remember every detail, every passionate moment, feeding hope on the assurance that no man could have acted with such tenderness, concern, and sensuous ardour towards a woman he did not love. On the verge of being convinced, she cupped scorching cheeks between trembling hands, trying to impose a band of caution around her pounding heart and riotous senses, and succeeding only too well when the voice of prudence whispered: "Love is hate's emotional twin—those whom we can love we find easy to hate."

Both passionate interludes had been initiated by Colt's fierce anger!

Seeking her usual antidote to depression, she saddled Cello and set off in the direction of the forest. Feeling the absence of motivation, her limp-wristed pressure on the reins, Cello chose the path leading straight into the clearing where they had been accustomed to meeting Abe. Rowan's involuntary jerk when she saw him strolling aimlessly, obviously awaiting her appearance, seemed to surprise him.

"I'm sorry if I startled you," he frowned. "Weren't you expecting me? I've just left Colt; he implied that you would meet me here."

He looked uneasy, his usual grin replaced by a thin-lipped line of worry.

"What did Colt say exactly?" Slowly Rowan dismounted and patted Cello's rump, encouraging her to graze.

"Nothing that made much sense—I only wish he had! Tell me, Lady Rowan," he appealed desperately, "what's gone wrong between Colt and me? I've no notion why, but his attitude towards me has undergone a complete change. There was even a time," he gulped nervously, "when he looked ready to beat the hell out of me—sometimes I wish he had, instead of banishing me without a word of explanation into the wilderness of Wales, supposedly to add scope to my work experience but basically, I suspect, because he can no longer stand the sight of me! Yesterday, when I received a message to return here immediately I thought my transgressions, whatever they might be, had been forgiven. Naturally I responded as quickly as I was able, driving all through the night, not even sparing the time to have a shave," ruefully he ran his fingers through a stubble of beard, "yet when I finally did meet up with the boss I found that nothing had changed. In fact, although I'd imagined it impossible his attitude was several degrees frostier!"

"Colt has been working under a great deal of strain," Rowan faltered lamely, realising that he had not the slightest inkling of the real reason behind Colt's actions. Reluctant to upset him further by explaining in detail, she decided to tread warily, to elicit as much information as possible without revealing the true circumstances.

"Didn't he tell you about the strike? I know he could have done with your help; he's probably asked you to return in case there should be further trouble on the site. I believe that long after such incidents, resentments remain simmering and are apt to flare up anew at the slightest provocation."

"Thanks for the vote of confidence," he smiled wryly, "but I think you know as well as I do, Lady Rowan, that Colt needs no help to win his battles, he thrives on conflict and invariably emerges victorious."

Gingerly as a kitten she side-stepped the subject and veered on a different course. "As you stated some time ago, Colt is working far too hard and as a result he's over-reacting to upsets which normally he would shrug off. Can you pinpoint the actual occasion when his attitude changed?"

"I sure can," Abe nodded emphatically, "it was the day you and I last met here in the forest. After leaving you, I made my way back to the car and found him parked alongside, almost as if he'd been waiting for me. Immediately I appeared he strode to meet me looking thunderous, and asked what reason I had for coming to the forest on my every day off. As he seemed in no mood to believe me capable of taking up any outdoor hobby, I evaded the question, and as you'd sworn me to secrecy about the orchids I could give him no convincing reason why you made weekly visits to the same spot. He then drove off looking murderous. That same night I received my marching orders."

His brow wrinkled as, deeply perplexed, he tried to fathom Colt's unreasonable show of animosity. Then suddenly he jerked erect, squaring his shoulders as if arriving at some decision.

"I'm going to have it out with him!" he exploded, so violently Rowan jumped. "I'll demand an explanation and refuse to budge until the cross-grained, horny buzzard has given me one!"

He began striding purposefully out of the clearing, then paused to cast an apologetic smile across his shoulder. "Heck, Lady Rowan, I'm sorry if I came over a bit strong—I know how much you love the guy..."

It was a long time before Rowan was able to move. Shock held her stunned, afraid as a cripple who has been miraculously healed yet is afraid to trust his limbs in case the happiness that beckoned should prove to be unreal, a figment of the imagination. Just a few words, one casually-worded sentence, had cured her of an inherited affliction, an inability to look kindly upon any Scot, and especially a Kielder; a determination to settle old scores, to nurse old grievances, to sacrifice herself as a martyr to the cause of family honour, when all the time, deep in her subconscious, had lain buried feelings too traitorous ever to be exhumed. Abe's careless pick of words had penetrated the deep crust of prejudice and heaved them to the surface, so that she could no longer deny herself the glorious relief of admitting to herself that she *really did love the guy*!

The transition from inertia to animation was swift once the realisation struck her that Abe, ignorant of his role of devil's advocate, was rushing to destroy her last tenuous chance of happiness. Colt's pride had been battered, was as weathered as the Kielder Stone. To be forced to apologise and to publicly admit to a marriage gone badly wrong would be bound to topple him into a state of lasting bitterness!

She rose swift as a Valkyrie towards the mêlée of battle, racing Cello out of the forest, across wide stretches of marshland and over the shoulders of fells, chancing every treacherous short-cut in an effort to overcome the time lapse and arrive at the dam before Abe.

A sob of relief blocked her throat when she breasted a rise and saw his car moving slowly along the gravelled road leading down to the base of the plateau.

"C'mon, Cello!" she urged through gritted teeth as she encouraged the mare down a slippery slope strewn with boulders. "I wouldn't normally ask you to risk damaging a forelock, but it's vitally important that we get to Colt first!"

As if horse-sense had managed to communicate that her mistress's future happiness was as stake, Cello re-

sponded with surefooted speed, negotiating all obsta-
cles, then racing flat out across the floor of the valley.
The contest between flying hooves and speeding
wheels ended in a dead heat on the fringe of a crowd
of muttering workmen and strangely-idle machinery.
She sensed that something was wrong even before
Abe's snapped enquiry:

"What's going on? Why aren't you sodbursters
working?"

The nearest group of workmen spun round to face
him, their mud-spattered faces solemn, anxious eyes
shaded by the steel rims of protective helmets.

"There's been a cave-in in one of the tunnels!"

Rowan's heart leapt, anticipating the workman's
final horrifying words. "Kielder's in there, but
whether he's been buried by the fall or trapped in the
tunnel behind it, we don't know yet." One of his
companions nudged his elbow and nodded, indicating Rowan's tragically, immobile presence. "I'm sorry,
ma'am," the speaker mumbled, "I wouldn't have
broken the news so bluntly... I didn't know you were
there... Don't you worry," he attempted to sound
hearty, "we'll get the boss out, never fear."

But fear was already clawing at her heart. "You
must!" she gasped, gouging desperate fingers into
Abe's arm. "Why is everyone standing about, why
aren't they *doing* something?"

White to the lips, Abe put his arm around her
shoulders and began guiding her through the crowd of
hushed, subdued workmen, dispensing with any time-
wasting attempt to get her to return home and wait for
news.

"The tunnel in question is over a mile long but less
than ten feet in diameter," he explained, hurrying her

through a parting of workmen. "Colt's been worried about its safety for some time, slight rock showers and a constant fall of dust have indicated an unreliable stratum, which is why he was anxious for the concreting to begin, why he carried out periodic inspections to ensure that safety precautions were being observed to the letter. In all probability that's what he would be doing when the cave-in occurred."

He bit off his words when the fringe of the crowd parted and they were abruptly confronted by a mass of granite boulders spilling out of the tunnel. Half a dozen men were sweating shoulder to shoulder, their helmeted heads ducking beneath naked light bulbs strung on wires fastened to the roof of the tunnel, clawing, heaving, grunting in the confined space, progressing slowly and cautiously in case one uncharted move, the dislodging of a buttress, should precipitate a second fall of rock.

"Oh, Colt...!" Rowan's despairing sob caused Abe to wince. "You *can't* be, you *mustn't* be buried beneath all that rock!"

Keeping an arm wrapped tightly around her shaking shoulders, Abe called out to a man directing the rescue operation:

"How's it going?"

Muttering a hasty instruction to his second in command, the man clambered down the rock pile towards them. His features were unrecognisable beneath a layer of grime and sweat, but Rowan's pleading eyes found a small trace of comfort in an expression set with determination, in a tone of voice echoing with a cautious optimism she sensed was not adopted for her ears alone.

"As you'll probably appreciate," he addressed Abe, but kept pitying eyes upon Rowan's agonised face, "we're having to proceed slowly and with extreme caution, but we've managed to clear a gap at the narrowest part of the rockfall where it meets the roof of the tunnel, so creating an airflow which alleviates our most pressing problem, that of ensuring that the boss is in no danger of suffocating however long it might take us to free him."

If he's still alive!

The unspoken doubt hovered in the air between them and was written upon the grave faces of men used to facing danger every day of their working lives, men as tough as the granite they blasted from the quarries, as basic as bedrock uncovered by the steel teeth and blades of their mechanical monsters. Yet many of them were having to swallow hard to disperse lumps in their throats; some were using the backs of grimy hands to brush away tears which, if challenged, they would have sworn were beads of sweat.

As if from a far distance, Rowan heard her own surprisingly steady voice querying: "Is there any chance that you might be mistaken about Colt being trapped inside the tunnel?"

The man to whom she had appealed grimaced painfully, then cleared his throat. "I'm afraid not, ma'am—he and I were just about to go inside the tunnel together when I turned back to issue instructions to a ganger, he was mere seconds in front of me when part of the roof caved in, but whether he was caught beneath the fall or merely trapped behind the blockage is what we have yet to discover."

"I have an idea!" Abe peered into the mouth of the tunnel, his gaze fixed upon the site of operation. "I reckon that gap you've opened up might just be wide enough to allow a man through. There's just a chance," he glanced apologetically at Rowan, "that Colt might be lying injured, in need of first aid. Every second might count!"

"We've already considered that course of action and discarded it as being too risky." Rowan's surge of hope was depressed by the grated rejection. "The weight of a man's body could exert sufficient pressure to dislodge a vital cornerstone in this jigsaw of rocks and send tons of stone tumbling inward. The weight of one boulder dropped from a height could crush a man's skull as easily as a hammer could flatten a matchbox."

"Dear Rowan, so slim and slight you barely cast a shadow—I swear your supple, silk-clad limbs could be threaded through the eye of a needle!" Rowan cringed from the painful recollection of Colt's teasing words.

Instinct cautioned her to hold a tight rein upon an hysterical desire to scream at men who seemed content to stand gossiping while her husband could be dying, his life-blood slowly seeping away. Somehow she had to rejuvenate these plodding, slow-moving men, had to make them see her not as a woman, but as an instrument that might have been fashioned especially for such a situation.

"I could do it!" Even she was amazed by the strength of purpose running through her words.

"You?" Abe swung round, astounded. "I couldn't possibly allow it, Colt would have my guts for—"

"I can...I must!" she insisted, hanging on grimly to control.

"But, ma'am, it's far too dangerous—we don't know what conditions are like behind the barrier, and even if you did manage to wriggle your way through without mishap, you might be injured, even killed, by a second fall of rock!''

Calmly, almost as if she were sympathising with the man for his lack of insight, she reminded the worried overseer: "And if Colt is behind there so might he be!'' Then, so simply and convincingly that they were rendered bereft of further argument, she confessed what was in her heart, what she had only just admitted to herself. "In which case my life wouldn't matter, because without Colt existence would become meaningless, I'd have no reason left for living.''

There was not one man present whose expression was not full of admiration for the slight, courageous girl who could hardly bear to wait until a makeshift harness had been fashioned from rope and fitted over her shoulders and beneath her armpits so that once she had negotiated the gap she could be lowered without risk of injury on to the floor of the tunnel; not one man whose horny fists did not knot with fear for her safety when with her pockets stuffed with various items of first aid and with a powerful torch secured to a broad leather belt fastened around her waist, she was given help to clamber up the pile of loose rock before she dropped to her knees and began inching along on all fours through the dark aperture, out of reach of helpless watchers.

Abe's voice, sounding demented with worry, encouraged her passage through the tight tunnel of rock with jagged points that gouged into her shoulders and pierced sharp as daggers through leather pads strapped around her knees. He was holding the rope attached to her harness, feeding it inch by inch through his fingers as she moved.

"Don't hurry, Lady Rowan, take it as slowly as you can, feel out every bit of rock in front of you before you move! When you're through the barrier give a tug on the rope so I'll know when to begin lowering you down into the tunnel!"

She made no attempt to reply. If her whole mind and being had not been centred upon reaching Colt she might have been overwhelmed by the panic-stricken horror of once again being entombed as she had been on the occasion, many years before, when Colt had been her rescuer. Now, as then, the darkness was intense, the atmosphere of danger oppressive, the fear of being buried alive in a tunnel of stone lurked hysterical as a scream in the back of her mind. But this time it was she who had been cast in the role of rescuer, she who had to maintain control over an ice-cool mind and precise, carefully deliberated actions, because her love for Colt transcended all fear, because his life and her future happiness depended upon the outcome of the exercise.

A hiss of fright escaped her tight lips when the ground fell away beneath her groping hands. Gingerly she eased one hand behind her back to give a tug upon the lifeline, and immediately Abe responded:

"You're through!" His far-off voice sounded choked. "Now for the tricky part. Wriggle your way forward until your legs are clear of the rocks—don't be afraid of falling, the harness will hold your weight and there are three hundred guys out here all itching to take the strain on the rope. Do you understand, Lady Rowan? For Pete's sake, if you're in any difficulty give us a yell!"

She tried to respond, then discovered to her horror that she could not. Tension had a grip upon her vocal chords, dust was clogging her nostrils and though her teeth were gritted, her lips tightly compressed, the taste of dust was acrid on her tongue.

"I'm all right!" she finally managed to croak, then, impelled by a sense of urgency, she sucked in a current of clean air and yelled. "Everything's fine, let's get on with it!"

Seconds later she was dangling over the edge, swinging in mid-air with the wall of rock behind her. Slowly, jerkily, she was lowered to the floor of the tunnel. Immediately her feet touched the ground she discarded the harness and groped for her torch. The beam of light wavered as erratically as her trembling hands around two solid walls bearing signs of construction; over the barrier of rock through which she had crawled, then into a maw of darkness where the remainder of the tunnel stretched. She tightened her grip upon the torch and pointed the beam downwards, mumbling a desperate prayer for Colt's safety as she scoured the floor for some sign of him.

When the beam of light fell upon a jacket sleeve, a sheepskin collar, then burst like flame around a fiery, belovedly-familiar head, a wave of relief weakened her courage and her vision was blinded by a swift, hot spill of tears. Fiercely she blinked them away and sank down on her knees beside the inert figure lying with arms outflung, eyes closed, and one leg buried to just below the knee beneath a fringe of fallen debris.

"Colt!" She bent over him sobbing, showering tears of grief and relief upon his senseless head. "Oh, God, he mustn't die! Please let him live for my sake!"

Reminded of the purpose of her mission, she exerted a tight rein upon her emotions and steeled herself to carry out the instructions she had been given, looking for signs of bleeding, for evidence of serious injury, sliding a trembling hand against his neck and being rewarded with the discovery of a faint but steady pulsebeat.

"What's happened down there?" Abe's voice echoed around the pitch-black cavern, demanding an immediate answer.

"I've found him!" she responded in a high-pitched cry, tremulous with delight. "He's alive and in no immediate danger, but please, Abe, tell the men to hurry, we must get him out of here!"

CHAPTER TWELVE

LIFE INSIDE the castle had reverted almost to normal. All work of interior restoration had been suspended in order to ensure that peace and quiet, that was an essential aid to the master of Falstone's recovery from severe concussion, could be strictly maintained. Mercifully, his only other injuries were a broken leg and a bump on the forehead sustained when a glancing blow from a falling rock had knocked him unconscious. Now all he needed was time to heal his wounds and patience to withstand idleness forced upon him by the doctor's strict injunction to rest quietly with his mind relieved of business matters and his injured leg, encased in plaster, subjected to the minimum of pressure.

But during the week that had passed since his accident Colt had proved beyond doubt that patience was not one of his virtues, and as Rowan crossed the hall she winced from a hail of words being let loose behind the door of the master bedroom and hesitated, expecting the worst, when a door slammed, preceding someone's hasty exit from his room. Training anxious eyes upwards, she waited and saw Abe, looking red-faced and furious, rushing down the stairs towards her.

"What on earth's going on?" she began scolding. "Surely you're aware that the doctor has insisted upon Colt having the maximum of peace and quiet?"

"In which case, it's a pity he wasn't left in the tunnel," Abe snarled in aggravation.

"How can you say such a thing!" Her cry of reproach caused him a shrug of discomfort.

"Heck, I'm sorry, Lady Rowan, but the guy's turned dead mean, pouncing like a frustrated tiger upon anyone foolish enough to enter his lair! In spite of the doctor's instructions to the contrary, he insists upon receiving a daily report on the dam's progress, yet nothing I do or say seems to meet with his approval. In fact," he clamped, looking suddenly accusing, "just a few moments ago when I made some reference to your bravery—having no notion that he'd been kept completely in the dark about the part you played in his rescue—his temper reached flashpoint. I'm to consider myself fired," he concluded bitterly, "together with every other man on his staff who was, to quote his own words, *criminally irresponsible, slow-witted*, and *cowardly* enough to allow you to put your life in jeopardy!"

"Oh, Abe, I'm sorry!" she gasped. "Perhaps I'm to blame for his ill-humour. He does hate being isolated—mindful of doctor's orders to ensure that he's forced to rest and to talk as little as possible, I've visited him myself only when I was sure he was asleep. But I promise I'll explain to him that you and the rest of the men were given no choice, that I was so determined to do what I did that nothing you could have said or done would have forced me to change my mind. Please," she begged, "don't mention a word

about dismissal to the others until I've had a chance
to speak to Colt."

"Very well, if you say so, Lady Rowan." His
expression was a mixture of relief and puzzlement.
"But I'd advise you to get your timing right—to wait
until after the brute's been fed, perhaps, when with
luck you may find him purring!"

When Abe had taken his leave she wandered into the
morning room, stalling for time, anxious to sort out
her thoughts. She could not explain even to herself her
reluctance to come face to face with Colt. She loved
him desperately. During the hours she had sat on the
floor of the tunnel with his head cradled upon her
knee, numb with worry, stiff with cold seeping into her
bones, that fact had been forcibly rammed home.
Though the men had worked like beavers, it had taken
long, painstaking hours to clear a way through the
rock barrier, and during that time, while Colt had remained unconscious, she had had time to think, time
to plumb the depths of the love she felt for the husband she had almost lost—could still be in danger of
losing—and to realise that although he had given her
no grounds for hoping her love might be returned, she
would be content to exist for the rest of her life on any
morsels tossed from King Kielder's table.

As she had kept watch by his bedside day and night
for the first few anxious days after his accident, hope
had been encouraged by the number of times her name
had been mumbled past his lips, yet immediately he
had begun showing signs of recovery she had shied
from confronting his grey, enquiring eyes and had
bolted from the room, returning to hover only when
she was certain he was asleep, gazing hungrily, her
heart in her eyes, before flitting away silent as a wraith

whenever the flickering of eyelashes or a lightening of his breathing had warned that he was on the verge of awakening.

She was jerked from her reverie by the sound of a second commotion. This time his victim was Nanny. Bristling, panting with indignation, she flung open the door and stood quivering on the threshold clutching an armful of crumpled bedlinen.

"I can't stand another minute of this!" She glared at Rowan as if holding her personally responsible for Colt's ill humour. "He's found fault with every meal I've set in front of him; he's refused to obey the doctor's orders and now," she quivered visibly, "he's insisting upon returning to his own bed, saying he absolutely refuses to spend another day propped up like a doll against lace-frilled pillows! For days he's been enquiring about your whereabouts, demanding to see you," she accused. "For heaven's sake, bairn, do as he asks, then we might all get some peace!"

"I will, Nanny," Rowan decided quietly, realising that the moment of reckoning could be delayed no longer. "Just give me a few more minutes and I promise I'll do as you ask.

When a slightly mollified Nanny had withdrawn, closing the door behind her, Rowan drew in a deep, steadying breath and clenched her fists tight, willing fluttering nerves to subside, her wildly pounding heart to revert to its normal beat. Then she squared her shoulders and swung towards the door, but before she could step forward it crashed open, revealing Colt smouldering dangerously on the threshold.

"You shouldn't be out of bed," she faltered, stunned by the shock of seeing his powerful frame supported by a stick; by a face contrasting deathly pale against the dark silk of his dressing gown, and by a livid bruise forking like lightning over stormy grey eyes.

"No, I should not," he agreed savagely. "In fact, I imagine my doctor, if he should see me now, would be appalled. But you left me no choice, did you, Rowan?" She backed away when he stomped inside the room, visibly aggravated by a restricting plaster cast. "As you didn't bother to respond to any of my messages I was forced to come in search of you."

"Please sit down, Colt," she trembled, near to tears. "I was just about to visit you, I would have done so sooner...I never dreamt you'd be so foolish!"

"Didn't you, Rowan...?" When suddenly he dropped into a chair all fire seemed to die out of him. "Isn't that how I've always appeared in your eyes—a jester aping a king, a rich clown who imagines money can buy him love?"

"No, Colt," she whispered through a throat so tight it hurt. She was standing a few feet away from him with head downcast, nervous fingers lacing, bruise-dark lashes spiked with tears. "Far from appearing foolish, you've always struck me as being an extremely rational person, one who's sure of his aims and certain how best to achieve them."

She winced when harsh laughter grated from his lips, recoiled from a question thrown contemptuously as a bone to a grovelling hound. "Do I look like a man who has everything he wants? I climbed high and fell low," he admitted with a grimace of defeat that was completely alien to his character, "some might say that I've received the just deserts of an upstart crow who pressed his suit upon an unwilling dove." He rose to his feet looking spent, utterly weary.

"Abe told me about the part you played in my rescue," he clipped so coldly she flinched. "Your actions were foolhardy, nevertheless, I'm grateful for the concern you must obviously have felt."

Rowan's taut string of endurance suddenly snapped. "So grateful that you've threatened to fire every man who struggled to save your life?" she flared. "What makes you so blind, Colt, so insensitive to love?"

His stick clattered to the floor as he grabbed her close to him. "They allowed you to put your life at risk—I'll never forgive them for that!"

The heavy thud of heartbeats filled the silent room while their glances clashed, held, probed, then became transfixed, startled by a glimpse of reality too ethereal to be believed. It took all the courage she possessed to chance being rebuffed, becoming an object of pity or, worse still, ridicule.

"The men tried hard to stop me, Colt," she told him simply, "until I explained that if you were to die I should have no wish to live."

She had not thought it possible for his pallor to increase, for a quiver to rake across a mouth so hard-bitten.

"Don't feel sorry for me, Rowan," he threatened. "I can take anything but pity!"

"Then take my love, Colt," she pleaded, laying her defeated head against a dark silk lapel, "for pity's sake, take my love!"

Her heart responded with a leap to the crush of arms savage with longing, to kisses that drowned her in ecstasy, to passion that swept her off her feet, lifted her, tossed and buffeted, into a stormy vortex of desire that drained her of misgivings and convinced her beyond doubt of his urgent, violent need.

"You *do* love me...!" she accused dreamily when he finally allowed her to draw breath.

"And have done for most of my life," he breathed the shaken confession. "Even when I was a child, you represented the unattainable, a being as rare and distant as a princess in an ivory tower. For many years," he whispered against her still, attentive ear, "I've travelled the world with your image stamped upon my heart—a memory so treasured no other woman could live up to it, a dream so fragile, so desirable, that I was almost afraid to return in case I should find you changed. You are the present I've saved up all my life for, my darling, and I found you exactly as I'd hoped, as unspoiled and untainted as the animals and birds you so fiercely protected. Unchanged in every respect," he loosened tender, trapping arms to administer a gentle shake, "to the point of having retained your mistrust of Scots, and of a Kielder in particular. You put up a hard fight," he sighed, his eyes clouding with painful memory, "a fight I felt certain I'd lost when you charged me with blackmail and accused me of spending money in an attempt to purchase love."

"A love that you'd already won, King Kielder," admonished his most faithful and loving subject, "a love born on the night of the hunter's moon that will shine constant as sunrise every day of the rest of my life."

Filled with remorse by this reminder of a night when desire had overruled the demands of conscience, humbled by her generous refusal to condemn, Colt hugged her slender body close and with his eyes fixed hungrily upon a mouth sweet as honey, groaned in an agony of loving contrition the words she had waited so long to hear. "Precious croodlin' doo! If only I could tell you how much I love you—if only I could tell you *all*!"

THE AUTHOR

Margaret Rome began writing at night
school under the tutelage of a man who
"instructed, coaxed and at times even
bullied us to reach heights we had never
thought to accomplish." Her first
Harlequin romance novel, *A Chance to
Win*, was published in 1969. Now, with
over thirty Romances to her credit, she
confesses that "it's still a thrill to see my
name in print." Margaret lives with her
husband and son in Northern England.